ROAD TRIP HOME
A Bahá'í Vision of Hope

First Edition Design Publishing
Sarasota, Florida USA

Road Trip Home
Copyright ©2016 Steven E. Ellis

ISBN 978-1506-908-52-6 AMZ
ISBN 978-1506-903-26-2 PRINT ISBN
978-1506-903-27-9 EBOOK ISBN
978-1506-903-51-4 AUDIO

LCCN 2016955901

November 2016

Published and Distributed by
First Edition Design Publishing, Inc.
P.O. Box 20217, Sarasota, FL 34276-3217
www.firsteditiondesignpublishing.com

Cover Photo Credit: Martin Pugh

DISCLAIMER:
This is a work of fiction, however the spiritual message it conveys is real. Some of the characters are based on actual people whose names have been changed to protect their privacy. Other characters (e.g. Rose) are fictional and any resemblance to actual persons, living or dead, is purely coincidental.

Library of Congress Cataloging-in-Publication Data
Ellis, Steven E.
    Road Trip Home / written by Steven E. Ellis
    p. cm.
    ISBN 978-1506-903-26-2 pbk, 978-1506-903-27-9 digital

1. FICTION/General. 2. /Religious/. 3. /Spiritual/.

R6285

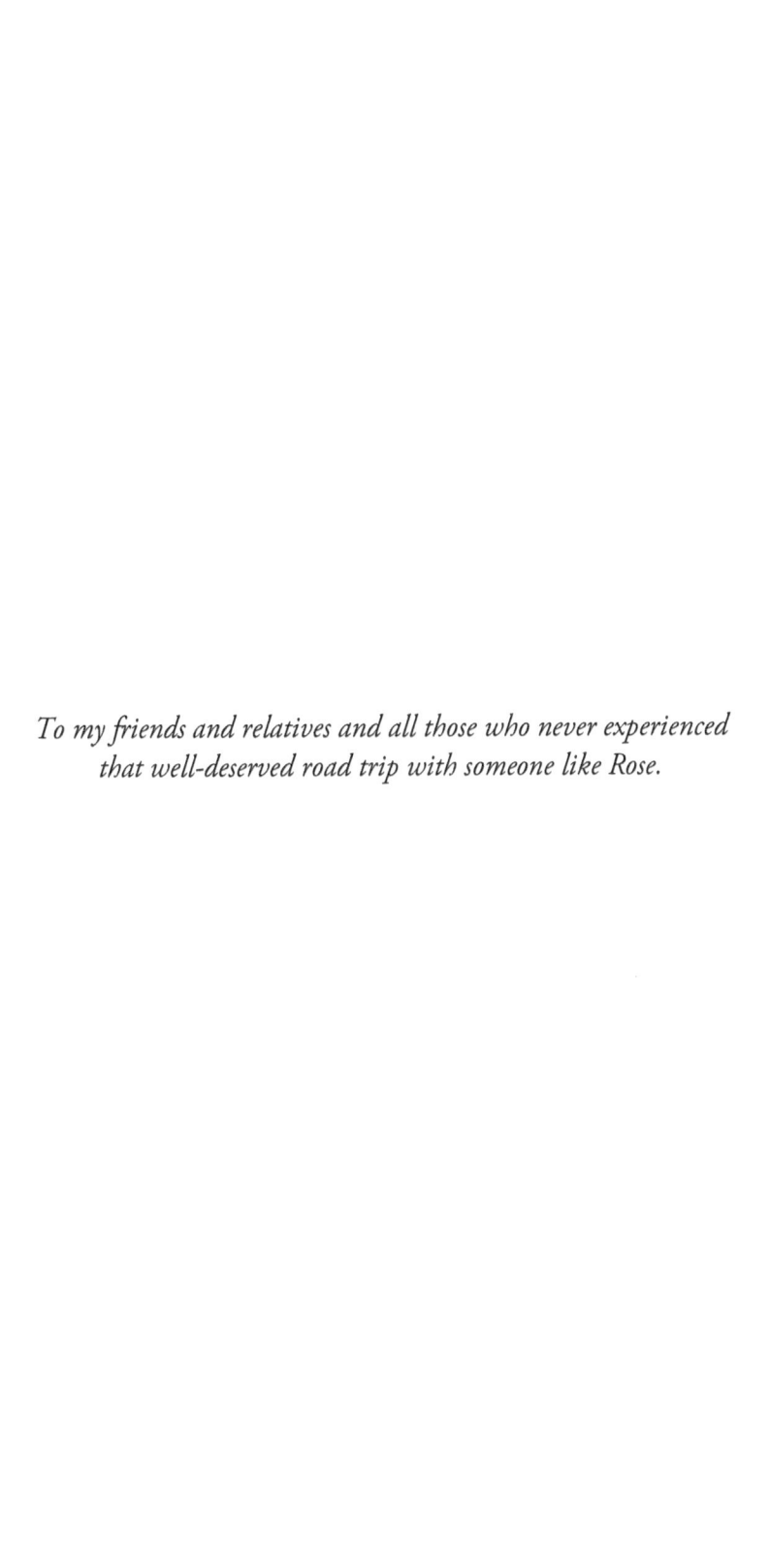

To my friends and relatives and all those who never experienced that well-deserved road trip with someone like Rose.

IT'S A WRAP

When I arrived home for lunch, my wife Sonia was in a busy scurry—cleaning. She was quiet. I knew that meant she was thinking through something important. She did that often. When she had something on her mind to work out, she would go into this quiet mode and start cleaning. I learned over the years not to disturb her when she was in this mood because she didn't like to engage in conversation, so I thought, *this, too, will pass.*

I sat down to eat lunch and watch *Perry Mason* like I did nearly every day at noon. When I got up to put my bowl away, my Sonia suddenly breezed through the kitchen with an armload of laundry and announced, "I'm moving to Oregon next spring. You can come with me if you want." She didn't even break stride as she disappeared down the hall and off into the laundry room.

There I stood, wondering what to make of her statement. I quickly followed her into the laundry room and asked, "What do you mean, you're moving to Oregon?"

She stopped right where she was. A look of hopelessness came over her face as she turned to me. "I just can't take another winter here."

I knew she meant it. We had been in Alaska nearly eight years now, and for the last three of them we had been talking about leaving. We loved it in many ways, especially the people. Then again, Sonia was ill, and the long, cold, dark winters were becoming too much for both of us. I was ready, too.

I had come to realize that there are trade-offs no matter where one lives. There are wonderful things to discover and experience, and there are some things that aren't so wonderful. I never did well in the city or where the sky was unusually cloudy like it was in Anchorage. I was happiest living inland where the sun shined frequently, and access to wide-open spaces was readily available. So agreeing with her was not difficult. I quickly replied, "I'm ready!"

The agenda was set for the next nine months. We would prepare to move to Oregon, to Eastern Oregon that is, where there are wide-open spaces and plenty of sunshine. It was October, which meant I had to sell my business while deciding on a new place to live and work. I also had to make all the necessary arrangements for our move. We still had a teenage daughter at home as well. It was going to be a complex project, but we were ready.

I informed the people where I worked of our decision. It wasn't long until all of our friends and associates knew about our plans. They showed disappointment when hearing of our upcoming move, yet encouraged us with best wishes.

Several years earlier, my daughter had asked me to accompany her on a service project that she had volunteered for as a school assignment. There was a small soup kitchen in downtown Anchorage called Bean's Café that provided free meals for people in need. She and I were to show up there and help serve. I thought it was a good thing to do, both for my daughter and as a service to the people. After going once and getting to know a few of the volunteers, I decided to continue at their insistent invitation.

Over the years, I became a regular at Bean's Café. While serving there, I experienced an opportunity to work with several Alaskan Native women. I sincerely enjoyed their company and found myself looking forward to the weekly visits at the café. These women had an unfamiliar way of dealing with things that totally amazed me. They seemed to be able to put people at ease and say the right thing in the right way, which was usually in an indirect manner. I also noticed that their outcomes were generally peaceful, and in some way, unifying. Serving people who live on the cold streets of Anchorage, who were often intoxicated and angry at society, was no easy task, yet these women did it so well.

One elderly woman was especially outstanding. Her name was Rose, and she took a liking to me, or at least I thought she did. She would always greet me with a warm handshake and make sure I had something to drink. She would sit me down and inquire about my family, my work, and my life in general. In fact, she often got quite personal with me, but she never pried and I never felt the questions she asked were inappropriate. They were always loving and sincere. She would fold her hands over her round belly, lean forward a little, look into my eyes as if to quiet me for a moment, and then ask me something general—the conversation eventually leading to more intimate details. Rose wondered what I thought about various political issues or current world events and why I thought the way I did. Sometimes she would offer a perspective different than mine and ask my opinion. I always enjoyed talking with her and eventually came to trust her, comfortably sharing my personal thoughts and feelings. I never felt harshly judged or condemned in any way. In fact, I often went away feeling better about myself and more hopeful about life in general. I came to like this gentle eighty-three-year-old woman very much, so I dreaded the time I would have to tell her I was moving. When I did tell her, she didn't even flinch. She just looked at me with her dark, smiling eyes and slowly sat back in her chair. "We all do what we have to do," she replied, then slowly stood to go back to her work. She was quiet the rest of that day, making only small talk. She didn't say anything more about me moving until just before the end of my shift when she asked, "When will you be leaving Alaska?"

"Probably sometime next summer," I responded.

She paused for a moment as though calculating the time, and then, throwing a towel over her shoulder, she smiled big and gave me a hug. That was one woman I was really going to miss.

As the months went by, I kept Rose informed of the progress of our move. She was always very kind to me—being informed of our move didn't change the way she treated me at all. One day I was explaining to her how I purchased a large truck with a twenty-foot van on it to move our belongings. I had bought one eight years earlier when we moved to Alaska from Oregon, and by selling it for more than I paid for it, our moving expenses were reduced considerably. I planned on doing the same thing for our return move. I was explaining in detail how we were planning the trip. I told her that Sonia would be driving our Bronco, and I would be driving the big truck and towing a small camp-trailer. Our daughter was going to fly down to Oregon and stay with my son, who had already moved back. Another couple we knew from Alaska were also moving back to Oregon. We had decided to all travel together.

Rose subtly informed me, "I was thinking of going down to Washington to visit my family sometime next summer, but I don't drive, and I can't fly."

"Why can't you fly?" I asked.

"My sinus condition," she replied. "I get intolerable face pain and headaches from the sudden elevation changes. I can take slow changes, like in a car, but not in planes."

"Maybe you could travel down with us," I suggested.

Glancing down, she said softly, "That's a possibility, but I wouldn't want to put you and your family out."

"You wouldn't be putting us out at all," I assured her. "Why don't you think it over? You are welcome, and we would be happy for your company." She agreed to consider my offer.

A few weeks passed without seeing Rose. I missed my regular weekly session at the café, so I hadn't talked with her for a while. I was busy phasing out all the activities and projects I had been involved in. I had been writing two books and was busy with so many other activities and projects that I felt overwhelmed. It was wintertime; I was extremely busy, and yet, I was getting depressed again. When it happened last winter, I was able to ride it out somehow. This time the pressure was too much. I couldn't shake the feeling of grief in my chest that weighed on me, so I made an appointment with a psychiatrist. His diagnosis of Seasonal Affective

Disorder came with a prescription for medication and a special light for people who suffer from light deficiency. I slowly began to feel better and was able to stay focused on my tasks. I was busy closing out projects and activities in preparation for our move. I also had to arrange for a place to live and a location to establish my business in Oregon. I was very busy and focused, so telling Rose I was resigning from my weekly post at the café was just a routine decision that had to be made. I went to the café on my scheduled day and informed her it would be my last, as I had so many things to do in preparation for the move. She acknowledged my decision with one of her kind smiles and continued with her work.

I had forgotten about the possibility of Rose traveling to Oregon with us until it was nearly time to go. Remembering, I casually asked, "So, are you going to Oregon with us this summer?"

"I think I might be able to do that," she replied, "but I would like to talk to you about it sometime first. There is a groundbreaking ceremony being held at a new Native healing center near Palmer. I would like to invite you and Sonia to attend. Maybe we could talk about the trip then."

"I don't know," I moaned doubtfully. "We're so busy getting ready for our move. I don't think we can add another activity to our agenda."

"It's a very special ceremony," she pleaded. "Audrey Hathaway bought the building and property and would very much like to see you there."

Audrey is an Alaskan Native healer who uses traditional herbs, drumming, songs, chants, and prayers to help those who need healing. She is well known and respected by the Native people and the medical community. I had met her before and found her fascinating.

"We'll have lots of good Native food for you to eat," she said enticingly, followed by belly laughter from her and several Native women who were working close by. It was funny to them, but I was clueless to the humor.

"Okay," I said. "Still, I have to ask Sonia if we can work it in."

Rose stopped, turned to face me directly, and then stood up real straight. "I would really like you to come." She held her hand over her heart and stood motionless, smiling, awaiting my commitment.

"All right," I said reluctantly. "I'll be there."

She gently nodded her head and returned to work.

The dedication of the Native healing center was in the spring, which in Anchorage means June. Spring, or "breakup" as it is called, begins in April. They refer to spring as breakup because that's when the ice begins to break apart and float down the rivers. In Anchorage, around the middle of May, over about a five-day period, nearly everything sprouts green. The cottonwood, willow, and alder all leaf-out at once and spring arrives. But June is the month to be outdoors. The sun is up twenty-two hours a day, the temperatures are in the sixties, sometimes even in the seventies, and it's generally sunny.

It was June, and we were making the final arrangements to move sometime in late July or early August. Because it had taken us ten days of travel when we moved up to Alaska from Oregon, we were planning on a ten-day return trip as well. It was 3,027 miles from the front door of our apartment in Anchorage to the front door of my mother's house in Tygh Valley—our temporary destination in Oregon. We would travel approximately three hundred miles a day, which would require six-plus hours of daily driving. The Alcan Highway was paved the whole way now with just occasional patches of gravel where the road was being repaired. These were the details rolling through my mind as I headed to the ceremony.

I only knew a few of the people at the dedication ceremony. There were three long tables set up with food, some of which I had never eaten before, including raw whale blubber called muck-tuck, dried seaweed, and seal oil. I filled my plate and sat down with Sonia and Rose to eat. The ceremony following the meal included prayers, drumming, chanting, and a few short talks. It was pleasant and inspiring. Even so, I was anxious for it to end so I could get on with my tasks. The activities were nearly over, and I was so preoccupied with other matters that I forgot to talk to Rose about traveling to Washington with us. It's not customary among the Native people for them to open up the subject when someone else is offering something, so Rose hadn't said anything either.

A physician friend of mine from Eagle River was getting ready to leave. While looking my way, he asked loudly, "Grayson, when are you leaving for Oregon?"

"In July or August," I replied.

He wished us well and proceeded to the parking lot. When I looked back at Rose, she was smiling big and looking at me with an inquisitive expression on her face. I wondered for a moment what that was about and then remembered her asking to talk with me regarding the trip. Walking closer to her, I asked, "So, what was it you wanted to talk to me about, Rose?"

"I would like you to sit down here and listen to me carefully," she replied, pointing to a small bench. "Please don't comment until I finish, and then I would like you to go home and think about what I have asked before you respond. Is that okay?"

"Yes, that's fine, Rose," I said.

"I want to make you a proposition," she continued in a quiet, sincere voice. "I would like to ride with you down the Alcan to Washington where my daughter lives. That is, I want to ride with **you**, just the two of us in your moving truck. I know you're a writer, and I have read some of your work. I like the way you write and the way you think. You have a good heart, and I can speak to it without reservation."

"Thank you," I replied.

She stopped abruptly and sat with statue-like stillness, staring at me. I realized I had spoken out of turn and had not kept quiet as she had requested. When she saw I had realized my error, she smiled one of those quick teeth-baring grins some of the Alaskan Natives do, bowed her head for a moment as if to find her place, then raised her head and continued. "I would like to publish a book, but I am having trouble writing what I want to say. I have tried several times. I even tried a computer. I still haven't found anything that works for me. I was hoping you could help. I would like to bring a tape recorder on the trip and record what I have to say while you listen. Also, I would like you to ask questions and carry on a conversation with me. When we have finished our journey, I would like you to write what we record, and then submit it for publication. I want nothing from the sale of this book. I only want you to do whatever it takes to get it published. Now, you go home and think it over, and then let me know. Do you understand what I am asking?"

I had to snap out of my stupor, for I found myself lost, imagining the reality of her proposition.

"What's the book about?" I asked curiously.

She just stared at me with soft, tear-filled eyes, and finally replied slowly, "**A spiritual vision of hope for mankind**. Now go!" she insisted. "We'll talk soon."

All the way home I kept scoffing at what she had said—"a spiritual vision of hope for mankind." *Oh boy, who does she think she is?*

What does that mean? I wondered. I couldn't get it out of my head. I didn't know of any spiritual vision of hope for mankind. In fact, the spiritual future of humanity seemed rather dismal to me. I had wondered about it nearly all my life but had essentially given up hope. Experiences in my youth had assured me I was a spiritual being and that there was so much more to life than what appeared in this short material existence. I had contemplated the questions of death, the afterlife, this life, and the possibility of other lives. I had investigated religions, read spiritual books, talked to everyone who would listen, read everything I could get my hands on about spirituality and religion, and temporarily had become certain of the purpose of life. But my enthusiastic interest had dwindled with time. Somehow, things changed. The more pressing concerns seemed to just take over my life—college, children, work, friends, responsibilities, stress—all causing the spiritual part of me to just fade.

I would love to have a spiritual vision of hope! I thought. I had been down the conventional spiritual path—go to church, do what you're told, and don't dare ask any probing questions. When I did ask, I was usually given the same parroted answers that never made sense to me.

Maybe to the real believers it does, I thought. Maybe I just wasn't ever a **real** believer. Maybe I just needed to accept the superstitious-sounding answers that were given to me whenever I questioned the conventional perspective. Maybe! Maybe! Maybe! I didn't know what was right and true, and I hadn't known for years—in fact, decades.

I was just doing what everyone else was doing—going through the motions of life as though they mattered somehow, yet feeling empty, as if something seriously important was missing. It had been especially true during this last year. I had blamed it all on depression. But I was probably depressed because my life didn't seem important or meaningful enough. I had read a verse from Danté that I thought summed up my life quite well:

"When I had journeyed half of our life's way,
I found myself in a shadowed forest,
For I had lost the path that does not stray."[1]

That was it. I was forty-seven. Three of my children were now living away from home, and I was on the threshold of being asked to consider again all those questions I had wondered about when I was nineteen. What am I doing here on this earth? What is my purpose here? What is anyone doing here? Does anyone really know? Does anyone else ask these questions? If they do, why doesn't someone say it? Are we all afraid of the answers? What if there aren't any answers?

So far there hadn't been any answers that felt right or made enough sense that the majority of people could agree upon them. And now, some old Alaskan woman wants me to listen to her for ten days while she resurrects all those difficult-to-bear feelings again. Was she crazy? Was I crazy for even considering her proposition? *Would she lay on me some Alaskan Indian thing?* I wondered. I didn't know. Maybe I would just listen to her talk and at the end of the trip tell her I am not up to writing the book. No, I didn't want to do that either. I might as well listen to her talk for ten days instead of listening to my own thoughts. *So be it,* I decided. *I'll just do it, and deal with it.*

Finally, the day came. The last items were loaded into the big truck, and I closed and locked the door. It's a hollow feeling when you're getting ready to move, and you walk through an empty house where you have lived for several years. I stopped for a moment in the living room and just took it all in. Years of life here, and now it's over. I felt a nostalgic melancholy swoop into my chest. It was from love—love of my family and our experiences here. For the most part, the experiences were good. Sometimes they were nearly unbearably difficult, and other times abundantly joyous. They all contributed to the love that was so strong in my family. I gave the house a big smile, closed the door, and walked away. Sonia and I had already said our good-byes to friends and co-workers, so we settled into our vehicles and pulled out of the driveway.

We headed to Palmer, which was just an hour away, to spend the night with some friends. We were to meet up in Palmer with Franklin and Annie, who were also moving to Oregon and planned on traveling with us. When we arrived, we helped them with their final packing and loading which we finished late that night. I didn't sleep well. I'm sure none of us did as we had quite a journey ahead of us. I ran through all the things I could think of to be sure we were ready. A three-thousand-mile journey through Alaska and Canada's northland can be trying. It pays to be prepared.

DAY ONE

IT TAKES A VISION

R ose arrived at our friend's house in Palmer the following morning with her suitcase and a large, woven, open-topped travel bag. She looked happy and excited. I showed her the truck. When we were ready to go, she stood nervously by the truck cab—shuffling back and forth. I warmed up the truck and helped Sonia get ready. Before long, Sonia rolled her window down and called to me. I went over to the Bronco to see what she wanted.

"I think Rose is going to need some help getting in and out of the truck. Maybe you could help her with that."

"Of course!" I replied, feeling thoughtless. Immediately I set my attention on helping Rose. First, I loaded her travel bag into the cab. I had already packed her suitcase in the Bronco with Sonia. I then set about helping Rose into the truck. After a bit of trial and error, we figured out a safe and easy way for her to get in and out. I checked with everyone to see if they were ready, climbed into the truck, and announced on the CB radio, "Forward Ho!"

It was finally happening. It was August 22nd, and we were on the road. Rose and I were in the big truck pulling a nineteen-foot camp-trailer. Sonia was behind us driving the Bronco. Franklin, Annie, and their newborn baby Scott were behind Sonia in a Ford pickup truck, pulling a U-Haul trailer. Annie's parents, T.J. and Alene, were in their car taking up the rear. T.J. and Alene lived in Tillamook, Oregon, and had come up to Alaska to see their new grandson, Scott, and to help Franklin and Annie with their move. They also wanted to drive the Alcan as a vacation. So there we were, a caravan of four vehicles, ready to drive a three-thousand-mile journey while trying to stay together.

I looked at my watch. It was about 9 a.m. Annie and Franklin had to care for their four-month-old baby boy, so it had taken a while to get ready.

Finally, we were traveling up the winding grade out of Palmer to the plateau region of the Copper River Basin. It's a curvy two-lane road with little traffic except an occasional local resident, delivery trucks packing freight, and motor homes with tourists. I had my mirrors set so I could see clearly behind me and down both sides of the truck. I was driving a manual five-speed with a two-speed rear end, giving me ten gears to play with. And play is what I did, because I was no truck driver! This rig had a Cummins diesel, which I had been told was a good engine. I also had a handheld CB radio wired to a magnetic antenna I had stuck on the cab of the truck. The antenna wire ran through the wing window and down across the dash onto the seat. From there, another wire ran underneath the dash to a hot wire, giving me power. The plug to the wires that attached to my hand-held CB didn't fit well, so I had it taped tight with black electrician's tape. I hadn't thought ahead to buy a coffee holder, so I had to hold my traveling coffee mug in my hand as I drove or set it between my legs. Sitting on the floorboard, just to the right of the gearshift, was a large houseplant that was too tall for the Bronco, where all of Sonia's other houseplants were. The darn thing was heavy on one side, so every time I went around a corner to the right, the plant would tip toward me. Sometimes I would have to reach over and hold it from tipping over onto the steering wheel, which made handling my coffee mug even more of a challenge.

On the other side of the seat sat Rose. She faced directly forward and perfectly upright with her hands folded in her lap. Her large woven handbag was at her feet. She had that scared, smiley look little girls have when they get to do something new and exciting. So there we were, going down the highway, talking and looking, listening and hoping this whole 3,000-mile excursion would be safe and trouble-free.

After some time I noticed Rose was laughing, but not out loud. She had her head turned toward the window as far as she could turn while hiding her face with her left hand. I knew she was laughing because her round short figure was bouncing up and down. She glanced at me and quickly turned back toward the window. For that brief moment, I noticed a big smile and a tear running down her face. "What's so funny?" I asked with a half-smile of my own.

She turned to me and exploded with laughter. She kept holding her face and trying not to laugh so she could talk, but something was just too amusing. Finally, she got it out. "You're so funny!" she spurted. "You should see yourself. You have a double-handed death-grip on that great big steering wheel. You're constantly looking at both mirrors with your head snapping back and forth while you operate the clutch and the gas pedals with your feet. Plus, you're shifting gears as you drive this curving, steep, narrow, uphill road while drinking coffee and talking on your CB! And you're doing it all at the same time while trying to keep that stupid plant upright! You're really scaring me, but watching you is hilarious!"

I looked at her, then at my feet, the mirrors, my hands, the coffee, the CB, the plant, and back at her. We stared at each other for a moment and then erupted with laughter. It **was** hilarious. We both laughed at how spastic I looked driving down the road. I had been under so much stress the last few years that focused multitasking was just an everyday-thing for me. Yet today, for some reason, it was just funny, and it felt really good to laugh so freely.

We were over our hilarity and settled in again. I felt more relaxed now and not quite so intense. We finally reached the plateau where the road wasn't so steep and crooked. Driving became easier, allowing me the opportunity to engage in conversation.

"I'm wondering if we could start now?" Rose asked hesitantly, waiting for my answer.

"Start what?" I said without thinking.

"Maybe we could start the conversation we spoke of before this trip."

"Sure, sure, any time you're ready," I replied anxiously.

"Wait a minute," she murmured as she bent over to get something out of her bag. She grunted a little as she shuffled around and pulled out a small cassette tape recorder. I slurped my coffee in partial reaction to what she was doing. I felt my heart rate go up and took a deep breath. I hated those things, especially when someone was recording me. I would immediately become self-conscious and stumble over my words, feel foolish, and forget what I wanted to say.

"What are you doing?" I snapped without thinking.

She stopped as though she was shot. Her eyes were full of dismay. She just sat there with the recorder in her hand. She didn't say anything and didn't move. Finally, she took a deep breath as though she had been holding it in, set the recorder down on the seat, and looked out the window.

"No, it's all right, I just forgot I guess," I said apologetically.

She turned back to me and said in a very soft voice, "I should have asked first."

"No, that's fine," I assured her. How was she to know how I felt about tape recorders? I knew she felt bad. It was her way, and the way of many of the Native women I knew. They were unusually sensitive to the people around them, which at times made them appear overprotective in the way they dealt with others. Rose was usually so in tune with my feelings and the feelings of others that she rarely did anything to cause distress or grief to another. It was like some kind of code of behavior, I guessed. I had noticed it before and admired it. Then again, I didn't understand how she was able to do it so routinely. She sat for a moment with her head down as if to ask for forgiveness—not of me, but from something beyond. I don't know. It just seemed that way.

"Your words mean a lot to me, and I would like to record our whole trip if you don't mind," she said.

"Yes, Rose, that's fine with me," I remarked, fidgeting around with my coffee cup, still feeling uneasy.

"I can tell you don't like the idea of having this recorder on," she said tenderly. "I hope you don't feel too bad about it. I don't like having to do it this way either," she admitted, "but if we're going to get this book written, we'll both have to endure it."

I assured her again that it was okay. I was actually feeling more comfortable with the idea already. She turned on the recorder as though forced against her will by some outside influence, then looked at me with pleading eyes and a gentle smile. She looked away, and then turned back toward me with renewed strength. Clearing her throat, she began, "As I told you when we first discussed this trip, what I want to share with you is spiritual in nature. I would like you to listen attentively and ask questions any time you like. Furthermore, I would like to record everything we talk about so you will have a complete recording of our conversation. Do you have any reservation about that?"

"No," I assured her, glancing at the recorder.

"I really don't know where to start, so I think I'll just tell you a story first." She paused and looked out the side window for quite some time before continuing. "I want to tell you a story about an elder from the village I lived in when I was young. At that time, there was this older man I knew who was in very poor health. Winter was soon to come upon us, and he knew he would not make it through another winter. Sometimes, rather than hold on to life, our elders would decide to take no more from their journey here, and silently prepare for their transition to the next world. This particular gentleman, who we called Phillip Eagle, began to take only small amounts of food, which hastened his weakening condition. One day he ambled off toward the sea. I did not see him go, but that evening my mother said she had seen him leave. This happened often, so no more was spoken of it, as it seemed a natural and normal thing for me. I was only ten years old and had not been out of my village yet. I didn't know other cultures did things differently. It was also before television and radio in our village.

"This time, however, when Phillip Eagle left our village, events took a different turn for him than expected. The following day, he came slowly walking back to the village. No one paid too much attention to him as this also happened occasionally.

"Later that afternoon, I was sent to a small stream to gather some special plants to go with our evening meal. When I arrived, I noticed Phillip Eagle sitting beside the stream. He looked up as I approached. I gave him a quick glance because I was surprised to see him. Normally, I would not have looked upon his face, as that would have been disrespectful. When I did glance at him, I noticed a subtle expression of joy, as though he had been waiting for me.

"When I arrived at the stream and squatted to gather some plants, he spoke to me. I did not look up. He said, 'I had a vision of you last evening when I went down by the sea. It was a great vision of importance to the people of our village.' He hesitated for a moment. 'You know that to every other generation or so, a great vision is given to one of the villagers that helps us through difficulties. But this vision was not only for our village, but for all the villages in the land. I am going to tell you what was given to my inner eyes.' He paused for a time before continuing. 'I saw you flying above the ocean waters. I saw canoes coming toward you from all directions—people from different villages and places—many that I have never seen or heard of before. Some looked very strange to me. The people were different in color and wore different clothing, and had different hats on their heads. All these people in the canoes were yelling desperately for help and assistance. They were yelling at **you**, pleading for your words that would help them. Even though all of them were yelling, they could not hear each other because they were all deaf. You were floating above the water speaking out, but nothing was coming out of your mouth, as you were mute. You had great words in your heart for the people, but you could not speak, and they wanted your words, but they could not hear. Then I saw you reach your hand out to the ocean below, and something came up from the water into your hand. You put it to your mouth to speak. Your words came out, and the people could hear your words. They all stopped rowing and sat up motionless, as if stunned by a jellyfish, but with looks of wonder, joy, and hope on their faces. And that was the end of my vision.' He then became silent. The whole time I had kept motionless, squatting by the creek with my eyes upon the water. After some time passed, and I was respectfully sure he had nothing more to say, I arose and returned to the village.

"Phillip Eagle's vision has haunted me all my life. I have looked for some method or instrument to speak through, to share with the people the special words that were later given to me. Every time I try to convey what I have discovered, I feel as though my tongue cannot speak what I want to say, and the people I talk to cannot hear me in their heart. I tried to write out my words by hand. I even learned to use a computer. Still, nothing has worked well for me. So I am hoping that this conversation with you will work. I'm thinking perhaps this tape recorder is the instrument Phillip Eagle saw in his vision." She looked at the tape recorder and snickered at something personally amusing which I did not understand.

"I tell you this, Grayson. The feeling I have in my heart is that I have been given a great vision of hope, yet I have been unable to write it out the way I want. Perhaps we will be able to do it together," she said hopefully. "I will do my best to tell you about it, and I am asking you to do your best to listen, and of course, to ask questions at will." She turned to look silently out the window.

I hadn't planned on giving this woman my full attention for ten days on the road. In fact, I had planned on having a relaxing drive, if possible, but that wasn't to be the case. After hearing about Phillip Eagle's vision, and seeing how serious and intent she was about my attention to what she was saying, I promised to do my best.

She was quiet and relaxed for some time after that, as though some major burden was lifted from her heart. Finally, she spoke again. "Tell me about you," she said seriously, looking down when I turned to look at her for a moment.

"Oh boy," I exhaled. "What do you want to know? Forty-seven years of life holds quite a lengthy story you probably don't want to hear."

"Tell me about this place where you and Sonia are moving," Rose urged. "How is it that you lived there? Tell me about it. Tell me about living there."

"Well, just for the record," I said, looking down at the recorder. "Where do you want me to start?" She was silent. I began before she could respond. "I moved to Tygh Valley with my family when I was nine years old. I loved it there. Before that we lived on the west side of the Cascade Mountains, in several places between the coast and Mount Hood. My father was a logger. He was disabled from several logging accidents. By the time he was forty-two, he had undergone seventeen major operations because of logging injuries. The places we lived before moving to Tygh Valley had up to sixty-five inches of rainfall a year and were heavily forested with trees, ferns, blackberries, moss, and other thick undergrowth. It seemed like it was always wet outside from the incessant rain, so I didn't like playing outdoors much. However, Tom and I did play outside on occasion when the weather was good. Tom was my younger brother, who was a year and a half younger than me.

"We had relatives who lived in Tygh Valley that we used to visit. Tygh Valley was about forty miles east of Mount Hood, which was about a two-hour drive from where we lived. Dad would sometimes pace around the house and all of a sudden exclaim, 'Let's go to Tygh Valley where the sun is shining and get out of this rain!' We would pack up a few things and head out. Dad would say to us boys, 'You just watch. As soon as we get to Pine Grove the sun will be shining.' It seemed he was always right. Pine Grove is just on the east side of the Cascade Mountains, near Tygh Valley. The yearly rainfall there is less than ten inches, and there are over three hundred days of sunshine every year." I popped up my eyebrows at Rose, trying to give greater value to living in Tygh Valley. She just nodded her head and looked forward. "We moved to Tygh in 1961, and I loved it. My mother said that once we had moved into our new home, Tom and I were hardly ever in the house until after dark. We loved living there because we could play outside most of the time." I paused for a moment, reminiscing about those childhood years of playing in the woods, swimming in the river, climbing the bluffs, hiking the canyons, exploring, fishing, hunting, and riding my bike. I regained myself and proceeded. "Do you want to know all these details?" I asked curiously.

"Yes, you're doing fine," Rose said. "But tell me about your grandfather."

"Which grandfather?" I wondered why she had asked that when I hadn't mentioned either of them.

"Once when we were working at Bean's Café, you said you had a grandfather who often prayed for you and had been vital in your life some way. Tell me about that."

"Well, that's a whole different story," I replied. "I was talking about my **spiritual** life when I said that."

"Then tell me about that," she asked. "How did your spiritual life get started?"

"Get started?" I repeated. "Well, I don't recall having much of a religious upbringing, but I can tell you about some of my experiences."

"No," she said. "I mean your **spiritual** life, not necessarily your religious life. Do you know what I am saying?"

I thought for a moment. "I suppose," I said. "Nevertheless, as I recall it probably began with going to church."

"Yes, of course," she said, nodding me on.

"My grandpa used to take my brother and me to church when we were young. I don't remember too much about it. He went to the Assembly of God church, which was quite evangelical and expressive in those days. Grandpa was very strict about his religion. He didn't drink or smoke, and he never swore. He didn't like television or anyone playing cards in his house. I guess he thought they were demonic in some way. He was very strict with my mother when she was growing up. She couldn't wear lipstick or nylons, for example. I remember that Grandpa would pray for what seemed like an hour every night. He would wait until everyone was in bed, then, dressed in his pajamas and robe, he would kneel down on the floor with his head bowed in a great big chair and pray, loudly and emphatically. I thought of him as a very religious man, and if I ever became religious, I wanted to be just like him. At least that's what I thought when I was young.

"I can remember going to church on Wednesday nights. It was scary though," I remarked, recalling those early years. "People would chant and moan, throw their arms up, holler, pray, and bow to the floor just to rise up again. Some would go up to the altar where the preacher was. They would talk, quietly at first, and then they would burst into an uproar of praise that sometimes led to tears. Occasionally they would talk in tongues, fall on the floor, and then roll around in a kind of fit. At least, that's what Dad called it. All I can remember is that it was mostly elderly people. Of course, I was only five, so everyone seemed old to me. I also remember Sunday school. Those memories are not necessarily pleasant either." I looked at Rose for understanding.

Rose looked back and smiled. "Why not?" she asked.

"I remember not wanting to be there and watching the clock. Most of the teachers I had seemed phony to me. They were almost always women, usually young ladies. They would come in with what appeared to be a pretend smile and start talking about Jesus and how he loved us and how he suffered for us. I didn't understand what all the fuss was about. I just wanted to eat and then go outside and play, which is what we did after Sunday school class was over. But the teachers would go on with these little felt figurines on a felt board about Jesus and the lambs. I didn't understand why they always talked about the lambs and how Jesus was the Lamb of God. It just didn't make sense to my young mind. Then I recall a little girl throwing up in the classroom. We were all so hungry that the rest of us got sick too. The classroom never smelled the same after that. That was church as I remember it—people doing strange things, and unpleasant experiences."

I paused for a moment and looked out the window, checking my mirrors and the caravan of automobiles behind me.

"But something must have happened there," I continued, "because somehow I grew up with a belief in God. I don't remember the details of that belief, except I knew he was there; he was watching, and I had better behave."

I thought about it for a few minutes and then remembered more.

"I think my belief in God and my understanding of having a relationship with him was fostered when I was about nine or ten from my reading a series of faith-based books about The Sugar Creek Gang. They were stories about a group of boys living near Sugar Creek, Indiana. They told of the adventures and mysteries the boys were involved in. Each story was written to teach lessons in morality and to help young boys develop a relationship with God. It did that for me. I do remember feeling confused by the occasional biblical reference that sometimes didn't feel real or possible to me. But I liked reading those stories, and they had a profound spiritual influence on me.

"I also remember a specific incident that confirmed my belief in God. It made me feel certain he existed and that he was near. It happened one time when I was about ten years old. Do you want to hear this?" I asked.

"Yes, please," Rose prompted. "This is exactly what I want to hear." She seemed pleased.

"We had a small Pomeranian dog named Ruff," I said. "I loved that dog. He was our family dog for several years, which at my age felt like a lifetime. One evening we were sitting at the dinner table. Our house sat only about eighty feet from the roadway. We heard a car go by, and the dog barking at the car. We heard brakes squeal, a thud, and then nothing but the car motoring on down the road.

"Dad jumped up from the table and looked out the window toward the road. 'Ruff's been hit!' he cried. He pushed his chair back from the table and headed for the door. 'You kids stay right here,' he demanded as Tom and I jumped up to follow him.

"We watched out the window as Dad went out to the road. He threw something out of the road into the ditch and then bent over the dog. The car that hit Ruff was an old Buick with detachable fender skirts. The dog had been hit so hard by the car that it knocked the skirt right off. Dad picked up the dog and carried him past the house to a shed out back.

"After a short time, he came back in the house. 'I'm going to have to put Ruff out of his misery boys,' he announced decisively. 'He's so badly hurt, he won't live, and I don't want to see him suffer.' Dad headed for the bedroom to get the twenty-two rifle. Tom and I looked at each other briefly, and then ran to Dad, begging him not to shoot Ruff. He was firm. We started crying and kept begging, but it didn't do any good. Dad went out the front door, closing it behind him. Tom and I ran to the bedroom and threw ourselves on our beds, crying miserably. I remember praying with all my might for God not to take my dog. I remember praying hard as I listened for that gunshot. I prayed and listened, prayed and listened. Suddenly, we heard the front door open and Dad come in. We both jumped up and went out to see what was going on.

"Dad was standing at the door, wiping his feet, holding the rifle by the barrel with his head down. He looked up at my mother. 'That was the damnedest thing I've ever seen. That dog was bloody and unconscious, and his eye was popped out of his head and laying on his cheek when I left him in the shed. I was sure he was near dead. But when I went back out to the shed and opened the door, there he sat with his tail wagging, his eye back in his head, and just as happy as though he had good sense! I guess he's going to be all right. I've never seen anything like it.' Tom and I just looked at each other, beaming with relief and joy. Something happened to me at that moment. I knew then, not only was there a God, but he hears and answers prayer. I silently thanked him and went about my day.

"I have to stop talking for a moment," I said to Rose. "You can turn that off if you want." I nodded at the recorder.

"No," she pleaded. "I would like to let it run for the whole trip. Please don't worry about it being on, and don't feel you have to keep talking just because it's there. Just be yourself, please."

I needed a few minutes to grieve again. Every time I tell that story the grief of nearly losing Ruff overwhelms me.

I finally continued with my story. "We did lose Ruff a few years later. One day after school, my mother told me he had been hit by a car again. He deserved it I suppose, because he was always chasing cars, and we couldn't seem to get him to stop. Mom asked me to remove Ruff from the road and bury him, as Dad wasn't home at the time. I went out to the road to find Ruff. He was lying dead on the edge of the road. His little heart had been squished right out of his chest and was lying beside him on the roadside, still attached. I picked him up, flung his heart up on top on his stiff body, and carried him out back to bury him. I went to the shed to get a shovel. No tears this time. I'm not sure why, but something inside of me seemed to say, *I answered your prayer and gave him more life than what was to be. Be thankful for that.* And I was. I buried him and walked away.

"Death is so final!" I blurted loudly.

Rose jerked her head around, looking at me solemnly. "Yes, it appears so, doesn't it?" she said with a gentle smile.

I needed some time. We sat quietly with the recorder running. Annie's dad, T.J., went whizzing by, pulling his little Honda car right in front of me. He came on the CB. "Hey, Big Koala. Tail-gunner here! We gotta find a restroom quick!" he snapped.

The map showed no towns for miles ahead, so I reported back, "If you can find a wide place where we can all pull over, we can use the restroom in the camp-trailer." He gave me the "ten-four" and sped off. "Restroom break!" I announced on the CB to the rest as I saw T.J.'s brake lights come on ahead of me.

We took turns using the restroom in the camp-trailer while the rest walked about to stretch their legs. It didn't take long before we were ready to go. It was quite an ordeal for Rose to get in that truck. She was elderly, short—maybe all of five-foot—and heavy. She did everything slowly and with care, whereas I was coffeed-up and in a hurry most of the time. You can imagine the two of us trying to work together. I had to help her in and out of the truck every time, but I didn't mind. I really liked her and was happy to help her in any way.

"Blinkers away!" T.J. proclaimed as he sped off. We all fell in and took off down the highway again. Rose already had the recorder on. I didn't see her turn it on, but it had a slight rhythmic squeak that let me know it was running. She must have turned it on after I helped her in and while I went around checking tires, doors, and hitches before climbing into the cab.

"Where do we go from here?" I asked, glancing soberly at Rose. Obviously, I was still not over my grief. In fact, I felt a little upset that I had to tell the story about Ruff again. I was hoping for happy traveling, but I was feeling down instead.

"Hey! I thought you were going to tell **me** a story," I reminded Rose. She smiled and readjusted herself in the seat.

"Yes, we'll get to that," she said. "I can't share my story with you until I find **you** first."

"Find me?"

"Yes. I want to understand you a little more first, and hear about your life and your search. It helps me connect with you better," she explained.

"Okay," I agreed with a sigh of surrender. "I understand." I really did. I knew that if you wanted to talk intimately with someone you had to wade through the outside shell to get to the real inner person. Generally, people are not ready to reveal their inner thoughts and sentiments without first establishing a feeling of safety that can only be formed with time, shared experience, and conversation—from the superficial to the profound, from the outward image to the true inner self. Whew! What a line of esoterica I was feeding myself. *Half-truths,* I thought, *all true, but debatable at every turn.*

I could have intimate conversations with people immediately—just go right to what I want to say and say it. That was my way. From what Sonia told me, it was the way of most men—get to the point up front, and explain your position afterward. Explain! Explain! Explain! Women are different, however, especially the Alaskan Native women I had met. Rose rarely talked that way. Instead, she would start gently, maybe with a story, probing my feelings with subtle questions. Then silence. More stories or conversation, building a theme I didn't even know was developing, urging my thinking along until I **self-discovered** the very understanding she was wanting to express all along, but didn't. Why? It took me a long time to figure it out. It's a spiritual thing, I determined, not to make waves of conflict if you can prevent it. That was Rose's way. I tended to say what I wanted up front, brave any defensive response, and then charge on with explanations. Her way was different—gentle leading without being presumptive, sincere questioning as though trying to find her way. I liked the way she communicated, but I had no idea how to do it. It was a peaceful way, and maybe sometime if I asked her about it, she would show me how to do it. *I'll do that*, I thought. *I'll do that for sure.*

I was feeling better now, so I asked again, "Where do we go from here?"

"Well, you told me about your spiritual experience with your dog Ruff and your reading of the Sugar Creek Gang books," Rose summed up. "Where did your spiritual interests go from there? Did you think about spiritual matters when you were young, or when did that come about?"

"Well," I began, "after Ruff died, I don't remember thinking much about God. I didn't go to church except once in a while when Grandpa would come to visit and talk me into going with him.

"I do remember attending Sunday school for a short time when I was about twelve. I had been hiking with several of my friends in Tygh Valley when we had quite a lengthy conversation about God and spirituality. We all decided that maybe we could find the answers to our questions at Sunday school, so we agreed to attend together. I can only remember going a few times before becoming discouraged again. I remember at that age the lot of us had numerous questions about life, God, and death. However, the teacher kept directing us back to her prepared lesson, avoiding the questions that were puzzling us so. I remember how serious we all were about learning about God and ourselves, yet the lessons we were being taught, and the stories we were being told all seemed . . . so . . . fairytale-like. That's what I called it. It all sounded so unrealistic—not unlike the stories of Santa Claus and the Easter Bunny. It seemed to me the congregation just wanted us to believe and pretend like they did. After attending for a few months, and without our questions being answered in any meaningful way, most of us quit going.

"Up through high school, I had no spiritual life to speak of that I recall. My parents didn't go to church or talk much about God or

STEVEN E. ELLIS

spiritual matters. They did live ethically though, and encouraged good moral behaviors like truthfulness, honesty, cleanliness, and fairness.

"The teenagers I associated with rarely discussed spirituality. I recall camping one time when I was about fifteen. We slept on the ground on a hill near an old millpond. There were no lights, and the starry sky was bright and beckoning. Several of us boys counted falling stars that night. We talked about the expanse of the universe and all we knew about atoms, stars, and space. Eventually, we came to a paradox that puzzles me to this day. Someone asked, 'Where does the universe end?' Another answered, 'It never does.'

"'But it has to,' I argued. 'It's impossible for it not to have an end. Suppose you put a sign out there that read: *The End of the Universe*. There has to be something on the other side of that sign! Even if it's just space; it's something. There has to be something forever.' Yet, forever also seemed impossible. We puzzled over that for some time until someone heard something scary, which ended our philosophizing that night. But, that thought has stuck in my mind ever since. It is one of those mysteries that I can't get my mind around. It seems to evoke parallel questions about God and life and death, but there doesn't appear to be acceptable answers to those questions either, except in religion. And that's another story."

"Yes, that **is** another story," Rose acknowledged. "Tell me, what did you do with that experience?"

"Nothing at the time," I admitted. "Well, not until years later, anyway. Maybe my curiosity about it was always there. In fact, I'm sure it was, and still is. To this day, I have no meaningful answers—at least none that I'm satisfied with."

"So what happened next?" she inquired.

"Well, throughout high school I was just a normal teenager. I did my schoolwork, played sports, liked girls, bought a car, and had a job during the summer. I don't remember anything significant happening that inspired any spiritual interests. When we were out drinking at times as teenagers, spiritual matters occasionally came up, but the conversation was never able to go anywhere meaningful,

26

probably because of the alcohol."

I thought for a moment. "I did have a general discontent, like something was missing, but I didn't know what. Anyway, I don't remember anything significant until after I was married."

"Lunch time!" blasted over the CB. T.J. and Alene went screaming around me in their Honda. We were getting close to Glennallen, Alaska, where we planned to have lunch. Our conversation was yanked back to the present by T.J.'s lunch announcement.

Glennallen had a big restaurant and lodge located in a large, old building on the west end of town. It had a huge parking lot, which we needed. Next door to the lodge, there was a convenient gas station. Inside the lodge there were numerous animal heads mounted on the walls. One was a large buffalo head. I wondered: *Why did they have a buffalo head in an Alaskan lodge?* It just seemed odd because I didn't think there were any buffalo in Alaska. I asked the waiter about it. He surprised me by telling me there **were** wild bison in Alaska. In fact, there were two separate herds.

While waiting for our meal, I told Sonia about the difficulty I was having with the large plant in the cab of the truck interfering with my driving. I asked her if it would be alright if I gave it to one of the people in the restaurant. She agreed. One of the waitresses was happy to take it, and I was relieved to be rid of it.

DAY ONE

THE WHY OF IT ALL

We had a hasty lunch, as everyone was anxious to get some miles behind us. We knew we had a long trip ahead, and we wanted to complete it in ten days. That meant we had to average three hundred miles a day, which was quite a chore. My big truck, when loaded and pulling a camp-trailer, had a maximum top speed of sixty miles per hour on a straight flat road. Much of the road was winding and steep, with potholes, frost heaves, occasional gravel, and was at times under construction. We also had a four-month-old baby that had needs, let alone the seven adults. Then there were restroom breaks, fuel stops, picture stops, meal stops, and assorted other stops. Sticking to driving three hundred miles a day required a vigilance that was difficult to uphold. Nevertheless, we surrendered to the requirements and proceeded down the road to our first night's destination: Tok, Alaska.

Rose lost no time after lunch. She often appeared easy going and unconcerned about what was going on around her, but I was beginning to see that she was different than I had first thought. We weren't even out of town when she reached over and turned on the recorder, making sure I saw her by grunting a little and scooting around in the seat when she did it. I glanced over at her hurriedly, catching her eye for a moment. I saw in her face that it was just what she wanted. I didn't say anything, and neither did she.

We made a right turn at the junction on the east end of

Glennallen and headed out across the upper Copper River Basin toward Tok. There were no towns through this area, just a few scattered, small villages. The terrain was mostly muskeg, some random trees, and a distant mountain range with huge snow covered peaks. It was a beautiful drive with only pleasant distractions.

Rose remarked, "You were telling me about your spiritual experiences as a young person. You mentioned something happened after you were married?"

"Oh, yes, after we were married," I repeated. "Sonia and I were married in March of 1970 when we were seniors in high school. I went to work at the sawmill in Tygh Valley while Sonia continued with school. We made an arrangement with the school principal that Sonia would bring my homework home and then return it to school for me so I could finish my senior year. It worked out well, and I was able to graduate. We lived in a small mill-house, which felt like our own. After a year or so, I remember going through a life-changing period. I was nineteen-years old, with a beautiful wife, a newborn son, and a hot new car. I had my own house where my friends could come and party. Even though I was not of legal age, I could buy beer at the local store. The woman who owned the store knew me and let me get away with it. So there I was at nineteen with everything I had ever wanted—a home, a family, friends—what else was there? Well, that winter it hit me—what else **was** there? Really! Was this it? I looked around me at some of the older men who worked at the mill. Some of them had worked there for forty-some years, nearly all their adult lives. They would sit around in silence during break, drinking coffee and smoking cigarettes, at least many of them did. The others would walk around for ten minutes, quietly and solemnly, as though waiting to return to work so they could feel normal. Most of them didn't make enough money to own their homes. Few ever went on vacation, except occasionally during hunting season. I looked around me and said to myself, 'Is this it? Is this what I am going to do for the rest of my life? Come to this mill every day and work hard for a measly wage while the stockholders get richer? Retire someday as an old man who had no joy or meaning in life—never doing anything or going anywhere—like the rest of these guys? That's not going to happen to me if I can help it!' I remember telling Sonia that I felt like a toadstool—just pop-up, live, and then die, with no meaningful purpose in life! I felt like I was just another tiny, meaningless grain of sand on some immense ocean beach. *There has to be more to life than this!* I remember thinking. I didn't know what it was, but I was going to find out. Because if this was it, something was terribly wrong. I guess I could say it stirred in me a kind of depression, mixed with anger, fear, rebellion, and search. I am sure it was obvious to others in my life, at least the adults, now that I look back on it, but no one said anything to me. Sometimes when we had parties, and the young people I knew were together, I would talk to them and ask them questions about life and its purpose, but no one seemed to care much or have any satisfactory answers.

"Then one day a young man who was a hippy-friend of mine came by to visit. His name was Butch. We had a lengthy, meaningful conversation about spiritual matters. I told him about the night I had slept out with the guys, and the conversation we had about the end of the universe, and how I wondered about life and its purpose. He suddenly jumped up off the couch and went over to his house next door where he had just moved in. He came back with a book about spiritual matters. Well, that was it. I read that book, and then another, then another, and then another. I read everything I could get my hands on about God and the spiritual path. There seemed to be something compelling about them that helped address my numerous questions.

"I had acquired a new job as tallyman at the mill, which required me to count and record the boards by grade and length as they came out of the planer mill. Sometimes it was slow, or sometimes there would be a breakdown that gave me time to read. I read every day, nearly all day, everything I could find about spiritual matters. Many of my friends noticed a change in me and thought I was crazy, but I knew I was on the right path to something important. Somewhere in the **spiritual approach** to life were the answers to my gnawing questions. I read the holy books of many religions. I loved what I read. Every day I felt high, detached, and joyous—maybe not all day, as I was still going through ups and downs. But at least I was on to something good. It set me out on a path of search that has not ended to this day."

I paused and looked out the window. I felt defeated. Here I was forty-seven years old, reminiscing about my spiritual journey, and realizing that I still had not satisfied my hunger to know what life was all about. There were times I felt I knew. Yet, something kept pulling me back to day-to-day life, which felt distant and disconnected from my real purpose. I couldn't reconcile the two for some reason. I felt unfaithful to my true self and was now depressed about it again.

Rose snapped me out of my self-pity stupor. "What a great story," she affirmed in a comforting way. "I think everyone has an interesting life story, and they are all wonderful, but yours is especially interesting. You mentioned before about your father dying when you were young. Was that during this period?"

"Yes, it was. He died when I was twenty-one. It challenged my newly found spiritual beliefs terribly," I whined. "I was so sure about life and death and the spiritual life afterward, and his spiritual life afterward, but I still grieved terribly. And I still do." I paused for a moment, as the emotion of grief from losing my father visited me again.

"It's all so permanent!" I insisted. "I mean, one day he was here, the next he was gone. Gone! Good-bye! Poof! Death just upsets everything! If it weren't for death, we wouldn't have to worry about who we are, where we came from, where we are going, the purpose of life, hell, heaven, reward, punishment, and such. But because of death, all those questions pester the mind and demand an answer. There's no avoiding them. They have to be answered, but quite frankly, I've failed to find anything that makes sense to me or anything I can feel certain about, and I've been around!" I took a deep breath before continuing. "I've read nearly all the sacred books of most major religions. I've sought out holy men. I've been to different churches and places of worship. I've attended their studies and meetings, and still I'm left unsettled. There are just no meaningful answers that satisfy the inquisitive mind and heart. Oh, yes! Every religion has an answer to nearly every question. However, so many of them are simplistic and incomplete, or even superstitious, or way out in the fantasy zone somewhere. Obviously their religious holy men couldn't find the answers either, or they wouldn't have made up such foolish stories and rationales in response to valid questions. I'm a little hot about this, as you can tell."

I looked over at Rose. She looked back and smiled, making me feel understood. "I'm sorry," I sighed. "It's just frustrating. I have always wanted to know. I want to know who I am, really. That is, **what** am I, in the whole scheme of things? I was born forty-seven years ago, and I don't remember anything before that. I was just born into this life. I had nothing to say about it, who my parents were, what I was going to look like, or what I was going to be like for that matter. So where was I before that? Where were we before birth? Did we exist before that? These are valid questions, aren't they?"

Silence filled the cab for a spell. "But that's not the really important question here," I continued. "That's not what really concerns me now. As time has gone by, I don't really care much about where I came from or the fact that I can't remember anything before birth. The real important question is: 'What about after death?' See! There it is again. Time is going to go on forever. Will I go on forever? Do I just get born and then die? Dead! Gone! Asleep, without dreams! A meaningless lifespan that's just a blink in the great eternity? If that's so, what's the point of living, especially for the millions that live in agony, poverty, disease and oppression? Why do people keep trying? Why not get it over with?

"I know why." I blurted out. "Because there **is** more to life than this measly eighty-year lifespan. Otherwise, nothing about the life of humans makes sense. If there is more to life than what we readily perceive, what is it? Now, that's the real question. And besides that, how do I know what's true if someone were to try to answer that question? Everyone has a different answer! Oh yeah, there are similarities among the religions and the spiritualists, but their explanations vary so much that I am confused about what is true? I would like to know. I would just like to know." I was finished. We rode for a while without either of us saying anything.

"Rose, I didn't mean to get all wound up like that," I apologized. "It's just that life is perplexing enough that I can't give up the search for meaningful answers."

"Don't feel bad," Rose replied. "These are the questions that haunt us all. Don't you worry, I am sure you will find the answers to your questions." She gave me a great big smile. There was also a kind of twinkle in her eye as she said it. Maybe from a tear, but it must have been a happy tear because she started giggling gently to herself for nearly a minute. I didn't know what was funny, but it didn't matter. I was quiet. I didn't want to talk anymore.

Here I am again, I thought, *right back where I have been time after time. Frustrated! Wanting to know and understand, but short, always short of the answers. Maybe once in a while I get a little bit of truth, just enough to keep me searching, but never enough to make me feel content.* I didn't want to think about it anymore. I focused on the beautiful snow-capped mountains in the distance and started going through the checklist in my mind that I needed to keep fresh regarding the safety and progress of our trip. *Focus on that*, I told myself. *That way I don't have to think about all those questions of life. There! Done!*

Oh, but it wasn't done. Rose finally spoke. "Your heart is rich," she said, "rich with wonder. What greater wealth is there than this?" She turned to me with her question.

I glanced at her, but this time she looked different. She was sitting upright. Her eyes seemed firmly controlled and focused. It was like her jaw was set, and yet she had a pleasant smile. How did she do that? She was serious, very serious, and intent with what she was doing and saying. I didn't know what she meant by "rich with wonder," but she soon continued.

"The whole purpose for me making this trip," she said, "is to address the questions you have just proposed so emphatically, and many more. It's rare that a person has a chance to sit down undisturbed and convey to a friend, a brother, a fellow man or woman, a deep truth that has been revealed to her mind and heart.

And this is what I wish to talk to you about on this journey. For the length of this trip, I would like you to listen carefully. Please let your mind and heart consider what it is I have to share with you, for indeed, it is well worth your time and thoughtful attention. I offer this story to you as a gift, in the same way it was given to me. I am presenting it to you as a sincere truth. I hope you will be able to consider it as such when I have finished sharing it with you in its entirety."

Rose paused while contemplating her next thought. "It is more than just a story though, Grayson," she explained. "It is a description, an explanation, a perspective of the purpose and reality of our life here on this planet, in this human condition. I earnestly request your complete attention and open-minded consideration of what I will say, and when you write about this, I hope you will invite your readers to give it the same attention I am asking of you.

"You have been searching for a long time, Grayson. Your quest has not been in vain. The All-Knowing Spirit knows of your efforts, and you will not be disappointed. You may have a tendency to judge what I am going to tell you as I am sharing it with you. However, I am asking you to put off judgment until you have the whole story, the whole perspective. It will make sense as a whole, but the independent parts are more difficult to understand without having the whole picture. It's like examining a puzzle, one piece at a time, and then placing each piece in a box. You can look at each piece carefully, over and over, one at a time, and you will never see the whole picture. But when you put them all together the way they were intended to fit, you will see the whole picture and each part will make perfect sense."

She paused, silently gazing out the window. "Nearly everyone, at some time in their life, asks the questions you have just expressed. Some search for answers repeatedly; some give up; some satisfy themselves with simple and often superstitious or immature answers. Others search endlessly, but most everyone considers them at one time or another. I am going to suggest to you there is only one place to find any potential for reasonable answers to these questions, and that is in the teachings of religion."

I glanced at her with doubt, questioning her statement.

"Where else?" she asked with a shrug. I had no answer.

She then gave me a slight nod of assurance. "The new-age, non-religious spirituality of modern times tries to answer these questions as well, but can find no common ground. Science tries to deal with them somewhat, but science can only answer the **how** of things. That is, science considers how things work, but it struggles with the why. I have come to understand that the answers to the why of things come only from the sacred words of the great spiritual teachers of the world's great religions. Look around you and observe carefully. Religion is the only resource available that deals directly and nearly exclusively with spiritual matters."

I couldn't hide the expression of concern on my face. Rose saw it. She took a deep breath and quietly sat back in her seat for a while before picking up where she left off. "I know the word 'religion' turns many people off—maybe even you. I don't blame you if it does, given the known history of religions and their sometimes superstitious and authoritarian practices. I am asking you to please set aside what you think you know about religion for a while. Let me use that word without you allowing your feelings about it to interfere with your ability to freely investigate a different concept of the word. Can you do that for me, Grayson?"

"I don't know," I responded. "I don't know if I can do that. How do you mean?"

"Just decide to let the negative emotions you have about religion remain unexpressed in your heart. I am not suggesting you deny them. Just let them stay still. You can do this. You know how to curb your impulsive, negative emotions. I'm just asking you to do it while on this trip. You can reconsider their value anytime afterwards if you want." She started to giggle, probably at my serious face as I imagined addressing my emotions like I would a dog: *Stay! Okay, now run!*

Her infectious giggling caused me to burst into laughter myself. "Okay," I said. "I'll try to curb any negative emotions about the word 'religion' while on this trip."

"Thank you," she breathed with relief. She relaxed, sat perfectly still, and gazed straight out the front window, collecting her thoughts. "The Creator of all things," Rose began, "the one true God, according to the sacred writings of the known great religions, desires only goodness and happiness for the human beings. He provides a path to this goodness and happiness when he discloses what is real, true, and good through his prophets and messengers. I suggest to you that the truth you have been seeking, and the meaningfulness in life you have been searching for, lies revealed in the words of the sacred scriptures. But for many, the answers to their questions remain partially hidden in these sacred texts. Not because God hides them, but because people have been misled by misconceptions and distorted beliefs that prevent them from understanding them clearly. This usually originates from misguided or spiritually immature religious leaders, who have **misinterpreted** the words of the holy books, leading others to perceive reality and their purpose of life improperly. This improper perspective of life and reality is the cause of considerable confusion and unhappiness in the world. My intention during this journey is to share with you a more meaningful and acceptable concept of our reality and purpose as human beings on this planet." Rose paused, giving me some quiet time to contemplate what she had said.

"Wait a minute," I murmured cautiously. "If true understanding and the potential for happiness comes from religion and the holy books, then why aren't things stated more clearly so we wouldn't be so confused?" I turned my head to face her, and then refocused on the road, waiting for her reply.

"That's a good question," she confirmed. She paused for a moment. "The Creator wants the human beings to know and experience freedom and liberty. If everything were made perfectly clear—simply handed to us—there would be no personal searching, no discovery, no independence, no freedom, and no free will. We would be like puppets. For our own sake, the answers to life are not just simply given to us. They require effort and learning.

"You asked earlier," Rose reminded me, "how is it that you and I can sit here and have an intelligent discussion of our reality and purpose when we have no knowledge of life prior to our birth, no understanding of where we came from or how we got here, and no clear comprehension of what happens to us after this life, except such as our beliefs may dictate? And you observed that most everyone, at some time or another must ask themselves these questions: 'Why am I here? What is my purpose? Where did I come from, and where am I going?' It **is** important that these questions get answered, Grayson. Otherwise, like you said, what is the point in living, suffering, working, having children, and so on, if we are unclear about our true purpose?

"My intention over the next several days is to convey, as best I can, a more complete and understandable concept of the reality and purpose of the human existence as revealed in the spiritual books and teachings. I want to show you a new perspective—a new paradigm— that you will find inviting and delightful. Imagine spirituality and religion free of superstition and fantasy, harmonious with your experiences in life, consistent with your heartfelt feelings on these matters, and reasonable and logical to your open mind." Rose went quiet, giving me time to process these ideas.

I was mulling over what she had said between sips of coffee. I liked what she was saying, but I was skeptical. I had heard similar statements before. I felt a little like I was her captive in the cab of this truck, albeit a voluntary one. Still, she intrigued me. "I will try," I said finally, "I'll really try to be open-minded and attentive." She smiled and nodded several times. We were good.

It was late afternoon now, and both of us were tiring. We rode in silence a while with only the squeak of the tape recorder, the hum of the tires on the road, and the steady droning vibration of the truck's big diesel engine. It all seemed to hypnotize my mind. I was feeling road-rummy, as Dad used to call it.

A question came to mind that had been puzzling me. "Rose, how come you call human beings **the** human beings? I have heard Native people do that before, and I have always wondered."

Smiling, she answered simply, "It honors them."

As I drove on, I was thinking through everything we had just talked about. There was something missing though, something here and now, something about day-to-day life in this world, something perhaps not spiritual, but still prominent and important. It was the state of affairs in the world in general that was tugging at my attention. I couldn't stay silent.

"No!" I exclaimed suddenly. "You know what? Yes, all these things we just talked about do still concern me, like my purpose in life, death, and that sort of thing. But there are other issues that cause me serious concern as well. Maybe because I'm older, or more worldly oriented—I don't know. What I feel looming is the collapse of everything going on around me. I see it every day. I hear about it every day from others. The economy, for example, appears like it could collapse at any time. Some people have excess while others live on scraps or sometimes with nothing. Work is harder to find, especially with decent pay. It now takes two to three people working in each household to live reasonably well. Many are just barely surviving. Some move in with friends or relatives. Some lay in the streets."

I paused for a moment. I was getting worked up again. "Healthcare! The healthcare system is falling apart. Insurance and good healthcare are so expensive and confusing that few people can even afford the necessities. Education is failing. Our nation is slowly—no, not so slowly—rapidly becoming less educated. Political leaders are polarized and impotent to solve the social problems that plague us. Religions have failed to exorcize their superstitions and authoritarian ways, making them collectively unattractive."

I gripped the steering wheel harder and tried to focus on the road even as more frustrating words poured out of my mouth. "I see violence becoming more active in our daily character. The news media discussion groups yell at each other. People use ever more violent, aggressive language, even in general conversation. We have become a culture that tolerates and glorifies anger and violence. Violent words. Violent, forceful leadership. We glorify violent sports, violent entertainment, aggressive business and work practices, and aggressive, competitive problem solving. Our media engages in loud, uncivilized, angry, and hostile discussions. We impose war on other peoples and nations and kill innocent people regularly. We glorify and make heroes out of soldiers of war. We tolerate violent computer games and other make-believe games of violence. I mean, I see problems!"

I paused long enough to catch my breath, but I was definitely wound up. "Marriages are in disrepair!" I lamented. "Drug use is rampant! Do you know how many people are taking mind-altering drugs?" I turned quickly toward Rose, but I was too worked up to stop and wait for an answer. "I see it regularly in my work when I interview patients. It's now **rare** to find a single person who is not regularly consuming some sort of mind-altering drug—either legal or illegal. They rely on antidepressants, pain medications, marijuana, alcohol, caffeinated energy drinks—all these and many more. All these drugs alter the mental and emotional state of the people we deal with every day. Is there anyone out there not altered? Some, I suppose," I continued, answering my own question, "but few."

"It's crazy! I don't know—I'm just saying—these things worry me, Rose. There is more, but it upsets me and depresses me to think about it. I see everything around me progressively declining. I hear others worrying about similar things every day, so I know it's not just me. I'm worried, very worried! I'm scared for our future. The whole world just seems to be unraveling. You told me you were going to talk to me about a spiritual vision of hope for mankind. We need hope and security, socially and materially as well! We need it badly! I read a couple of books lately that identified the historic process of societies that decline into barbarism. The signs include the ill-treatment of women, increased tolerance of violence, excessive attention to something-for-nothing in games of chance, the glorification of vigilantism, poor education, violent competition, corrupt leadership, and excessive substance abuse. Those problems of the past clearly describe the direction some of our social conditions are moving today! I'm worried."

Rose sat quietly. Her face was calm, but her eyes were downcast. Her thumb stroked a loose piece of torn seat-cover—slowly, rhythmically, meditatively.

We drove on in silence for a long time until I thought Rose wasn't even going to comment on my rant. Maybe I had said too much. Finally, she spoke.

"The material and social future of mankind is intimately linked with our spiritual future, Grayson." As she turned her body toward me, her empathetic eyes caught mine. In them I saw that I hadn't overstepped any lines. "I will talk to you about both matters, giving you a vision of hope that encompasses issues of daily life in this world, as well as those pertaining to our spiritual reality. And, I will tell you about a clear pathway to achieve that vision of hope. This is my promise to you." She raised her eyebrows, checking to see if I understood, and then added, "But not today. I need to rest for a while." Rose shuffled around in the seat to acquire a relaxed position. She left the recorder running.

We rode in silence. The tension left my chest, and somehow I felt calm. At first I thought it was because I had emptied myself of so many concerns. It came to me, though, that I felt better because Rose had understood me without judgment.

Soon our caravan pulled into the town of Tok. We began looking for a place to stay for the night. We found a nice campground right in town that catered to tourists, RVers, and campers. It was called the Gateway Salmon Bake. Outdoor salmon bakes were widespread throughout Alaska during the summer months. They usually consisted of an outdoor pavilion with tables and chairs, often covered with netting or screens to keep away pesky mosquitoes and no-see-ums. Salmon bake hosts usually provided barbequed salmon—lightly smoked with local alder, and a variety of salads. This particular salmon bake had alder smoked, honey-glazed salmon, halibut, beef ribs, reindeer sausage, buffalo burgers, and seafood chowder. Our happy caravan feasted with delight.

After dinner, I drove Rose to a local motel, securing her a room for the night. She was moving slow and acted stiff after the day's ride, appearing a little stoved-up, but made an effort not to show it. T.J. and Alene stayed at the same motel. The rest of us stayed up for a while, relaxing and comparing notes about the trip so far. We headed to bed around eleven o'clock even though there was still a little light in the sky—such is a summer day in Alaska. Five of us, including the baby, slept in the camp-trailer, which was tight, but we made it work. As I lay there with my face turned toward the short wall between me and the restroom, I tried to think about what Rose had said. My mind kept wandering, vacillating between the responsibilities of the trip and everything Rose and I had talked about. I couldn't think about what she had said at this point and get too enthused about the whole book project. I was tired, and my brain needed to rest. I remembered something I liked though, something that let me go to sleep with calmness. Rose had promised she would address my spiritual **and** day-to-day life concerns, give me a vision of hope for our future, and offer a means to achieve it. I liked that. I looked forward to hearing more tomorrow.

It's About Purpose

It seemed to take forever to get going that morning. We woke up around 6:30. There was a baby to feed and change, and then breakfast for the adults. I went to pick up Rose—she was ready. We had to gas up the rigs, check tires, make coffee, and use the restroom before hitting the road. Finally, we were traveling again—into a stretch of road that, for the next few days, was going to be among the worst of the whole trip. I remembered it well from when we traveled north eight years earlier. Our planned route was from Tok, Alaska, to Haines Junction in the Yukon Territory of Canada. The road between these points, while nearly all paved, was mainly a narrow two-lane highway. Its true challenge was the frost heaves. Built through muskeg and tundra—essentially a boggy, shrubby, nearly treeless northern wetland—the road freezes in the winter, expanding and rising in places. When the surface thaws somewhat during summer, the road sinks in random places, making for a terribly rough, roller coaster-like ride. Nonetheless, we had a plan, and we set out with determination.

We were barely out of town when Rose confided, in a kindly, measured tone, "I'm not sure how to convey what I have to share with you today." She paused thoughtfully for a few seconds before continuing. "Perhaps I'll just dive in and see how it develops. Is that all right with you?"

"Sure," I agreed indifferently. She was serious, focused, and energized. I suspected she had been up for hours preparing because she seemed ready to talk. As for me, I was just there, driving that big truck, drinking my morning coffee, and heading home which was all I cared about at the moment.

"Yesterday you expressed frustration about not knowing what your reality and purpose are as a human being. I would like to talk about that today. These matters are important. I have a lot to tell you. It will take quite some time." She turned and looked at me. I had already forgotten about expressing those concerns, but I didn't care either way. I had given my word to Rose that I would listen, and I didn't have a preferred subject at the moment.

"Well," she began, "the first thing I want to express today is this: we, the human beings, in our eternal reality—our true reality—are spiritual beings. I say this without doubt because it is intuitively within us to know this, and it is stated quite clearly in nearly all the world's sacred scriptures. I'll quote one example for you:

'Man is, in reality, a spiritual being, and only when he lives in the spirit is he truly happy.'[2]

"This means our spiritual self, or our soul, exists consciously and is attached to our material body in such a way that it can perceive and experience the physical world we live in through the outward and inward senses of the body. Our true reality then, that is, what is real and eternal about us, is not this material body." She slapped her thighs to emphasize her physical self. "And it's not the brain or the senses we possess, but, rather, it is our soul which is the spiritual driver, so to speak, of this material vehicle we call our body.

"Unfortunately, many in our society have gradually come to believe, through improper influences and perceptions, that we **are** this material body and that our material life on this planet, as we see it, is what is most important. However, all spiritual teachings suggest something different. The holy books of the world explain that our reality, our eternal soul, is attached to this body in some inexplicable way, and that we, our soul, uses this body to experience life in this material world. Therefore, our reality is spiritual, who we are is spiritual, and the reality of our experiences is spiritual. I have heard people say we are spiritual beings having a physical experience. This sums it up reasonably well, I think. But I would like to add to this and say: we are spiritual beings, having a physical experience **that has a spiritual purpose.**"

I listened and liked what I heard. Rose continued, "One might wonder: 'So what is the purpose in having an eternal soul?'" She raised a finger as though to signal me to wait. "Sacred writings teach us that we have been created by a superior spiritual being whose reality is beyond our comprehension and understanding. Therefore, to fully understand our own purpose—our own reality—on our own, is likely impossible because we are inferior to that superior being who created us. Something inferior can't understand the thinking, purpose, and reality of something superior. Just like a rock can't know what it's like to be a plant; a plant can't know what it's like to be an animal, and an animal can't know what it's like to be a human. So we can't know, **on our own**, what the Creator intended as our purpose when he created us."

I looked at Rose, disappointed.

"It's all right, Grayson. Here is the good news. We can get a **vision** of our reality, a **belief** about our reality, a sufficient **understanding** of our reality to proceed in life with joy and confidence. We can do this because the Creator has expressed, repeatedly throughout the ages by way of the teachings of great prophets and messengers that our purpose as human beings is to recognize and discover the one true God. Through our discovery and ongoing efforts to learn about him, we come to love and glorify him in our daily lives. One of the best ways to express our love and glorification of God in this life is to find the means to be of service to, and function harmoniously with, our fellow human beings." She paused, giving me time to let that soak into my brain.

"We do this," she went on, "by expressing in our everyday actions the spiritual behaviors emphasized in the sacred books. The spiritual behaviors are numerous, but they include such wonderfully developed attributes and characteristics as love, compassion, kindness, wisdom, forgiveness, tolerance, forbearance, trustworthiness, justice, fairness, and truthfulness. These and all other spiritual virtues have been explained and demonstrated to us by the great prophets. **Part of our purpose**, then, in this life as human beings, is to make efforts to acquire and express spiritual attributes, because they are the highest and most developed spiritual reality our soul can attain."

"Our soul, which operates through this body, comes into this world at birth without any of these spiritual qualities," Rose elaborated. "It is through the experiences of this earthly life that our soul has the opportunity to develop them. We are assured in the great spiritual teachings that the purpose of this life is to develop the character of our soul by acquiring the spiritual attributes of God, which will benefit us in both this life and in the afterlife."

Rose was quiet for a while, and so was I as I thought over what she was saying.

"Let me give you an example," she said suddenly while rearranging herself in the seat. I wasn't quite ready, for I was still trying to appreciate what she had just shared, but I set it aside and listened carefully as she had requested. "This entire earthly life we are now experiencing might be compared to our physical life while in the womb of our mother. While in the womb, we developed eyes, but could not see there. We developed ears that could only barely hear there. The sense of touch has no known purpose there. Taste has no meaning there. Fingers have nothing to do there. A brain with the potential for thinking exists, but has nothing to think about there. Limbs for carrying out tasks have no tasks to perform there. So why do we spend an entire nine months developing all this potential? We develop these attributes while in the womb so we can function well in **this** world. It is the same with our purpose in this earthly life. Our souls are here, having this physical experience, that we might develop spiritual attributes that will be beneficial and useful for us both in this earthly life and in our eternal life to come in the spiritual world. I'm talking about the life that exists after our physical body dies, and we find ourselves born into the next existence as purely spiritual beings. And, just as a child in the womb cannot perceive this world, we, in this earthly world, cannot perceive the life of the spiritual world that exists after death.

"It is important to understand, and to try and accept with true humility, that we are essentially born ignorant of our purpose, our origins, and our future spiritual reality that exists after the death of our body. Yet anyone who takes a moment to maturely contemplate life, surely will conclude that there must be **some** purpose to our earthly existence—to our life, and the lives of others. Otherwise, our lives and the lives of everything else in the universe would be senseless, worthless, and meaningless.

"My intention over the next several days is to share with you more about the purpose and reality of our lives as conveyed by our Creator in the spiritual teachings of the holy books, but in a way you may have never heard before. I hope not only to make sense of this earthly life for you, but also to make it exciting and meaningful. I hope to help you find purpose in all the intricate experiences this earthly life has to offer—purposes that relate to our **true reality** as human beings."

She paused for a moment to readjust herself in the seat again. "Knowing the true reality of our life and purpose allows us as human beings to pursue the wonders of our earthly life and make sense of our experiences. Knowing our true reality and purpose makes our relationship with the entire creation a learning experience. This is where the souls created by God find the best possible environment for developing into mature spiritual beings and subsequently into a unified, loving humanity, with both a meaningful purpose in this life, and as it pertains to our eternal spiritual life."

She stopped and remained motionless, staring at the road ahead in a fixed-like state. Eventually she took a deep breath, sighed, relaxed back in her seat, and turned to stare out her window.

Wow! What a mouthful she had just blurted out. *Was she done?* I wondered. *Dare I say anything, or would I be interrupting?* I tried to grasp it all. It was a lot to take in. Something inside me declared, *I knew it! I knew somehow we were essentially spiritual beings with a spiritual purpose!* I liked this idea, but it provoked numerous questions. I decided to ponder on it for a while because I didn't know yet exactly what I wanted to ask.

Rose suddenly turned her head back to face me, and resumed her talk. "You see, Grayson, what I want to talk to you about on this trip is spiritual in nature, and yet ever so practical in its application to this material life. Humans, for the most part, only receive approximately eighty years of earthly life. I have been gifted with a few more than average." She chuckled, delighting in her good fortune. "Yet, when we look around at the creation, we must face the fact that time has existed for billions of years in the past and will surely continue for an unlimited time forward. We live a very short life here between two great eternities: the eternal past and the eternal future. Our little eighty-year lifespan is less than a blink in the totality of time. That's why we feel compelled to ask and seek out the answer to the question: 'what is the purpose of this short life?' I believe, with certainty in my heart, that its purpose is spiritual in essence. Our life here is like attending a spiritual school, and everything about the physical experience is training in spiritual matters. We are being taught, and we are learning, to be loving, wise, just, kind, generous, forgiving, and tolerant beings. Many of us are unaware of this, yet it doesn't change the fact that we are all learning spiritual ways, even if we don't know it, don't try, or don't care. In fact, even if we are resisting, we are learning. At least, the potential is always there. This is the way of the creation. The creation is perfect in every way for our spiritual development. It cannot be outwitted, changed, or conquered. It is what it is. It is a learning experience created out of love, all for our own eternal joy and goodness."

"So," I interrupted without forethought, "why do you think we have such a tendency to place so much attention on material concerns and less on our true spiritual purpose then?"

"Human beings sometimes lose sight of their true purpose and begin to think this material life **is** their real purpose," she replied without pause. "They direct their attention toward the wonders of the classroom of their physical experience, forgetting it's **what** we are learning here that's important. We humans can become so attached to the classroom of this material world that we even begin to alter it to fit our material wants. Notice I said wants and not needs. Pretty soon the classroom is altered, and the stresses caused by this alteration become unbearable. That's where we are now in the modern world. We have so altered our societies and the environment we live in from its original intent that the stresses on the mind and soul are making it difficult for people to cope. War, crime, drug abuse, violence, mental illness, immorality, and numerous other distorted behaviors can only worsen as we lose the joy of living true to the purpose of our existence. This diversion will most likely continue until we awaken to our spiritual purpose, through natural consequences and effort, and begin to act in accordance with our spiritual reality. Then, we will collectively place less importance on the material model of reality we have created and more on the one that gives meaning, purpose, and joy to all of us."

"Hold it! This is going too fast!" I insisted. "Just give me a minute to take this in." I had interrupted her again, but she seemed pleased. I was trying to understand what she was saying. I thought about it for some time without comment.

After several minutes, Rose asked, "Shall I continue?"

"Sure, I'm ready," I answered, as I couldn't really formulate any questions at the moment.

"Why do you think the most admired, the most respected, and the most revered human beings in society are those who are the most loving, the most wise, the most kind, and the most generous? What attracts us to those who selflessly contribute to the good and betterment of the people they are privileged to associate with on the planet? It is because we know intuitively, deep in our soul, their behavior exemplifies our highest and most complete purpose as human beings!

"If you look closely, you will find both religion and science confirm that learning, especially learning how to be loving human beings, is a major feature of our true purpose in this life. Most religions and spiritual paths teach this and our most outstanding people emulate this. It is our highest purpose in this life, day in and day out. Each day, all day, we have the opportunity to learn, to show forth love, to graciously receive love, and to work in our daily activities to contribute to a better world."

She paused for some time, probably because I was deep in thought. "I hear you thinking," Rose presumed. "Are you wondering how science helps affirm our purpose to be loving human beings?"

I looked at her quickly and nodded, a little startled by her ability to summarize what I was thinking.

Chuckling a little to my reaction, she cheerfully continued. "Let me share with you one example of how science has validated that learning, and learning how to be loving human beings, are part of our true purpose.

"Due to modern technology, people in the healthcare field have developed highly sophisticated equipment and techniques that sometimes bring people back to life who have been clinically dead for a time—even up to an hour after their so called 'death!' Through body cooling, CPR, and defibrillation techniques, they have been able to revive people whose hearts and brains ceased to function for a short time. Thousands of people have been brought back from near death through modern knowledge and technology that never existed prior to the last fifty years or so. Now here is the interesting part: many of the people who were revived, had what is called a 'near-death experience.' That is, while they were technically dead, their consciousness, or soul, arose in a disconnected way from their bodies. They were able to experience this world **and** part of the spiritual world by being detached from their bodies as free spirits for a brief period. They were then able to return to their bodies and tell others about their experience. Nearly all these people saw or experienced beings that already had passed from this world—they saw friends, parents, grandparents, or other relatives. A great many of them relate how they were informed during their near-death experience that their time on earth had not ended, and they were going to have to return to their bodies. Nearly all also experienced the presence of an all-loving Being. Additionally, they nearly all reported that their near-death experience taught them that the purpose of this life is **to learn** as much as possible, to **learn to love** as much as possible, and to express that knowledge and love by contributing to the joy and betterment of others." While tilting her head a little to one side, she smiled at me as if to say, *what do you think about that?*

"Now that's far out!" I said in amazement.

"Yes, and it's in direct harmony with what the spiritual teachings have conveyed throughout time. Does it make sense to you? Does it feel right in your heart? Is it consistent with what you have learned as a human being in your life?" Rose prompted, awaiting my answer.

"Well . . . yeah!" I conceded. "I can easily agree with that, but is it really that simple?"

"Describing our basic purpose might be that simple," Rose agreed, "but it's acting on it consistently that's challenging!" She laughed—as did I.

"Oh boy! Now there's a truth I can confirm!" I nearly shouted. It felt good to laugh. A short silence accompanied us a mile or two down the road before I repeated my question. "Rose, is it really that simple?"

"Yes, it is," she affirmed, nodding with a reassuring smile. "It's just that simple and that beautiful. The purpose of the holy books and the entire purpose of religion have been, and still are, to help us attain unto this highest and most complete spiritual purpose. What greater feeling than to give or receive love? What greater benefit than to have understanding and wisdom so you can express your love in ways that are purposeful and meaningful to others? I'm not talking about a learning or knowledge that consists of facts and figures. I'm talking about acquiring true wisdom and real knowledge of ourselves, the creation, the Creator, and our relationship with all things. What could be more fulfilling than to contribute regularly to the betterment and joy of others? Aren't these heavenly qualities? And isn't it a type of hell not to be able to express love, to harbor hatred, to be despised, to be ignorant or foolish, or to be only a taker and never a giver?"

"I can agree with you there," I murmured, struck by how her questions were addressing those I had asked only a day ago.

The CB suddenly cracked to life. "Big Koala, do you read me? This is Baby Buggy." It was Annie.

I fumbled with the CB, pressed the button, and responded. "Big Koala here."

"We stopped to take some pictures of a momma moose and her calf. We're a ways behind you, but we'll catch up soon."

"Okay, ten-four," I responded. This was the very reason we used CBs while traveling as a caravan on a three thousand-mile trip through a wilderness with no cell service. With four different vehicles, the likelihood increased for someone to stop for something without the people up ahead being aware of it. Someone might take a turn or pull off for fuel while the others go whizzing by trying to catch up, leaving everyone confused as to where everyone else is. We were glad to have the CB radios. My handle was "Big Koala" because the truck I was driving had the image of a big koala bear on the side. Sonia's handle was "Little Caboose," and T.J. and Alene's handle was "Tail-Gunner." We were coming upon a small roadside station, not more than a wide spot in the road, so I pulled over to wait for Franklin and Annie to catch up. Sonia, T.J., and Alene did the same. "Sorry about that," I said to Rose. "Go ahead . . . you were saying?"

"Let's wait until they show up. We can talk once we get going again."

It wasn't long before I could see them coming in my rear view mirror. Annie's voice came over the CB when she saw us. "Here we are!"

"There's a station here if you need fuel," I announced. Annie said they could use a break, so we got out of the truck and waited for them to pull in. We did our usual routine: gas up, walk around, stretch, and use the restrooms. The people at the station were accommodating, and it wasn't long before we were ready to go. I checked with Sonia to see how she was doing. All was well with her and the Bronco. She did tell me that at one point where the frost heaves first began, both wheels of the nineteen-foot camp-trailer I was pulling had bounced completely off the pavement! She suggested I slow down on the rough parts of the road so I wouldn't lose the trailer. The trailer was snugged up so tight behind my big truck that I couldn't see it very well in any of my rear view mirrors, so it was a good thing Sonia was keeping an eye on me from behind or I might have wrecked that trailer. I made a point in my mind to be more careful when driving through frost heaves. It wasn't long before we were pulling onto the highway again.

I don't know why I asked the next question, but I thought I might as well ask Rose some of the things that had bewildered me for years since she was on a roll. "Rose," I asked, "how do I know for certain there **is** a God?"

She looked at me thoughtfully for a few seconds. Clasping her hands and placing them between her knees, Rose pulled her shoulders up, sat forward, and stared out the front window, motionless. Finally, while still regarding the road in front of us, she began, "First, you must fast, consuming nothing but water for three days, and pray. Second, go into nature where you can see no one, where you can hear nothing of humans. Look about yourself and take in all of nature. Hear it, see it, smell it, touch it. Finally, cry out loud, 'Are you there, Lord?'" She looked at me in silence. I looked at her, waiting, before catching the twinkle in her eyes.

Suddenly she erupted in loud, cackling laughter. She got me. She laughed and laughed, looking at me and then looking away. I didn't think it was that funny, but she sure enjoyed it. Wiping away a tear, she gave me the sweetest, most loving smile, and abruptly reached over and cast her left hand upon my chest. "If you seek proof of the existence of God, you will find it here." She held her hand motionless a moment before lightly tapping my forehead and saying, "Not here." She turned away slowly, sniffing, and searched in her bag for a tissue. I felt like someone had just opened me up and rearranged my insides. I don't know why or how, but something had just happened to me that I couldn't get my mind around—I really didn't even know how to try. I drove in silence, trying to adjust.

We rode quietly for some time before she gave me a more detailed answer to my question. "Grayson, for the most part, nearly everyone believes in a God in some way. At least most people say they do.

However, they differ in their explanation of what God is. Even those who are agnostic, claiming they are unsure about the existence of God, acknowledge there is some source or force from which all things have come. Everyone acknowledges there is a creation, and that acknowledgment, in and of itself, presumes a creator of some kind."

"What do you mean, 'it presumes a creator of some kind?'" I asked.

"Everything in creation substantiates that all action is preceded by a cause. Therefore, creation must have a cause, a creating force, a creator. Now, some choose not to call it God, and instead refer to it as some kind of initializing power. Nonetheless, it exists. Even atheists understand this. For the most part, they reject the concept of God conveyed by religion. Therefore, they say they don't **believe** in a God. It's undoubtedly the description or the concept of God that they don't believe in. Nearly everyone understands there is an unknown generating and sustaining force in the universe, whether they refer to it as God or by other names, while others refuse to associate that force with any title that might imply the existence of a God. So be clear on this. No matter what we call it, or perceive it to be, or whether we believe in it or not, most everyone acknowledges the existence of something that brought us into being. I will refer to that generating and sustaining force—that something—as God, hoping your experience with the word will not cause prejudice toward what I am going to say. So, as I did with the word 'religion,' I am asking you to put away your preconceived concepts of God for a moment—just for a while—for it isn't possible to fully understand a new or different concept unless you are willing to temporarily suspend your current perspective. If the newly conveyed concept doesn't make sense to you or feel right in your heart, you can always return to your previous one. But please, will you give it a fair try?" She looked at me for acknowledgment.

I nodded in response, "Sure, sure, that's fair."

"There are reasonable evidences of the existence of God for those who may feel unsure in their heart. Let me suggest to you that one can know God exists by his signs." Rose glanced at me to see my response. I looked back at her, saying nothing, waiting for more. "You know there is a God by his signs," she repeated. "There are endless signs in the creation that give evidence to a creator. I'll give you an example. Where I live, and where you have been living in Alaska, there are moose. We see them, so we know they are there. But how do you know when one has been, say, near your house? You know one has been near your house by the signs he leaves behind. A moose leaves tracks in the snow or in the mud or sand where he has walked. We know by these tracks that he has been there even though there is no moose standing there to see or touch. We know the moose has been near when we see the ends of the willow eaten off. We can also tell from this about how tall he is. We know where he goes by his tracks. We know if it is male or female by the pattern of its urine in the snow. We know there was more than one if there are more than four separate tracks. We know if it is a large or small moose by the size of the tracks, and the length of the stride. We know when it was in the area by the degree of decay in the tracks, and the warmth and texture of the scat. By these signs, we know for sure a moose has been around, and we can know several things **about** this moose by the nature of the signs it has left.

"So it is with God. We know he exists by his signs, and his signs are plentiful and infinitely present. We ask the question: 'Is there a creation?' We look about ourselves and behold the evidence. The signs are all around us, so we also know there is a creator because the signs of a creation are overwhelmingly in our face. The existence of a creation proves the presence of a creator. Next we might ask: 'How do we know there is only one Creator, like the monotheistic religions say?' We look about us and see many things, many powers, many lands, rivers, mountains, and creatures. This many-ness points to the existence of a singleness or a one-ness. Yet, when you look around, where will you find oneness or singleness? Nowhere. It belongs to God alone! The signs in nature and its composition of many-nesses testify to the singleness of its creator." She paused for a moment, rubbing her finger and thumb together in a slow rhythmic motion. "Let me say something more here," she picked up again. "This world we live in is a world of contrasts. The existence of certain things proves the existence of others. Darkness proves the existence of light. If there were no darkness, we could not know there is such a thing as light. Now think about that for a minute." She looked at me to see if I was paying attention. "You could not know there was such a thing as light if there was no contrasting darkness. This is what I mean by reading these signs in nature. Therefore, by reading the signs before us, we can determine the existence of other things. This creation has contrast so we can know things. It all supports our purpose as human beings to learn. Without darkness we cannot know light, without ignorance we cannot know knowledge, and without hatred we cannot know love. And so we know there is a God, and we can know about that God, by looking to the natural world of creation to behold the signs of the Creator revealed within it." She stopped.

I jumped in. "My father used to say he didn't need to go to church to talk to God. He would say that when he was in the barn milking our only cow, he could talk to God right there, and it felt more real to him than it did in church. He used to say that he believed in the God of nature, but was unsure about the God they spoke of in church."

"Oh, how profound that is!" Rose exclaimed. "How interesting that he saw the truth about God in the signs of nature. Apparently, he read the signs of creation and from that he knew his Creator. Many people have the problem of perceiving the God of religion as **different** from the God of nature. This usually occurs when the human beings inaccurately interpret certain sacred scriptures literally. Consequently, they begin to describe the one true God in limited, finite, human-like, or superstitious terms that contradict what we observe as the Creator of the natural world."

"I don't know of any religion that teaches that!" I asserted. "I, too, have always had a conflict in my heart whether to believe in the God of creation, revealed in the 'signs of nature,' as you call them, or to surrender everything I understood about nature, life, and reason to accept what felt like a superstitious explanation of God taught by some religious groups."

"Too bad," she remarked solemnly, "because in reality they are one and the same. How could it be different? When you read sacred words yourself, with an open and detached heart and without the influence of immature interpretation, and you look upon the creation, you will know that the God of creation and the God of the holy scriptures revealed by the prophets, are one and the same. You know this by the signs in the creation, and by the signs left in your heart from reading the revealed word of God. Listen to these sacred words pertaining to this matter:

'*The understanding of His words and the comprehension of the utterances of the Birds of Heaven are in no wise dependent upon human learning. They depend solely upon purity of heart, chastity of soul, and freedom of spirit.*'"[3]

She stopped talking. My head was swimming. I had nothing to say at the moment, but Rose did.

"So, is there a God?" she asked bluntly, staring at me with piercing eyes.

"It's pretty apparent to me," I replied.

"And how do you know?" she continued.

"Like you said, the signs are everywhere." I swept my hand before me, following it with my gaze as I looked out at the landscape before us. There was nothing more to say. We both became silent. My question was answered—a question that had perplexed me for a lifetime was summed up in a few short minutes by this wise old woman. I looked over at her, and she looked at me as though she had heard me thinking. She erupted into laughter, and so did I. We laughed freely again. I don't even know why. I just know it felt good.

"There is a story about a beetle," she started in again. "And not one of those musicians," she snickered. "He was a proud, shiny, black creature with limited sight. He could only see clearly for a few feet. The other small creatures told him about a great mountain that was so large, he could not pass over it in a lifetime. He did not believe this could be true, so he went to find this mountain called Denali. He walked in the direction of this great mountain. He went uphill and downhill, crossed muskeg and streams, and climbed through tundra. When he arrived at the mountain, he continued to walk uphill, but did not recognize it as being any different than any other hill he had traveled. He kept walking. Looking before himself, he exclaimed, 'I see no great mountain, therefore, as I expected, it does not exist.'

"And so it is with humans. The evidence and signs of God are so great, and we are so used to them before us; we don't recognize them for what they really are. There is a saying: 'You can't see the forest for the trees.' And so it is with us. The presence of the signs of God, that creating and sustaining intelligent force of the universe, are so evident we don't recognize them as such. Because these signs are always present, it makes it difficult to detach from the creation we exist in to look at it objectively. We can only do this with our intelligence, because our intelligence is supernatural. It allows us to rise above nature, above our immediate perspective, and get outside ourselves to interpret the creation as an observer. Because of the influences of our parents, friends, associates, and society, we learn to interpret our experiences and the creation as we are told, which may not be as it really is. We have to get out of the trees and see the forest, look beyond our limited beetle vision and see the mountain, break free from the interpretation of creation as it is imposed upon us, and instead, objectively witness the signs of God before us. When we do this, I think there is little room for doubt about the existence of God."

Rose became silent again. After a little while, she added, "Mature contemplation can only lead to a humble conclusion that we are ignorant and powerless compared to the wisdom and power that exists in that creating and sustaining Force behind all things. I urge you to have faith and confidence in that Force and to consider it the same as the one true God identified in the sacred scriptures. This is all anyone really needs to know. In fact, faith in him is just about all you will ever need—here and in the next world. I want to give you these holy words to remember:

' . . . *thy faith shall be sufficient for thee above all things that exist on earth, even though thou possess nothing.*'[4]

"Grayson, whenever I give you holy or sacred words, be sure you record them exactly as I give them to you. I'll explain why later." I assured her I would. "Don't forget these sacred words. If you take anything into your heart and make it permanent and real, make sure it is this verse—it shall be sufficient for you eternally. Observe the signs of God in the creation, and put your trust, confidence, and faith in the Creator of those signs and in the words of the great prophets. That is the best I can give you for now."

We were quiet for a while, but I needed to summarize it verbally to be sure I understood.

"So, I get it like this," I began. "There is one true, creating, sustaining force in the universe we call God. We know it exists by its signs, but we are unable to explain it. So, it's like our higher power, whatever we perceive it to be?" Rose looked at me with her most serious face. She stared at me as though to look right through me.

"Not exactly," she said softly, as she slowly turned to look out the window again. "The great prophets of the world have always directed the human beings toward faith in the one true God, explaining that he is unknowable, unimaginable, and unperceivable. That's why he is God. He is **beyond** our limited mental ability to grasp. So, when people say things like: 'My God wouldn't do something like that,' they are talking about the God they have devised in their own mind. When you say that one can turn to their higher power, 'whatever you perceive it to be,' then you are talking about turning to a mental image or perception—a God of one's imagination. But God can't be perceived or imagined. To worship or turn to an image of God in one's mind is no different than turning to a stone image and worshiping it. Neither is the one true God. Both are false images or, as it is often said, false Gods. You have heard atheists say that some people worship their imaginary friend. They are right. That's why many people won't believe in God, because those who are trying to convince them there is one are describing an image they have created in their own mind. That's why atheists are one of the human beings' best protections against idol worship and superstition. They won't let us get away with worshiping the concepts of our own imagination or the things that are untrue. Well, at least they are willing to call us on it and point it out."

Rose paused and sat perfectly still for some time before continuing. "I have already made it clear to you that I believe there is a God. We know religion supports this because that's what religion is all about, but science also supports the existence of a god." She looked at me—I must have looked puzzled because she went on to explain. "Even the most educated and most intelligent and respected scientists in the world conclude that all matter and energy in the universe 'came from something,' or some might say, 'it came from nothingness,' or 'we don't know where everything came from,' or 'it came about randomly.' The key words here are 'came from'. These statements all admit and identify the same unknown, unknowable, unperceivable, creating and sustaining source of all things in the universe that people of religion refer to as God, or Jehovah, or Yahweh, or Allah, or Wakan Tanka. These are all phrases and words used to identify the same thing. The great prophets describe God as the All-Mighty and All-Powerful. Science also knows this to be true by virtue of the scientific laws of the universe.

"What scientific laws are those?" I asked.

Rose's eyes seemed to look straight through me as she contemplated her next thought. "First of all," she said slowly, "the force it took to create the Big Bang, or the ongoing banging, or whatever the beginning was or is, had to be a force **equal to** or **greater than** the sum total of the matter and energy it created. Think about that. That's a lot of force! And that's why God is referred to as the All-Mighty and the All-Powerful! Let me give you an example. If you were to place a 100-pound stone on a table and attempt to push it off, it would take more than 100 pounds of force to accomplish it, otherwise it could not happen. That stone will never randomly acquire the energy to move off that table. It cannot happen on its own. It takes the expression of potential power to move that stone. That's a scientific law. In the same way, the creation of the universe did not come about **on its own**. It took an equal or greater amount of potential force to bring it into being, and that's an incomprehensible amount of power." She looked at me and smiled. "How powerful **is** God?" she marveled, nodding her head.

"Similarly, whatever the intelligence is which brought the creation into being, sustains it, and created all the intricate relationships that exist within it, requires a knowledge superior to that found in the entirety of the creation itself. It follows logically that the intelligence wrapped in all the complexities of the universe could not come about by anything less intelligent than everything in the creation. That's why God also is called the All-Knowing and the All-Wise. He had to have superior knowledge in order to create such a complex and interrelated creation. And that's how, I believe, religion and science both, in reality, acknowledge the same creating and sustaining force many of us who speak the English language call 'God.'" She stopped again and sat still, but she wasn't silent for long.

"Some time back, the astronomers who work with the Hubble telescope had a two-week window where they had no scheduled activity for the telescope. They decided to point the telescope at what was thought to be only dark space, just to see if there really was anything out there. They were looking into a very small area of the cosmos, about the size of space you would see while looking through a straw at arm's length. After two weeks, the images taken in that tiny, previously thought to be dark space revealed greater than one billion galaxies, each with more than two billion stars, stretched out endlessly. So I ask you: how great is this creation? And I ask you, how great is the God that created it?

"The one true God is not what we imagine in our minds. He is not a mental image, concept, or thought. He is beyond all imagination, all conception, all thought, and all words. He can't be seen. He can't be heard. He can't be described. He can't be sung," she paused, "and he can't be whistled either." We looked at each other and laughed. "He can only be known to exist and adored here, in your heart!" She slapped her palm to her chest. "God has placed within all human beings—in that soft, tender place in our hearts where we are vulnerable and feel compassion and love—the capacity to recognize the truth of his existence and to have faith in the supremacy of his being." She held her hand to her chest tightly for a long time before she said more. "I have no words beyond this," she said with a sigh, as she removed her hand from her chest and sank into the seat.

Her silence was brief. "Yes, I do have more words," Rose announced, sitting up and beaming at me with a smile. "I want to share these words of sacred scripture with you that pertain to this subject:

'*With the hands of power I made thee and with the fingers of strength I created thee; and within thee have I placed the essence of My light. Be thou content with it and seek naught else, for My work is perfect . . . .*'"[5]

She slumped in her seat again as if spent from the exertion of talking. Leaning her head against the side-window, she shut her eyes and rested.

For the first time in my life, the reality of God was satisfyingly clear. Past confusion was gone. A lifetime of inner struggle was over. I didn't have to search or debate about the existence of God or try to get a mental grasp of his **being** anymore. I knew. If I were completely honest, I had known all along. He is, and he is what he is. He was beyond my limited capacity to understand fully, and that was perfectly okay. In fact, I liked it—I loved it!

I turned my attention to the beauty of the mountains, the sky, and everything around me as I drove. It all seemed alive, as though it was all smiling at me and my newfound understanding. It felt good. *I'm going to soak in this for a while,* I thought. I drove on in peaceful silence.

Rose, who I had thought was napping, slowly moved to look out the side-window. Something about her posture seemed to say *don't talk to me now.* I, too, felt a need for silence. My energy was diminishing even though my mind was filled with new ideas. Still, I didn't want to think anymore, because my brain was full like a saturated sponge. I went on a kind of auto-pilot which is what happens when my mind does its processing without me being very conscious of what it's thinking about. We rode quietly for a little more than an hour, the recorder still on, neither one of us bothering to turn it off.

I knew it was getting close to lunchtime. It wasn't long before T.J. was on the CB telling me it was ten minutes to twelve. It was his way of saying, "It's time to eat." I started looking for a wide spot in the road where we could all pull over and have lunch. We would fix lunch in the trailer instead of eating out. It was too expensive to eat every meal at restaurants for ten days.

After traveling for several miles down the road, I announced on the CB, "I can't seem to find a place large enough for all of us to pull off the road. I guess we'll have to park on the shoulder for lunch." Not more than five seconds went by before I heard on the CB, "No, you won't! This is the Canadian Mounted Police, and you're not allowed to park on the shoulder of the road. You keep on going until you find sufficient parking for your party. Is that clear?"

Surprised by the unexpected remark, I asked, "Who is this?"

"This is Officer Vincent of the Royal Canadian Mounted Police, and you're not allowed to park on the shoulder of the road."

"Okay, Officer," I said respectfully. "We'll find a place to pull off the road and stay off the shoulder."

"That would be good. Drive safely," he said.

"Did the rest of you hear that?" I questioned over the CB. Everyone acknowledged and said no more.

We drove on for another twenty minutes until we came to a place where we could pull completely off the road. With almost choreographed efficiency, the ladies were in the trailer fixing soup and sandwiches while the men inspected the rigs. The view from our makeshift restaurant was spectacular. We were on a highland plateau where we could gaze at the beautiful snow-capped mountains in the far distance. It felt like we were in a photograph on top of the world.

DAY TWO

HOW DO WE KNOW?

We were hungry, and the hot soup felt good. We enjoyed our lunch and some easy companionship before taking care of travel necessities and preparing to return to the road. *We had better get moving before the after-lunch sleepiness sets in,* I thought. After cleaning up from lunch and making sure our picnic area had no debris left behind, it was time to board. I helped Rose into the truck. Then I ran around and hopped into the driver's seat. While fastening my seatbelt, I heard Rose turn on the recorder. *Oh, here we go,* I thought. I really didn't feel ready to dive right back into any discussion because it demanded my focused attention. Frankly, I wanted a little break, but it wasn't to be. We were barely rolling down the road—in fact, I hadn't shifted out of second gear yet when Rose started right in.

"Before lunch, we were talking about the existence of God. Well, during lunch I remembered something I wanted to share with you. In Buddhism, there is a story," she began, "about several blind men and an elephant. These men had never heard of an elephant before. Each man was asked to touch the creature before him and then describe it.

"One man reached out and felt the trunk of the elephant. 'The elephant,' he explained, 'is like a large snake, writhing with great power.'

"The second man reached out and felt the leg of the animal. 'No,' he said, 'the elephant is like a large tree, standing straight and strong.'

"A third man reached out and found the tail of the elephant. 'These elephant animals are not as you say,' he declared. 'It is more like a tall, slender twig-like animal, whipping about.'

"The fourth man reached out and felt the elephant's ear. 'No,' he said, 'the elephant is more like a large leaf-like plant that moves about on the air.'

"And so, you see, limited perceptions result in diverse realities. That is, whatever you behold is limited to your own perceptual ability. If all seven billion people of the world were asked to look at the creation and describe the Creator, based on his signs in the creation, what do you think the results would be?" She looked over at me with her head tilted slightly, waiting for me to answer.

I cautiously responded, "I suppose everyone would give a different answer."

"Of course!" she exclaimed. "And who would be correct?" she questioned, looking at me again, holding her hand up as if to say, *don't answer*. "We might say that everyone is correct, but that is difficult to accept. For example, someone might observe a grizzly bear killing a moose calf and declare that this is a sign that God is vicious because he is the one who created this world. Whereas, another might look at a pit-bull playing with a kitten and say that this is a sign that God is gentle and loving. Consequently, some will say they are acting like God and feel justified in being violent, whereas others will say being God-like means to abhor violence. So then, what is true about God and what does God want from us? How can we interpret him through his creation when the creation holds so many conflicting signs?"

"I'm confused," I admitted.

"You should be! The world of creation doesn't make any sense by itself. Remember, this world of existence we live in is a world of contrasts, created so we can observe and learn. We look at the creation and try to get an idea of God the Creator by reading the signs about him in his creation, and yet, it just gets confusing. The different ways to read the signs of God in the creation are countless."

"What's your point?" I asked, feeling defeated. "I thought we could know about God by observing the signs in the natural world. Are you now saying we can't?"

"The point is this," Rose explained, "in the same way interpreting moose tracks requires a wise, experienced hunter who is knowledgeable about reading the signs left by a moose, interpreting signs in the creation that reflect the nature of God also requires wisdom and knowledge. **And that is the purpose and role of the great prophets**." She let silence fill the cab as time ticked by.

"Did you get that?" she inquired several minutes later. Speaking slowly and carefully, she rephrased her statement. "One of the main roles of the great prophets is to help us **properly** interpret the signs of God inherent in the creation." I could only nod. I was still unsure of her point.

"Let me try it this way," she paused. "The world contains opposites and contrasts so that we may acquire knowledge and understanding, like I said before. Merely reading the signs of creation in order to know the one true God, without having any idea what we are doing, results in limitless contradictions. We need guidance **directly from the Creator** to correctly understand him and his purpose for us. That guidance comes **from** the Creator **through** the great prophets of the world's great religions."

Okay, I thought, *I'm getting this now.*

Rose continued, "Now, one person might say that God told him to help someone in need. Another might say that God told him to kill a person who he perceived was doing evil. So we must ask the question: 'Does God talk to all of us?' If he does, why does it appear that he tells some to be kind and others to kill? Grayson, listen to this carefully. God speaks directly to no one. He inspires hearts with goodness, but he does not speak in a language directly to each human being, and he **never** inspires evil."

"How is it you think **you** know what is true?" I asked, challenging her conviction.

She paused and averted her gaze toward the floorboard. She sat motionless for a moment before heaving a deep sigh. "By the time we finish this trip, Grayson, you will know why I speak to you with such certainty. For now, I ask you, please, just consider the possibilities of what I am sharing with you. There is so much more to tell. I am asking you, first, to take in these concepts without making any conclusive judgments on them as we go. Instead, try to grasp the whole perspective of reality I am attempting to convey. When I am finished, you can re-evaluate everything and reject it, accept it, or do with it as you please. However, unless you are willing to seriously consider what I am saying, and regard the whole perspective with possibilities, you will not be able to hear the spirit of what I am sharing. If you think your heart is filled with a fixed knowledge, then there is no room for other options. If you think you already know the truth, then it is impossible to learn anything more. Only when you consider another person's perspective as real, at least temporarily, can you learn something. I am not saying what you already know is wrong. Oh, no! I am just hoping you will open-mindedly consider the beautiful vision of our purpose and reality that I am trying to describe. Would you like to try that?"

"Sure," I said, nodding my head in agreement.

"I am glad to see the sincerity in your face. Thank you for your understanding," she replied with a warm smile. After gathering her thoughts, she continued. "I was saying that God speaks directly to no one, remember? **Except**," she asserted "except to the great prophets. What makes them the great prophets is that God speaks, or communicates, directly to them and to them only!" She paused and sat motionless.

"I am going to give you a little different understanding than what you are used to hearing about the great prophets, but first I want to give them a different title. Many people believe that a prophet is one inspired by the spirit of God, who tells us of future things that are true. While there is truth in that, the prophets are so much more. The great prophets include names you are familiar with—Moses, Jesus, Buddha, Krishna, Muhammad, and others. Each of them not only spoke as inspired by the spirit of God, but also behaved as directed by God himself. Many people already believe this. The words of the great prophets, their deeds, behavior, thoughts, and ways were all directly influenced by the Holy Spirit emanating from the Creator. This did not come about as a result of personal choice or effort. It was **bestowed** upon them, or **infused** into them, by the spirit of holiness from the God. Each one of them spoke of the spirit of holiness coming upon them, but related it to their followers in different ways. To Moses, the Holy Spirit appeared as a voice from the burning bush; to Jesus it came in the likeness of a dove; to Muhammad it came as the voice of the angel Gabriel; to Buddha, through the Lotus flower. All of them described the appearance of the Holy Spirit differently, yet each was visited involuntarily. They did not attain to prophethood through effort; rather, they were called and empowered by God alone. They did not ask for it; it was given to them. Once this occurred, their words, deeds, actions, and everything about them were influenced directly by God through the Holy Spirit. I am declaring to you that no other person does or can receive this kind of direct influence."

She paused for a moment to gather her thoughts. "Now follow this carefully, Grayson. These great prophets are different than all the rest of the human beings in these distinguishing characteristics. First, they are inspired by God to speak or write powerful, influential, holy words without the need of forethought or contemplation. Second, their actions are harmonious with their words, and they submissively, with no personal resistance against their perpetrators, endured persecution, hardship, betrayal, disownment, torture, ridicule, and sometimes death without resorting to any behavior inconsistent with the spirit of holiness. They behaved this way throughout their given time on earth, making them distinguishably holy. No one else can do this even for an hour, let alone for a lifetime! Because of these distinguishing characteristics, I am going to give you a new title for these great prophets. From now on I'll refer to them as **manifestations of God**."

I looked at her with confusion. "What?"

"The word 'prophet' does not adequately describe their true reality," she remarked, "but **manifestation** does. To manifest means:

to disclose or to make known, by revealing and exhibiting distinct signs. So, a manifestation of God is one who reveals in his words and exhibits in his behavior the truths, signs, attributes, and will of God. He does this through his speech or writing, and he makes God evident by demonstrating the will of God in his words and deeds. The ancient prophets, or manifestations of God, were so outstanding, so remarkably different, that they spiritually influenced billions of souls for thousands of years. They were not normal people. Their words and deeds were so spiritually unique that they remain highly distinguished from the rest of humanity."

Rose turned in her seat to face me. "Consider this: suppose we were aliens from space on a mission to visit this solar system, and, let's say, we landed on the moon to observe the earth and its creatures." She was smiling as she continued. "Now suppose we had some form of technology, like a computer, that contained detailed information regarding the history of earth. Then suppose we asked our all-knowing computer, 'Who were the most influential people ever to have lived on the earth?' I'm suggesting to you that the computer would list the great prophets, or manifestations of God.

"Of the many people in history who have been influential for short periods of time, and of whom you might have read about in various books, none compares with the enduring influence and popularity of the manifestations of God. They each spoke with a truth and behaved with a holiness that has resonated intuitively with responsive hearts and souls for centuries.

"Grayson, seriously consider this idea, at least temporarily, so you will have a chance to take in this great vision of hope. The manifestations of God alone give influence to all that is good and protect us from our own destruction. Were it not for them, the people of the world would most likely destroy the world and themselves. They alone give understanding to the purpose of our creation, the purpose of our life, the reality of our death from this world, and the reality of the spiritual existence that follows. I ask you: where else can you find anything that is sufficient to explain the reasons for our creation or the purpose of our life and death, except in their teachings?"

"Science might answer some of these questions," I suggested hesitantly, after a short pause.

"I don't think so," Rose responded. "Science might be able to tell us **how** life and death work, but not **why**. Scientists can explain how some things function in the universe, but if they were to venture an explanation of our purpose, the best they could do is merely offer their own varied opinions and theories, not facts—and that's not science. The manifestations, however, can help us understand the **why** about nearly everything, because that's part of their mission and purpose.

"I am getting a bit off track here, though. The main idea is that the most meaningful way to know God and understand the purpose of our lives is through the teachings of the manifestations of God. Nature gives us the signs of God's existence. Each phenomenon or living entity reflects truths about the Creator, providing opportunities for us to learn and develop spiritually. The best way to know if what we observe reflected in the signs of creation is harmonious with the will of God or not, is by the spiritual interpretation of natural phenomena by the manifestations of God. There, that's it!"

My head was spinning with questions and thoughts. "Hmmm," I groaned. It was the best I could manage. Rose happily took in the wide view ahead, as if I wasn't there.

Eventually, she added, "As I mentioned before, one way to know about God is through his signs in the creation. By observing both violence and selfishness in the world of nature, as well as love and kindness, it might seem that the qualities of God are both violent and loving. So how do we know which is true about God? I suggest we turn to the manifestations of God for these answers. They are the **only** ones who can properly interpret the natural signs so we can understand them correctly—just like the wise hunter who interprets signs left by a moose. We are assured in the sacred scriptures, Grayson, that God did not just create us in the world and leave us ignorant, stranded, and alone to figure things out unaided. He arranged for guidance to direct our experiences here through the words and teachings of the manifestations of God."

Rose reached into her travel bag and took out some peppermints. She offered me one and then took one for herself. I thought about what she had just said. "I have no problem with what you're saying," I remarked. "It makes . . . good sense to me. It raises lots of questions, of course." I looked at her for feedback.

She read me clearly and responded, "Yes, there will be endless questions. For today, though, I just want you to be clear about what I am suggesting—that there is a God and that he expresses himself to the human beings through the creation and through the manifestations. That's all."

"I understand that," I confirmed.

"Oh good!" Rose said with a sigh of relief.

"But Rose, I've read the words of most of these . . . uh . . . manifestations . . . and sometimes they are confusing to me. That is, they don't all say **exactly** the same thing. In other words, there are differences between them. How can they all manifest God, or speak for God as you say, if they say things and do things that are different from one another?"

"Excellent question!" she almost sang out, throwing her hands up and smiling as if I had understood something important. She seemed charged with energy again. She quickly looked down and began searching for something under the seat.

"What do you need?" I asked.

She said nothing, but kept feeling around on the floorboard. Rose was rather rotund, so bending over was difficult. She couldn't see down where her feet were, so she had one hand down rummaging around. With a look of delight, she sat upright and pulled out a small cardboard box I had left under the seat that had once contained some strapping bands. She started gently drumming on the box with one hand while she held it out in front of her with the other. Then she began to sing. It was an Indian song or a prayer of some sort, I surmised. It was somewhat familiar; I had seen the Native Alaskans drum and sing in their traditional way before. She was slowly twisting back and forth in a rhythmic motion as she sang. She sang beautifully but not in English. It was inspiring, gentle and soothing. She would lift her hands up and down as she turned left and right, raising and lowering her voice, all the time opening and closing her eyes, looking up and down and about her as though I wasn't even there. I felt a little disconnected just sitting there driving. I wanted to move and sing with her. It felt so primal, yet, naturally familiar. She soon slowed down—ending with some tender humming sounds through her heavy breathing. Her eyes were closed, and she hung her head silently. She had dropped her arms motionless by her side, as though she could no longer hold them up. I tried not to look at her and tried not to show any feelings for fear she could sense them. I didn't want to disturb her. I waited for her to cue me that it was all right to speak. Instead, after a short time, she replaced the box under the seat and picked up right where she left off.

"Many of the words and teachings of the great prophets, or manifestations of God, have been, over time, either misunderstood, incorrectly interpreted, wrongly taught by religious leaders, improperly recorded years later, omitted, or in some rare cases, altered. For all these reasons and others, some of the words of the manifestations appear inconsistent with one another, as you have observed."

She looked at me to see if I was paying attention. I glanced back at her, and apparently she thought I was. "It's additionally important to understand—now listen to this carefully, Grayson—each manifestation of God addressed a relatively small group of people in his lifetime. He communicated to them in **their** local language and according to **their** local tradition and culture. They did this to help the people understand their teachings as clearly as possible. However, those cultures, languages, and traditions changed with time. The teachings of the manifestations, therefore, may not be clear or make sense to later generations much less to neighboring tribes, nations, or cultures. Some of the teachings of the manifestations of God are eternal in nature, but some are relative to the times and conditions that existed during the manifestations' lives. So, yes, through his manifestations, God communicates truths that assist in our spiritual maturation or progress as human beings. And, because truth is relative, what was needed for spiritual growth in mankind's earlier history naturally differed over time and is different from what is needed today. In the future, different guidance may be needed to assist a more mature society in its continuing spiritual development. If you look closely at the words of the manifestations, you will find they all spoke the **same spiritual truths**. The golden rule, for example, is consistent throughout all religions and throughout time. The manifestations all taught love, compassion, truthfulness, forgiveness, mercy, kindness, tolerance, good deeds, and many, many other spiritual qualities. The **differences** in what they taught were in their **social teachings**, which were **relative** to the conditions of the people among whom they appeared, and relative to the stages of those peoples' spiritual maturity. Over the expanse of time, the human beings required different guidance in order to advance. It was provided by the manifestations in the forms of various laws, rules, rituals, ceremonies, methods of worship, spiritual disciplines, and other various patterns of behavior. Do you see that? It's crucial to understand, because it is why there appear to be differences between the teachings of one manifestation and the ones who followed later in time." Rose waited for my acknowledgment.

"Yes, I get that," I affirmed. "So, all the manifestations of God taught the same spiritual truths, but different social teachings, depending upon who they were talking to and what their needs were at the time. Is that what you're saying?"

"Yes, Grayson, that is exactly it!" she beamed.

It seemed so simple. If I had wanted to challenge her premise, I couldn't think of anything to ask.

"There is one more important spiritual principle I want to share before we arrive at Haines Junction," Rose said. "It is this: the manifestations convey God's will and wishes to humankind in a way that helps us **evolve and progress** spiritually. For example, a first-grade teacher will teach her class the basics in reading, writing, and social skills. When her students advance to the second grade, they don't abandon everything they learned in the first grade before starting to learn from the second-grade teacher. Nor do the students refuse to go into the second grade and insist on staying in first grade! No! We enter second-grade where the new teacher affirms what the first-grade teacher taught and then gives us more lessons, more knowledge, more learning, and more wisdom, relative to our capacities as second graders. This is the way it works throughout all the years of our schooling.

"It is similar with the manifestations of God and the religions that are associated with them. Each manifestation affirms the spiritual truths revealed by the previous manifestation. In addition, he clarifies misunderstandings, elaborates on some truths, conveys new information on some subjects, assesses the needs of the current society, and prescribes spiritual solutions for personal and social progress. This makes the prophets one in their essence and connected in their religions. This has been going on now for thousands upon thousands of years. Even so, this has not been, nor is it now, the general understanding of the people.

"I would like to conclude on this subject with what I believe are some very important spiritual truths. I am proposing to you that the world's major religions are not separate, but one. The manifestations do not teach different truths, but instead have taught one continuous, progressive, unfolding, timely, relative truth. Therefore, **they are all part of a single evolving spiritual faith or religion**. One of the manifestations of God put it this way:

'*This is the changeless Faith of God, eternal in the past, eternal in the future.*'[6]

"Wow, that's cool!" I blurted out with almost teenaged enthusiasm. The juvenile response reflected the sense of joy I was feeling from what she said. I had studied different religions enough to recognize their similarities, but never understood them this way! It really made sense to me. All the religions speak a connected truth. I had believed something like this for quite some time, but had never had anyone explain it in such a simple and reasonable way. It rang true . . . maybe intuitively in some way . . . I didn't know. All I knew is it made sense to me, and it felt right. I felt good about myself and my beliefs. It just all seemed to come together.

"Some may not think it's so cool," Rose remarked. "Some may feel their religion or their faith is demeaned by comparing it on an equal basis with others. Some people believe their religion is superior and the only **right** religion, whereas everyone else's is wrong. May the spirit of all that is good inspire us all to love, not hate; unity, not conflict; healing, not violence; tranquility, not discontent; joy, not despair; togetherness, not separateness; and peace, not war. This is what the manifestations taught. You know it is true by the evidences of the loving signs in your heart when you read their sacred words.

"I have given you a simple explanation as to why the religions appear different from one another. I have explained that all the manifestations contributed to the ongoing guidance from the God over time, and therefore, in reality, are all part of one faith—one religion. Still, there is more to understand and more evidence to this point which I will share with you more clearly later on. For now, I just want you to appreciate the value of the manifestations of God and the religions associated with them in helping the human beings understand God and their reality and purpose on this earth."

Rose was finished talking. She settled back into her seat, watching out the window as the shadows lengthened along the roadside. Whew! I had to let my mind rest. Rose had rearranged my thinking such that my brain felt a bit over-saturated again. I was glad she had asked me to record the conversations of this trip so I could hear them again at some other time. I was feeling overwhelmed by the profusion of new concepts. I looked forward to listening to the tapes once we arrived in Oregon so I could better evaluate what she had been saying.

It was approaching evening. I'm sure everyone was ready for a break from the road. Before long we pulled into Haines Junction, a little town in the Yukon Territory of Canada where you can continue on the Alcan Highway or turn and take a dead-end road to Skagway, Alaska. We stayed at the North Country RV Park. It was a nice, large, open-spaced park with plenty of room and quality services. I found a place to park the truck and camp-trailer. T.J. and Alene drove off to secure a room at a nearby motel, taking Rose with them. Franklin and I set up the trailer for the evening. Soon thereafter, we had a delightful dinner at a nearby restaurant. After a fine meal and a short walk with Sonia, it was time to sleep.

The pastel sky of evenings in the north was glowing out my window. As I lay in my bed, I contemplated the subjects Rose had spoken of—our reality as human beings, the proofs of the existence of God, and the oneness of the religions. One thing kept coming back to my mind. The prophets, or the "manifestations of God" as she called them, all taught the same, continuous, evolving truth. Oh, I liked that! *But is it really possible?* I wondered. How come no one ever told us about this before? It makes sense to me. It feels right and sounds possible. She did say she would elaborate more on it later. I looked forward to better understanding the possibility.

Before drifting off to sleep, I remembered a prayer I had learned from my mother when I was young. *Now I lay me down to sleep, I pray the Lord my soul to keep. If I should die before I wake, I pray the Lord my soul to take. God bless Mommy, Daddy, Tommy* (my brother), *and Laura* (my sister). *Make me a good boy. Amen.* I repeated it in my memory. A feeling of fear came over me as it sometimes had when I a child: *What **if** I die before I wake?* It was disconcerting. *Will God take me? If not, then what?* That's it! Tomorrow I'll ask Rose about heaven and hell and see what she has to say. That felt right. I smiled, pulled the covers up over my shoulders, rolled onto my side, and quickly fell asleep.

DAY THREE

WHAT COMES NEXT?

I t was morning. As I lay in bed, I thought about what Rose had talked about the day before. She had spoken to me about profound subjects with such clarity, ease, and conviction. It was clear that Rose was far more complex than I had originally known.

I remembered a distinguished gentleman who used to come into Bean's Café in Anchorage to talk with Rose. He was a professor at the college. I didn't know him, but others told me who he was. I used to listen to him and Rose talk about various subjects. Once when he was leaving, I heard him say to another person who was with him that Rose was surely an enigma. He said she was one of those rare persons who could easily communicate to the common people of the street as well as hold her own with any scientist, theologian, or philosopher on most any subject. I had heard another person say that Rose only had a grade school education, but she read all the time. She had committed to memory several books on spiritual matters and was well known as an outstanding public speaker. I was beginning to realize how unique this woman really was, and I was looking forward to hearing more from her.

Today, everyone was up early and ready to go. Our destination was Watson Lake, a small town in the Yukon Territory near the border of British Columbia. Once we were out of Haines Junction, I told Rose about my thoughts last evening and the little prayer I had silently recited. I confessed my long-standing curiosity, asking her,

"What about heaven and hell?"

"What about them?" she replied.

"Do they exist? What are they like? Do you know?" She raised her eyebrows in surprise, then slowly reached down to turn on the recorder. She silently turned her head and looked out the window. I didn't know why, but she did that often when I would ask her a question. I couldn't tell if she had her eyes closed, was upset about my question, was formulating her thoughts, was praying, or meditating, or talking to the Spirit. I learned when she did so, it was best to wait. She had heard me and would answer in her own way and in her own time. I drank my coffee, checked the rear view mirrors to see the caravan following me, and fiddled with the CB until she responded.

"I wasn't going to speak about that today," she said, "but when the spirit moves upon one's heart as it did yours last evening, then I must comply with it. It takes me a little time to prepare myself. What do **you** believe about heaven and hell?" She looked at me intently, waiting for my answer.

"I don't know!" I exclaimed. "I really don't. It has puzzled me all my life. When I was young, I was told in church if I was good I would go to heaven after I die, and if I wasn't I would go to hell. Heaven was a place where all people that were good went when they were dead, and hell was where they went when they were bad. It's just about that simple," I said, glancing at her for understanding.

"Well, yes, that about covers it," she said, looking straight at me without any expression.

"That's it?" I cried in surprise. She couldn't hold it in any longer; she burst into laughter. She had me again!

"You're so serious," she muttered, after catching her breath again. Then she clasped her hands together, sat forward, and put her hands between her knees. Then she stared straight out the front window and began to speak. "First of all, I want you to be sure about this simple fact: the afterlife, or heaven and hell, to use your terms, is impossible to fully know or describe." She didn't move. I looked at her, but she didn't react. Finally, she looked back and said, "Did you get that?"

"Yes, it's impossible to describe," I repeated.

"Good," she said with a nod. "No one can tell it, and no one could hear it if it were to be told. Human language doesn't have the words to describe it, nor the mental faculties to understand it." She paused for a few moments, and then continued. "It's like this. Life after death is as different from this life, as this life is different from the life in a mother's womb. Do you understand?" she asked, looking at me intently.

I didn't answer right away, so she reiterated, "Life after death is as different from this life, as this life is different from the life we had while in our mother's womb. Let's say you and I were twins," she looked at me with a quick glance and a grin that said *go with me on this, Grayson.* "Let's say we are in the womb of our mother, and she is eight months pregnant. Now, in the womb, it's warm and comfortable, but we don't know it's warm and comfortable because we have never been cold or uncomfortable to compare it to. It's dark, and for the most part, silent. We actually don't know that either because we have never experienced light and our capacity to hear is limited. We don't know about color, sound, food, physical pleasures, happiness, sadness, joy, taste, or touch. We don't think in words or visual images. Why? Because we haven't developed those capacities yet nor have we had access to environments where we could experience those things. Our development is so immature it seems nearly negligible. How could it be possible, therefore, to convey to either of us while in the womb the incredible wonder of the things we were about to experience after birth? Impossible! It's the same with life after death. The next world is vastly different from this world—so beyond this present experience that we have neither the environment to experience it nor the capacity to imagine or describe it."

"Well, that's depressing in a way," I grumbled, interrupting her.

"Don't jump to conclusions," she insisted. "Be patient and stay with me on this, Grayson. If the life beyond is as different from this world as this world is different from the womb, then it must really be something! For example, we know seven colors here in this world. That is, the colors we perceive are within the known color spectrum, like the rainbow. Do you know what I mean?" She waited for a response.

"Yes, I know about that," I conceded.

"In the womb, there was no color, no light. So what an immeasurable difference this world of color and light is from the world of the womb! To estimate a similar difference, we might speculate that the next world could contain colors and light spectrums far beyond our current experiences and imagination. That's not all. Perhaps there are other stimulants to our spiritual senses that don't even exist here in this world, and perhaps other senses as well! In the womb we were developing organs, limbs, and senses to experience **this** world. Yet, we had no need for them in the womb because the environment was insufficient to use them. We developed eyes to see but could see nothing. We developed ears but could hear very little. We developed touch but lived in a water world with minimal textures to experience. We developed taste with nothing to eat. We developed these things in preparation to use in **this life** here on earth. In all probability, it follows that we are developing some kind of spiritual sense organs, or faculties, or capacities in this world that will be used extensively in our spiritual life after the death of our bodies. Let's think about a few we know of so far. Some of the qualities or spiritual faculties we are developing in this life that we will need in the spiritual world to come are truthfulness, trustworthiness, love, forgiveness, kindness, faith, patience, and generosity. Yes," she said, looking at my puzzled face, "you are developing spiritual qualities in this world for use in the life hereafter. If you don't develop these spiritual qualities and faculties in this world, you will be deprived of your full capacity and ability to experience that which exists in the future spiritual worlds."

"Now that's far out!" I exclaimed after imagining the possibilities. "That's really far out."

"Isn't it, though?" she agreed. "Now of heaven and hell. As you are good in this world, or as you develop spiritual qualities and capacities like those I just mentioned, so will be your 'heaven.' And vice versa. If you get diverted in this life and don't engage in developing these spiritual qualities, then upon arrival in the next world you could consequently feel deprived, and have excessive feelings of want, need, and regret which can be a real 'hell.' Think of it. The worst hell here in this world is to feel inadequate, unloved, unwanted, unneeded, guilty, regretful, and unable to love and fulfill the needs of others. This results in remoteness from others and our true purpose. The worst of hells is to cause our self or others terrible misery and not know why or what to do to change it. This is what comes about when we don't develop our necessary spiritual qualities.

"Some religious teachers I had when I was young," Rose confided, "explained hell literally as an eternal fire, with pain, agony, and tortuous deprivation. This was the interpretation **they** had been taught. I don't think we should take these concepts literally by any means. Sacred scriptures do suggest that 'hell' **is** a lack of the better things. In this life we call it hell when we don't have the good things of life and have no means or capacity to acquire them. Whereas, we might refer to some things in this life as heavenly because we get pleasure from the fact that we have the capacity and means to experience them. The terms 'heaven' and 'hell' used in the scriptures are not **physical places**, but **spiritual conditions** experienced after death. They are not places where our physical body is going to go after it dies. When we die, our body returns to the earth, and we will never need it again. The resurrection spoken of in religion was not intended to be taken literally as a time when our bodies would come out of their earthen graves. It is instead referring to the resurrection of faith and spirituality in the life of the soul.

"In the life after the death of our bodies, our spirits will progress forward through endless spiritual worlds, or conditions of existence, that cannot be described. When we die there is not a judgment of heaven **or** hell, but a judgment that is consequential justice according to how we behaved and developed spiritually in this world. It's as though we land on a continuum in which one direction is a more hellish, deprived condition, and the other direction is a more heavenly, satisfying existence. We will naturally seek to work toward the one and away from the other. This spiritual progress is impossible to describe except to say that the mercy of God will propel our movement toward the more heavenly condition, as will the prayers and forgiveness of those with whom we have had experiences in this life, and as a result of good deeds others do in our name or on our behalf." She paused long enough for me to jump in.

"Now, wait. Let me see . . . that was just too much for me to grasp," I said. "Too much new information. Now, I need to think about this and see if I can understand it."

"Of course," she assented.

"Now let's take one thing at a time here," I insisted. "First of all . . . when we die our soul lives on. Is that right?"

"Yes, of course," she replied.

"Everyone?" I asked.

"Yes, everyone."

"Then we land on some continuum or something?"

She laughed. "Not exactly. You will pass into the spiritual world and find yourself spiritually developed to a certain degree, depending on how you have lived your life and on a few other vital factors."

"Vital factors? And what are those?" I asked.

Rose looked at me with a long, loving gaze, as if trying to decide whether to answer my question or not. She took a deep breath, turned to sit straight, and continued, "Your purpose in this life is to become aware of and recognize the one true God that created you and gave you life, and to love and worship that one true God. Furthermore, your purpose is to recognize his manifestation, as I mentioned before, and to make efforts to behave in accordance with God's instructions as conveyed by the manifestation. That's why the Christians say you must accept Jesus into your heart before you can enter heaven. It's similar to the Buddhists, who believe you must follow the Buddha and learn and express compassion in order to attain Nirvana, which is the same thing as the heaven spoken of by the Jews and Christians, or as paradise as it is often referred to by Muslims. One must recognize the one true God, and through faith, make efforts to behave in a way that is consistent with the teachings of his manifestations."

"Hold it," I objected. "I have heard people say that we are saved by God's grace through faith alone and that deeds have nothing to do with it. Are you saying faith and deeds are both necessary?"

"What you have heard from the Christian friends is undoubtedly true," she replied, "but once a person becomes a believer, faith in God and his manifestations, **and** compliance with his teachings are equally important."

"Well, then," I asked, "what about what people say concerning heaven and hell who have had near-death experiences, like you talked about earlier? Is what they're saying anything close to the reality you're talking about?"

"For the most part what they are saying is consistent with the spiritual reality conveyed by God through his manifestations, yes," Rose confirmed.

"Okay . . . what about those neurologists who say these so-called 'near-death experiences' are just hallucinations being caused by the brain being deprived of oxygen?" I challenged.

"Well, both could be true. It doesn't have to be one or the other," she countered. "To experience God, one doesn't have to have an experience that is unexplainable. The neurologist might explain **how** it's happening, but an explanation doesn't change the purpose or reality of the experience. Nearly all people who have had near-death experiences commonly have learned from their experiences that their purpose in this life is to learn and to love. And that, my dear friend, is exactly consistent with the Word of God as revealed through his manifestations. Nearly all say that their near-death experience was, essentially, indescribably glorious—again consistent with the descriptions from the manifestations of God."

"So are these experiences real?" I asked.

"I certainly think so," Rose asserted. "Even in the womb subtle sound and touch is experienced—just enough to suggest **something** exists beyond that world. It appears to be the same way in this life. Some will experience spiritual phenomena enough to hint of a life beyond. I think these experiences exist so we will become curious and investigate spiritual matters. Yet, as I said before, they can only be considered as extremely limited experiences of life after death."

"I have experienced some of those spiritual phenomena, but it was when I was young . . . and under the influence of psychedelic drugs," I admitted with reservation.

"Yes, many in your generation did have mind-altering experiences that caused them to investigate spiritual matters," recalled Rose. "However, I wouldn't necessarily call drug experiences 'spiritual.'" She took a short pause and looked at me with a raised brow. "At that time it may have caused some to awaken and search, but most lost hope and adapted to the deception of being successful that drives the materialistic model of reality that the majority of people live by today. But, enough about that."

I knew that meant we were not going to get into a discussion on that issue. Not now, at least. I quickly blurted out, "Now, more about hell!" I laughed, looking at her for agreement.

"Yes, hell. Think of it this way. Hell might be thought of as deprivation, want, need, fear, anger, loneliness, remoteness, lack, or attachment. I have heard Sunday school teachers tell children that hell is like a fiery furnace where one feels tortuous pain until one collapses. After you collapse, God renews you so you can go on feeling intense pain from the fire. Frankly, I think scare tactics like that are terrible—no, worse—they are abusive! It's some people's distorted, fear-based way of trying to instill compliant behavior in young children. Let's consider it figuratively though. Isn't deprivation, want, need, fear, loneliness, remoteness, lack, or attachment each like a burning fire, in that any one of them can cause us endless pain? Sure!" she asserted. "Hell, or the consequences of improper living, has no physical eternity because our body dies permanently. However, if it has the **qualities** of fire within the soul, then the soul will make efforts to change for the better. And if the soul doesn't make efforts, then it will continue to experience that so-called 'hell.' Hell, then, **is a condition**, not a place or a thing. That's one of the reasons why the manifestations of God guide us ever so persistently to develop spiritually. It's really what's best for us in every respect when considering our true purpose and reality as spiritual beings. Mature contemplation on this matter will surely arrive at the same conclusion."

"How do you **know** it's best for us?" I inquired. "I mean, where do you get your information on these subjects?"

She looked at me with an apologetic expression. "I'd really like to share that with you, Grayson, but please be patient with me. I'll answer that question as soon as I feel it's most meaningful to our discussion. Is that okay with you?"

"Okay," I murmured, "sure."

"Now, a little more about heaven," Rose continued, pausing for a moment. "Whatever degree of spiritual goodness we develop in this world will go with us to the life hereafter. Most assuredly, we will be filled with joy and gratitude with whatever amount or degree of love and spiritual qualities we have developed. This consequence is our reward, our heaven, and our eternal life. Keep in mind this is just a simple, limited explanation. There is so much more. I hope it helps you with your concerns about heaven and hell."

I grinned at her. I was smiling all over my being. I didn't even know why except I felt . . . joy . . . and gratitude . . . to use her words. Finally, so much confusion, disagreement, and conflicting concepts came together into a simple, affirming truth.

We were both quiet for a while before I asked: "Why do religions traditionally explain heaven and hell the way they do then? You know, like heaven having streets of gold and trumpets playing or hell containing fire and brimstone. Why do they explain things that way?"

Rose grew thoughtful. Finally, she asked, "How would you describe something to a little boy that you can't explain, and he can't understand?" Before I could answer, she continued, "You might tell a child that heaven is like having all the toys and candy he wanted, and hell is living without them. In other words, you would speak to that child on his level of understanding, making comparisons so he might get a glimmer of a notion regarding the consequences in the afterlife of his behavior in this life. This is the way the prophets, or manifestations of God, and religious authorities addressed the people when asked about heaven, hell, or the afterlife. Knowing it is not understandable or explainable, they sometimes drew comparisons that were better understood by the people they were addressing. To those who delighted in music, one in ancient times might have explained heaven as trumpets and harps playing. To people who valued riches, heaven might have been described as cities of gold and jewels. To those whose lives were torn by war, violence, and conflict, one might explain it as peace of mind or freedom from suffering, or, as some call it, nirvana. It's important to understand that the descriptions of heaven and hell that come from religious tradition were tailored to the people of a given time and place. They were devised to help people better understand the afterlife and the consequences of their behavior in this life. These descriptions were never intended to be taken literally or to be considered permanent conceptions of something that can't be understood. It's the same with what I have expressed. I have conveyed concepts that are relative to both you and me. These concepts are generally intended to give value to right living, to deter poor behavior, to enhance faith in God, and to give hope for a meaningful future and afterlife."

She sat back in her seat and turned to look out the window again. We rode in silence. As we approached a small Canadian town, I announced on the CB it was time for fuel again and a restroom break.

Our small caravan stretched itself out behind the single fuel pump of a little roadside store and café. I helped Rose out of the cab. We went into the store just to stretch and move about. As we were leaving the store, I glanced at the headline of the local paper, which read, "Violence Erupts Again in the Middle-East." My prior joy suddenly leached out of me. I was upset again. *When will the people and governments get together and solve our national conflicts? I'll ask Rose*, I thought, as we went about our business.

Once we were on the road again, I acquainted Rose with the newspaper headline and shared my feelings with her. I could tell she, too, lost her joy and was saddened by the subject. Then I saw her face transition from sadness to a relaxed contentment. She began, "I am going to say a couple things about politics. No. Instead of politics, I am going to talk to you about government and suggest two things people can do to help prevent international conflicts."

"As you know, Grayson, long ago the people of the United States decided to create a federal government that would oversee disputes between states and would take care of the states collectively in relation to other countries. The states at that time were furious about such a proposal. They did not want another higher form of government telling them what to do. It is understandable, and perhaps a natural and normal way to feel for people who had fought for independence. Adding another level of government would expand the possibilities of oppression, so they had good reason to be concerned. However, in the evolution of social order—from the institution of the family, to the tribe, to the city, to the state, to nations—expanding systems became necessary for the ordered life of evolving societies around the globe. And now, because we are living in a world community, government must be expanded to accommodate an international federation that will solve disputes and govern over international issues. So clearly, it is extremely important for the people to work toward expanding the concept of federalism to an international level. One nation's government, or even a few, should not be policing the world alone. It doesn't work, and it will lead to terrible consequences. Some people will resist an expansion to international federalism, but those with vision will see it as an absolute necessity and will support it. The United Nations is a good start, but it needs to be revised so **all** the nations of the earth have equal representation and influence.

"The next step is to encourage the people to do everything in their power to inspire our national leaders to make a binding international agreement to abolish war and violence as a means for dealing with national differences. This is critical! Each nation eventually must lay down its weapons created for international conflict and retain just enough to protect its internal affairs and to contribute to an international force created to oversee all international disputes."

She paused for a moment before continuing. "One more thing, please. I can't emphasize this enough. The **means for this** to be successful requires that the people's efforts to influence and encourage their governments must be non-partisan, non-violent, and law abiding. This is the spiritual way! It would also be best if partisan politics were eventually abandoned. They create a destructive disunity that causes stagnation and impotence of government, as the world is now witnessing." Rose's face was stern as she sat motionless, staring out the front window.

"Beyond this, I will say no more at this time about politics or concerns of government, and please don't ask me to talk about these issues. This is not the purpose of our conversation. My mission is spiritual, because that's what will cause things to change for the better. Let me explain why."

Rose paused for some time before proceeding. Returning to what inspired the conversation, she said, "Some people think that if we just had a better, more efficient government, the problems of the world like those in the Middle-East would be resolved. Even though I have talked about the need for expanding government to embrace international federalism, more government, or more efficient government alone cannot solve sufficiently the underlying problems plaguing the human beings. I believe the root of our problems is the decline in spirituality and morality among the people. Government does not and cannot stimulate spiritual or moral refinement. Dishonesty, distrust, deception, greed, avarice, and ambition spread like an infection when morality and spirituality decline in a civilization. Governments naturally respond to these conditions by creating more rules, laws, security, and oversight to make up for the loss. As any casual observer can see, it doesn't work very well because government cannot have any effect on the source of the problem. I feel confident that the world soon will come to realize that pure religion with true spirituality, and not just better government alone, is the most vital necessity for solving the world's considerable problems. When the spirituality and morality of the people improve, consequently so will the quality and efficiency of government. And the source and sustaining force of spiritual and moral development is found only in true religion, which is what I hope I am sharing with you."

She was silent. I waited for more, looking down the road and back at her—I waited.

"That's it?" I asked.

"For the moment," she replied.

The CB crackled, "This is Tail-Gunner . . . it's time for lunch!" Suddenly, T.J. and Alene passed me like a bullet. We followed behind them, riding for a while with only small talk about the scenery and the fine weather of the day. It appeared that the heaven and hell discussion had run its course, as had my concern over more efficient government. I had no pressing questions, and Rose was in a quiet mood. As we came around a bend, I saw T.J. standing beside his car, waving us down. He and Alene had located a small roadside diner. We pulled off the road to join them for lunch.

Something inside was nagging at me, and I knew what it was. Up until now it was just a feeling I would get at the mention of the word "religion". But suddenly, it became a strong feeling accompanied by a series of thoughts, and they were not good. I knew I would have to voice them to Rose, but I was afraid to because she had asked me to let it go. Tension started to build in my neck at what I was thinking. But it was time to order lunch, so I had to just let it go—for now.

DAY THREE

WHY AWRY?

We had our meal in the diner along with a number of other travelers. We shared stories and laughter while enjoying a wonderful view of the Canadian Rockies out of the large windows. It was a good time and a good lunch.

Soon it was time to go again. After a few photographs and some souvenir purchases, we loaded up and moved on. As I fastened my seatbelt, Rose turned on the recorder. For some reason, it triggered those feelings about religion I had noticed before lunch. I felt myself flush with discontent, which prompted me to tell Rose how I was feeling.

"I've been thinking, Rose, and I really can't go on with this conversation we're having without first getting this off my chest." I paused, trying to think of a way to say what I had to say in a sensitive way. My heart started to race, and my breath became short. "It's about religion," I said. "Not so much the word. It's about the pretending, the fantasy, and the fairy-tale aspects of religion that turns me off cold!" I announced bluntly. "I just can't get over it. Please, before we go on, I need to be heard on this." I glanced at her for understanding—she looked straight ahead without a response.

"I **really like** the spiritual aspects of religion, Rose. To me, they feel right, good, and true. But the religions themselves base many of their beliefs on stories that seem to be mere fantasies. It appears that if one wants to become a believer and wants to remain faithful, acceptance of fantasies and surrender to make-believe are required. I just can't do that! I can't reconcile my love for the spiritual with my disdain for pretending. When I try to accept religion as it's usually presented to me, I feel disingenuous, dishonest with myself, and plumb crazy. I just can't do it! I don't know how people do it. How do people accept fairytale-like explanations of their religions and then go on about their lives as though the things they are being taught are true and real when they **must** know in their hearts that something is not right?"

"And they have no say," I continued ranting, "nor do they discuss alternatives about what scriptures might mean. It's just a dictated belief system promoted by an accept-it-or-not or, worse yet, accept-it-or-else controlling style of leadership. The organized religions I'm familiar with seem to want to tell you what to believe and how to behave—not that those things aren't important, but it's the **way** they go about it that offends me. It doesn't feel as though there are options for choices or room for different opinions. It's like: 'if you don't like the stated beliefs of our church or faith or religion, then choose a different one that suits you.' The believers say, and they are told, not to probe too much or ask questions but 'to have faith.' Now I ask you: is that the way God wanted it to be? Is that the way of truth—just pick a religion that suits you and go along with it in blind faith? Shouldn't truth bring about harmony in one's heart and mind? Shouldn't a person's beliefs be compatible with life's experiences, and with what is real? Shouldn't we be encouraged to question and explore the meaning of sacred scriptures instead of just accepting fairytale-like explanations dictated by the clergy? Can you help me with this, Rose?" I asked, pleadingly.

I was done. I was shaking. I don't know if I was angry or just afraid I had exposed my soul to someone who probably believed differently than me. This could create conflict between us or even end this whole project, and I didn't want that. I was hoping I hadn't offended her. I looked over at her for feedback, then back down the road. I kept looking back and forth, waiting for a response.

Rose just faced forward, expressionless, with her hands together between her knees, rocking backward and forward ever so gently. It seemed like a long wait, but it was probably only a minute. Finally, she turned her whole body toward me in the seat, reached out and put a warm hand upon my tense shoulder, giving it a little squeeze. "You are such a brave man to say how you feel, Grayson. You are honest and brave. That's good. Honesty and bravery only lead to what is good and true. All your questions are valid, and it is an absolute necessity they be answered to your complete satisfaction before we go any further. The spirit has moved on your heart again, so this afternoon we will travel this path together that has been presented to us."

I looked at her. She was smiling, but with tears in her eyes. Her face seemed to beam with joy, shining intense love right out at me. I melted. I felt like I was six years old again, at home within the safe and loving care of my mother. "Thank you," I whispered, "I just wanted . . ."

"Please don't feel you need to explain or apologize," she interrupted. "I understand you are frustrated and need answers. So let's just do this," she said, as she turned to face forward.

I felt better. I sighed and relaxed into my seat. *Okay. I've got to hear this,* I thought. *In fact, I'm going to be tough on her and call her on anything that sounds questionable to me. I'm ready.*

"Grayson, I would like you to consider the possibility that the basic teachings of all the world's major religions were inspired by the one true God, and therefore, are true—Judaism, Christianity, Islam, Buddhism, Hinduism, Zoroastrianism, and some others—are all true. And I would like you to know that there have been other civilizations with legitimate prophets, spiritual seers, visionaries, and teachers, whose guiding words have either been forgotten or were never recorded."

Flushed with desperation, I asked, "What does that have to do with the concerns I just expressed?"

Rose looked at me and smiled lovingly. "Please, if you give me some time, and listen and explore with an open heart and mind, you will discover that these new spiritual truths I am asking you to consider, are consistent with how you feel in your heart, how you think in your mind, and with your experiences in the world—and yes, even with science. Are you willing to try this?"

"I'm sorry about my impatience," I apologized. "Please go on."

She rustled around in her seat and took a more relaxed position, which also helped me relax. It was a while before she continued. "The manifestations of God, who founded the world's great religions, did everything they could to communicate spiritual truths and teachings clearly to the people they were addressing. Some religious leaders, though, lacked spiritual maturity. They did not correctly comprehend the **spiritual meaning** of the words and teachings of the manifestations. As a result of their limited understandings, they became frustrated. Over time, they began to interpret some of the words and teachings of the manifestations in **literal,** or materialistic ways, hoping to simplify the religious teachings, to avoid confusion, and to unify the believers. That is, they sometimes took what was said word for word. Some might say they believed and acted on the **letter** of the word instead of the **spirit** of the word. It has been this literal or materialistic interpretation of sacred scriptures by the clergy that has caused religion to degenerate by varying degrees to incorporate fantasy and superstition." She paused. "Did you get that?" she asked, turning her head only slightly to look at me with one eye.

"Well, yes, I think so, I replied."

"When I use the word 'superstition,' I'm talking about believing in things that are not true or real. I'm not talking about fear of bad luck from a black cat crossing the road in front of you or worrying about breaking a mirror and having seven years of bad luck, even though these are superstitions," Rose explained. "I'm talking about interpreting sacred scripture and the lives of the manifestations in ways that are inconsistent with reason, inconsistent with the wisdom gained from our collective experiences of life, or inconsistent with what we know to be scientific proof of what is real and true. Are you clear on that?"

"Yes, I understand what you're saying. Thanks for the

clarification," I replied.

"It has been the subtle infiltration of superstition into religion that makes its believers appear to be pretending, which easily creates a barrier for those who are seeking spiritual truth, and consequentially causes you and others such frustration. Nearly all the organized religions in the world today are influenced by superstitious interpretation of scripture."

I snapped my head around at Rose's comment, feeling surprised.

"Now don't get jumpy about this," she cautioned. "There is a lot to explore and understand, and I'm hoping to give you sufficient examples to satisfy your many questions."

"But wait," I pleaded. "Let me understand what you just said. So you're saying that my feelings about religion," I hesitated, "are legitimate? They're okay with what you believe?"

"Yes," she nodded, without further explanation.

She waited, I guess, to see if I had any more questions before continuing. I didn't. I was surprised enough at this point that there just wasn't anything more to say at the moment.

"Okay," I said, "I guess that's it."

Rose held her chin with her thumb and index finger, intently contemplating her next words. "The scriptures given to us by the manifestations of God," she explained, "are the highest and most powerful expression of what can best stimulate the evolution and development of humans toward their destiny as spiritual beings. Their words affect the hearts and souls of people in ways that cannot be fully analyzed or understood. But some of the scriptures seem so complicated and so difficult to understand that we just want to ask: 'Why didn't the manifestations say what they had to say more clearly?' I will explain it this way—the words of the manifestations of God are for the development of the hearts and souls of the human beings. They inspire us to rise above the burdens and pettiness of daily life, to seek the spirit of joy and contentment. They move us to behave in ways that are right, good, true, kind, and loving, even though at times a line of scripture might not make perfect sense to our minds.

"It can cause confusion sometimes when a person tries to analyze and understand a difficult passage of scripture. So the question arises: how are certain scriptures to be interpreted or understood, literally— word for word as they are written—or figuratively, or should I say, symbolically? This is where agreement often breaks down. Some people, due to limited understanding and out of frustration to capture scripture with their minds, will resort to interpreting some scriptures literally, which really should be interpreted symbolically instead. They often argue their points to such a degree that separate sides emerge. Then, in order to strengthen their position of perceived righteousness, they sometimes emphasize that their truth is greater than that of their contender. This competition for what is perceived as righteousness, if not curtailed, can degenerate into arrogance and separation—the very opposite of the loving and unifying spirit the manifestations were actually teaching. Eventually, this contention can result in division into sects. This is one reason there are so many sects in the religions, and why the major religions themselves are often at odds with one another.

"I want to repeat these sacred words from one of the manifestations of God:

'*The understanding of his words and the comprehension of the utterances of the Birds of Heaven are in no wise dependent upon human learning. They depend solely upon purity of heart, chastity of soul, and freedom of spirit.*'[7]

Rose clarified, "The 'words' are God's teachings. The 'Birds of Heaven' are the manifestations of God. So, I am suggesting that the understanding heart will, with common sense, be able to tell when scripture is intended to be interpreted literally or when it should be interpreted symbolically. Those who purify their hearts and free their spirits will be content not to have to wrap their mind around everything, but will seek instead to let the spirit of the sacred words into their hearts. From this perspective, they will recognize the common truths of all the great religions. Common sense sees the commonality. It reveals how the path is one, not many. Sacred scripture is the food of the heart; it can only be digested there. The finite mind cannot partake of this infinite food without the heart's involvement or else it will be left confused by such an attempt. So you see. Out of some people's limited understanding and mental frustration, many sacred scriptures have been interpreted literally, which has led to the adoption of numerous, worthless and meaningless beliefs, rituals, ceremonies, and traditions. Consequently, many people don't want to be part of this type of religion."

She became silent again, but she was sitting perfectly still so I knew there was more to come.

"Grayson, there is something I want you to know in your heart. I only tell you these things so you will have a clearer understanding of what has happened in the course of religious history, so you can know what has led to the undesirable conditions of religion that cause you concern. My analysis and conclusion are not for the purposes of assigning blame or shame to any persons or to any religions. I am hoping we can have this kind of exploration of truth without the need to assign fault to anyone or any group. What has come to pass can always be interpreted as faulty in retrospect. So, instead, it is best we both look upon former times with understanding and forgiveness."

I nodded at how reasonable Rose's thinking was. I felt my former disdain begin to slip away along with the tension I had been holding in my neck and shoulders.

"There are some things I will not be able to explain satisfactorily to you or others. If you pay attention and observe with a detached perspective, you will find that people often become like sheep. They follow the group's thinking patterns without knowing they are being influenced and possibly misled by those around them. There are some extremely conservative people, for example, who cling to old, worn-out habits, beliefs, and customs out of a fear of losing something once thought to be dear. More liberal people may gravitate toward current trends of harmful excess without even knowing their peers are influencing them negatively. Not until people examine these truths objectively, with detachment, and in light of our true purpose, will they be able to understand. Not until they give up their lesser loyalties of secularism, racism, liberalism, conservatism, nationalism, and religious sectarianism, will there be opportunity to expand their unity to include the whole of mankind. Not until they recognize the members of the human family equally, accept the unity of religions as one continuous, evolutionary faith in God, and pull together in recognition of the one true God, will there be opportunity for goodness to prevail."

Rose quieted again. I was neutral. I had nothing to say yet. She sat silently, looking out the window, until I heard, "Examples—hmm," as she murmured to herself.

"Let's start at the beginning," she determined. "At least at the so-called beginning," she breathed with a big sigh. Let's use the story of creation as it is told in the book of Genesis from the Jewish Torah, which is also part of the Christian Bible. Here we have an example of how religious scripture can become superstition when interpreted literally. Seen another way, it is guidance for true spiritual understanding when interpreted symbolically. In fact, let's consider a couple of different stories.

"The biblical story of creation says that God created the heavens, that is, all that is observable in the sky above, and the earth and all that is upon it in six days. It goes on to explain what was created each day until the process was complete. If taken symbolically, it is clear that God first created something undeveloped and apparently of little importance, which he caused to go through a series of changes, culminating what currently exists. This spiritual, figurative, or symbolic interpretation is totally consistent with our collective observable experience, science, reasoning, logic, and the feelings of the heart. On the other hand, if this story of creation is taken literally, it appears to have happened in six twenty-four-hour periods, which is inconsistent with all observable experience, reason, and especially science. To this day, despite evidence to the contrary, some continue to interpret this story literally. This, as you have observed, is fantasy and superstition."

"I don't get it!" I barked in frustration. "It seems the only reason for that kind of thinking is just plain stubbornness. The only reason I can see for the clergy to continue to interpret that story literally and to teach it to their congregations is to separate themselves and their religion from others in an attempt to make them appear exclusively superior. There is no motive behind it except pride and arrogance as far as I can see. Isn't that the very opposite of the true spiritual path?"

I looked at Rose for clarification. She didn't answer me right away. I think she was letting me cool off. Finally, she resumed. "Literal interpretation of scripture that is obviously intended to be symbolic can cause the teachings of a religious sect or group to become distorted and superstitious, and sometimes even cause them to deteriorate into a merely materialistic organization. The revealed religions, like those I mentioned before, began pure and wholly spiritual. Over time they divided into different sects. Many of the sects slowly became infiltrated with material purposes—this-world purposes and this-life purposes—like acquiring excessive possessions, power, notoriety, wealth, popularity, and consumption. The true spiritual path, however, focuses primarily on the spiritual development of hearts and souls and not on worldly matters.

"Here is where the confusion comes in over time," Rose elaborated. "The development of spiritual qualities, like kindness, truthfulness, trustworthiness, generosity, and others we have discussed, gradually can become less important in religion. When this happens, the religion degenerates. Its principles and morality are given less value than worldly or material values. More attention is devoted to pursuing wealth, comfort, power, prestige, and security. None of these are necessarily undesirable or sinful, but focusing on them—giving them higher priority and greater value than acquiring spiritual qualities—leads to the degeneration of religions, as you have observed. Such degeneration puts it out of touch with the true spiritual path."

"Let me see if I understand," I interrupted. "Are you saying that religion starts out . . . let's say . . . true and spiritual in essence, but can end up decaying into superstition because of the literal interpretation of some scriptures that were intended to be considered symbolically, or even, let's say, metaphorically?"

"Yes," she affirmed with a quick nod. "Yes, that is exactly what I am saying. Let me give you another example. I started out by explaining the creation story from Genesis. If you read it thoroughly, and consider it symbolically, you will see how it is consistent with your life experiences and with reason and science. The point is this: the planet and everything on it evolved over time, as would a project that takes six days to complete."

"So, are you saying evolution is true?" I asked.

She held her hand up as if to stop us from engaging in that topic. "We will discuss that later. For now let's stay focused on the subject at hand."

"I'm with you," I agreed.

"Now, another example is the Adam and Eve story," she said. "There are two biblical stories of Adam and Eve that differ a little, and the story of Adam and Eve in the Muslim Quran is different still. But, generally, the story is that God created a single man and a single woman and gave them a garden paradise. They were instructed not to partake of a certain fruit in the garden, which they did anyway after being misled by a serpent. Consequently, this caused them to be banished from the garden paradise. Now, it would be silly to take this story literally, word for word. It is inconsistent with reason, experience, and wisdom. However, when interpreted symbolically, it has profound significance. There are many wisdoms to be extracted from this story, but I will give you just one possibility. This story demonstrates that obedience to God's instructions results in good and desirable consequences, whereas, yielding to selfish desires, symbolized by the serpent, and disobeying the guidance from the wise Creator, leads to hardship, pain, and suffering. Isn't this interpretation more harmonious with reason, experience, science, and intuition of the heart than an interpretation that considered the story literally?"

She waited now. I was lost in listening. A few moments passed before I realized she had stopped and was looking at me for a response.

"Of course," I blurted, "but that's so simple and not the way some religions teach it. In fact, this is exactly what I was talking about when I said religion becomes make-believe."

"I know," she replied. "Let's not get into all the possibilities. I just wanted to point out that religious scripture has spiritual implications. When the followers of the various religions could not understand the teachings and words of their great manifestations, they resorted to literal interpretations of some scriptures that eventually led to the current superstitious practices and pretense you so abhor about your religious experiences."

Silence. I looked at her, and she at me. I stared ahead, focusing on the road, while still trying to think of some argument or comment to what she had been explaining.

"What can I say?" I questioned. "It makes sense, and it just seems so simple that I don't know what to say. It just feels right; the way I have always felt. So where did they go wrong? Well," I continued to answer my own question, "because of their lack of spiritual maturity, they did not understand the words and teachings correctly, so they began to interpret them literally, and that resulted in the . . . the superstitious beliefs and pretending!"

"Yes," she said, in a soft fading tone. "And because of that, many people feel organized religion is meaningless and unfulfilling. To some, it is even repulsive. That's why, like you, so many today do not turn to religion even though most people say they believe in God and spirituality. How unfortunate, huh?"

"Yes, yes it is," I nodded sadly.

"Grayson, I want to be clear about what I said before. What I have just explained was to answer your specific question about the development of superstition and pretense in religion. It is in no way meant to condemn any of the religions. I talked about challenging ideas—the kind of ideas that would cause many to reconsider some of their beliefs. What I have expressed to you is purely for the sake of helping you understand what has happened over time, and what has caused religions to succumb to the superstitious beliefs and practices you have observed."

She was quiet for a spell and then turned in her seat to look at me directly. "I want to say something hopeful here because it's getting late, and I am sure we are going to be in Watson Lake soon. I don't want you to feel discouraged or depressed about what we have been discussing. There is great hope! I am going to show you how each religion has had, and still has, a glorious place in the spiritual development of humanity. I am going to show you how they all tie together and are really all parts of one great spiritual belief. I am going to show you how they can all be recognized as one faith, and how it is possible for the human beings to become a united people as citizens of one planet. I am going to revive that vision of hope your generation had in its youth, and I am going to give a great vision of hope for the youth of today and tomorrow. The Great Spirit has again addressed the human beings and pointed out the way. Stay with me, Grayson, in anticipation of this. I promise you these things before we are through with this trip. Are you with me?" she queried.

"Yes, Rose, I'm with you," I said hopefully.

We were close to Watson Lake where we would spend the night. T.J. and Alene had gone ahead and were calling in on the CB. They had located a place for Rose and them to stay. I asked them to meet me at the Watson Lake RV Park so they could transport Rose to the motel. It was easier that way because maneuvering the truck around town with a camp-trailer attached was difficult. It was raining hard as we pulled into the park. I helped Rose transfer to T.J. and Alene's car while Franklin helped set up the trailer. Sonia and Annie took off for the coin-operated showers, which Sonia later said reminded her of church camp when she was a child. After T.J. secured rooms for the night, he located a restaurant for dinner. He dropped Alene and Rose off there so he could come and shuttle the rest of us.

It rained off and on all night, but that wasn't the worst of it. It was the mosquitoes! Up in the front of the trailer where Franklin, Annie, and baby Scott slept, there were mosquitoes everywhere! They were in our trailer by the hundreds and thick outside! It was to be a difficult night—too warm to stay under the covers and too many mosquitoes to leave the covers off. Sonia and I didn't get bitten too badly because we had a curtain separating our bed from the rest of the trailer. Franklin, Annie, and unfortunately, little Scott, were badly bitten. Scott's little face looked like he had chicken pox! It was a hard night that all of us were eager to have end. We were up at first light, near four, hoping to get out of that infestation as quickly as possible!

DAY FOUR

CHAPTERS OF THE SAME BOOK

We had breakfast, broke camp, and were on the road quicker than any other day of the trip. Our desire to escape those mosquitoes was a great motivator.

I was the first to speak this morning as Rose and I left Watson Lake. I had been thinking about yesterday's conversation. "Well, I thought about what you said yesterday," I began, "about religion falling into superstition because of literal interpretation of scriptures and so forth. That's all well and good—well, not so well and good, but at least it makes sense. It explains what has happened to religions over time, but here's the problem. If nearly all religions have adopted some superstitious practices and beliefs, then what do we do now? I mean, that's depressing and leaves me right back where I started, feeling kind of lost!" I took a sip of my coffee, but before I could continue, Rose quickly responded.

"Grayson," she said abruptly, as she turned in her seat to face me directly. She waited for me to look back at her so she knew I was listening. "What I am going to share with you today is more important than anything I have shared with you so far. This will tie so many things together, just when it seems hope is lost." She grinned. "What I have to tell you today has never been thoroughly understood by the ancients, and is not, for the most part, widely known by people today even though it was intended for it to be common knowledge in the world by now."

She paused and marked her words carefully. "I'm going to start out with some background information first." She readjusted herself to face forward and relaxed in her seat. "What I first want to talk to you about this morning is what I refer to as **continuous revelation**. Continuous revelation is the belief **within a religion** that God has guided their people, over time, through a series of prophets or messengers. This is a basic belief in all the world's major religions. Nearly all religions, cultures, societies, and tribes believe the one true God has inspired a special Soul to enlighten and guide them with spiritual knowledge and goodness. Most religions moreover, believe this has happened more than once, resulting in numerous prophets or messengers whom they recognize **within** their Faith.

"The Jewish faith, for example, recognizes a number of prophets. Their holy book teaches that God promised not to leave mankind alone—that he would always send guidance through prophets. When Jesus claimed to give guidance to the people, however, and to teach the truth on behalf of God, the Jewish spiritual leaders at that time insisted that he did not fulfill the requirements of the Messiah according to **their** criteria." She paused without moving. "Why not?" she queried. "It was because, as I explained yesterday, they had begun to interpret some of their scripture literally concerning the Messiah, causing them to have distorted expectations of what he would be like. Therefore, when Jesus came and claimed to fulfill the scripture regarding the promised Messiah, they could not acknowledge him. They consequently denied him and have denied the claim of every prophet or manifestation of God since."

I looked at Rose, and she looked at me. This was an old story and a serious issue of contention between Jews and Christians. I knew it, and she knew it. Neither of us said another word about it. After a few minutes, she continued. "The Christians also believe in the prophets of the Jewish faith, which to them is contained in what is referred to as the Old Testament of the Bible, and of course they additionally believe in the teachings of Jesus. Thus, Christians believe that God sent spiritual guidance for thousands of years through all the Old Testament prophets **plus** Jesus. The Christians, however, also came to a point where they began to interpret some of the biblical teachings literally regarding Jesus' return. Because of those literal interpretations and the subsequent perspectives, they have come to believe there has been no further guidance by prophets or manifestations of God since the time of Jesus."

She looked at me as if to say, *do you follow me so far?* I was following her, but I wasn't sure what point she was making. Rose must have seen what she needed in my facial expression because she looked satisfied, turned to look straight out of the truck, and then continued.

"Now, the Muslims also believe in the guidance given by God through the prophets of the Old Testament, just like the Jews. They also believe in the teachings of Jesus that are in the Bible, just like the Christians. They additionally believe in the teachings Muhammad revealed, as recorded in the Quran. So, they, too, recognized continuous guidance from God throughout the past, and believe in the guidance of God up to and including God's word as revealed by Muhammad. However, because they also came to interpret much of their sacred scripture literally, they eventually formed their own perspectives regarding future manifestations. This has led them to believe there has been no further guidance by prophets of God since the time of Muhammad.

"The Hindus had many great teachers of truth over time as well, and so did the Buddhists. Consequently, they, too, believe in continuous guidance within their religions. Also, there have been great spiritual teachers giving continuous guidance in other parts of the world among various tribes, nations, and races of peoples. The point is, there is a universal belief that the one true God, in the past—get that? **in the past**—sent guidance and love repeatedly through great spiritual teachers or prophets. We can say with certainty that belief in some kind of continuous guidance from the Creator is universally recognized by believers in God, and the followers of faith and religion around the world."

She took a deep breath and let it out with a sigh. She sat still and meditative before continuing. "Not only do the religions around the world recognize continuous guidance **within** their religion, but they also believe the manifestation of God that founded their religion assured their believers of further guidance to come. Did you get that? Further guidance to come," she repeated.

"Yeah, further guidance to come," I echoed.

"To some, the further guidance to come was the promise of a Messiah, to others, the promise of the return of their own manifestation of God. Do you understand what I am saying, Grayson?"

"I think so," I replied. I looked at her . . . she was waiting for me to paraphrase what I thought she was saying. "Okay, let's see if I understand. You're saying that the religions around the world have promises and expectations of additional manifestation who will give further guidance to come. You also said that this spiritual guidance has been and will be, ongoing."

"Yes, continuously," she said.

"How continuous?" I asked. "Or how often?"

"Whenever the need was perceived by the Creator, he raised up a manifestation to guide the people," she said. "Therefore, the time element was always different. It was three thousand years or so between Moses and Jesus, but only six hundred years between Jesus and Muhammad. In the Hindu scripture, the manifestation of God, Krishna says,

'*Whenever and wherever there is a decline in religious practice, O descendant of Bharata, and a predominant rise of irreligion—at that time I descend Myself.*'[8]

"The point is this: the all-wise Creator knows best when we need guidance and what that guidance should be, and therefore, sends it accordingly.

"Now about the other point I was making," Rose reminded me, "the one about each manifestation of God assuring us of further guidance to come . . "

"Yes, I'm familiar with that," I remarked quickly, interrupting her.

"All right," Rose acknowledged with a nod. "Each one promised either his own return or the appearance of a future messenger, or manifestation. In addition, each manifestation that has come claimed to fulfill the hopes, expectations, and promises of the messenger who preceded him. Each manifestation brought a new spiritual life of truth and understanding to those dwelling in the spiritual decay of their old faiths. Each manifestation resurrected the dead from the tombs of ignorance, sin, and superstition, raising the human beings to a new spiritual life of truth, faith, and love. This is the true nature of God's one continuous Faith!" she declared. Her hands were trembling with excitement. I saw her quickly fold them on her lap.

We rode quietly for a little while before Rose picked up the conversation again. "The problems and conflict you see between the religions of the world," she continued, "often develop when religions begin to elevate their own manifestation above the rest, thereby separating themselves and their religion by considering theirs' superior to others. In turn, they develop their own criteria for the appearance of the next manifestation, or the return of their own, based on literal and often-times superstitious interpretations of their scripture. When things do not happen as they expect, they are unable to acknowledge the value of a manifestation when he does arrive. Yet, in spite of this confusion, some people do recognize the promised manifestation of God when he appears and become believers in his teachings, whereby a new religion is born. This is the way it has been for eons, and this is why it is perceived that we have so many religions today."

"Why so many?" I asked in frustration. "Why would God create so many religions?"

She paused and waited for me to settle down. She looked at me and smiled. In the sweetest, gentlest voice, Rose explained, "The human beings have separated the religions and given them different names, Grayson, not God. Jesus did not call his religion Christianity. Moses did not call his religion Judaism. Buddha did not call his religion Buddhism. The followers gave the religions their names later, causing them to **appear** as separate religions. The truth is, there is really just one religion,

' *. . . eternal in the past, eternal in the future.*'"⁹

She showed me those words by gesturing quotation marks.

"Now, here is the key to everything I have been trying to tell you. **These great world religions that have developed over time, are, in reality, phases or chapters of one ongoing continuous religion of guidance and inspiration from God to humanity!** The revelations, that is, the words of the manifestations of the world's great religions, are God's communication to mankind over time. The words of these great manifestations are the Word of God, and the only direct Word of God. They are his ongoing guidance to humanity. People already believe in continuous guidance **within** their religion as I just pointed out. The new idea I am asking you to consider is that continuous guidance from the God was going on long ago, and has extended through all the religions of the past right up to the present, linking all the religions together as one continuous Faith. So when a new religion appears to be born, it's not really a new religion, but the **renewal** of past religions, continuing God's ongoing guidance forward. Nevertheless, few people believe in all the prophets and all the religions. Most stop with the one they have been advised is special. They neglect to investigate the newest manifestation of God when he does appear, which causes them to reject his valuable teachings."

"If this is so," I remarked, "why do so many people see the major religions as different from one another? If they really are one continuous religion, why are they so different? Explain that one!" I waited. I had her, and I had her good. I sipped my coffee and grinned smugly—waiting.

Without missing a beat, she continued confidently. "Thank you, Grayson, I am happy to. What I have to say is very important, so pay close attention! The ongoing guidance from God, revealed through the words of the prophets or great manifestations of God, is progressive and relative in nature. That is, it is developmental in its characteristics, helping us to spiritually mature over time as human beings. It is so because human beings require different remedies for different stages of social maturity. That is what makes the religions appear different. Each religion brings a healing remedy tailored to advance humanity's spiritual progress. As humanity matures, develops, and progresses as a whole, changes are required in the approaches taken to guide it through further phases of development and maturity. Some social teachings and laws of former religions become obsolete and are no longer relevant to current needs. So the newest revelation from the latest manifestation changes some teachings and brings laws to fit the relative needs of the current condition of humanity. This is what makes the religions appear different from one another.

"Remember," Rose prompted, "A child in the first grade has different needs and requirements to help him reach a second-grade level of development than those of a junior high student who is striving to attain high school status. Likewise, humanity requires different guidance over time to assist its maturation, its development, and its spiritual and humanitarian evolution, so to speak. First graders have numerous games and crafts to facilitate their learning, which changes and becomes more academic by the time they are in high school. High school students are assigned extensive homework and writing assignments because they are mature enough to handle them. First graders cannot be educated this way because it would be premature, and undoubtedly, injurious.

"Here it is," Rose summarized, "revelation, or guidance from the Creator to humanity, comes by way of the words of the manifestation to help the human beings mature socially and spiritually. It is **continuous,** in that it has been going on throughout the past and will continue into the future, as I have just explained. And, it is **progressive** over time and **relative** to the needs and conditions of the people it influences. This understanding of progressive and relative revelation is a new concept, specific to our time and age. We are now mature enough to understand it, accept it, and act on it!"

Rose's voice was full of elation and wonder as she asked, "How beautiful is that? Do you see the potential in all this? Do you see the possibilities for religious unity around the world? We no longer need to fight over whose religion is right, or superior, or best! Instead we can choose to see them in their true relationship as continuous chapters of one ongoing progressive, relative, unfolding book of inspiration and guidance from the God. Not many religions. Just one!

"So here is hope fulfilled!" Rose exclaimed, raising her hands, palms upward in the air. "Here is how the swords of aggression are beaten into plowshares of peace. Here is where the lion of might, wrath, and violence lies down with the lamb of timidity and vulnerability. Right here, really, is the greatest potential for true world peace. Where else can you find such potential? How else can religious conflict in the world be overcome? What other time has afforded such opportune conditions? By what other means does it exist if not wrapped so carefully within these truths that I have just shared with you?"

Rose sat still and quiet for a minute, but I could tell she wasn't finished. The air around us vibrated with energetic excitement. "Grayson, the great religions of the world are all chapters of the same book of guidance. The pens that scripted those chapters are the manifestations of God who founded those great religions, and the hand that guided those selfless pens is none other than the spirit of God himself." She turned, her smile glowing at me, her face beaming with joy. Let me quote these holy words directly from the latest manifestation of God:

' . . . *all the Prophets are the Temples of the Cause of God, Who have appeared clothed in divers attire. If thou wilt observe with discriminating eyes, thou wilt behold Them all abiding in the same tabernacle, soaring in the same heaven, seated upon the same throne, uttering the same speech, and proclaiming the same Faith.*'"[10]

I was left speechless by what she had just shared and stunned by the possibilities. Suddenly, I saw with a new vision. My brain was being flooded with ideas so fast and furiously I could not keep up with my own thoughts. It was as though a new and larger hard drive with faster speed and greater capacity had been attached to my mental processor. *Could what she just said really be true?* The idea was battering against all the concepts and ideas I had constructed over a lifetime. My reality was undergoing a destructive whirlwind, while an army of reconstructionists simultaneously molded, patched, and rebuilt it with lightning-like speed and crystal-like clarity. I was trembling with excitement and immense joy!

This is just too good to be true, I said to myself. *Is it really possible to solve the problem of religious difference with these simple concepts? Could it really be this way?* I knew somehow, in my heart, that it was true—at least, I wanted it to be. And I knew I was now on a new journey with open-ended, unknown possibilities. Every time I thought of a question or a rebuttal to what she had said, it would be answered in my mind by this new concept. I couldn't find a flaw—not yet, anyway. I suspected there had to be one. It was too much for me to challenge at the time. I had to let my brain rest. Silence ensued. I glanced at Rose. She was looking out the window, relaxed and quiet. There was a car and a motor home parked along the road ahead. I slowed down as we approached them.

"Look at the bears!" Rose said joyfully. A sow and her yearling cub were feeding just off the road in the muskeg and willows. We slowed more to watch them as we passed. The folks from the car and motor home were taking pictures. It was a warming sight, but not an uncommon one in these northern territories. I had seen so much wildlife while in Alaska that today it meant little to me. *Stick to the road and the mission at hand*, I thought. I sped up. We kept going, riding quietly for some time.

"I've been thinking about what you said," I finally broke the silence without taking my eyes off the road, "and I can't think of any real argument or anything I could disagree with. But it does leave me with an obvious question." I turned to look at Rose, raising my brows at her to see if it was all right to ask.

She looked at me, smiling, and responded, "And that question is?"

"If all this is true," I began, "that God guides humanity through the words of his manifestations continuously, progressively, and relatively over time, then what about now? What about today? Who was the latest manifestation of God—Muhammad? If so, I don't think that's going to fly too well—not today in our country, anyway.

Besides that, I just don't understand Islam!" I complained.

Rose was smiling and her eyes where shining with tears. *Oh no!* I gasped inside, wondering, *was that the wrong thing to say?* I had underestimated Rose. Those were tears of joy.

"I really love you," Rose said. "You're so honest with your feelings. It makes it easy for me to share my story with you."

"Well, thank you, Rose," I replied, "but do you hear what I'm asking? Everything you just told me is well and good, but so what? Now what? Do you understand what I mean?"

"Yes, Grayson, I do," she assured me. "I have good news. There is more to the story." She giggled before erupting into gales of laughter, alternately looking over at me and out the window.

I began to smile, feeling my body relax. The next thing I knew, I was laughing, too, only this time I knew why without explanation. It was because I was so serious! So intense! *But that's because this is serious stuff!* I thought. *The most serious part of life! This is about life and death, eternity, truth, and everything that has puzzled me for my entire life.* It **was** serious, but not now. Not here. Not with Rose. It was serious, yet flooded with joy instead of frustration. It was truth without harshness. It was life and death with complete faith and acceptance. I liked this contrast, but I didn't know how to process it very well. Somehow, Rose seemed to always do that. No matter what the occasion, or the topic, or the situation, she could make me feel safe, reassured, and contented. I came to feel that way again even though minutes earlier my feelings had been much different.

"What if, like every time in the past, a manifestation of God **has** appeared anew? And what if, as in the past, most of the people do not recognize him as such? Could that be possible?" she asked, looking at me pointedly.

"Well, I suppose," I offered. I was wondering, *is she going to tell me that she is the latest manifestation with the latest guidance from God for mankind?* No, apparently not, at least not now.

Rose's voice broke my train of thought. "Every time in the past when a manifestation of God appeared, or proclaimed Himself as God's messiah, or God's prophet, or God's messenger, people initially rejected him and his message. Are you familiar with this in religious history?" she asked.

"Yes," I replied. "To my knowledge every one of these manifestations had been denied and rejected by most, at least in the beginning."

"True!" she affirmed. "Do you remember why they were rejected? That is, do you remember what I explained to you as to why they were rejected?" I paused, unsure of the answer. "Because," she continued after seeing me hesitate, "the leaders of each religion, over time, failing to understand the spiritual nature of their manifestation's teachings, began to interpret their scripture literally. Consequently, superstitions developed, causing them to adopt their own man-made expectations and criteria as to what the next promised manifestation would be like. They worked out how and where he would appear and what they thought he would teach and do. So when a manifestation of God **actually** appeared and began to proclaim the Word of God **differently** than the people expected, they rejected him. They rejected him primarily because they had been misled by the controlling nature and fear imposed upon them by their clergy. It's an old story that has been repeated throughout time."

"So to my point," Rose resumed, "if a manifestation of God has appeared since Muhammad, how would we know?" She shuffled in her seat, getting into what looked like a more relaxed position. "First of all, we probably can predict that whomever it was, like those gone before him, didn't literally fulfill the expectations devised by the leaders of the world's major religions."

"It had to be someone who **claimed** to be a manifestation," I interjected.

"Yes!" she said.

"He had to perform miracles," I continued emphatically.

"Well . . . about miracles . . . ," she paused. "Miracles basically are events that those witnessing them can't explain. So let's hold off on that one for a while."

"Okay," I mumbled, feeling I had been a little too excited and spoken out of place.

Rose steered the conversation a different way. "Let me comment on a few things about the nature of a manifestation of God. There is a sacred text that says,

'The proof of the validity of a Manifestation of God is the penetration and potency of his word, the cultivation of heavenly attributes in the hearts and lives of his followers, and the bestowal of divine education upon the world of humanity.'[11]

"We are also told he will speak or write with heartfelt inspiration ' *. . . beyond the power of men,*'[12] that moves people toward spirituality, goodness, and happiness. He will disclose profound spiritual truths and teachings that have not been acquired through human learning, but through the inspiration of the Holy Spirit. He will reveal sacred words throughout his ministry without forethought or preparation. He will guide his followers through changes that are progressive and relative to the time, and also clarify and renew the deep-seated spiritual truths held dear by former religions."

"Hold it a minute," I requested. "He will make progressive and relative changes? In what way?"

"Well, it is a historic fact that each manifestation of God proposed significant changes to the prevailing religion of his time. Like I was telling you earlier, such changes caused commotion among the religious leaders and followers. Jesus, for example, altered the Sabbath held sacred by the Jews. Muhammad, during one of his prayers, turned from facing toward the customary direction of Jerusalem to face Mecca. These are just two simple examples. The point is, the newest manifestation of God imposes necessary changes to old, worn-out, valueless traditions, beliefs, rituals, rules, and laws that the leaders of previous religions consider sacred and fundamental to their faith. The religious leaders find these changes unacceptable, even blasphemous, and thereby declare the new religion to be false. As I said before, this has been demonstrated repeatedly throughout history and is a predictable phenomenon.

"Now, back to my point. Do you know anyone in recent times who meets the criteria of a manifestation of God I just outlined?" she asked.

"Not me!" I said quickly and definitively. "If I knew of anyone like that I surely would have checked them out. Those I know of, who have proclaimed to speak for God, didn't fit those criteria or any reasonable criteria of holiness. Most of the ones I am thinking of were egomaniacs!"

"Yes, I know about those," she said, stopping me at the beginning of what was sure to become a rant, "and let me say this." She became very serious and spoke softly, as if handing me a delicate item of great worth. "I know of such a holy soul," she confided, "but I don't want to tell you about him just yet."

A long silence followed her pronouncement. I looked at her in disbelief.

"What do you mean you don't want to tell me about him yet? Why not?" I challenged.

"Grayson," Rose warned, "I don't want your prejudices to interfere with you hearing the sacred message he has given us for our modern times."

"What prejudices?" I barked defensively, before I even had time to think about what she had just said.

"We all have prejudices," Rose assured me, "and if I tell you a time he appeared, a name, a place, or anything, you will react with the opinions and attitudes you have developed over time which could hinder you from hearing the truth of his message."

"I can handle it," I protested. "I can deal with my own prejudices quite well." I looked at her, but she was immovable. "You are telling me that you know of someone who claims to be a manifestation of God for modern times, and you don't want to tell me details because of my prejudices. Is that right?"

She sat with her eyes closed, giving me time to calm down. When she opened them, she glanced at me with a pleading face. Speaking in a soft, kind voice, she said, "Please trust me. Please let me tell you about his teachings first, so you can evaluate them in your heart fairly, independently, and with true impartiality. Would you do that for me, Grayson?"

I sat stewing for a moment before surrendering. "Sure," I finally sighed, after a long pause. "I'm sorry. It just caught me a little off guard when you said I had prejudices."

"Everyone does," she continued. "We are born without prejudice of course, but through the interpretation of our experiences and learning, we develop them. You already know that most of how we interpret our learning and experiences comes from parents, friends, co-workers, educators, and clergy—it's the natural consequence of being part of a culture. Few people are truly free of prejudice and capable of evaluating and judging things without the interference imposed on them by the society in which they were raised. Please don't take it personally that I said you have prejudices. Everyone does. That's why, when it comes to investigating something new, it's important to make every effort to avoid any and all pre-judgments that might cloud one's understanding."

Once again, Rose had said the right thing, in the right way, at the right time. We were good. I was feeling better about myself again and was ready to proceed. "Okay," I announced. "Let's do this!" I had no longer spoken when Navigator T.J. came on the CB, "Liard Hot Springs is just five miles up the road," he reported. "Do you want to stop there for lunch like we talked about?" I looked at Rose. She nodded.

"Sure, T.J., that sounds good," I answered.

As we rode, Rose made one further comment: "Grayson, I promise to tell you more about the latest manifestation of God and his glorious teachings for our modern times. I want you to know that this is the whole point of my wanting to make this trip. We have several days left and plenty of time to walk this sacred path together. I hope you can stay interested in this great hope I have to share with you."

I looked over at her and said with a nod, "Yes, Rose, I am very interested."

Our conversation was on hold, so we both rode quietly, enjoying the beautiful scenery and the moments of silence. My thoughts were spinning, but I couldn't still my mind long enough to ruminate over what I had just learned. I willed my mind to remain silent, to run on auto-pilot. I was tired enough from lack of sleep that it seemed to work.

We took the exit into Liard Hot Springs. It wasn't long before we were pulling into a large parking lot. We had a quick lunch, using the accommodations of the camp-trailer and the amenities of the park. After a nearly sleepless, mosquito-plagued night, the morning drive had been slow and difficult over numerous steep mountain grades. "It seemed like we were always going up, up, up, or down, down, down," Annie commented.

We all agreed to take an hour's break to rest and enjoy the park. There was a long boardwalk through the tundra and muskeg to an open man-made pool, which was fed by natural thermal waters emerging from the heated depths of the earth. It was a wonderful place to relax. The day was sunny and warm, beckoning us to slow down and partake of the warm pool. Most of us were too tired from the short night's sleep to treat ourselves to the soothing thermal experience. Annie and Franklin walked out the boardwalk to the pool while Annie took a short swim. T.J. and Alene went for a walk together and took pictures. Sonia and I took a nap in the trailer. Rose sat in the shade on a park bench, reading a book. Eventually, she got up to pace about, enjoying the relaxing environs of the park.

DAY FOUR

A NEW THEME

It was such a nice mid-day break at the park, but we knew we had to keep going to get our three hundred miles in for the day, especially since much of it had already been slow going. Finally, I said what everyone was thinking, "Well, I guess it's time to keep moving." Everyone reluctantly agreed and quickly moved to their respective vehicles. As soon as we were all lined up and checking for traffic before pulling out onto the highway, Rose changed the tape and turned the recorder on.

I felt refreshed and was actually eager to engage in conversation. My brain had rested, and now I was ready for more. Without giving it much time or conscious thought, I started in. "You mentioned earlier that the religions all taught something that was the same for all of them, yet differed in some other way. I was thinking about that, and I couldn't remember what you had said. Could you help me with that again?" Rose was used to my questions by now, and this afternoon she took right off with an answer.

"Well," she began, "let me start by saying that most faiths and religions have very similar spiritual teachings. They may recount them differently because of language, culture, times, and conditions, but in their essence, they are the same. Here are a few of the teachings that are similar: there is a loving, creative force many refer to as God. There is an afterlife, which is consequential to the way we have lived our lives. Our reality is that we are spiritual beings. Our purpose is to develop spiritual characteristics, virtues, and qualities, such as . . . " she paused. "I am going to list a number of these virtues so you can get some idea as to the scope a spiritual life has on our individual soul and on our society. I'm talking about spiritual qualities like kindness, love, tolerance, truthfulness, forgiveness, righteousness, fairness, justice, wisdom, generosity, thankfulness, sacrifice, refined manners, gentleness, joyfulness, humility, courage, patience, unity, reverence, compassion, loyalty, respect, moderation, obedience, detachment, trustworthiness, reliability, excellence, peacefulness, perseverance, modesty, chastity, purity, and numerous others. These are among the many spiritual teachings common to most religions.

"The major religions of the world also have differences, which primarily pertain to their social teachings expressed in rules, laws, values, and principles. I will give you a few examples of them. They include when and how to pray and worship; when and how to observe holy days; what behaviors are forbidden, and what is considered acceptable; marriage and divorce laws; the use of different calendars to mark time, and aspects of life that are most important, and those of lesser value. These differences exist because the societies and civilizations of the past were so diverse. For guidance to be effective and meaningful, it had to be tailored to their specific needs and capacities. And, as I disclosed earlier, religion is progressive over time, which by its definition, requires each religion to be a little different as well."

"How is religion progressive?" I interrupted. "I don't understand that very well either. I mean, I get the idea of the first grader needing certain guidance that is different than a high school senior, but how were the various religions progressive, or as you said, developmental, or evolutionary in some way? How did that work? Am I making sense?"

Rose was patient. She paused for some time and then asked me for clarification. "So, do you want to know how the major world religions effected a progressive improvement upon humanity over time? Is that it?"

"Yeah, that's it!" I replied.

She continued, "One way, for instance, is in the effects they had on the civilization of humanity. That is, the religions influenced people in such a way that their ability to work, live, and worship together became ever-expanding and more unifying within the size and complexity of their population. Ancient religions primarily influenced small populations of people. Communication was simple, and limited travel capacity didn't allow for an extended economy. The effects of the guidance of the early manifestations usually didn't extend initially much beyond a given tribe or small population. It did, however, have a unifying effect on that group of people, affecting behavioral expectations, simple laws, local rules, and forms of worship that helped create order, love, and unity among them.

"Over time, the guidance of God given in the form of inspired revelation to subsequent manifestations became more encompassing, more complex, and more inclusive. It influenced how populations of people, perhaps of a common region, engaged in their relationships regarding culture, communication, and trade. Again, it created conditions of peace, love, and unity, which contributed to the greater good of a given population. Gradually, the spiritual guidance given by the manifestations created a unifying influence on the complex development of civil systems necessary for larger, more diverse populations to flourish. Consequently, cities developed, and eventually nations, to the point where we now are on the threshold of a unified **world** community. We now live in a world where travel is possible within hours to any other place on the planet. Commerce is interactive worldwide. Communication is nearly instantaneous from one point of the earth to multiple points in varied forms. Races, cultures, and nationalities are intermixed. Civilization is becoming so complicated that the ways and means of the past are no longer sufficient to carry us into a world civilization. Here we are on the brink of a unified world, but feeling like it's on the verge of a sure collapse. Why? Because we, the people of the earth, are for the most part unaware of the guidance and rules of engagement that will unify us. So what are they, and where do we find them? I propose to you that it's in the guidance from the latest manifestation of God."

She paused soberly and sat perfectly still, staring downward as if trying to see straight through the floorboard of the truck to the pavement below. Suddenly, she took a deep breath, and let it out. Her body kind of melted with the outgoing breath. She turned and looked out the window for a moment, and then back at me with a serene look. "What is progressive revelation?" she asked, restating my question. "Let me give you another perspective. Let me see if I can give you some ideas to consider.

"Revelation from God through his manifestations is essentially an unveiling of truth—that is, the manifestation uncovers or makes known what was previously unknown in the world. He does this through his words and his actions. What isn't seen, or known, or understood is that he also releases, in some mystical way, a renewing, reforming spirit upon the hearts of the people of the earth. People, in some mystical way, pick up on this renewing spiritual broadcast of what is right, good, true, and real as it pertains to our reality as spiritual beings. People all over the planet are affected by the release of this renewing and reforming spiritual energy. Because of it, societies are thrown into turmoil as they struggle to adjust to the progressive influence of this effusion of spiritual energy and truth. In these two ways, the new revelation causes a forward or 'progressive' movement in the spiritual transformation of souls and in the social development of mankind.

"Human beings throughout the planet have lived nearly the same way for most of our known past. Ask yourself, what happened in the mid-1800s that caused such a torrent of new information and knowledge to come about so suddenly and to continue to this day?" She waited for my answer. I looked at her and back to the road, feeling a little puzzled. "It was the appearance of a manifestation of God!" she proclaimed with emphasis. "There had been a new revelation and an unprecedented release of spiritual energy, knowledge, and goodness showered upon the earth, affecting both the need and the remedy for personal and social change and progress. Look around you and behold!" She extended her right arm out fully before her, palm upward, and swept it from left to right as she followed it with her eyes, as if showing me the entire world in a new light. "Reform, progression, transformation—these are the words that describe the last one hundred and seventy years. Never before has the planet been so connected in nearly every way. Oh, yes, there is conflict, but it is just the normal struggle associated with change and progress, especially during this time in history when it is on such a massive scale. It is, and will be, tumultuous, but we will survive and eventually flourish as a unified world community." She stopped. She was silent again. The squeak of the recorder, and the steady hum of the truck engine filled the void. I couldn't think of anything to say.

"Souls are changed," she started in again. "Gentle, open, loving hearts are responsive to this new outpouring of spiritual energy. People are learning and they will continue to learn the importance of kindness, love, and truthfulness. They are now learning and will continue to learn that the people of the earth are one, that what you do to one person affects everyone, including yourself. They are learning and will continue to learn, peace, not war—oneness, not separateness—equality, not 'we are better than . . .' or 'they are less than . . . .' We are learning and will continue to learn, happiness, not sorrow—forgiveness, not wrath—acceptance and tolerance, not anger and violence—understanding, not prejudice. These are the ways of the spirit, and these are the unfolding progressive effects upon the human beings by the latest manifestation of God. This is the way of progressive revelation. Throughout history, the teachings of every manifestation infused humanity with a new spirit. Each time a manifestation appeared, God's message proved more profound, more expansive, more enveloping, more complete, more complex, more transforming, evolving, improving, and advancing.

"Over time this renewal induces a transforming effect on humanity, gradually causing societies to flourish. Eventually though, the religion runs its course and becomes diminished in its ability to be a useful cause for improvement or social progress. At that point, a new manifestation appears. The process begins all over again, moving humanity forward, directing it down a path of advancing evolution to its intended destiny on this planet, and leading individual souls to their personal spiritual salvation.

"History, as we have been taught it in school, may not bear this out clearly. What we have been taught is a fragmentary view of history, heavily infused with stories of conquest, war, trade, politics, and other worldly matters. What I am sharing with you now about the manifestations' role in human advancement is an aspect of history seldom considered and rarely told. Most of humanity's spiritual development is only written about in retrospect. Even then it is seldom pursued. If you were to investigate the past by exploring the abundance of knowledge available today, you would know what I say is true. You have to observe with a detached heart and an objective eye."

She started giggling again, pretending to take her eye out and to look around with it. We were there again—laughing until we were tearful. *What fun this woman is*, I marveled. *How is it that she can be so serious one minute and be laughing uncontrollably the next? It must be her detachable eye.* That thought doubled me up in laughter again.

We quieted as we drove along. Rose was content to sit still and look out the window. Ten minutes went by before she even moved. Then she reached down into her bag and pulled out a small book with a nice-looking cloth cover. I was unable to see the title. The book had a small piece of torn paper sticking out of the top and a nice beaded bookmark. "It's going to be a little while before I'm up to talking," she announced as she opened the book.

For quite some time we rode to the hum of that big diesel engine. Rose would read for a while, and then close her eyes and sit meditatively before continuing her reading. Finally, she laid the book on her lap, stretched her arms and shook her hands out a little, then returned the book to her bag.

"So far we have had a great discussion, just as I had hoped we would. We have discussed some important truths that I trust will help you embrace the rest of what I have to say. We have discussed the reality of our purpose as human beings—that is, generally, to know and to love, and more specifically, to know and love God. We have explored how our life here in this world is to develop our soul by acquiring and developing spiritual qualities, traits, and virtues. I have shared with you that spiritual guidance has been given to us continuously throughout time, and progressively through the ages, by way of the manifestations of God. I pointed out that the manifestations renew the spiritual truths of the past while simultaneously giving us an expanded and deeper knowledge of ourselves, God, and our place and purpose in the universe. Finally, we have seen how acquiring such knowledge provides for a progressive, mature, evolving human condition. This is where we are right now. **From this point forward**, I am going to share with you the spiritual truths and principles that have been given to us by the latest manifestation of God. Truths specific to our time and age that will help us mature, evolve, and develop individually as souls and collectively as a world society. Are you ready?" She looked at me for a response.

"Yes, I'm with you," I said.

"Do you have any questions about what I just said?" Rose inquired.

"No, I'm good," I responded anxiously. In fact, I was eager to hear what was next.

"Okay," she said quietly. "Let me start this way. Now remember—just as a teacher at the beginning of the school year gives you a brief vision of the direction you will be moving toward in your learning, I am going to do the same at this point. However, what I am going to outline may be difficult to understand at first because it is new."

Rose paused as if to measure out her next thought. "Each of the manifestations of God who have appeared throughout time had a major theme to their revelation. We might call it an over-arching concept that permeated their specific message. Moses emphasized the law of God. Jesus emphasized loving each other—to love our neighbor as ourselves. Buddha's central themes were compassion and detachment. Krishna focused our attention on the reflection of God in all things. Muhammad's teachings revolved around the need for submission to the will of God. The latest manifestation of God also has a central theme to his revelation. **The spiritual principle most critical to our development as individual souls, and collectively as a world community right now, in our time, is unity!"**

"Unity?" I repeated in an ethereal tone.

"Yes, unity! Now let me clarify. The idea of unity has endless implications, but I am going to define it for you like this: **unity is a heartfelt condition of peace, love, and harmony in human relations, free of conflict and the struggle for dominance.** This spiritual principle permeates all of what I am going to tell you from this point forward. It is the major theme of the most recent revelation of God to the human beings. The application of this spiritual theme will propel humanity's spiritual and material development into a future age. It is by the conscious, constant, and confident application of this spiritual principle in everything we do, making it our highest priority among all things, that will help us deal effectively with all the problems that face us in the modern world!"

I glanced at her doubtfully.

"Yes, that's right, Grayson. I mean all of them!" she stated confidently. Listen to these sacred words from the latest manifestation of God:

'*The well-being of mankind, its peace and security, are unattainable unless and until its unity is firmly established.*'"[13]

A meditative silence ensued before she continued, "Imagine a couple—a man and woman—who, out of love for one another and out of their desire to comply with the wishes of God, have agreed to place this idea, this spiritual principle, as the highest and foremost objective in their relationship. What could be better than always to show love, respect, kindness, and tolerance toward one another? What kind of marriage would it be if a couple made every effort to do this above all other things? Imagine the effects it would have on their children if they made every effort to avoid using harmful, hurting words or emotional or physical violence upon them? How safe and loved the children would feel! Just think what potential it gives for the children to grow up as loving, kind, happy human beings.

"Think of the effects on your community. **What if** all the people where you lived in Anchorage, or any other place in the world for that matter, consistently tried to apply this principle in their lives? What would that community be like? Can you imagine it? Do you feel its potential? Do you feel the fear, the caution, the distrust, the suspicion melting away? The effects of unity have that power!

"And what of the nation?" Rose expanded on the theme. "Look at the terrible conflicts going on now between people and various groups in our country. People are arguing and fighting to such a degree that good decisions, policies, laws, and ideas are difficult to discover or implement. Look how people are defensive toward one another as a result of decades of social, commercial, and political aggression. Now imagine what the nation would be like if the people applied this one spiritual principle. Think of the relationships between differing races, employers and workers, students and teachers, young and old, parents and children, the wealthy and the poor, the educated and the ignorant, the blessed and the unfortunate, the right and the left, the conservative and the liberal. What if the people collectively implemented this principle as the highest priority in all their relationships?

"Now consider its influence on an international scale. Look how the world would find peace. True peace! So essential is this theme of unity for our time and age that the manifestation of God clearly instructed his followers,

'*Conflict and contention are categorically forbidden.*'[14]

"Now Grayson," Rose said, as she scooted around in her seat into a more upright posture, "some might think that unity is impossible, but I am telling you it is only impossible if we continue to believe it is. Here is where faith comes in. If you believe that God exists, and that he guides us through his manifestations, then you are empowered through faith to apply this principle of unity regularly in your life. You are **empowered** to do it! This empowerment is what's known as God's grace."

I must have had a skeptical expression. I was about to say

something when Rose, perceiving my concern, continued assuredly, "I personally know people the world over who are intentionally employing this spiritual principle of unity regularly. People like you and me—everyday people from every race, nation, religion, and culture you can think of—are busy now, today, working together in unity. It is the most wonderful thing in the world to experience. I have seen it, felt it, lived it, and I will never give it up. Once you have experienced it, life can never be the same without it, and you will do everything in your power to retain it."

She turned and looked at me with a great big smile. Giving me a single, firm nod, she turned to gaze out the side-window. I was thinking about what she had said and was about to comment when again, without notice, she proceeded with her thoughts.

"This theme of unity," Rose explained, "this overarching spiritual principle, also encompasses a recognition of the oneness of all things. We have already discussed that there is just one God. We have looked at how all the religions are connected, over time, as one progressive Faith. In addition to these onenesses, this central theme of unity includes a belief in the oneness of humankind. We are guided by the spirit of the age to consider all people as true brothers and sisters—a single family regardless of nationality, class, race, gender, culture, social or economic status, or any other form of difference."

She was quiet for a moment. Her breath was becoming short and rapid, and her hands were trembling slightly again. She took a deep breath and sighed. "Imagine relationships built on love, peace, respect, truthfulness, kindness, tolerance, and understanding. Imagine relationships free of the manipulative tactics of shaming, imposing guilt, denigrating others with words, threats, or curses, aggressive arguing, and other tactics humans have devised to exert power over each other. Imagine if those were absent in all relations from one person to another—right up to the relationship of one nation to another. I tell you it is possible. It is happening, and it is a reality that will continue to develop over time. The people of the world have the choice to resist it or embrace it, but it will proceed, because this is what the manifestation of God has prescribed for our modern age. Unity is to be the means and the ends in personal relationships, families, organizations, and governmental relations. Everything about the teachings and guidance from the latest manifestation of God has to do with unity and oneness! Everything! Unity is the spirit of this age! It is the whisperings of truth in the wind. It is the feeling you get when you are with your favorite people. It is the culmination of the hopes and intentions of all former manifestations, fulfilling their purpose, teachings, and missions, to bring us to a mature enough time and place that universal unity could be realized. The time is now, the responsibility is ours, the need is clear, and the means are available. Each principle and truth I will share with you throughout the rest of this trip has to do both with attaining unity and with applying it.

"'The ends justifies the means,' is a principle the human beings have commonly practiced now for centuries. But this practice is no longer effective or acceptable. No! The means must now be consistent with the ends. True peace is achieved by peaceful means, not by violence. Loving relationships are achieved by love, not anger or coercive force. The unity of the human beings is achieved by means of peace, love, and harmony, and the avoidance of conflict, aggression, and violence. This is our **goal**, and our **mission**! And unity is the **way** and **means** to achieve it!"

She was silent for a moment. My mind was whirling. "Is there any confusion about what I just shared with you?" she asked, nearly breathless. "What I want to know is, are you clear about unity and its importance?"

I thought about it for a moment. "Well, I think so," I replied. "I mean, I'm just trying to take it all in. Who wouldn't want to live in a world where unity existed? It sounds like a utopia or a paradise—at least potentially." I thought about it for a minute longer before continuing, "I've heard people talk about utopian societies. They usually say that it doesn't sound like much fun—a world of robotic, smiling, perfect people."

"That's not the way it manifests itself, Grayson," she interrupted.

"That comes from former writers and naysayers with limited vision and immature understanding. I suspect that they imagine it that way because they have never experienced true unity nor made the necessary efforts to employ it or achieve it. They have only experienced the pretense of unity, similar to what you noted earlier as part of your religious experience. Once you have experienced true unity, you will know how really wonderful and real it is. So, I ask you again. Is the concept clear?"

"Yes, I think so," I answered. "I'll just need some time to think about it. Then maybe I'll have some questions."

"Okay," she said, turning away in her seat. She sat quietly for several minutes.

"Human beings are at a crossroads," she suddenly remarked. "Disunity is threatening to destroy everything good that has been developed in the world. Educational systems are failing, the family unit is under challenge, the economic system is in serious disarray, politics and governments are at a standstill in effectiveness, international relations are tense and fragmented, travel, trade and communication are ever more increasingly vulnerable, just to name a few. We witness all this disarray without any agreeable means on the horizon to avert the ongoing chaos. I invite you to carefully consider unity and its vast implications and potential as the primary means for addressing the diverse problems that are stifling social betterment and improvement. Pertaining to this I want to share the following sacred verse with you from the latest manifestation of God, who wrote,

'*So powerful is the light of unity that it can illuminate the whole earth.*'"[15]

After a short pause, she concluded: "If not unity, then what? I ask you, seriously!" Rose was through.

The hum of the engine and the noise of the road filled the atmosphere of the cab. I couldn't listen with attention anymore. It was getting late. I was hungry and looking forward to a meal and rest.

Unity, hmm. There had been moments in my life when I experienced unity. It actually made me feel really good—peaceful-like and hopeful. Yet my demons of doubt were whispering again. I decided not to think about it for now. I concentrated on the road, on the trip, where we were, how far we had to go, wondering if we would have any troubles, what life would be like in Oregon. *I'll just daydream the time away until dinner*, I planned. But it didn't turn out that way.

"Do you think this can really happen?" I blurted without thinking. "I mean, behave in ways that are peaceful and loving all the time, or even most of the time? How is that possible?" I guess I couldn't keep my mind off the subject.

"It happens this way," she said. "First of all, it's the theme of the age, and God is infusing us with the power of his grace to achieve it. That is, the power to apply it consistently is provided as a result of our making the effort. You hold it in your heart. You practice it in your thoughts, your feelings, your decisions, and your actions. You do it on faith that it is the right thing to do. You do it consciously, constantly, and confidently. You keep trying your entire lifetime because it's the proper and right way to behave and to be. When enough people practice this, it begins to affect society in ways you can only imagine at this point.

"Can you imagine, Grayson?" Rose went on. "Do you know what it is like to live in a society where nearly everyone can be trusted? Where nearly all fear and suspicion of one another is absent? Where people are not in aggressive competition for your money or your time or your resources? Where you are respected and accepted for who you are, as you are? Where other people consider you as their equal or with even greater honor? I have! It's nearly impossible to imagine what it is like until you have experienced it. But like all behavioral change, it takes time. Change occurs with faith and effort, and it influences others until nearly everyone participates.

"All the spiritual truths and principles I am sharing with you come from and support the eventuality of unity in personal relationships, families, governments, businesses, religions, nations, cultures, and races. This is the extent of its encompassing power.

"Furthermore, unity is, and always has been, the highest aim and purpose of the religions. Up to this point there have been small populations in various places where unity has existed for limited periods of time, but in this time and age it will affect the entire population of the earth. It is our true purpose and our highest and most noble calling as human beings in these modern times!" She paused briefly as she thought through her next comment.

"As I mentioned earlier," she continued, "I want to emphasize that unity means both our thinking and behavior must encompass the principle of oneness. That is, if unity is our means and our end goal, then it requires we firmly believe in our hearts in the spiritual principle and truth of oneness."

Interrupting her, I asked, "What did you mean by that again?"

"For example," she said, "we should consider that when people say they worship God, no matter by what name or term they use for that Force, or that Great Spirit, there is only one God and it is the same one God worshiped the world over."

"What about those who believe in many Gods, like the ancient Greeks?" I questioned abruptly.

"No," Rose shook her head. "I am talking about those who say they worship the one true God of creation and revelation, who are worshiping the one creating and sustaining force behind all things in the universe. Remember the story of the elephant? We may all describe God differently, but it's the same, nonetheless. Because there is only one God, there is also only one religion. One continuous, relative, and progressive truth revealed to the people over time by way of the manifestations of God.

"Furthermore, the people of the earth are one. That is, they are like different colored flowers of one beautiful garden of humanity, or like the different notes that comprise a harmonic symphony of souls. Each contributes its God-given share to the beauty of the whole, no matter how limited or abundant one's qualities or gifts are.

"Remember, Grayson, it is ignorance and lack of maturity that causes some people to consider certain groups of people as superior or better, and other groups of people as inferior or less-than. People the world over are human beings. They all want to be happy. They all want to work and provide a living for their families. They all love and want to be loved and accepted. They all feel pain and heartache at their losses. The people of the world are one people and deserve to be treated as such! Unity means we think about, feel, make decisions, and act on the truth that all people are one. It means we avoid, with conscious effort, anything that prompts us to consider any group of people as either inferior or superior to another, regardless of what country they are from, what their religion is, what race they are, what gender they are, what income level they have, what culture they are from, what language they speak, or for that matter, how short they are."

I looked at her quickly, wondering what she meant by that. She giggled into her palms. I, too, had to smile. I had been listening so intently that she caught me totally off guard with her humor.

"I guess I didn't know, or at least never thought about these things as having anything to do with unity," I said.

"Well, if you think about it honestly for a moment," Rose counseled, "you will surely conclude that if we are going to foster relationships of love and peace, we are going to have to think about and feel about people who are different than us in ways we are not generally accustomed. This is what each manifestation does. He gives us new teachings, new ways of thinking, feeling, and behaving that challenge us to grow spiritually and become better people—this stimulates individual spiritual development as well as social evolution as a whole. I want to re-emphasize this. Everything I have conveyed to you so far, and all the spiritual truths and principles I will share with you from this point forward, have to do with creating and sustaining our growth and evolution in unity! This is the heart of what religion was intended to be. The human beings, repeatedly throughout time, lose sight of this intention. However, God periodically brings forth a special Soul—his manifestation—to redirect our attention back to this purpose." Rose turned her head to look out the window, signaling her desire to be silent again.

After several miles, I had an urge to speak. "I have to say this, Rose. When we first started this trip, I was leery about this whole project. Quite frankly, I didn't think you would have anything to say that I hadn't heard before. I was wrong. What you have shared with me so far is difficult to deny. I keep saying to myself 'this makes so much sense; it feels so right.' I wonder how it could be that no one has presented these concepts like this before? What I mean is, I have heard most of these ideas before, but never presented in such a way as to tie so many things together into one . . . one . . . " I struggled for words, " . . . one truth! I mean, never before have I heard it in such a way that helps tie everything together so well. Purposes of life, God, religion, where we fit in! I mean, I like it!"

"Thank you, Grayson," she said softly.

I felt good. I felt better than good! I probably couldn't explain why, but it was as though a great cloud was lifting from my mind and heart. I felt light, happy, and mostly . . . hopeful!

We pushed hard on the road that day, arriving late in the evening at Fort Nelson. It had been a long day, but the conversation had been enlightening and the scenery beautiful. We had driven past Muncho Lake, one of those sparkling, turquoise-blue lakes fed by the glacial waters of the north. We passed by three giant mountains of solid granite that dominated the landscape majestically against the wide blue sky. We saw deer, something we hadn't seen on this trip until today. They don't thrive too well any farther north. We also saw caribou, wild goats, and even buffalo.

All the caravan members were road-weary by the time we arrived at the town of Fort Nelson. We found a large parking lot and pulled in together to discuss where we would stay for the night. As we were discussing our plans, we noticed the nearby Fort Nelson Hotel. We decided we would all stay there.

We had dinner in the restaurant, and later that evening, went swimming in the indoor pool. It was a nice break from the rigors of travel and camping. When I went to bed, I tried to recall the subjects Rose and I had discussed that day, but I was too tired to focus. I fell asleep immediately and didn't wake until Sonia nudged me to get up.

DAY FIVE

LET'S BE ONE

By nine-thirty, we had showered, eaten, and were on the road again. It was a warm, sunny morning, and everyone seemed happy and refreshed. Before leaving town, we filled our automobiles with fuel at a local gas station. I was the last one in my vehicle, yet intent on the object of our journey—keep moving. Rose seemed nervous. She didn't say anything in particular to give me that impression. She would smile at times and then her face would return to a solemn seriousness. I didn't give it too much thought, or I would have said something, but I waited.

Rose turned on the recorder, and then sat quietly watching the road go by. Finally, I told her, "I really like what you had to say yesterday. I can't remember it all, but it just felt right and gave me hope."

She gave me a quick look and a smile. "Thank you," she said tenderly.

"Where do we go today?" I asked eagerly, while drinking my coffee and checking my side mirrors.

Rose let out a big sigh, covered her face with both hands, and then dragged them downward as if to wipe something away. She began, "Some of what I want to talk to you about today is very difficult for me," she said. "I have deep-seated emotions about a few things, and much of it is not good. I still will try my best to share with you a beautiful, wonderful, and urgent spiritual principle given to us by the manifestation of God for our time and age. I'll begin with some positive news. These spiritual truths I am sharing with you from the most recent manifestation were given to us more than one hundred years ago!"

I looked at her, puzzled by the comment.

"Yes, these teachings, given to the world for our spiritual and material development, were revealed in the 1800s," Rose continued. "When a manifestation is inspired with a message from God and begins to reveal it to the people, the knowledge and truths of this new guidance are showered, in a spiritual sense, upon all the souls on the planet, which, in turn, causes the human beings to awaken and change."

"Wait a minute," I insisted, "What do you mean, it's showered? Like some kind of pixie-dust or something?"

"Something like that," Rose smirked. "What I am saying is the inhabitants of the earth, that is, those whose hearts are receptive in some way I don't understand, are affected by the newly revealed truths, ideas, and principles, even though they may have no direct physical contact with the manifestation or his written words. Maybe it's like a broadcast in the spiritual realm, and people with active spiritual antennae respond to the broadcast or something." She laughed. "We can witness the evidence of this by reviewing recent history, paying particular attention to the sudden changes that began in the mid-1800s. Changes that started then are still transforming the world and its people today. These truths and teachings I am sharing with you may not seem so new and revolutionary today, but to the world in the 1800s they were extremely challenging. Furthermore, if you consider them carefully, you will realize how they remain relevant and meaningful, and how our world is in greater need of them today than ever before.

"Remember yesterday the subject was unity and oneness? I told you all the truths and principles given to us from the manifestation for this time and era relate to and support a central theme of unity." She paused, closed her eyes, and took in a deep breath. Then, letting out a big sigh, she uttered, "Specifically at this moment," she said, "I want to address the importance of racial unity as it pertains to the oneness of all people.

"The manifestation of God has lovingly addressed all the human beings, saying,

'Ye are the fruits of one tree, and the leaves of one branch.'[16]

"Further to this subject he wrote,

'Close your eyes to racial differences, and welcome all with the light of oneness.'[17]

"This spiritual guidance inspires us to consider all people as part of the family of human beings. No matter what color they are, what color their parents were, where they are from, or what their ancestral origin might be, people are one. My ancestors were mostly Alaskan Native Tlingit. However, my grandfather was Russian."

I shot a surprised look at Rose.

"You didn't know that, did you?" She smiled.

"N-no," I sputtered.

"Racial unity is such an important spiritual teaching. It should be obvious to most people how necessary its implementation is if we are going to achieve true unity. This is especially so in America, the so-called 'melting pot of the world.' The horrors inflicted upon the people of color in this nation and others are evident and available for everyone's review. I am going to make an effort today to avoid discussing those atrocities. Let me just say that race relations in the United States have improved. This is undeniable. However, the long-term effect of racism in America, and of course, many other countries as well, is still carrying forward through the generations its destructive subjugation of people of color.

"Today the effects of an earlier overt and rampant racism are this . . .," she paused to measure out her words. "The evil effects of racism that pass from generation to generation have dual consequences on our society. One of the consequences of centuries of overt racism is the subconscious sense of superiority it creates and passes on to those of European descent—the white people. Notice I said subconscious. This means, for the most part, Caucasians aren't even aware they think this way, but they do! The subconscious attitude of superiority imposed on them through the generations has the potential to manifest itself every time they deal with people of color. This attitude of superiority not only perpetuates racism subconsciously, but sometimes it is even imposed intentionally on subsequent generations by parents, family members, and other close associates. Simultaneously, it is reinforced in the culture and by educators, government policies, business practices, and every other aspect of society, making it an institutionalized reality. History books reflect it, and neighborhoods separated by race exemplify it. There is racial profiling, racial jokes, blaming, scapegoating, jobs and means disparities—the list goes on and on. The fact is that racism continues until we recognize that we **all** play a part in it. It has been and still is a harmful evil that we cannot continue to perpetuate. We defeat it by making conscious efforts to wisely implement this spiritual teaching from the manifestation of God:

'*Close your eyes to racial differences and welcome all with the light of oneness.*'"[18]

"Do you think that I am prejudiced toward people of color?" I asked without thinking.

"We are all influenced by the long-term effects of racism," Rose replied. "But please, let me explain to you the other negative consequence of racism."

She paused for a moment. "Before I get into that, let me say this first. If racial equality is to occur, then an important contribution the white population can make is to be consciously involved in assuring that people of color are equally placed in decision-making positions in all aspects of our society. To have equality also means to have equal power, and equal power means to have equal rights to decide. Until people of color have equal power in decision-making positions in our society, there will be no racial equality. As long as it's white people **giving** people of color equal rights, it means people of color still don't have them. It means the white people have the power to give equal rights or take them away, and that is not equality."

Rose looked stern and focused. Her breathing was shallow, and she was frowning. I saw her shake her head as if to say "no" to herself.

Then she sat motionless and remained quiet for some time.

"I want to say that each generation is getting better over time in dealing with this issue of racism," Rose commented. "We are moving ever so slowly toward oneness, which is best hastened by our collective conscious efforts.

"Now, about the other long-term effect of racism. The ongoing generational effect of racism inherited by people of color is the tendency to develop an excessive sense of suspicion toward white people and all the social and civil systems of society as well. This is because most systems are created and controlled by white people who are affected subconsciously by an overtly racist past. This is not to say the suspicions that people of color harbor are invalid—in fact—quite the opposite. There are many reasons for people of color to be suspicious. However, one of the best ways people of color can apply this spiritual principle—'Close your eyes to racial differences and welcome all with the light of oneness'—is first to understand that **excessive** suspicion is a natural, but **undesirable** consequence of living through generations of racism. It can, and does, contribute to the propagation of racial tension if one reacts with excessive suspicion to every situation. So it would be better if we consciously discerned the truth of every situation carefully, responding only to those situations that truly justify suspicion, while making every effort not to respond with suspicions of racism when unwarranted.

"These are the spiritual tasks before us. These are the principles that will stop the hellish pain of generations of racism. This is how we all can contribute to a more unified, peaceful, loving society and culture—by consciously making every effort to close our eyes to racial differences and welcoming all with the light of oneness, and by looking with wonder at the beauty that is our diversity. This is one of the expressions of the Holy Spirit in our age. Just think of how much fear and agony we can avert in the world by fully applying this simple yet profound truth."

Tears rolled down Rose's wrinkled cheeks. I felt a shame come over me. I knew then the answer to my question. I was prejudiced, maybe not intentionally, but subconsciously. How could any of us escape it, having grown up in a society where everything reflected an attitude that people of color were inferior to white people? How awful! How very evil and awful are the effects of racism. I was surely affected by it, and to some degree, contributing to it.

"You're right, Rose," I admitted. "I'm really sorry." I reached out and put my hand on top of hers which she had placed beside her on the seat. She quickly pulled her hand out from under mine and then slowly reached over to clasp mine so as to make them side-by-side. She looked at me tenderly, waiting. I knew what had just happened was a gift from the spirit. I had acted with subconscious superiority by placing my hand on top of hers without asking, as though I had the right and power to comfort her. She had reacted suspiciously by quickly pulling her hand away, but then moved it to a position of equality by holding it next to mine—side by side. It felt good. It was like we both knew—*we can do this*, because this is our true destiny, to be one loving, peaceful, united, diverse family of human beings.

Rose made one more comment on race unity. "The world is changing quickly, and the issues of race inequality are diverse and dynamic," she explained. "For those who are overtly racist and for those who unknowingly, subconsciously, and ignorantly perpetuate racism, we can hope that through better education and enforcement of appropriate civil laws, through exemplary, unifying behavior and through heart-to-heart discussions between people of different races, with time, racism will fade from existence. For all of us, tolerance is required. Tolerance of one another whether we are the perpetrators of racism or the recipients. Love—love is needed, and acceptance of one another for who and where we are in our spiritual development. Empathy is needed for the feelings of one another, and sensitivity to one another's circumstances. Caring and listening ears are needed to validate one another's feelings without judgment or explanation. Will and effort are needed. A willingness to learn, and efforts to make change, will both speed our much needed recovery. May we all be empowered by the spirit of the age to treat each other with extreme kindness and respect and rid ourselves of this terrible social sickness forever. This is the call of the spirit of unity in our modern time."

We rode on for some time before Rose began her next subject.

"Unity, being our highest and most prized spiritual aspiration, has numerous aspects to it." Rose paused, humming a little to herself, as though she were looking for the next thing to say. She found it, and with a quick nod and a smile, proceeded.

"Another spiritual truth, or principle, I would like to talk to you about today is the elimination of all forms of prejudice. What I mean by prejudice is thinking of others who we don't know, or who are different than us, in negative ways or in ways that consider them inferior or less important than ourselves. Negative 'pre-judgment' of anyone perceived as different is one of the most destructive attitudes preventing healthy human relationships. It inevitably leads to personal, social, and even international conflict. When people believe that their family, their town, their country, their tribe, their nation, their values, their religion, their politics, their way of life, their food—whatever it may be—is better than anyone else's, it presumes that others are inferior. This arrogance is the foundation of prejudice. It can't help but lead to conflict and separation of people from one another, which is the very opposite of unity! What could be more immature? Really!" Rose wrinkled her nose in disgust. "Prejudice—of any kind—is merely a form of ignorance," she continued. "It is based on a lack of **true** understanding of those who we perceive as different, who are then judged as being inferior or wrong.

"I already spoke to you about racial prejudice, but there are endless other expressions and forms. Look at the destructive effects prejudice is having on our society today. Look at the terribly destructive conflicts between political parties. It is so divisive that our governmental representatives have become nearly impotent to make meaningful decisions or to help heal the social and economic problems that plague our country. Conservatives are camping up against the liberals, and democrats against the republicans. There are prejudices against the poor, who are often looked upon as lazy or entitled takers. There are prejudices against the rich, who are considered greedy, insensitive opportunists. The results of prejudice are clear, and unarguably destructive to the unity of the human beings.

"This is a new day. The Spirit of Holiness is inspiring and empowering us to overcome these prejudices by making conscious, constant, and confident changes to the ways we think and behave toward one another. We are encouraged not only to stop considering those who are different than ourselves as inferior, but to make efforts to consider everyone as our equal and to take time to understand and become informed and knowledgeable about why others think and behave the way they do. These conscious efforts to learn about and understand others, move us out of ignorance. It allows us to understand and appreciate difference and diversity in the world, and that's what most people are, just different! And beautifully so!

"Sometimes people develop a perspective that differences among the human beings are moral issues of right and wrong. That is, people might think that if others do not think or act like they do, then the others must be wrong, or because we do something different than others, what we do is right. It could be that we just do things differently! What I am suggesting to you is that most of the time the differences we have from other people are just that—differences."

She sipped from a water bottle before continuing on the subject. "People most often develop these prejudices from the influence of their culture. Some cultures, for example, demonstrate less worth for their elders than others, and some clearly show a disdain of craftsmen and professionals. Elimination of prejudice requires us to reexamine our own culture, our family's beliefs, and even the teachings of our own religion, discarding any beliefs, attitudes, and behaviors that are not based on truth. These are among the ways we engage in the elimination of prejudice.

"My hope is that all people will decide to contribute to a new and better world by thinking and acting on the spiritual principle that humankind is one. Let us look toward acceptance and love of one another. Let us seek out peace in all our relations with those we know to be different than ourselves. Let this terrible, immature, childish, and selfish prejudice be destroyed and replaced with tolerance, acceptance, interest in, and concern for, all our fellow human beings.

This is the clear message from the manifestation of God for our time. This is what the Creator wants for us and from us. Unity! A condition of peace and love in all human relations! May it come to be considered our highest moral value and the foremost spiritual priority in everything we do. We would do well to cause unity to take precedence over everything else. This is the call from the world of the spirit. This is the remedy for the problems that afflict the human beings—unity first—in all things! We can all be certain about this if we look deep within our hearts to that place inside where we feel love and compassion. The manifestation of God for our time wrote,

'*This goal excelleth every other goal, and this aspiration is the monarch of all aspirations.*'[19]

"That is how exalted the station of unity is!"

I waited for more, but Rose quietly settled back against the seat. I thought about what she had said for a few minutes. "I absolutely agree with you, Rose," I finally concurred. "For me, personally, this has always been my thinking—well, maybe not always—but I do remember a song from the sixties by Joe South, titled 'Walk a Mile in My Shoes.' I was a teenager then, and I really liked the song. Of course as a teenager I wanted others to understand **me** because it seemed that no one did. I also consciously began, as you put it, to think about what it would be like to walk a mile 'in another's shoes,' so to speak. It helped me to feel empathy and respect for other people, even people I really didn't like. Once I learned to listen and learn about the lives of others, I inevitably felt different about them than I had before I knew them. I have prejudice toward angry, aggressive people, but I have learned they are often just genuinely worried and fearful about something. I think because they really don't have the knowledge or skills to alleviate situations peacefully, they resort to anger and violence. Does that make sense to you?"

"Yes, Grayson, it sure does. I have my burden of prejudice as well. White people have caused me and other people of color so much pain and agony over the years that I have to fight off my own prejudices and hatred constantly. The Spirit of the Age has taught me to replace every thought of hatred with a thought of love; every inclination of avoidance with an effort toward fellowship, ignorance with understanding, and difference with oneness. I am getting better with time and practice." She started giggling. She looked at me with her hand over her mouth. We were both laughing again.

"Isn't it beautiful? Isn't it hopeful?" Rose asked with elation. "That we have been given these useful, effective, and meaningful spiritual tools to deal with our current issues and problems. It gives me hope. The true spirituality of religion is a great gift to the world. How practical! How reasonable! How hopeful these truths are in our struggle to free ourselves from superstitious, immature, and imaginary beliefs."

"Yes, very hopeful!" I agreed. "I mean, it gives me something specific to work on, not just some pie-in-the-sky 'won't things be nice when' ideas. I like it! Thank you, Rose," I said affectionately. "Thank you for giving me the opportunity to share your vision, your beliefs, and this project. I just had no idea."

"You're welcome, Grayson," she said humbly. "You're very welcome."

We rode for a while as I pondered what she had been saying. Suddenly a thought came to mind. I asked Rose, "What about patriotism? Is that a form of prejudice?"

Rose paused for a few moments before replying. "Well, it can be if one puts loyalty to one's country above the greater unity of mankind, or if one thinks and behaves as though our country is always right, or our country is best, or our national interests are always justified, no matter what. This kind of thinking assumes that the people of all other countries are inferior or of secondary importance, a true prejudice. In fact, most wars are due to this biased viewpoint. Promotion of 'loyalty at all costs' is not unlike the brainwashing tactics used to keep gang members in line, where they eventually become willing to murder others out of loyalty to their gang. Nationalism can be the same way. We have been given spiritual tools to deal with this problem in a practical and unifying manner. The manifestation of God guides us to think, to make decisions, and to act with confidence on **new** principles. He wrote,

'It is not for him to pride himself who loveth his own country, but rather for him who loveth the whole world.'[20]

"He also wrote,

'The earth is but one country and mankind its citizens.'[21]

"It is by the application of these spiritual principles and truths that the negative effects of an excessive nationalism and patriotism can be reasonably controlled and subjugated. It would be preferable for this more mature way of thinking to replace the ignorant bias and limited loyalties of patriotism and nationalism that can be so destructive in the world. To consider ourselves as citizens of one homeland, to regard all people as equally valued members of an extended family—this is the true spiritual way. Let me share with you another verse from the manifestation of God pertaining to this subject:

'This handful of dust, the world, is one home: let it be in unity.'[22]

"I would like to clarify something before we leave this subject. Prejudice is a judgment or bias based on an ignorant misunderstanding or misinformation of others. For example, sometimes the rich are blamed for being greedy, dishonest, or selfish. If one judges all rich people thusly, then that is prejudice. If one comes to know several wealthy people, through investigation, understanding, and true knowledge, it will become apparent that many are selfless, giving, kind, and honest. Some rich people may indeed be greedy and dishonest, but just as it is said, 'You can't judge a book by its cover,' so it is with human beings. Human beings are, or should be, evaluated fairly based upon their actions. A person who frequently lies is by definition a liar and cannot be trusted to tell the truth. A person who repeatedly takes things without permission is a thief and should not be trusted with another's property. So, a judgment of others, based on their demonstrated behavior is not a prejudice. It is an evaluation based on known facts. Even at that, we can't go around disliking or expressing anger and aggression at everyone who is imperfect in some way because that would include all of us!

"We are guided by the manifestation of God for this day to

consider the faults and immaturity of others with a sin-covering eye, and not to expose or emphasize one another's faults. The manifestation of God wrote,

'*Breathe not the sins of others so long as thou art thyself a sinner.*'[23]

"We are even instructed to avoid backbiting, cursing, or reviling others, because these actions have a devastating effect on society. In fact, the manifestation informed us that backbiting is so harmful that it

'*. . . quencheth the light of the heart, and extinguisheth the life of the soul.*'[24]

"So the proposed solution to dealing with prejudice," Rose concluded, "is to avoid prejudgments, to look at others with the eye of oneness, to become informed and knowledgeable of others, to trust them according to their behavior, and to avoid fault finding and backbiting at all costs. These are among the many rays of the light of unity. These are the spiritual principles and truths that will improve the souls of the human beings and thus the world's societies at large."

It hardly seemed possible that we had talked the morning away. Before we knew it, navigator T.J., who was some miles ahead of us, broadcast news over the CB of a nice restaurant about thirty minutes ahead. Annie had read about it in *The Milepost*, a book about traveling the Alcan Highway. I looked at Rose. She smiled and relaxed in her seat. I, too, felt relaxed and at peace. It was a good day, a beautiful day, with beautiful people and beautiful scenery. I enjoyed taking in every bit of it. We were beginning to see a few houses, so I knew we were close to a settlement again. Soon we turned a long, sweeping corner, and a small Canadian town came into view.

T.J. was at the side of the road, waving and pointing to an open gravel parking lot. We pulled in and parked. There was a nice-sized restaurant across the street. As I helped Rose out of the truck, T.J. reported, "It's Sunday, and there are a lot of people in the restaurant, but there's plenty of room for us." We readily marched across the street for lunch.

Once we had finished our meal and were preparing to leave the restaurant, several people came shuffling in, laughing and talking. I had my back to the door, so I didn't see them. The waitress gathered up some menus and ushered the group past our table to be seated. As they passed, I noticed one of them had a black cape-like top on with a tight priest-like collar. *Minister or priest*, I quickly assessed as they walked by. When they arrived at the table, the same person turned around, and I noticed it was a woman. *Interesting!* I thought.

Soon we were on the road again, talking about our trip, how far we had to go and how lucky we had been to be without breakdowns so far. I commented to Rose about the woman minister in the restaurant, asking, "What about women as priests or pastors? What do you think about that? I read recently that women have now surpassed men in the work force in the United States, but their wages still remain less than what men receive for the same work. What about all that?" I took a quick glance at Rose and waited for her answers.

She grinned. "Well, I guess we have found our topic for this afternoon."

I relaxed, looking forward to having my questions answered as soon as Rose was ready.

"Do you remember that the truths and teachings I am sharing with you from the manifestation of God were given to us in the middle to late 1800s?" Rose questioned.

"Yes," I replied.

"And do you recall that I told you how the Creator gives us guidance through the manifestations according to our needs and capacities to help us spiritually mature and develop, both as individual souls and collectively as a world society?"

"Uh-huh," I muttered.

"One of the guiding spiritual principles given to us by the manifestation of God for this time in history," Rose asserted, "is for us to recognize and implement equality for women. Surely, it is not too difficult to understand that women and men should enjoy equally all the benefits this life has to offer. Equality for women in status as human beings is an undeniable reality! Equality means having an equal right in all things. Equal legal rights, equal pay, equal opportunity, equal access to education and development, equal social status, equal say in all things, and equal influence in all decision-making are just some of the more obvious aspects of true equality.

"Another feature of equality means equal power. Having equal power means having an equal right to decide! Equal pay for the same work, and the right to decide on that equal pay by being equally represented in government, business, and all other aspects of human life and society are part of this. Of course this includes women having equal rights with their husbands in the decision-making processes for the family—equal say in how their children are raised, how money is spent, where to live—everything! The days of subjugating any human being are finally over!" Rose exclaimed. "Thank God!" she added.

"The struggle for gender equality has been hard fought by women for a very long time. Surely it's time for men to join them. Old, biased beliefs, such as how men are somehow superior to women, or that God intended for men alone to rule and be the decision makers, must be abolished. It is time for men to awaken from their indifference and help this happen. They need to guarantee that women have a say in how things are done in society. For the most part, men are still predominantly represented in positions of power and decision-making. Think therefore, of the great potential men have at this time in history to influence the implementation of gender equality. Here is a distinct opportunity to do something profoundly loving—to give equality, generously and happily, to that half of the world's population that has been subjugated throughout time. What an opportunity! What a sacred mission for men to engage in!

"I want you to consider something else," she said, pausing for a minute to rearrange herself in her seat. "Until now it was not time, nor was it possible, or wise, to fully implement the spiritual principle of gender equality. Consider the time of Jesus or even 630 years later with Muhammad. Human beings were not ready, not mature enough to learn and fully implement this principle of equality. But we are now!" she exclaimed with certainty. She was worked-up, sitting on the edge of her seat.

"I want to say something else about the role of men and their relationship with women," she went on. Pursing her lips, Rose closed her eyes and bowed her head in silence. Raising her head up, she said, "I want you to know that equality means women and girls deserve the right to be uniquely respected and therefore protected from all forms of violence inflicted upon them by men." She gazed at me sternly and earnestly, never taking her eyes off mine. "The tolerance of violence against girls and women in the world is completely unacceptable. It includes such atrocities as domestic violence, rape, and the ravages of war! Men must forego their barbaric attitudes of dominance and entitlement as it pertains to women, and collectively transform the way they perceive their relationships with women to one of absolute equality and respect. This is the true way of holiness! This is one of the most profound expressions of love and righteousness men can demonstrate!"

She sat back against her seat and turned to look out the side-window. We rode for some time in silence. Rose took in the forested view, and I took in what she had said. I was thinking about my life, wondering if I had been doing my part on this issue.

"There is a lot to discuss on this subject." Rose said, seriously. "In America, for example, there has been a great struggle for women's equality, which has included efforts to pass an equal rights amendment to the Constitution. As I recall it historically, many inferred the equal rights amendment would give women the right to behave in ways some considered immoral, like the right to engage in military combat, or that the amendment would uphold the right to abortions. These, as well as a number of other related concerns, began to create a multitude of different conflicts. This essentially stopped progress on the endeavor. Of course, this is a legal issue that is separate from the spiritual approach to equality I am sharing with you. However, it shows how the idea of equality provokes questions as to what it really means as we attempt to apply it in society. I want to be clear on this, Grayson, that the spiritual principle of equality I am sharing with you is not about an equal right to express one's lower nature," Rose instructed. "The spiritual principle of equality for women does not suggest an open license to be violent, vulgar, immoral, or disrespectful, just because some men are. Instead, it is the implementation of the right to equal status as a human being.

"Let's consider one of the morality issues that has hindered progress toward equal rights legislation for women. It's a big one—abortion. There are few issues that get people more heated and argumentative. Let's look at it, though, from a spiritual perspective, which is not to take issue with its current legal or social aspects. You recall that I shared with you that our purpose as human beings is to acquire knowledge and to love unconditionally. Well, we learn from the most recent manifestation of God that life begins at conception. We also know from him, as well as from former manifestations, that to take a life is wrong. In light of this wisdom and guidance, to remain consistent with our purpose to be loving human beings, and for those who choose to walk the spiritual path, how can abortion ever be considered a legitimate issue of true equality?"

We looked at each other momentarily and then both turned away in silence. The answer was clear, and we both knew it. I ventured a comment, "You know this idea might not go over too well with some in modern-day America?"

Rose shrugged her shoulders. "What I have pointed out is a spiritual understanding that is already part of many people's perspective," she replied. "On the other hand, it may not be the most popular. Let me share something with you. Some of the people in America, and in other parts of the world as well, practice what they believe to be a legitimate aspect of democracy. They think that if some issue is popular, or that the majority of the people believe something, then it must be true or acceptable. In other words, the standard of truth, or the means by which they determine right or wrong behavior, is by popular opinion. If that's what they want to believe, if that's what they want to act on, then they certainly have that freedom. Still, just because something is popular doesn't make it true or consistent with our spiritual purpose as human beings.

"There are other standards by which people determine what is right and true as well," she continued. "Some believe that the proper standard is determined by the Constitution of the United States. Some think that science alone has the ability to put forth such a standard. Some believe that their particular religion is the right model of truth. I am suggesting that the standard by which we can best judge what is right, good, and true for the time we are now living, is the guidance given to us by the one true God, through his manifestation for **this day**. Who else, or what other organization created by the human beings, can possibly claim the right to do this?

"Carefully consider this," Rose challenged, "Has the standard of public opinion brought peace, love, and happiness to American life? No, not by any means. Has the American Constitution or government provided these things? How about modern religious organizations or science? The human beings would do well to ask themselves, 'By what standard do we determine what is right behavior and what is not?' I am sharing with you a set of spiritual standards, a means by which we can measure and evaluate proper behavior, and a set of principles by which we can live in harmony with our intended spiritual purpose as human beings. They may not all be popular at this moment in time, but they are presented here for everyone to consider."

I didn't think either of us would comment further on the subject of women's rights, as it seemed clear, but I was wrong.

"There is more on this subject," Rose remarked. "Equal rights does not mean equal function. Men and women are biologically different. I surely hope there is no need to elaborate on this," she smiled mischievously. "Women alone give birth and have the natural potential to breastfeed their babies. Furthermore, women are generally better equipped mentally, spiritually, and emotionally to nurture, care for, train, and educate children through the early years of children's lives. Nurturing in early childhood is crucial to the proper development of healthy adult human beings. Consequently, appropriate education and training of young girls and women in the art and science of childrearing should be given the highest priority.

"In addition, women in general are more merciful, compassionate, and intuitive than their male counterparts. There is no reasonable debate on this, and it is clear to all those who observe objectively with wisdom. However, men too, can and should contribute significantly to the care, education, and training of children. There are numerous ways men and women are different, and we have to remember that equality does not mean the same. Equal rights, equal station, equal say, and equal status are all part of this. Women can, do, and will, in some cases, dominate men in certain activities and positions of society. In some activities and positions, men will outnumber women. It is natural and normal that men and women have different biological qualities and traits that make them generally more capable in some areas than in others. These are not issues of inequality," she assured me. "The issues are equal rights, equal say, equal power, equal opportunity, equal influence, and equal status—with some different functions specific to their womanhood. May it be so."

Rose yawned, and then turned her head to look out the side-window. She must have been tired because within minutes her eyes were closed and her head was nodding. I drove for a long time with her sleeping beside me. I was mulling over everything she had said. I guess we both needed the break. It was a peaceful time with nothing along the route but trees, blue skies, and the occasional bird flying overhead.

Finally Rose woke up. Stretching her arms in front of her, she breathed, "Oooh! That felt good. Sometimes a short nap is just the ticket." She sipped a little water from her water bottle and replaced the cap. After a few minutes, she stated, "There is a little more I want to share with you on the subject of the oneness of humankind that we began the day with. I want you to know that the spiritual principles I have talked about so far, and those I will share with you for the rest of the trip, are to help the human beings transition to one world community and to sustain it well into the future. The spiritual principle of the oneness of humankind, then, includes a vision of one worldwide community of people, peacefully united in all aspects of society, and supported by respect and the cultivation of differences in cultures and lifestyles. It means we treat each other, all the human beings, equally with loving-kindness and sincere concern. This is the way of the spirit for those who seek the path of love and unity in modern times." She took another drink and returned to her silence.

I stared out the front of the truck, focused on the road. I wanted so much to be of those who walked the path of love and unity.

We spent that night at Tubby's R.V. Park in Dawson Creek. The RV Park was nice with an abundance of large fir trees which I hadn't seen since being in Oregon. It was encouraging that we were getting closer to home. We were becoming proficient at travel now. It didn't take us long to set up the trailer, attend to our maintenance details, and be ready for a meal. We decided to eat at Boston Pizza. It was a fine meal, made better with laughter among good friends. After dinner, Rose left with T.J. and Alene to spend the night in a small motel. I was getting used to "living on the road." I imagined it must be what the life of a long-haul trucker is like because after several days now it was beginning to feel like a routine job.

This trip with Rose, though, was nothing like anything I had experienced before. It was a reality check, for sure. In fact, it was a reality changer! I could tell something was happening within my being, and I liked it. I knew my life would never be the same after this trip, and I didn't care. *Hope is like that*, I thought. And I had hope.

DAY SIX

MANY NEW PRINCIPLES

It started raining hard in the middle of the night. I didn't want to get out of bed and deal with driving in it, but it had to be done. Franklin, Annie, and little Scott were up, so I mustered the energy to rise from my warm bed to take on another day. I made coffee while Sonia fixed a small breakfast. We were quick about getting the trailer ready, and preparations for leaving went smoothly. *Ah, that rain is proving to be a good motivator,* I thought. T.J., Alene, and Rose showed up looking refreshed and eager for the day. They had already eaten breakfast and were ready to go, so out onto the wet roadways we went.

Not too far out of town, we met with construction. We were now traveling on a muddy gravel road, interspersed with rough pavement. I was trying to negotiate the road safely while attempting to make good time. *Yeah, right,* I thought. *Safe and easy is a better idea.*

I had been thinking about something since yesterday when Rose spoke about the need for equality between men and women. I decided to ask her about it this morning. "Rose, I was just wondering . . . is the manifestation of God for our age a woman?" I took a quick gulp of my coffee, glanced at her to see her response, and waited. She sat quietly without the least twitch of a response. "Maybe I'm getting ahead of things here, but since you put such emphasis on equality of men and women, I thought perhaps . . . I mean, you keep talking about the manifestation of God for this day, and I don't even know

152

who that is!" I felt kind of intrusive with my statement and hoped I hadn't offended her.

"No, he was a man," she said assuredly.

"Uh-huh," I added, nodding my head. Both of us were quiet for a spell. "You said he lived in the 1800s?"

She quickly looked over at me with an expression that said, *why are you doing this when I told you I didn't want to discuss this yet?* At least my guilt made me interpret her expression as such.

"Yes, he lived from 1817 to 1892."

I scanned my brain for information that might help me guess who he was. There were numerous religious movements that sprung up in and around the mid-1800s. I knew of several Christian groups that had been initiated at that time: the Seventh-Day Adventists, Jehovah's Witnesses, and the Latter Day Saints, or Mormons. I was familiar enough with these religions to know that none of them taught what Rose was telling me.

Before I could ask another question, Rose bowed her head slightly and said, "He was a Persian man and was from a place now called Iran."

"Iran?!" I exclaimed. "He was Iranian?" I was momentarily shocked by the possibility.

"You see," she said, looking directly at me. "There has been so much bad press over the last several decades about Iran that nearly all Westerners have developed a prejudice about the Iranian people. I ask you sincerely, does it matter where the manifestation of God comes from? It was said during the time of Jesus that nothing good comes of Nazareth. Does it matter what his race or gender was, or what language he spoke? I think not! What remains important is the content of his message and the purity of his character."

She paused and said slowly, "I will tell you about him today." She smiled like a little girl with a secret, excitement dancing in her eyes.

"The manifestations of God all had a two-fold station. One is their human station, in that they appeared like all men. They slept, ate, drank, carried on daily tasks, worked, felt pain and joy, and had families."

"Jesus didn't," I interjected.

"Yes, true, he didn't marry," Rose conceded. "His mother and siblings count as having a family, though. However, the fact of his remaining unmarried had nothing to do with his spiritual station. It was merely a factor of his human circumstance.

"The other station of the manifestations is the divine, or God-like characteristic of their spirit, which is bestowed upon them by the Creator. This is what allows them to speak and act as influenced directly by the emanations of the Holy Spirit. This is what makes them distinguished from the rest of us. This is what makes them one with God. This is what Jesus meant when he said, 'I and the Father are one.' They speak and act as prompted by a direct connection to that creating and sustaining force behind all things in the universe we call God."

"So, who was he? Do I know him? Is he a popular known figure?" I flung out these questions as quickly as I could, eager for her to tell me.

Rose replied, "The name given to him by his parents was Husayn Ali. The world knows him by his title name, which is how they did things back then in Persia. He is known as Bahá'u'lláh."

"What?" I questioned, confused.

"Bahá'u'lláh. His name is pronounced like this: 'Baa (as in back) - haw' - oh - law,' with the accent on the haw." We were both silent for a moment.

"Baha - oh—" I tried to pronounce his name. Rose helped me a few times until I could say it properly.

Rose explained, "It was a common practice in the old world to give people title names. Not unlike Jesus, who was known during his early years as Jesus of Nazareth. His title name was Jesus Christ, which meant Jesus the Anointed One, or the Messiah. The title given to Bahá'u'lláh translates into English as 'The Glory of God.'"

We were quiet for a few moments. I think Rose was letting me integrate this new information.

Finally, I said, "You were right, Rose. I understand now what you meant by me being prejudiced. My first thought was, 'How could any divine prophet, especially for the new age, one who claims to be giving a message for the problems of the modern world, come out of Iran of all places?' I see now that my own bias jumped right up to challenge the possibility immediately. I wouldn't have believed it possible, at least not as sudden and forceful as it was. This might take me a while to overcome," I said, sheepishly.

"Well, don't worry about it too much. We all have biases. Recognize it for what it is. Try to stay focused on what is real and true, and don't let the influence of your past prejudices block your heart from hearing his message. That's what's really important.

"Think about this for a minute. You know that Moses received the Ten Commandments from God and that people all over the world have tried to live by that guidance for centuries. The positive influence of those commandments in the world is incalculable. When Moses gave that guidance to the people, they had a hard time accepting him as the bearer of a message from God. Why was that? Primarily, it was because he had been raised in opulence in the house of Pharaoh. Another obstacle was that some considered him a murderer because when he was younger he had killed a man while defending another. Think of how difficult it was for the people at that time to overcome their pre-judgments of Moses. Think how hard it was for them to accept his message from God and not be deterred by his upbringing and history.

"Look, too, at the life of Jesus. Because his father was considered unknown, he was looked upon as dishonorable by the people. Consider how difficult it was for the people to overcome their prejudices and listen to what he had to say. And yet, observe how his life and teachings have affected goodness in the world for over two millennia. This has always been God's way of keeping us focused on the importance of the message rather than on the messenger."

She was silent for a moment. I had nothing to say. She had obliterated my concern that an Iranian could be the manifestation of God for our time. Suddenly she raised her hand as though to stop me from speaking even though I wasn't about to say anything. "I will tell you a little about the life of Bahá'u'lláh." She said his name with such reverence and respect.

"He was born near the edge of the city of Tehran in 1817 to a wealthy family. His father had a prominent position in the city with the government. His mother related how he never cried or showed restlessness as a child. As was customary among families of stature in Iran, he received a simple childhood education at home. The subjects of education in those days in Iran usually included reading, writing, study of the Quran, and poetry. Beyond this he had no formal education, nor did he attend any of the theological schools that were readily available at the time. He was acknowledged as being extremely wise as a child by all those who met him, often solving difficult adult problems. He married at the young age of eighteen. His chosen occupation was to comfort those who were weary and unhappy, and to feed and care for the poor and hungry, using his own resources.

"When he was in his thirties, he was cast into a stench-filled dungeon and chained for promoting spiritual beliefs that appeared to oppose the accepted beliefs of Islam. It was during this imprisonment that the Holy Spirit moved upon his soul and his mission as a manifestation of God was revealed to him. In an attempt to suppress the influence of the new religion he was teaching, and in response to the urging of the powerful Islamic clergy, the government exiled him and his family to Iraq. Similar circumstances in Iraq led that government to exile him to Turkey, which was part of the Ottoman Empire at the time. Because he was known and loved by all who met him, no matter where he was, and because of the spiritual truths he was teaching, jealous clergy interfered yet again. Eventually he was exiled to the prison city of Akka, which is in present-day Israel. His life and that of his family was full of ridicule, imprisonment, exile, poverty, and extreme hardships. He was poisoned by those who were jealous and eventually condemned to a beating for teaching a new approach to religion and spirituality.

"Like all the manifestations that have come to humanity, he had an innate knowledge of all things. He lived his life harmonious with the Word he was teaching, and his teachings were consistent with his actions. This is something that no one but a manifestation of God can do. He endured hardship, suffering, and harsh cruelties with radiant submission and a humble serenity. Many of his followers who believed in his station and teachings, people he dearly loved, also were harassed, tortured, and killed by fanatical opponents, causing him incessant grief. He wrote these words to the soul of mankind:

'*My body hath endured imprisonment that ye may be released from the bondage of self.*'"[25]

Rose's voice quivered with emotion.

I didn't even know this man, this manifestation of God, Bahá'u'lláh, but I too was moved and felt empathy for him and his followers. *How awful*, I thought.

Rose stared out the side-window until she had collected herself. "That's all I will tell you about Bahá'u'lláh at this time," she finally concluded, "unless you have questions pertaining to his life."

"No, that's fine," I said. Of course, I wanted to know more, but I didn't have any specific question at the time. Besides, it seemed like Rose wasn't really up to talking at the moment. We rode for more than fifteen minutes without speaking. We both probably needed some quiet time.

Finally, Rose shuffled around in her seat and started to tell me more. "Let me share with you another basic teaching given to us by Bahá'u'lláh. This is one of those spiritual truths that was not given prominence by former manifestations. Its emphasis is new and specific to our time and age, just like the other spiritual principles I have been sharing. In his assessment of the needs of modern times, Bahá'u'lláh identified blind imitation as one of the most challenging impediments to acquiring knowledge, intelligence, and wisdom. Blind imitation means to follow the beliefs, customs, and actions of those who have lived before us without due consideration. It means to believe and behave as our forefathers did, or as dictated or demonstrated by politicians, the leaders of religion, famous people, or other influential people, without personally assessing the value of such beliefs and behaviors. Bahá'u'lláh proposed to overcome the entrapment of blind imitation by teaching us to apply the spiritual principle of independent investigation of truth.

"Independent investigation of truth," Rose explained, "means to believe and act in ways that are free from the control, influence, and opinions of others. It means to take personal responsibility to investigate matters thoroughly before incorporating them into our beliefs and behaviors. Consider that for a moment. What is more foolish, more stunting of one's understanding and wisdom, more irresponsible, or more unfaithful to oneself than to never question what we are told or to never personally seek truth or understanding? This is the age, and this is the time, when this spiritual principle is critical to our survival as human beings. This is one of the spiritual remedies that will help heal the present human condition.

"Independent investigation," she continued, "means to investigate matters for oneself, impartially before believing or acting as those before us did or as those presently around us do. Observe the conflicts in human relations carefully—from the simple disagreements between individuals to the more complex discord and strife between different religions, political groups, or national ideologies. Much of this conflict, as you are surely aware, is due to mindless imitation of entrenched traditions, beliefs, and behaviors promoted and enforced down through the ages."

"Yes," I interrupted. "It reminds me of a story they use in modern business training programs. May I?" I asked.

"Sure," Rose said.

"It's about a young woman who has invited her mother over to help with Thanksgiving dinner. The mother is putting the turkey in a large cooker when the daughter exclaims, 'Don't forget to cut the tail off that turkey!'

'Why?' asks the mother.

'Well, you always did, Mom, and so did Grandma.'

'That's because Grandma had a small cooker, and you couldn't get the turkey in without cutting the tail off first,' replied the mother. 'And I inherited that cooker, so I did the same thing. However, with your large cooker there is no need to cut the tail off this turkey.'

The young woman gave it some thought and then responded,

'Well, I'm going to do it anyway because that's the way we've always done it.'"

"What a great story!" Rose laughed. "I like that, but in your story there was no harm done. Believe me—wars are fought over things just that foolish. So I ask you to be sure and put in your . . . ," she paused, "in **our** book, how important it is that the human beings consider seriously the value of this simple yet profound spiritual principle emphasized by the manifestation of God, Bahá'u'lláh. There is great confusion in the world right now because this principle is not being implemented well. There is an enormous volume of information being disseminated immediately and constantly by television, radio, internet, smartphones, and other media. New technologies compete in relaying massive amounts of information, which can be confusing, contradictory, misleading, and outright untrue. One person might say something and soon millions repeat it or transfer it to others without even knowing if it is accurate. So we have a spiritual obligation to ourselves and to others to personally investigate all matters thoroughly and impartially before we believe or act on unsubstantiated information! This includes everything I am telling you! You have to contemplate these matters, investigate them for yourself, and weigh them against reason, science, your own experiences, and the true collective experience of the human beings. Then weigh it in your own heart—that place where love, kindness, and goodness prevail in your feelings. And, for me, I also assess matters in accordance with the teachings of Bahá'u'lláh. If something is harmonious with all of these things, then you may want to accept it as true, believe in it and act upon it with confidence. If it is inconsistent with these criteria of truth, then set it aside and move on.

"I think it's time for the human beings to have a collective investigation of truth. It is time to lay aside our superstitions, our worn-out, worthless, or meaningless customs, behaviors, and beliefs. It is time to take a fresh look at what we have been taught about religion and understand it in a whole new way. It is time to re-examine our philosophical ideologies that drive the modern ways of society and re-design them to fit the needs of a modern time and a new age. It's time to read the sacred scriptures ourselves, taking the message into our hearts, and acting upon them as they inspire us.

"So, among the major teachings of Bahá'u'lláh for this day is the elimination of blind imitation and the implementation of its twin principle, the independent, impartial, and personal investigation of truth. These are among the most vital needs facing humanity and the surest means for healing the social ills of our modern world."

We were both silent for a while. Finally, Rose said, "It should be evident to most that holding on to ancient religious beliefs and traditions is causing a great deal of conflict among peoples and nations of the world right now. These conflicts cannot be resolved until the people abolish all archaic beliefs in the superiority of their own religion, stop listening to the superstitious rhetoric of some of their misguided leaders, and re-examine and seek out the truth about their own faith. It is this same thoughtless imitation of past beliefs and behaviors that is responsible for conflict and disputes at nearly all levels of our societies, as has been the case for a long time. What is being offered to us now, at this time in history, is the opportunity to overcome our immaturities by consciously applying these new spiritual principles in our lives.

"These principles, and others taught by Bahá'u'lláh, have profound potential to help the human beings mature spiritually and to deal more appropriately with the problems that plague modern society. I want to share these sacred words with you, which were written by Bahá'u'lláh:

'Should the lamp of religion be obscured, chaos and confusion will ensue, and the lights of fairness and justice, of tranquility and peace cease to shine.'[26]

"He also wrote,

'The winds of despair are, alas, blowing from every direction, and the strife that divideth and afflicteth the human race is daily increasing. The signs of impending convulsions and chaos can now be discerned, inasmuch as the prevailing order appeareth to be lamentably defective.'"[27]

She remained silent for a moment and then noted, "When I give you a quotation from Bahá'u'lláh, please quote it word-for-word in our book. I'll give you references for them later." She looked at me for a response.

"Yeah, sure, I'll do that, Rose. I promise." She then became quiet.

I eventually broke the silence. "How come I haven't heard about Bahá'u'lláh before? I mean, if he wrote or said all this and has claimed to be the manifestation of God for our time, how come I haven't heard about him? You would think that anyone making such a claim would be thoroughly investigated by the people and either be pronounced a heretic, or if he really did prove out, people would be flocking to him. So what's the deal with that?"

"Well, have you heard of the Bahá'í Faith?" she asked, looking at me cautiously.

I thought for a moment. "Yes, come to think of it, I have. Is that what this is?"

"Yes!" she said joyously. "Those who have personally investigated and believe in what Bahá'u'lláh said and wrote are called Bahá'ís. It's pronounced like this: 'Baa-highs', with the accent on the **hi**."

"Bahá'ís?" I repeated. "Now I remember what I heard. I heard about them being persecuted as a minority religion in Iran. So most Bahá'ís are Iranian?"

"Goodness no!" Rose answered. There are more than five million believers worldwide in more than 100,000 localities around the planet. According to the Encyclopedia Britannica, the Bahá'í Faith is the second most widespread religion in the world, second only to the composite of the Christian religion. The Bahá'í Faith is represented by more than 2,000 different tribes, races, and ethnic groups and its literature has been translated into more than 800 languages. There were several hundred Bahá'ís in Anchorage, and you met many of them. Furthermore, there are Bahá'ís in the small community where you are moving to in Oregon."

"You're kidding me," I interrupted.

"No, I checked before we left Anchorage," Rose giggled. "I also checked on these statistics before we left, so be sure to record them accordingly."

"Just like they're recorded," I said, glancing at the tape recorder.

"Good. So you see from the statistics at least that the Bahá'í Faith is widespread. Many have heard some information about it. The Bahá'ís actively share these new spiritual teachings with others who show interest. It's just what passes for news in the world is usually something negative, disastrous, or sensational in some way. New ways of thinking, believing, and behaving don't get coverage—especially news about new religions! As you pointed out earlier in this trip, many people in today's society have negative feelings and perspectives about the word religion. Their preconceptions prevent many of them from investigating the Bahá'í Faith. Then there are those who are satisfied with their religion and don't feel a need to consider anything else. However, there also are many who are dissatisfied with their religion, or don't have any religion at all, and feel unfulfilled in their spiritual life. It's these people who most often investigate the teachings of Bahá'u'lláh, become believers, and then endeavor to implement these spiritual principles and teachings in their lives."

"So, you're a Bahá'í?" I ventured.

Rose gave me the most tender, affirming smile and said, "Yes, Grayson, I am a Bahá'í."

I nodded and tried to put everything she had been talking about together with the little I knew about the Bahá'í Faith. My thoughts were broken by T.J.'s voice coming over the CB, "Break time! We're just ahead of you. Less than a mile up." Soon I saw T.J. standing beside his parked car on the roadside, waving me down again. He quickly ducked back into his car to get out of the rain. I pulled over so we could take a short break.

We had been driving through a steady rain for a while, and I was feeling tired. It was mid-morning and the truck cab was warm and vibrating gently as we traveled down the road. I had been pushing for weeks to get this trip underway, and after several days on the road I was beginning to feel exhaustion catching up with me. I was glad Rose was with me, otherwise staying awake could have been difficult.

I looked over at Rose and she, too, looked tired. Her face sagged a bit, making her appear older this morning. *This is a difficult trip for an 83-year-old woman*, I thought.

The recorder on the seat next to Rose was still on, though neither of us had said anything for half an hour. Finally, she took in a deep breath and began, "We have plenty of time before lunch for me to share the spiritual teachings of Bahá'u'lláh pertaining to economics. Shall we do that?" She paused and looked over at me.

"I'm ready," I said as I rallied myself to sit up in the seat and be attentive.

"Grayson," she began, "as I emphasized to you previously, all the spiritual principles I am sharing with you serve to fulfill our purpose as human beings and relate to the theme of our age—unity. It surely is evident to you that we can never have peace, love, and unity among the human beings until we deal appropriately with the grossly unfair distribution of wealth that exists throughout the world. The extremes between the haves and the have-nots, the wealthy and the poor, are glaringly apparent. Unnecessary, unjust, and unfair accumulation of wealth by the few, while the many suffer needlessly from an appalling lack of means, is a reprehensible and shameful condition. This economic imbalance exists in human societies nearly everywhere. Furthermore, it is increasingly obvious that the current approach to economics is lamentably defective and impotent in its ability to solve the serious economic needs of an ailing world civilization. I could go on in detail for hours on the terrible injustices being perpetrated by the current systems of economics. I could relate to you the degree of suffering by the young, the sick, the poor, the under-privileged, and the disadvantaged, but I prefer not to recount it. If a person isn't aware of it, given the abundance of information and exposure made available by our technology, then they have to be intentionally ignoring it, denying it, or asleep."

She looked at me and started to laugh. I must have looked half-asleep myself, or maybe she just had to laugh to release tension because the subject was too disturbing to her. I wasn't sure. I smiled and acknowledged her humor.

"Remember, these principles and truths I am sharing with you were given to us by Bahá'u'lláh well over a hundred years ago. He advised us that these were the solutions to the problems facing humankind in modern times, and they would continue to be relative for the next thousand years or so, at least."

"Thousand years?" I retorted.

"Yes, these spiritual teachings and principles are to guide us through the next thousand years or more, until the next manifestation appears."

"So, it will be a thousand years before a manifestation of God shows up again? Is that what you're saying?"

"Yes, according to Bahá'u'lláh, a thousand years—or more! But let's not change the subject," Rose answered.

"I want to share with you several practical spiritual principles pertaining to economics that were untimely to implement collectively in the past, but are very pertinent today. These are principles and truths that specifically fit the needs of our modern time. They are spiritual solutions to the current problems of economic dysfunction and disparity." She had my complete attention.

"The first of these principles," she began, "which is really not new, is the voluntary sharing of wealth and abundance with the poor. Because the humans are one family, it is evident to anyone with a sensitive heart that to hoard wealth while others live in need is spiritually immature and selfish. Since we are, in reality, spiritual beings, whose purpose is to develop a loving, kind, and generous spirit, then it is evident that sharing one's abundance benefits both the giver and the receiver. Giving voluntarily of one's wealth to help the less fortunate is one way to contribute spiritually and materially to fair wealth distribution.

"This same principle pertains to certain rights and privileges that a civil and mature society provides its members. Economic fairness is not just about money, but also about social privileges, opportunities, and services. We all have a personal and social responsibility to see that everyone is educated and helped to escape the bonds of ignorance that burden so many people. Social provisions, such as equal access to education, adequate healthcare, loving care for the aged and the disabled, and the necessary provisions for widows, single parents, and orphaned children need to be provided out of the abundance that exists collectively in a society. It's a disgrace that some live in opulence while others suffer from a lack of adequate services or even the basic means for survival in these modern times. So when I tell you about the spiritual solution toward economic justice, I am not just talking about a fair and just distribution of monies, but also about the provision of goods and services in a fair and equitable fashion to guarantee that humanity develops as a whole rather than in a disproportionate way."

"Some would say," I interrupted, "that the wealthy have earned their wealth, and that it is only fair that they should be able to keep it. Also, many are complaining today that redistribution of wealth reeks of socialism. What about that?"

Rose answered, "Remember me explaining to you that the principles and truths I am sharing with you from Bahá'u'lláh support our given purpose as human beings, which is to work toward being wise and loving souls? Well, it's spiritually immature to amass wealth at the expense of others and to live in luxury while others suffer from lack of means. No one really profits because it is inconsistent with our true spiritual purpose. The kind of love, caring, and sharing proposed here for our fellow human beings is something most everyone teaches their children when they are young! So, for grown adults to behave contrary to this is really immature," Rose asserted.

"Let me answer your question about socialism," she said. "For the most part, those who use the word to refute these principles do so because of their limited understanding about what is really being proposed here, and it is not socialism as a political ideology as they know it or imagine it. To implement these principles is not the same as adopting an archaic man-made form of government or philosophy. These are spiritual solutions based on the spiritual truth that humankind is one, making these social concerns worthy of true justice and fairness."

I interrupted again. "Some people say that everyone in America has an equal opportunity to succeed and be wealthy. Look at all those who were underprivileged, and through their own efforts, became successful. What about that?" I asked.

She looked at me for a second with what appeared to be disbelief. Sighing deeply, Rose said, "Let me say, Grayson, there is little, **real**, equal opportunity in our society. We have laws that attempt to make it that way, but socially there is a serious lack. Everyone has an opportunity for a good education, **if** you can afford it, or **if** you live in the right neighborhood, or **if** the subculture you are born into supports it. Everyone has the opportunity for a good job, **if** you can get hired, and **if** your family and culture happen to provide the necessary education, training, and skills. Everyone has the opportunity to work up the same economic ladder, **if** enough variables come together to support such an endeavor, and **if**, as is sometimes the case, they have the heartlessness to take advantage of others on their way up. There are numerous iffy variables that are not equally and fairly available to all.

"It is true that there are some people from less fortunate backgrounds who have been financially successful, according to the modern definition of the word, and who were fair, honest, kind, and even spiritual people. They would tell you honestly that it was a particular set of fortunate circumstances and people in their lives that made their success possible. Many would tell you there were certain miraculous-like events or circumstances outside of their control that occurred to them or for them. For some, it was the existing social conditions of moderate fairness and equality that lead to their success. And yes, these partially developed conditions did play a role. Even so, you have to get inside people's lives to see that equal and fair opportunities are not nearly as abundant as we would like to imagine."

She suddenly sat upright, remembering, "I saw a cartoon once, or a drawing that demonstrated this quite well. There were three small boys who loved baseball. One day their favorite baseball team came to town. They had no money to get into the game, and there was a fence around the park so they couldn't see the game. Behind an old garage they found three equal-sized boxes. They quickly grabbed the boxes and dragged them over to the fence so they could stand on them and watch the game. As they stood on the boxes, only one boy was able to see over the fence because he was taller than the other two. Some would say that the boxes gave the children equal opportunity because the boxes were all the same height. But because only one boy was privileged with height, only one was successful in his efforts to watch the game. That's the way it is in society. True equal opportunity is far more complex than what most of us understand.

"Some people become financially successful because of their enormous efforts and sacrifices. Some inherit their wealth. Some take advantage of others to acquire it, and some come by fortunate circumstances to attain it. There are numerous variables, too many and too complex to address at this moment. But what we can do, and what is righteous, is to make collective efforts to assure real fairness and equal opportunities and provisions exist for all. For the boys watching the baseball game, it would mean each box would be tall enough to provide each child with a view of the game.

"Religion, true and pure religion, as I believe I am sharing with you, require the development of spiritual qualities, traits, and virtues that lead to a change in the character of human beings. It is these spiritual characteristics that can best contribute to meaningful solutions for better economic conditions. Think of what it would be like if people were focused on developing fairness, honesty, trustworthiness, loyalty, responsibility, and honor in all their business and human interactions and relationships. These are spiritual qualities. Take a fair and honest look at how business and economics operate in today's world and consider how different it would be if these spiritual characteristics were implemented: fairness in prices, fairness in wages, fairness in job allocation, and honesty in all business dealings."

I snapped my head around in disbelief.

"Yes, honesty!" she repeated.

"Oh, sure," I spouted sarcastically. "That means no fine print, no legal jargon that few can read or understand, and no entrapping others into economic disadvantages . . . why not expect honesty in advertising, too? Ha! That's a joke."

Rose just looked at me and waited to see if I was finished with my outburst.

She continued, "The Bahá'í sacred scriptures say this, *'Truthfulness is the foundation of all human virtues.'*[28]

"Yes, truthfulness! Imagine the effects of truthfulness on the economy! It alone would transform our economics. Grayson, a just and fair economy never can be established without these spiritual qualities being present in the character of man. And their development is dependent upon our **belief** in them, in their Source, and in our willingness to act upon them with confidence."

It was a lot for me to take in. Rose quietly left me to my thoughts for a few minutes. A flash of lightning streaked down from the clouds, followed several seconds later by a huge boom of thunder, stirring me out of my musings. Rose wisely chose the moment to continue her discussion.

"Another spiritual principle necessary for the development of a fair world economy," she related, "is the re-apportionment of funds for military purposes. Funding for war has always been, and continues to be, a financial drain on peoples and nations. Means should be developed so that security for all nations would be provided by a collective international force. I will speak to you more about this later, but for now I just want you to consider the excessive expenditures allocated to defense. They are enormous. They drain nations of an unreasonable portion of their wealth that could be put to better civil purposes for the benefit of all. This, too, is a spiritual approach to economic fairness.

"Another distortion in modern economics," she continued, "is the truly unfair and disproportionate distributions of unearned wealth collected as interest on money loaned, or on dividends and other profits from investments. Credit cards, business loans, personal loans, and investment loans are all economic methods of making money from interest charges. Profits are also acquired from purchasing or trading stocks, bonds, real estate, and other financial investments. The spiritual approach is that profit made from interest charges on loans and returns acquired from trades and investments should be tempered with fairness, moderation, love, and compassion.

"Yes! I really did say those words," she assured me, looking at my puzzled face. "Love and compassion! Observe around you the injustices perpetrated by those who control the wealth. Consider the effect of unjustly high interest rates on the misled poor and the entrapment of debt on the sometimes weak-willed, unfortunate, or misinformed ones of our society. It is a disheartening situation. Look at the excessive accumulation of wealth by the investment system at the expense of the poor who are **doing the work** that accumulates that wealth! This is not a fair or a just system. It is an aggressive, heartless, hostile scheme. It upsets me terribly, and I really don't want to go there."

She took in a deep breath, let out a big sigh, and turned to look out the window again for some time before continuing on the subject.

"Another spiritual solution to economic disparity," Rose finally said, "is that everyone who is able should work to provide some kind of goods or services to humanity. Of course, this excludes children, the elderly, and the disabled. To work and to be of service to others are parts of our spiritual purpose as human beings. How can we learn to be loving and wise if we are not engaged in service to others in some way?

"This principle applies to everyone up and down the socioeconomic ladder. The poor should do everything they can to work and be of service in some way. It lifts human dignity not to be dependent upon social services for support. And the wealthy, too, should work and make their contributions to the social good. What is the difference between someone who lives on welfare when they could be working and a wealthy non-working person who lives in luxury from the excessive money accumulated on interest and gains from their investments alone? There is little difference! Both are living off society while personally providing nothing meaningful!

STEVEN E. ELLIS

Neither is contributing to the social good. Both are taking and not giving.

"Investors say their work provides capital for jobs and businesses at a risk of loss. Like their so-called risk is a contribution that excuses them from working and being of real service to society! It is true we need people who will provide capital in the form of loans for economic development. However, that doesn't mean it has to be set up as an ongoing profit-making game of chance such as now exists in the investment world of economics.

"There are fair business models that already exist in the world that do much to overcome economic disparity. These business models distribute profits among the workers, the owners, and the financers while eliminating the disproportionate distribution of profits to their investment sectors.

"We are called by the spirit of the age to work in a trade or profession with an attitude of service to humanity. And we are enjoined by the manifestation of God to excel in our work. These, too, are among the spiritual principles that will bring economic fairness, prosperity, and happiness for all the human beings.

"It's important we look at this subject from the standpoint of our true reality. We are spiritual beings with a purpose—to become better at expressing love. To work and be of service to others is one of the greatest means we have to show our love for others and for the Creator. So the attitudes surrounding money for nothing, financial independence, or having enough wealth so one never has to work, are selfish, immature approaches to life that only distract people from their true purpose. This is why gambling is taboo in religion and within mature societies around the world. Gambling fosters a behavior of trying to get something for nothing. Look at what is going on in society today. The hope of a lucky financial windfall seduces the minds of millions, distracting them from their real and true purpose. So rampant is this attitude that many state governments are now dependent upon funding from state-run gambling lotteries! Yes, dependent! Even the economic system at the level of Wall Street has become a giant game of chance based on what will, or what will not, be valuable in the future. A system of economics engaged in such vulnerable speculation surely contributes to uncontrollable economic fluctuations that constantly disrupt the social order.

"These are among the spiritual principles given to us by the Creator, through his latest manifestation, for properly developing an economy that is fair, just, and dependable. Contemplate them carefully, individually, and collectively, and I think you will see the truth of what I have shared with you. Further, I suggest that if you consider the economy carefully, you will come to realize, as will the experts in economics, that there are no other practical solutions available. The desperate measures now being taken to patch up the failing economic systems are having minimal effects and can, at best, provide only temporary relief.

"Humanity has a choice in all these matters. Whatever the choices, there are consequences. There are consequences to every decision we make and this needs no explanation. The direction being propagated by our collective choices now do not bode favorably for our future. It is easy to see how they will continue to worsen until these God-given spiritual principles and truths are realized, accepted, and put into practice. The spirit of the age is one of oneness, Grayson, not separation; cooperation, not competition; trust and fairness, not opportunism and advantage over others. Remember, all these principles are an expression of the spirit of the age, which is unity and oneness. And not just here in America, but worldwide!

"I hope I have adequately explained the true unifying spirit to you as it pertains to fairness and justice in economics," Rose concluded.

She rested silently. I was nearly dizzy from the thoughts that were spinning through my head. Like many people, I had consciously engaged in endless contemplation and speculation about the economy. Until now I had never been presented with any novel ideas for dealing with it, and certainly never such as the combination of principles Rose had just suggested.

"I'm going to have to give this some deep thought," I told Rose. "It's just too much for me to reflect on right now. I mean, you proposed so many things all at once that I'm going to need some time to think about them before I can even comment or ask a question."

"I'm not surprised," Rose said lovingly. These ideas deserve a lot of time. They are about our social and spiritual survival." I had to agree with her there.

"I threw a lot at you all at once. I was really on a roll there," Rose admitted. She looked at me and started laughing again, as did I. Her on a roll, and me dizzy and confused. It wasn't just funny, it was hilarious. **We** were hilarious!

All was well. I felt good driving down the road on my journey to a new life in Oregon. I realized not only was I going to a new life in Oregon, but there was a new life being formed in my heart and spirit. Hope was rising! Hope for the future. Hope for my future, my children's future, and, in fact, hope for the whole of mankind! I hadn't felt this way for a long time. A few old demons of doubt might still try to pull me down, but I felt confidence building inside.

"I love you, Rose," I said without thinking, feeling a little bit embarrassed.

"I love you, too, Grayson," she said, in a soft, heartfelt voice.

Tears of joy filled my eyes and blurred the road. I didn't care. For the moment, everything was good.

SCIENCE AND MORE

Before long navigator T.J. was talking on the CB again. He said there was a small park ahead, just off the road a piece where we could pull in and eat lunch. It was called Bijou Falls and was frequented by tourist and locals for its beauty. Before long, I could see the sign directing us into the park.

There was a large empty parking lot at the end of a long driveway. No one was there, probably because it was raining so hard. I swung the big truck in a half circle to park with the nose of the truck against the outer barrier of the parking lot and my camp-trailer protruding into the center. Sonia, Annie, and Alene fixed soup and sandwiches in the trailer while the rest of us stayed in our vehicles to keep from getting soaked. When lunch was ready, Franklin ran out in his hoodie to deliver soup and sandwiches to the rest of us. Rose and I ate in the truck. It was so humid that the truck windows steamed up enough that I couldn't see out at all.

When we were through with lunch and ready to get moving again, I called Franklin on the CB to guide me as I backed up to leave the parking lot. Rose and I wiped down the windows, and I reported on the CB that I was ready. I started to back up when I heard Franklin say, "Forward!" over the CB. For some reason I thought he meant "proceed as you are," so I kept backing up. Again he stated, "Forward!" but louder and more emphatic this time. Suddenly I felt some resistance in the truck as though I had hit something. I stopped quickly. There was silence for a moment. Rose and I looked at each other with surprise. The CB crackled to life. "We have a little trailer damage here," Franklin reported. I was immediately upset. How could this happen? He was guiding me and still we have an accident! I put my hat on and jumped out into the rain. The trailer was jackknifed against the truck. I had backed the truck right into the front corner of the trailer. I climbed back into the truck and pulled it forward to release the entanglement. The right side of the trailer was considerably damaged. The whole outside wall was knocked off to the side by a foot. The door wouldn't close, and there was a large opening between the wall and the front that would make it impossible to drive without rainwater and mud filling the trailer. I had already made plans for this trailer if it were to break down on the trip. It was an old 1973 Terry. It wasn't worth much, but it worked well for our purposes. But not anymore. Not now, and not in the middle of a soaking British Colombia rain. I was so upset I told Franklin, "Let's just empty the trailer and leave it right where it sets!" We were too far from Dawson Creek to go back for repairs, and besides, that would take an extra day or two. "Let's just leave it!" I repeated, exasperated.

"Now don't get all in a hurry," Franklin demanded. "Let's see if we can fix it." After I cooled off, I dug the toolbox out of the back of the Bronco while Franklin pulled out a handyman jack and some tools from the back of his pickup. We went to work. After an hour of engineering in the rain, we got the wall back where it belonged and the door to close. With ample duct-tape, nails, and sheetrock screws, we made the trailer travel-worthy again.

We were back on the road. I felt somewhat better now that we had sufficiently repaired the trailer, but I was wet and cold, which caused the windows to steam up again for the next several miles. Finally, I worked my way out of my wet jacket, stuffing it behind the seat with Rose's help. I soon warmed up and began to feel more relaxed. My mind was racing with thoughts of what Rose had shared, jumbled up with my own past experiences, studies, and learning. There was just too much going on in my head. I could hardly remember the things she had shared—only bits and pieces. I couldn't even formulate any decent questions. I decided to stay focused on the driving and let my brain rest this afternoon. But that wasn't to be.

We were many miles down the road this time before Rose turned on the recorder. She must have seen the reluctance in my face. Soon afterward, she asked: "Are you okay? You seem a little distant."

"I guess my brain's just tired," I said. "That trailer wreck upset me. Plus, you have shared so much new information, and I have tried to consider so many new concepts—I feel like I used to in college. I'm trying to integrate these new principles and truths, as you call them, and it's making me feel a little overwhelmed. I don't know how to assess things anymore. I don't seem to be able to tell what is true and what is not, or what I believe and what's questionable. I'm just taking it all in. I like it, don't get me wrong. In fact, it's giving me a feeling of great hope again. It's just challenging to put it all together."

We were both quiet. A full stomach combined with a full brain were giving me an after lunch lull. Finally, Rose reached over and gently rubbed my shoulder. "You're doing fine," she said. "Nearly everyone feels the way you do when presented with a considerable amount of new information. Don't worry, this, too, shall pass." She paused and smiled at me tenderly.

"Since you feel some confusion about how to determine what's true for you anymore, let's consider what good criteria for truth might be. In other words, how do people determine what is true and what is not?" We looked at each other without comment, which I guess meant we were ready to proceed.

"Sometimes people say 'go with your gut,'" Rose began. "What they mean by this is when they read or learn something that scares them, confuses them, or challenges them, they get an undesirable feeling in their emotions and most likely reject whatever they read or hear. If they get a feeling of hope or if they get no feeling at all, then it is more likely they will at least consider the new information presented to them. These feelings they experience are sometimes called intuition or even inspiration.

"Now, intuition and inspiration are fascinating, and they have great value for creative purposes. But they are also vulnerable to deception when determining the truth of things. A skilled or convincing speaker can easily manipulate these emotions and promptings of the heart. Look at advertising, for example. It has become such a well-developed science that people are often easily persuaded to purchase goods or services they may not want or need. There are endless examples, but I think you are sharp enough to understand that relying solely on intuition, emotion, inspiration, or just gut feelings may not be the most mature way to evaluate what is true in the world."

I didn't say anything. I was just listening.

"Some people will say the best way to determine if something is true or not is by logic or reason. If something is rational, that is, if it makes sense to their mind when weighed against their own experiences, then it must be true. This, too, has great value, yet it doesn't appear to give sufficient **proof** that something is true.

"Some say it doesn't make any difference if something feels right or if it is reasonable. They might say, 'If it was good enough for my parents, or my people, or my country, or my religion, then it's good enough for me.'"

"Like that old gospel song, 'give me that old time religion . . . '" I began to sing.

"Yes, that's it," Rose laughed. She paused for a moment. "Many people consider reliance on tradition to be sufficient for determining truth. They will believe something that has been believed and perpetuated for generations and never question its validity. We discussed this earlier today. Needless to say, this criterion for determining truth has numerous problems and if you are paying attention and are observant you will notice how easily it can retard social progress and unity.

"Another criterion for determining truth is to accept without question what religious, political, or governmental representatives say. People often believe and follow without question whatever they are told by those in positions of authority. For obvious reasons, this criterion for determining truth is inadequate by itself. Now, experts and those in authority are extremely valuable to us, but to rely on them solely, without clear understanding, would make us like puppets. We would be surrendering our free will to the dictates of others. The vulnerability of this approach to truth is also evident.

"I want to propose to you that none of these methods is sufficient by itself, but what if one were to use them collectively in determining truth? Would that be wise? What if someone presented you with a possible truth, and you evaluated it rationally and intellectually, and it seemed reasonable? What if you weighed it against your experience in the world? What if you were able to evaluate it with the collective experiences of fifty or so other people, and everyone found it consistent with their collective experiences? Then what if it were presented to experts in the field, and they agreed to its validity? You also determined it 'felt right' after assessing your 'gut' feelings. Would you now say that it is true?" She looked at me for a response.

"Sounds good to me," I said half-heartedly. "It also sounds like a lot of work!"

"Yes, it does," she agreed. "But is this proof?" She waited for my answer.

"Well, no, I guess not **real** proof. It depends on what we are talking about here. If there is no proof, I guess it is only a good theory."

"Yes!" she said emphatically. "It might be a great theory! It might even have a high probability of being accurate. We don't know for sure. So, how do we prove something?" she asked. "Well, that's the role of science! Science is essentially the study of phenomena of the natural world. Through the process of experimenting, and testing causes and effects, science can determine if theories are true. Therefore, one of the best means we have for determining truth is to weigh everything against the best science currently available—I mean, what else do we have?" She stared at me with a little grin on her face.

"Nothing I can think of," I replied.

"Grayson, I'm suggesting that the human intellect is one of the fruits of the human soul, and that the greatest expression of that intellect is science. I suggest that true science is the apex of human understanding. It allows us to merge intuition, inspiration, tradition, reason, and experience to arrive at provable conclusions and real truths. It is the means by which the human beings have escaped the bonds of ignorance and arisen to demonstrate their ability to be supernatural spiritual beings."

I snapped my head around to look at Rose, as though to question her statement.

"Yes, supernatural," she repeated. "Because we employ our intelligence through science, we are enabled to escape the bonds of nature and **rise above** the constrictions imposed on other creatures, which makes the human beings truly supernatural.

"Let's look at the life of the human beings consequential to the development of science. We have gone from cave dwelling to living in skyscrapers. We progressed from daily foraging for food to growing, producing, and delivering foods. The development of farming has changed from subsistence to abundance. We moved from face-to-face conversations to communicating long distances instantly from telegraph, to telephone, to the World Wide Web. From walking as a form of travel, we now transport ourselves at hundreds of miles per hour in the air and nearly as fast on land. We built space crafts, left Earth's atmosphere, traveled to the moon, built an international space station, and sent one space craft beyond our own solar system. We explored the depths of the ocean around the planet. We penetrated the surface of the earth to extract useful resources. We developed medical science from bloodletting to antibiotics, prosthetic limbs, heart transplants, and even brain surgery, giving us the opportunity to live fuller lives with less disease and pain. And now, we have artificial intelligence and 3D printers. Yes, science gives us supernatural powers! It provides us with the potential to express our inherent capacities as human beings to understand, channel, and control nature. We are empowered to rise above that which is purely natural and change things to our own advantage and to the benefit of other creatures on the planet.

"Clearly, science is among the greatest gifts bestowed solely upon the human beings by the one true God. Without it we would be like all the other creatures, totally subject to the dictates of nature. Our capacity for science is one of the evidences of our being created in the image of God. Science is our servant and a bringer of joy to our lives. It moves us forward, sweeping away ignorance, useless and damaging false beliefs, and worthless superstitions. It can serve our best interests, and the best interests of all creatures. The human beings would do well to consciously, faithfully, and joyfully adopt it. May it be so!"

She sat very still and quiet for a moment, and then suddenly raised her hands as though she had found something. "Here is a direct quote from the Bahá'í writings," she said, measuring out her words precisely:

'*The virtues of humanity are many, but science is the most noble of them all.*'"[29]

She looked at me with a smile and continued with another verse:

"'*It is a bestowal of God; it is not material; it is divine. Science is an effulgence of the Sun of Reality, the power of investigating and discovering the verities of the universe, the means by which man finds a pathway to God. Through intellectual and intelligent inquiry science is the discoverer of all things.*'"[30]

Rose held her fingers contemplatively against her cheek. "So, can we say that science is the best means for evaluating truth?" She gave me a quick, smiling glance, and then answered her own question. "Perhaps, but let's consider. What science discovered one hundred years ago is sometimes disproven today, as scientific methods and equipment have developed and improved significantly over time. Therefore, I believe it is safe to say that truth, even scientifically proven truth, is **relative**. Relative, that is, to time and other associated variables, and relative to everything that affects the assessment of a given theory or idea. Even scientific proof is not absolute proof, but a relative truth.

"Take for example, the characteristics of water. Early people knew that water always ran downhill. It was a truth, I am sure, they could all agree upon. However, it was later determined that water could and would run uphill, against gravity, if in a vacuum. That's what happens when you remove air from a straw; the water moves up and takes the place of the air. So the new truth was that water runs downhill and sometimes uphill when the conditions are right. The truths about water and how it behaves were discovered over time by scientific means, and the truths that developed about the behavior of water were relative to the scientific understanding at the time.

"Probably one of the better understandings one can have as a human being is to know that all proposed truth is relative—relative to the time, conditions, and variables involved in determining anything. So, to accept current scientific conclusions is probably the **very best** we can do in determining truth at any given moment. And to do so collectively invites unity among the human beings, which, as I have already shared with you, is both the means and the ends in the attainment of our individual and collective spiritual purpose."

Rose paused for a minute and sat perfectly still, gazing out the side-window. "We might conclude at this point," she said slowly, choosing her words carefully, "that intuition, tradition, reasoning, logic, and reliance on experts are all valuable, but still limited criteria for determining truth, with science being the culmination of them all. Furthermore, I think it's fair to say we can conclude that all truth is relative."

Before I even had a chance to assess what she had said, Rose was off running with another thought. "Now, what about religion?" she asked. "What about the role of religion in determining truth? I have already explained to you that the revelation of God to the people—that is, the words inspired by God through the manifestations—is the truth given to us by the Creator of all things. Remember me saying that the revelation of God helps us interpret our experiences in this world so we know what is true? And how science tells us how something works or occurs, but not why? The revelation of God tells us our purpose as human beings, which is something science cannot do. The manifestations teach us how to behave to fulfill our purpose; science cannot do that either. True religion tells us about our reality as spiritual beings, again something science cannot do. I believe, the best criteria we have for determining truth, therefore, is to accept the best science has to offer, balanced and harmonized with the loving guidance given to us by God through his most recent manifestation, Bahá'u'lláh! Consequently, for something to be considered true, it must be consistent and harmonious with both modern science **and** true religion. This is one of the spiritual teachings emphasized by Bahá'u'lláh for modern man. He teaches us to abolish ignorance, superstition, and worn-out traditions and beliefs, and calls us to a higher, more mature, evolved, and developed approach to life. In this day, the religion of God confirms science, and science confirms true religion. Bahá'u'lláh urges us all to adopt this approach joyfully. Here is a quotation from the Bahá'í sacred writings pertaining to this principle:

' . . . *religion must conform to reason and be in accord with the conclusions of science. For religion, reason, and science are realities; therefore, these three, being realities, must conform and be reconciled. A question or principle that is religious in its nature must be sanctioned by science. Science must declare it to be valid, and reason must confirm it in order that it may inspire confidence. If religious teaching, however, be at variance with science and reason, it is unquestionably superstition. The Lord of mankind has bestowed upon us the faculty of reason whereby we may discern the realities of things. How then can man rightfully accept any proposition that is not in conformity with the processes of reason and the principles of science? Assuredly such a course cannot inspire man with confidence and real belief.*'[31]

"Further to the subject," she continued, "I would like to point out that science needs to be balanced with spirituality to be meaningful and useful to our purpose as human beings. The use of scientific discoveries without spiritual guidance can result in the development and use of dangerous technologies and inventions that are harmful to humans and other living creatures on the planet. Some that come to mind include the use of nuclear and biological weapons, or technologies that poison instead of nourish, or destroy instead of create. Further to the subject are social sciences that mislead instead of guide, or enslave instead of liberate. Our modern world is out of balance. Right now it is heavily weighted toward science and technology that supports a materialistic society, which is considerably out of touch with its spiritual purpose. This imbalance has seriously damaging effects on society. The unabated development of some modern technologies without the influence of true spirituality is causing great distress in the world. The need for science to be harmonious with the loving spirituality of true religion should be clear to all.

"The influence of true spirituality and religion on science can help the materialistic world with all its excesses change into something more meaningful, useful, and consistent with our true purpose. While the application of science in understanding religious concepts and truths can help leave behind any worthless, meaningless, or immature religious beliefs, traditions, rituals, and superstitions that stifle spiritual development.

"The cleansing of religion with the application of pure science and the sanctification of science through the spiritual influence of the words of the manifestation of God is bringing about a complete transformation to society. This road to our destiny may be difficult, unpredictable, and painful at times, but the outcomes are hopeful and glorious. Whew!" she resounded. "I hope that came out well."

She looked at me and started to laugh. We were both laughing at our intense seriousness. We were a funny couple. Soon we settled down, riding in silence for some time again. I was thinking about what she had said.

"Rose, are you saying that going with your gut, your intuition or inspiration, isn't necessarily good?" I looked at her for feedback. She didn't respond. "And . . . what was it? Our collective experience . . . and tradition . . . and . . . oh yeah, reasoning. Did you say that none of these were sufficient or useful?" I asked.

"Of course they are useful, and they all have validity in determining truth," she replied. But true science, when balanced with the Word of God, **includes** and **envelops** those criteria you just mentioned. Intuition, reasoning, and tradition are extremely vulnerable to error when relied upon exclusively. So it is best to train your mind with good science and your heart with the loving word of God. Then your intuition, your reasoning, and your interpretation of tradition will find harmony and peace within. You will then have the best possible criteria for making decisions in your life that are harmonious with your true purpose as a human being.

"Remember, the spiritual principles and truths I am sharing with you from Bahá'u'lláh are specific to our time in history. If you think about it for a minute, you can easily understand why it was impossible for science and religion to be considered complementary in the past. One reason is that science has been in development for only a short time in the world. Another reason is that religion has historically held great power and influence over the multitudes. And because religion was often steeped in superstition and tradition, it made it nearly impossible to implement good science. However, the time has now come for balance in our material and spiritual development. The time has come to apply the spiritual principle of harmony between science and religion consciously and confidently in all human endeavors.

"You asked before about evolution and creationism," Rose continued. "You wanted to know which was true. Let me use this subject to exemplify the value of implementing the principle of harmony between science and religion in exploring truth.

"Now Grayson, I have given speeches on this subject several times in the past, so I think I'll just talk through it like I usually do. Is that okay with you?"

"Sure," I remarked, "whatever you want, Rose." She paused a few minutes before beginning her talk on evolution.

"The controversy between religious creationist and scientific evolutionists is an unnecessary contention created by two groups of people whose beliefs are in opposition to one another and who feel they have something significant to lose by looking at any other possible explanation of truth other than the one they have adopted," Rose began. "For the creationists, they feel their faith would be jeopardized if they considered anything other than that which has been taught to them by their religious authorities. Many cling to their beliefs vehemently, in spite of all the rational and scientific evidence that challenges those beliefs.

"The evolutionists feel all would be lost that is conducive to sound reasoning, science, and liberation from superstitions if they were to consider the possibility of a God and a six-day creation as presented to them by the creationist theory. Both groups cling to their own models of reality, their preferred ways of thinking, their own 'inner map of the world,' which has been imposed upon them by the dictates of their faith or their profession. The Bahá'í sacred writings give great insight into this divisive issue and provide a welcome understanding of our creation and its evolutionary nature that neither detracts from one's faith in God nor conflicts with sound scientific evidence."

Rose looked at me and popped up an eyebrow, as if to ask if I was on board with what she was thinking. I quickly gave her a slight nod and turned back to my driving.

"Let's look at the creationist's view," Rose went on. The Judeo-Christian teachings suggest that if the biblical story of creation is taken **literally**, human beings appeared on earth suddenly, approximately 6,000 years ago, on a certain day, and in the exact same form as we are today. Furthermore, they believe that humans were created in the image of God. When interpreted literally, this suggests that the physical body of humans is like that of the Creator. It is true that some religious people believe in the possibility that scripture can be understood symbolically, which would instead mean that the six-day creation story **explains** an evolutionary process. For example, the six days **could have** stood for six very long periods of time, or the six days could represent how we have gone through a series of processes to arrive at our current development. But this is not what the creationists believe.

"Now, let's consider the theory of evolution. Scientists say, based on scientific evidence, that humans went through an evolutionary process to reach their current stage of development. They say that sometime during the early formation of the earth, a single life-form came about. Others suggest that a diversity of life forms originated.

Whatever first developed, or however it occurred, life began to differentiate, depending upon varying environmental influences and conditions. Over a very long period of time, as the various life-forms continued to develop and change, humans came about, and following the same process, matured to the state and condition we observe today. Now remember, this is a **theory** based on an interpretation of scientific findings. Science has proven that creatures evolve over time, but the entire process of our beginning and evolution is still obscure and therefore remains in the form of a theory. Theories, as you recall, are reasonable attempts to explain something based on a known set of facts.

"Current science proposes that if we were able to follow our ancestry back, we would find that humans, along with primates like chimpanzees, orangutans, and gorillas, all descended from a common pre-human, pre-primate type creature that carried the potential for this differentiation and development. Thus, to some scientists, this suggests that humans are merely a more highly evolved primate than the others just mentioned. The concern in the religious community is that this view detracts the supremacy of humans from the other animals and denies the supreme nature of God as well. This idea is unacceptable to the religious community.

"Do you see the problem?" Rose asked. "One of the two opposing views that spark the debate is a conclusion by the scientific community that humans and other primates evolved from a common ancestor, or a pre-human, pre-ape-like creature, and therefore the humans are just a highly evolved primate. The other view, held by many in the religious community, is that God literally, suddenly and completely, created the universe and all its components, including humans, approximately six thousand years ago in a six-day period.

"Let's consider the possibility of evolution for a moment. It is evident to most people, when tracing the origin of human beings back through an evolutionary process, at some point there **had to be** a common ancestor. It might even be necessary to go all the way back to some kind of an agreed upon beginning, like a big-bang moment or a specific time that the creation of the universe began in some other fashion. The point here is not to decide **how** it all started, but to agree there was a beginning that was common for all life. All life appears to have a common beginning, which, in reality, means we have a common ancestry. The point of contention comes in, as I have already noted, when considering how and when human beings appeared upon the planet and what their relationship was to other creatures.

"I am suggesting, Grayson, that there is a way to reconcile these two opposing views that is harmonious with both science and religion. What I would like to propose neither detracts from the superior station of humankind nor negates the sovereign station of God. Neither does it disagree with scientific evidence when evaluated objectively and free from the influence of the secular scientific theories that attempt to explain the evidence.

"The manifestation of God, Bahá'u'lláh, affirms the sovereignty of the Creator and tells us that the creation has always existed and that it is an **ongoing** process that has neither beginning nor end, as is reflected in the nature of the Creator. God, by virtue of his eternal nature, has no creator and had no beginning. Therefore, God has always been creating, and therefore, there has always been a creation."

"Wow, that's profound!" I exclaimed as I tried to absorb the reality of what she was saying.

"The creation of our planet was an evolutionary process," Rose continued, "which has taken an unfathomable amount of time to reach its current stage. In the development of the earth, conditions were right for the formation of life. We might say it was 'programmed' into its development at the time of its creation by its all-wise Creator. When God created our universe with its principles and laws of operation, it was inherent in its evolutionary nature that it would bring forth a multitude of life forms, one of which would develop into human beings. It is stated in the Bahá'í writings that the human being did not start out in its present form, but evolved from a form containing the potential to evolve to its current state, not unlike the embryonic development in the womb. From conception, it is merely a single-celled organism containing the potential to grow into a fully developed human being. Eventually, an embryo goes through a process where it takes on a form resembling a small, worm-like creature, then to something that looks like a seahorse, and eventually to a recognizable human fetal form.

"I believe there is a harmonious explanation of creation and evolution that is consistent with both science and religion. We could say that the Creator, or creative Force we refer to as God, set in motion the universe wherein we exist. I already proposed to you evidences of a creator, and I think if the scientific community considers it thoughtfully, indifferent to the superstitions proposed by some creationist, they would most likely be able to agree on the probability disclosed by the evidence. We should be able to agree as well that the nature of our evolution is not fully understood, but that we did evolve and change over time. We could say that the religious story of creation is true as well if we interpret it **symbolically** and not literally. This is to say that God, or the creative Force behind all things, did not create the human beings **physically** in his image, but instead created us spiritually in his image, giving us the potential, through our intellect, to reflect multiple spiritual, God-like traits. Traits like intelligence, love, kindness, truthfulness, generosity, mercy, forgiveness, and numerous others associated with God. Considered in this light, it's easier to realize the supremacy of the human beings over the animals. Animals were created with no capacity to intentionally or consciously develop spiritual qualities. Thus, humans were created in the spiritual image of God and have physically and spiritually evolved over time.

"What I am proposing is that we accept what science has discovered with a slightly different interpretation of the scientific data and an alternative interpretation of religious scripture that conforms to reason and science. When religious doctrine and scientific facts are interpreted less dogmatically and less competitively, they can find this common ground of truth. True science and true religion are like two wings of the bird of truth. The flight of truth is not possible with one wing. Both are complementary and necessary to the other. In the Bahá'í writings we find,

'*God made religion and science to be the measure, as it were, of our understanding. Take heed that you neglect not such a wonderful power. Weigh all things in this balance.*'[32]

"So for the teachings and concepts of religion to be true and free from superstition, they must be harmonious with science and reality, and for science to be protected from materialistic and unethical practices, it should conform to the spiritual wisdom of true religion. This is another spiritual principle revealed by Bahá'u'lláh to assist the human beings in their progression toward love, unity, peace, and security."

She was finished. I knew so because she ended with a big sigh and a nod of her head, as though to say: *Done!* She sat quietly looking out the window for quite some time. I, too, was quiet. What was I to say? I had no arguments. For some reason, it just felt like she had summed up what I had always wanted to believe but didn't know how to express. It was just a common sense, matter-of-fact solution to an age-old social conflict. She brought it together with such sweetness, such completeness, and such . . . unity! Yeah, that was it!

"It's a unity thing, isn't it?" I said finally, looking over at Rose. She just turned to me and smiled, not just a regular smile, but a smile of contentment and confirmation that I had, indeed, begun to understand.

We were entering a town of about 10,000 people called Quesnel. Since the trailer was pretty well damaged, and we were all tired, we decided to stay in a motel. Traffic was heavy, so we parked in a large open lot while T.J. and Alene went to find us a place to stay. After checking in at our motel and taking a little break, Franklin, Annie, Sonia, and I decided to walk across the bridge that spanned the Fraser River and have our dinner at the renowned Heritage House Restaurant. T.J., Alene, and Rose drove to the restaurant in the car. We discovered the restaurant was extremely crowded. As soon as it became clear we were not going to be served for quite some time, we decided to eat elsewhere. We found a place nearby called the River-Rock Pub and Restaurant. It had been a long, rainy, testing day, and we were all weary from travel. We sat for quite some time after dinner, talking and relaxing.

After a short walk back to the motel and a shower, I was nearly asleep before hitting the pillow.

DAY SEVEN

SPIRITUAL TRUTHS

"**D**id you feel that earthquake last night?" Franklin asked, as I walked into the eatery for breakfast. I hadn't felt anything, so I told him he was dreaming.

"No, he wasn't!" Alene exclaimed. "I felt it, too." Others around the table were agreeing with her, so I guessed I was just too dead to the world to have felt it. Anyway, there had been an earthquake and I missed it, but I didn't care. We had experienced several each year in Anchorage, so they weren't a big deal to me anymore. The group ate breakfast rather quickly, and we all proceeded to our respective vehicles. We had the routine down now and everyone was anxious to cover some ground.

I was in a strange mood. I get that way periodically. I didn't want to be around people; I didn't have much to say, and I didn't want to talk. When I am feeling that way, I prefer to have something to focus on. Driving would be the ideal activity for the day.

I had become accustomed to Rose having something prepared to talk about when I didn't have any questions—at least that's the way it seemed to me. There were endless questions that would pop into my mind at various times, but I was beginning to find more pleasure in anticipation of what she had to say next than in getting my questions answered. Besides, if I waited, it seemed she would somehow get around to answering them whether I asked them or not. So today I just waited for her to start, not really caring much either way.

"Today, I want to talk about the importance and value of justice." Rose looked at me as I took a quick retracted posture.

"Justice, huh?" I pretended to understand, but really I was instantly confused. I immediately had feelings of apprehension and fear, and wondered how justice fit the spiritual path we were exploring.

"I hope I can express in a meaningful way how considerably important and essential justice is for unity, tranquility, and harmony among the human beings. It, too, is one of the spiritual principles emphasized by Bahá'u'lláh to help us in our modern times.

"First, let's get a clear understanding as to what justice is. Let's consider justice as having two realms of expression. The first is in the personal behavior of individuals one to another. The second is in the decisions and actions of human institutions—like the institution of marriage, the educational institutions, or those pertaining to governments. So let's begin by considering justice as it pertains to the thoughts, behavior, and actions of individuals toward one another. One of the general definitions of justice means to conform one's behavior to what is right, good, true, and fair." She paused for a second.

"Well, that's a big order right there," I remarked.

"It gets bigger," she countered. "Justice also means to conform to what is right, good, true, and fair as indicated by the Word of God." Rose saw the look of confusion on my face. "Yes! That's how justice was understood and defined in the dictionaries prior to this century. However, over the last fifty years or so, people have slowly discontinued using spiritual connotations in their conversations and writing, resulting in the gradual removal of such definitions from modern dictionaries. So modern definitions of justice do not define it the way I just did.

"To understand the spiritual principle of justice given to us by Bahá'u'lláh, we need to consider justice as it was defined a century or more ago. In doing so, we could then say that the principle of spiritual guidance emphasized for this time in human history is that it is in our best interest, and in the best interest of all human beings, to strive to conform our thinking, decisions, and actions to what is just as explained by the manifestations of God. Bahá'u'lláh places such high importance on this principle of justice that he called it *'the best beloved of all things.'*[33]

"Do you have any questions about what I am saying so far?" she asked.

"No, I guess not," I replied. "It's just a little unusual for me to think of justice that way. I usually think of justice as some kind of punishment or harsh enforcement of rules or laws. So I guess that means if I try to be fair in all my dealings with others, and try to do what was right and good, and always seek out the truth of matters, then I would be acting with justice? Is that what you're saying?"

"Yes! That's it precisely, Grayson," she confirmed.

Rose thought for a moment. "Another definition of justice means to render what is due to others, which includes that which pertains to reward and punishment. But the sacred writings of Bahá'u'lláh make it clear it is not for individuals to punish others in their personal relationships with one another. That expression of justice is for social institutions. In our personal relationships with people we are to forgive them, and, as Jesus taught, to turn the other cheek. We manifest justice to others by conforming our behavior to true spirituality and by forgiving others for their immature behaviors. Does that make sense to you?"

I nodded without comment.

"I want this to be really clear to you so you can make sure it is understandable in our book because I don't want people to think the principle of justice emphasized by Bahá'u'lláh gives anyone the right to enact punishment on others in any way. It does not! That's the role of social and governing institutions that make decisions and enforce them for the good of us all."

We were silent for a time.

"What if, Rose," I began, "What if I had a neighbor who was selling illegal amphetamines to children? Should I just forgive him?"

Without even a pause, she answered: "You would personally

forgive him, in that you would not personally attempt to punish him for his behavior. You have no right to do that. Instead, you would be obligated, out of righteousness, goodness, truth, and fairness, to report his behavior to the proper authorities so that the appropriate institution could deal with his illegal behavior justly. This is another way individuals can help manifest justice in the world.

"Now, remember I said there were two expressions of justice, one for individuals and one for institutions. The individual conforms his behavior to what is just, whereas institutions render justice by additionally allocating reward and punishment according to what is earned or due. If there is going to be unity and tranquility in the world, then institutions must make this one of their highest priorities. For justice to be rendered properly, institutions cannot decide or act with excessive leniency. On the other hand, they cannot use excessive force or act with tyranny either. Justice is that middle place, that place of moderation that best urges, educates, and trains perpetrators of wrong toward maturity, and proportionally rewards desirable behaviors.

"Take, for example, the institution of marriage. Let's say two parents are lenient and forgiving of everything their children do. The outcome is usually unruly, spoiled, selfish children. This is not good for the children, for the parents, or for society. Now let's say the parents are excessive in punishing their children for every little thing they do wrong. This is not just either, but abuse. If undue force is used as the hand of justice to control children, it will result in rebellious, angry, and violent young adults. This is what happened to your generation."

I frowned at Rose, puzzled by her comment.

"During the first six decades of the twentieth century, institutions were extremely authoritarian in nature. Many of their executors were aggressive in their demeanor—verbally, physically, and horrifyingly, even sexually abusive. The outcome was a generation of rebellion. Your generation rebelled against nearly everything, but most didn't know why. I suggest it was because of the authoritarian and unjust styles of institutional leadership. These styles existed in religion, education, parenting, law enforcement, and government, prompting that whole sixties counter-culture movement. But enough of that."

I had noticed whenever Rose said "enough of that," she was touching on something that aroused her anger. I wondered if I could develop the same kind of self-control to divert negative thinking. I barely had time to pursue that thought before she continued speaking.

"So think how important justice is in the world. Look around you at the problems you witness and observe how the consistent implementation of justice would help improve so many social problems and bring greater peace to our society. Consider also how many of the other principles I am sharing with you are expressions of justice. Like the need to bring equity to our economic condition. That is, the institutions involved need to make fair and just decisions that would give relief and comfort to the poor while also relieving the rich of the spiritual burden of managing wealth that can divert them from their true purpose. True justice requires equity and fairness. Fairness indicates that all should have a realistic share of the abundant wealth that exists on the planet while participating in the work required to create and sustain that wealth. It is the means to ensure that each receives what he has earned and what he is due, according to his efforts and contributions.

"Three other principles I shared with you, the elimination of prejudice, blind imitation, and superstition, are also expressions of justice, in that they are ways we can conform to righteousness. The equality of men and women is justice. Equal rights for all is justice. The elimination of torture and tyranny is justice. The avoidance of extreme leniency is justice. Equitable, affordable, and accessible education and healthcare for all is right, fair, and just. To personally investigate all things, free of traditional and social pressures, is justice." She paused; she was thinking intently.

"Let me quote directly from Bahá'u'lláh. He said,
'*The purpose of justice is the appearance of unity among men.*'"[34]
She looked over at me, smiling. "So you see, it comes back to unity again. As I said before, all things that are right, fair, and just in

this age promote conditions of peace, love, and harmony among the human beings. If you consider justice fairly, I think you will see how harmoniously and effectively it contributes to the unity of mankind.

Rose paused and sat very still, measuring out her next words. "One might consider the golden rule the most perfect justice in the treatment of individuals toward one another. To do unto others as you would have done unto yourself. To do good—to be understanding and forgiving—this is the spiritual way.

"There is a metaphor in the Bahá'í writings that helps us understand how to treat one another. It goes like this:

'If others hurl their darts against you, offer them milk and honey in return; if they poison your lives, sweeten their souls; if they injure you, teach them how to be comforted; if they inflict a wound upon you, be a balm to their sores; if they sting you, hold to their lips a refreshing cup.'[35]

"This is a wonderful expression of how kind and loving we should try to be to one another as spiritual beings."

"So, if a man were to come into the restaurant at lunch to rob it, should I just forgive him and let him do that?" I asked.

"I don't think so," answered Rose, "because that is not an offense just against you. It's an offense against everyone in the restaurant and the restaurant owner. You and I would have the obligation to protect the owner and everyone else in the restaurant from that offender the best we could. We protect and defend others, as this is just, and we protect or defend ourselves from perpetrators of violence or any other kind of aggression. The important thing to remember is we should not personally enact punishment on perpetrators. That's for institutions. If we were to do so personally, we would be acting with vengeance and vigilantism, and that's not justice. Am I being clear on the difference?"

"Yes, you are," I assured her.

We rode for a while without talking. My mind was spinning again. New information, new thoughts, trying to integrate them into what I had experienced in my life. What I knew, or thought I knew, was shifting.

"Institutional justice isn't only about reward and punishment,"

Rose asserted. "It's about rendering what is right, good, true, and fair which **might** include punishment or reward. It is also about teaching, training, educating, guiding, and nurturing individual offenders toward personal, social, and spiritual maturity. True justice helps people overcome their immature ways by providing them with appropriate assistance that might change their behavior for the better. Punishment and reward can evoke just about any desired behavior temporarily, but for it to be lasting, conscious, and sincere, it must be combined with true education and training. That requires the allocation of resources necessary for it to come about. This might be considered an expression of **divine** justice because out of love it endeavors to facilitate the individual soul toward its true spiritual purpose.

"For example, let's say a person is a chronic thief—a behavior deplored in all societies. What would be just for a person who has, let's say, scammed thousands of people out of millions of dollars? Probably imprisonment—that might be just. Restitution? Paying back what was stolen? That might be just. But what is **divine** justice in this case? How do we help contribute to the mental or spiritual recovery of persons who error so grievously? Maybe they could be required to interview a hundred people who have been victims of such a crime, so as to hear their stories of loss and the pain they suffered as a result. Maybe they could be involved in educational workshops that help them develop a heartfelt consciousness of the consequent pain and suffering their actions imposed on others. Perhaps they could be trained to such a degree that their rehabilitation allows them to become involved in aiding others to overcome their tendency to thievery. Maybe then, the goal of justice is spiritual rehabilitation in addition to due punishment. Wouldn't this be better than punishment alone?" She paused for a moment. "Or leniency! Neither has demonstrated the ability to change behavior effectively in a conscious and lasting manner.

"So you see, justice is more than simple punishment and reward. It's the avoidance of the extremes of forgiveness and leniency on the one hand and of tyranny and torture on the other. It's the middle way of moderation. It's about training, educating, and guiding souls to fulfill their true spiritual purpose. It's about helping them learn to love, to mature, and to progress as a human being—to bring about a condition of peace, love, and harmony in human relationships—a true heartfelt unity. This is the purpose and value of justice. You can understand why it is critically important to everything we do on the planet. May it reign with intention," she pleaded, flinging her arms open as though to embrace the whole world.

After a short silence, Rose added, "Sometimes, though, people are so damaged and the current methods of rehabilitation are so inadequate, the implementation of justice requires harsher measures." She looked at me gravely. I nodded in sad agreement.

I saw T.J.'s brake lights come on up ahead; his blinkers signaled a turn into a rest stop. It was time for a restroom break already. *Must be the abundance of morning coffee*, I thought. Alene came on the CB announcing the break. I shifted down my big diesel truck and pulled into a small rest area with a view of the Rocky Mountains of British Columbia. It was a sunny, beautiful day. I had seen some farmland and forests with trees similar to those in Oregon. I could tell we were getting closer to home, and the familiarity felt good. After a short break and checking our vehicles for safety purposes, we climbed aboard and were off again.

"I've been thinking," I prodded gingerly, to see if Rose was interested.

"What's on your mind?" she asked seriously.

"Well, I've been listening to you for several days now, and I have to say, I really like everything you have shared. It makes sense to me, and it all feels good." I paused for a moment, searching for words.

"Ex . . . cept . . . ?" she urged me on.

"Well," I glanced away so she couldn't see my face. "Except this. Why do we need **organized** religion? I mean, can't we just adopt these ideas, and then wouldn't we have a better world? Religion can be so confining, so . . . controlling, so . . . unnecessary! Isn't just living these ideals enough without having to be part of an organized religion? Haven't we evolved sufficiently to do without it? Many people think religion is archaic and unnecessary, especially since there has been so much damage in the world in the name of religion. And there is so much childlike pretense, and as you said, superstition."

Rose listened without moving a muscle. She just stared straight out the front of the truck—expressionless.

"You know," I continued, "this is what many people think nowadays. At times I don't feel much different, given my experiences and what I know about organized religion in history. Aren't we modern enough to solve the problems of the world without structured religion?" I guess I thought I had made my point because I became silent. I figured since Rose wasn't saying anything either, she must have understood my concern. The feeling in the cab of the truck was solemn. It felt like maybe I had taken everything she had shared and completely discounted it. I felt bad, but I knew I had to say it because it was how so many people felt, and I knew it. I hoped she wasn't upset with me. "I'm sorry," I said finally, "it just came out."

"No, this is good, Grayson," she said, excitement shining in her face. "This is good. I have been wondering how to address this issue, and now you have given me the opportunity. I agree with most of what you said. Many people **do** feel this way, and you can't blame them, given their experiences and their understanding of religious history."

She paused, formulating her words. "Why do we need organized religion?" she said, repeating my question. "First of all, let's remember that nothing good created in society is sustainable without order and organization. There is no debate on this. It's the same with the development of spiritual characteristics and virtues. It takes motivation, inspiration, education, training, skill building, and systematic organization. A review of social studies clearly bears this out. So **organization** isn't the problem. In fact, it's a must! It's the **way** things are organized that causes concern.

"Something else contributing to the aversion of organized religion is that most people's knowledge of religious history is negative. History, as it is generally taught, is primarily a politically slanted record of expansion, conflict, and conquest, with far less attention given to social life. It was typically recorded by people who noted the more sensational and negative outcomes of religion because its positive influences were more difficult to assess and far less interesting to record. So the perspective modern human beings have about the historical influence of religion on society is seriously distorted by these limiting factors. Perhaps we could expand on what we have read or been told by additionally taking a look at the beneficial influence religion has had on humanity.

"As you know, all people have the capacity to do good or to do things that are not so good. The teachings of Bahá'u'lláh tell us that all the goodness in the world of humanity comes from the influence of the manifestations of God and their subsequent religion."

I looked at her with skepticism.

"Now, hear me out, Grayson. This is another spiritual teaching from the manifestation of God for our time. He says:

' . . . the still greater task of converting satanic strength into heavenly power is one that We have been empowered to accomplish . . . The Word of God, alone, can claim the distinction of being endowed with the capacity required for so great and far-reaching a change.'"[36]

"But I know people who have nothing to do with religion," I argued, "who are good, honest, spiritual people—in fact, great people!"

"Yes, I do, too, Grayson. But what I am suggesting to you is their goodness was influenced, either directly or indirectly, by someone who **did** have direct contact or experience with the sacred words of one of the manifestations. The positive influence of religion is like the ripples in a pond when it's raining. Each ripple affects another, then another, and so on. So it is with the human beings. The words of the manifestation of God inspire goodness in the heart of a believer, whose behavior is consequently changed for the better. That behavior influences others to do likewise, which affects others, and so on. The source of goodness in the world is the Word of God in the heart of man. It is like a seed of goodness that sprouts, blossoms, and then fruits more righteousness among the people. Pertaining to this

Bahá'u'lláh revealed these beautiful words:

'The Word of God is the king of words and its pervasive influence is incalculable. It hath ever dominated and will continue to dominate the realm of being. The Great Being saith: The Word is the master key for the whole world, inasmuch as through its potency the doors of the hearts of men, which in reality are the doors of heaven, are unlocked.'[37]

"The people you know who are good people may have had no **direct** involvement with religion, but no one is formed in isolation. In all likelihood, these good people were influenced by other good people who **did** have direct contact with religion. Contacts like parents, grandparents, teachers, coaches, friends and mentors. Also, keep in mind how they were affected by the culture and society around them that was permeated with religious influence.

"I am going to suggest to you that it is the decline in the spiritual influence of religion—that is, true religion—which is the cause of most problems in the world today! Yes, the social ills you observe today in the world are because the spiritual influence of the Word of God has been slowly diminishing. I am suggesting to you that the remedy for the ills that plague our society lies in the direct influence of the Word of God upon the hearts of the people."

I shook my head skeptically. I wasn't so sure.

"Put another way," Rose explained, "as the spirituality of religion declines in the world, social disorder increases everywhere, and in every way." She paused. "Did you get that?"

I nodded.

"True religion gives clarification of our reality and our purpose. True religion creates the opportunity for greater development of honesty, truthfulness, kindness, wisdom, generosity, trustworthiness, justice, and other desirable traits in the hearts of the human beings. True religion, through its social influence, leads to greater equality, prosperity, and freedom for all people. True religion, with its disciplines, laws, and ordinances, results in greater happiness, unity, harmony, and attraction among the people." She stopped and looked intently out the front window for a few moments. "I want to quote Bahá'u'lláh on this matter," she resumed. He wrote these very words,

'Should the lamp of religion be obscured, chaos and confusion will ensue, and the lights of fairness and justice, of tranquility and peace cease to shine.'[38]

"Well, I can't disagree with that," I remarked. "You keep using the term 'true religion.' So, what do you mean by that, exactly?"

"I am talking about religion that is as free as possible from authoritarian leadership; beliefs in things that are not true or real, hypocritical and pretentious behaviors, and meaningless ceremonies and rituals. Furthermore, I am talking specifically about religion based on the authentic words of the manifestations of God, even though identifying the authenticity of the exact words and teachings of the great prophets of the past is difficult. I'm also talking about a reasonable interpretation of those blessed words, and not those infiltrated with superstition. Moreover, I am talking about religion that nurtures the spirit of holiness with loving-kindness, the way the manifestations did.

"I hope I have made it clear to you that I believe the religions of the past are equally true, and that the essence of true religion still exists therein. Literal interpretation of their holy words and the subsequent introduction of superstitions have caused them sometimes to appear otherwise. The essence of their spiritual truths sometimes is obscured by the outward semblances of what they have become. Therefore, when I say 'true religion,' I'm talking about religion that is pure, unadulterated, and free of superstitious misinterpretations of its authentic holy text. Maybe I should be saying 'pure religion' instead of 'true religion.' Does that work better for you?"

"Either way works for me, now that I'm clear on what you mean," I assured her.

"Remember when I say to you that religion is the cause of all that is good in the world, I'm talking about religion in its purest form," Rose advised. "I'm talking about a more pure form of religion as it was in the early and more unencumbered days of Judaism, Christianity, Islam, Buddhism, and so on, when the focus was on the spirit of the teachings. I'm talking about those aspects of religion that are free from developed superstitions, blind imitations, and man-made forms and rituals. Remember, there is just one religion of God. What we perceive as different religions all are links in the chain of the same one true faith. Each one starts out pure and renews the same eternal truths of God. Each one has a springtime of exuberant awakening and renewal, a summertime of growth and development when great civil and social improvements are forthcoming, an autumn of harvest when each one brings forth the fruits of its influences on society, and each one has its winter, when it generally goes spiritually cold and dark. For the most part, the wintertime of religion is when it becomes superstitious and controlling, and loses its way. This signals the time for another manifestation of God to step forth in the world and start the renewal process of religion all over again. The goodness in the world is due to the lasting effect each religion has had on society. All the goodness in the world comes from the teachings of the manifestations of God and the subsequent religions that came about in response to those teachings. This is what I am inviting you to consider."

As Rose paused to take a drink from her water bottle, I carefully twisted the lid on my traveling coffee mug to take a sip. *Spiritual seasons*, I mused, *that's an interesting idea.*

Rose continued, "Each time religion declines, the people move away from the spiritual truths and behave in less desirable ways. This continues generation after generation until people eventually become more selfish, greedy, crude, crass, dishonest, untrustworthy, violent, and even barbaric. Haven't you recently observed people becoming more disrespectful of one another, more afraid, more anxious, more stressed, more prone toward substance abuse, more aggressive, and more suspicious of others? I ask you, do you witness chaos and confusion in today's society? Do you see how it has worsened even in your lifetime? To me, it has become glaringly obvious that the people have a hard time agreeing on anything because they have lost their bearings of what's right, good, and true."

She looked at me, waiting. I had nothing to say. We both knew it was true.

"When societies decline, Grayson, they usually degenerate one generation at a time until it becomes evident that a spiritual renewal is needed. Then the people begin to investigate everything in search of something that will help. I foresee our society soon deteriorating to such a point that people will start to investigate and search everywhere for truth and hope, including all the religions and their various sects. Some will put their hope in various governmental, political, or social movements, expecting a solution. Some might rely on science or technology for answers. Some might believe a prosperous economy will solve everything. But nothing will prove sufficient. Any of those remedies will give only temporary relief and result in false hopes. They will always end in dismay. Eventually, the human beings will seek out the wisdom from the latest manifestation of God, recognize the truth in his teachings, and a renewal of spiritual goodness will surge throughout the world. Purpose and hope will be restored; life will take on meaning; social institutions will be redesigned to fit modern times; political and business integrity will be established, and all potential for a better society will be forthcoming.

"My belief is that the decline of civilization, the chaos and confusion that people observe on a daily basis, is due to a decline in spirituality and true religion. I feel confident our hope lies with faith in God and in his guidance as given by his manifestation for our time, Bahá'u'lláh."

Rose paused and looked out the window for a spell. When she broke her silence, she said, "As you have observed, Grayson, much of the conflict in the world, both past and present, can be traced to organized religion, and this has prompted efforts to discard it. But as religion fades from society, as it has been doing for some time now, and chaos and confusion ensue, it will eventually prompt a renewed interest in spirituality and a collective search for true and meaningful religion. I hope this helps you understand the true value and necessity of religion in its pure and intended form. We need religion for the achievement of our personal purpose in life as well as for the improvement and future development of a divine civilization on the planet. Here is a direct quotation on the subject from the words of

Bahá'u'lláh:

'Religion is the greatest of all means for the establishment of order in the world and for the peaceful contentment of all that dwell therein.'[39]

"I hope that you will consider the true value and need for religion in the world, Grayson. Perhaps the aversion to organized religion can be recognized for what it truly is. There is a saying, 'Don't throw the baby out with the bath water.' It applies to organized religion, too. If we separate out the undesirable aspects of religion and understand them for what they are, then we can recognize religion's true value for what it is. This is something that requires open-minded investigation and a mature approach to what is real and true."

We were silent again. I could tell there was more coming, because Rose was tense.

"Let me say this," she continued. "Religion—that is, true religion, pure religion, true spirituality—creates an awareness and a consciousness in the human heart of the invariable presence of God in one's life. One develops an appreciation, a fondness, a respect, and a love for that Presence, and a desire to please it. That's the way love works. One becomes fully aware of God's ever-present bounty, guidance, protection, grace, and loving kindness. Consequently, our heart becomes motivated out of a deep respect and love for God, which helps us be better people. Furthermore, one develops an awareness of the consequences of one's actions that begins to move us away from those things that cause the heart pain, regret, and disappointment, toward those things that bring joy, happiness, harmony, peace, love, and unity. It's the awareness of the ever-present God that allows one to change immature behaviors to those more desirable and spiritually attuned. You eventually learn, at least as you get older, there are consequences to every choice. God has wrapped natural consequences into the ways of the universe! They will naturally visit upon us, either in this life or in the life to come. The Hindus and Buddhists have a term for this. They call it karma.

"Think of the behavior of an immature two-year-old child. You can tell the child not to do something, like, don't take a cookie off the table, and yet they will go around behind the table and try to sneak it. They sneak because they know there will be consequences if they are seen or caught, yet really believe if no one sees, they can get away with it. They do this because they have no consciousness of the ever-present God. So we train and educate children with kindness, love, and truth, about his loving presence. Over time they begin to develop a respect, a love, a knowledge of their true self and their purpose and reality in the universe. Consequently, they begin to behave in ways that are far more desirable than if left to their own lower nature, which, if left untrained, will lead to unruly, uncouth, disrespectful, crass, selfish, and even violent behaviors. I am suggesting to you that the development of the ever-presence of God in the consciousness of the human being is created and nurtured by religion only. Bahá'u'lláh says this:

'*Every good thing is of God, and every evil thing is from yourselves.*'[40]

Rose sat thoughtfully for a moment, looking out the window at a hawk making lazy circles in the sky. She resumed, "The problems facing us individually, and those confounding societies around the world, cannot be solved solely by better government, economic prosperity, the application of good science, or by any other means unless there is a spiritual reformation in the hearts of the human beings. All these institutions are important and necessary and deserve serious attention. However, if social institutions are comprised of people whose spiritual, moral, or ethical integrity is lacking or absent, then those institutions cannot serve the needs of the people well. But when the hearts of the people are influenced with true spirituality, human relationships mature and provide opportunities for all aspects of society to function properly. Then everything is better. This transformation of hearts to true spirituality comes from a spiritual relationship with the manifestations of God—thus the need for true and pure religion.

"Right now, many people feel discontented about what they perceive as excessive governmental interference in their lives. They think reducing government will make everything better. What they don't realize is that as society decays, and the behaviors of the population around them become less spiritual, more laws and oversight are required and implemented to make up for that decay. That's what is going on in today's society. Due to the loss of the influence of true religion, spirituality fades. Common social behaviors become less and less desirable. More and more laws, protections, oversight, and security are implemented to make up for that loss. However, law, security, protection, and oversight cannot and will not become so omnipresent and effective as to replace the reality of the ever-presence of God in the hearts of the human beings.

"Take the workplace, for example. As work ethics decline, more and more rules and policies are written and more and more human personnel are allocated to enforcing them. Why? Because many workers don't care or they aren't trustworthy enough to be left unsupervised. And those workers don't care because they feel the people who own and run the companies have lost their morals and ethics and don't care about them. You can observe this happening at every level of society if you just look closely. People behave well when they are observed, but not so well when left unsupervised, especially when they are tempted without consequences. Why? Because they can get away with something! We, as human beings often choose the easy, selfish way if we perceive no consequences. With a rightful consciousness of the ever-present and loving God, we know we are always accountable, and therefore we make better choices."

"Hold on," I objected. "I know people who are spiritual or religious who believe in the ever-present God and feel accountable to him, and they still choose wrong sometimes. What about that?" I insisted.

"Sure," Rose replied softly. "It's the natural way of the spiritual path. People who are living in the presence of God also struggle with right living. It's hard work being a spiritual human being. That's probably why we get a lifetime to work on it. We all fall short of our intentions at times. We even intentionally make wrong choices even when we know we will suffer from the consequences. But a population of human beings consciously living in the presence of a loving God have far greater potential to be better people than if they had not developed that consciousness. Really, it can't even be compared.

"This world might be considered the school-ground of life. It is not our eternal home. We are here to learn spiritual qualities and virtues, and there is a wide margin for error. We have the opportunity to make mistake after mistake until we learn to do things better. God's design is quite merciful if you think about it. If we were severely punished for every wrong behavior, or if consequences were harshly enforced, life would be pretty awful. Our life experience on this earth is the learning center for the development of our eternal soul. It's perfect in its design and flawless in its function. One can only see this when it is considered in light of our real purpose to learn true knowledge and wisdom, and to learn to express joy and love in everything we do and be."

"And be?" I asked.

"Yes, we are human beings, not human doings." She laughed and then looked at me, still grinning. "Human beings . . . not human-doings!" she repeated, erupting into laughter again. I just smirked. It was funny, I guess, but more so to her than to me. "I suppose we're really human-be-doings," she said, choking it out with such laughter that I could hardly understand her. She laughed so hard she teared up again. Finally, she let out a big sigh and wiped the tears from her face with a tissue.

It then became quiet in the truck for a while. All I could hear was the drone of the engine and the hum of the tires drumming a rhythmic sound that pacified my brain. I was tired from trying to think and understand everything Rose was saying. I was trying to integrate what she had said with everything I had experienced in life, and trying to see if it all fit together somehow. *Is all this really true?* I wondered.

"So you see," Rose finally broke the silence, "the human beings can't live without religion, that is, without true religion and spirituality. The consequences of the decline in spirituality and pure religion here on earth are chaos and confusion, fear and discontent. I feel confident the time will soon come when people will arrive at this understanding collectively. In fact, it is already happening. It's just that they don't know what to do or where to turn for answers. I believe soon there will be a resurgence of interest in spirituality that will spark a worldwide investigation of religion. As a consequence of this collective investigation, most of the people of the world will conclude that what I am presenting to you is a truth they are happy to live with. I can foresee a mass movement to adopt this Faith as the standard of living and social development throughout the world. These teachings and truths presented to us by Bahá'u'lláh are a very special gift, Grayson, intended for all the people of the earth, and specifically addressed to our modern times."

She paused for a moment and looked out the window. Then she sat up straight and in a raised voice, as though speaking to the whole world, exclaimed, "It is a great day to be alive!" She sat erect and silent afterward with her eyes closed, breathing heavily. Then she slowly relaxed into her seat. I knew that was the end of the conversation. It was like a great, big period at the end of her exposition on the importance of religion.

It is a great day to be alive, I thought. *Yes, it just might be.* I felt a little more hopeful. From what she was telling me, life seemed promising again. *Could this be possible? Could this be what I have been searching for, waiting for, hoping for? Was it all as simple and reasonable as what Rose had been explaining?* I was full of mixed feelings. I felt both excited and hopeful while also cautious and skeptical. I had been down this road of hope before and ended up disappointed. Somehow this time it felt different. I couldn't reconcile my feelings at this point. There was too much conflict. To divert my attention, I began to review in my mind how far we had driven, where we were going to stop next, and all the things I needed to do to ensure this trip was as smooth as possible for everyone. No matter how I tried to distract myself though, I couldn't help coming back to the questions percolating under the surface. *Is this it? Is this really it? Is all this true? Is this really possible? A new religion for our time—a renewed one, a clean one, a pure one, a now one. Is it possible that a manifestation of God recently appeared and most people didn't even know it? Is that really possible? I guessed so, because it happened that way every time before.*

There was no reason for it not to happen again. Wow! If this is the case, it truly is a great day to be alive! I thought. I looked over and stared at Rose, smiling. She looked back and waited for me to speak. "It **is** a great day to be alive!" I boomed in a thunderous voice. She grinned widely, her eyes smiling. It felt good.

It was getting near lunchtime, but I hadn't heard from T.J. yet. He was somewhere behind me. I couldn't see him in my mirror, but I knew he was back there somewhere. I saw a sign that read, "Truckers Welcome Ahead." I decided today I would make the call for lunch before T.J. got a chance. I grabbed the CB and announced, "Lunch break ahead."

T.J. came back, "Tail-gunner here. Yes, we're ready."

We found the small truck stop. It had a large, paved lot with plenty of room for us to pull off and park. We all agreed that we were getting tired of restaurant food, so we fixed lunch in the trailer instead.

DAY SEVEN

MORE SPIRITUAL TRUTHS

After lunch, I helped Rose into the truck. As I was climbing in on my side, I saw her change the cassette tape in the recorder. She took the used tape and stored it in her little carrying case full of tapes, then placed it gently in her travel bag as though it were something precious. I checked in with everyone over the CB to see if they were ready to proceed. I received a "ten-four" from each vehicle. We were off again.

I was thinking about what Rose had said about the importance and value of true spirituality and religion when she started right in with a new topic.

"I would like to share with you another spiritual principle from Bahá'u'lláh," she proposed.

I looked over at her in anticipation.

"Surely you recall me telling you that unity is the central theme of the Bahá'í Faith, and I suggested to you that the most desirable condition a human being can experience in relationship to others is unity. I explained that unity is a heart-felt condition of trust, understanding, love, and peace with others. So I ask you, what could be more hopeful in the world than a condition of global unity? Nothing!" she emphasized as she answered her own question. "It becomes especially evident how desirable unity is when we contrast it with disunity—relationships characterized by distrust, fear, suspicion, hatred, conflict, violence, and its worst expression, war.

"Good relationships, distinguished by peace, love, and unity, are really dependent upon quality communication. Science has shown that the most troublesome and violent relationships are those consisting of individuals whose immaturity or lack of skills limit their ability to communicate well with others. Consequently, it has established that the one single factor that best contributes to unified relationships is the ability of individuals to communicate clearly and effectively without allowing their conversations to escalate emotionally to verbal or physical aggression. Good communication leads to understanding, and understanding leads to more unified relationships. This has been well proven. So to help us communicate more clearly with others, and to become a more unified world community, Bahá'u'lláh prescribed the adoption of a single world-wide language and script."

"I heard recently," I chimed in, "that English is now considered the language of business around the world. So it looks like that's already happening."

"Yes, it is happening," Rose acknowledged, "but remember these principles were put forth over one hundred fifty years ago in the Middle East! As you might imagine, they were not well received or understood at the time. Inhabitants of little villages knew next to nothing about the rest of the world. Most of them had never traveled more than ten miles from their place of birth. When Bahá'u'lláh spoke to them about a world language, they weren't sure where the rest of the world was, let alone how to implement this principle. Remember, these principles were given to **all** the people of the earth to guide humanity through the next thousand years or so before the next manifestation appears. A single universal language was a challenging issue then. Today, it may not be so difficult to fathom. Unless, of course, the universal language was one other than English, then you and I might have a different feeling about it." She looked at me inquisitively.

"Well, I suppose I would," I said proudly, not realizing how I was displaying my subconscious sense of superiority again. My nation-centric bias had raised its ignorant head, and Rose noticed I'm sure.

But she didn't say anything. We were both silent. I thought it over for a few minutes and then remarked, "Yeah, you're right. I don't think I would be much of an advocate if I had to learn a different language."

"Well, you may not have to. Who knows?" she speculated. "Bahá'u'lláh said that in addition to teaching our children their native language, a universal language should also be adopted or created that children could learn. Eventually, everyone would enjoy the unifying outcome of being able to communicate more clearly with everyone else on the planet.

"Some may resist this, you know, feeling they are giving up something sacred and dear. That's a natural response. I hope for the sake of more peaceful relations with others and for the sake of unity among the diverse peoples of the earth that the human beings will make the necessary sacrifice to implement this unifying spiritual principle." She paused, thinking. "Do you know what sacrifice means?" She asked abruptly as she turned to look at me. "It means to give up something of value for something of greater value."

I got it.

We drove only a short distance before Rose took off on another subject. "Another spiritual principle I want to share with you this afternoon is the importance and merit of knowledge and wisdom." She scooted around in her seat, trying to get comfortable. "First, I would like to share with you this quotation from Bahá'u'lláh pertaining to wisdom:

'Above all else, the greatest gift and the most wondrous blessing hath ever been and will continue to be wisdom. It is man's unfailing protector. It aideth him and strengtheneth him. Wisdom is God's emissary and the Revealer of His Name the Omniscient. Through it the loftiness of man's station is made manifest and evident. It is all-knowing and the foremost teacher in the school of existence. It is the guide and is invested with high distinction. Thanks to its educating influence earthly beings have become imbued with a gem-like spirit which outshineth the heavens.'"[41]

She paused for a bit, then added, "It is said that knowledge is power, and it is. But without the guidance of spirituality, knowledge can become a power used for gaining unfair advantages over others, destruction, aggression, oppression, and even war. You see it all around us in the materialism that dominates our modern society."

"What do you mean by that?" I asked.

"I mean, you see immature people using their knowledge for personal gain at the sake of loss for others. Nuclear weapons, for example. Scientific knowledge has given us nuclear power. Now here is a power that can be used foolishly or with wisdom. And what was the first thing humans did with that knowledge?" She looked at me and kept right on talking. "Yeah, that's right, they built nuclear weapons—tens of thousands of nuclear weapons, many of which are still poised for use, should they decide to do so. True wisdom might be the use of nuclear power for safe, positive purposes and not for destruction. And so it goes for most everything. Knowledge might give you power, but wisdom directs it in beneficial ways. So I'm not talking about knowledge acquired to gain advantage over others. I am talking about knowledge and the acquisition of wisdom, which is the appropriate application of knowledge in light of its relationship to our true purpose as human beings. As I mentioned before, our true purpose as intended by the Creator is to acquire knowledge and learn to apply it in loving service to others. I am talking about an understanding of knowledge and wisdom that enhances our material life and the lives of others while supporting the development of our eternal soul and its life and purpose. So, you might be wondering, 'How is this different than what is going on in today's society?'" She looked at me, smiling. I just smiled back and waited, knowing full well she would explain it.

"Let me explain," she continued. "Earlier, I told you that the Creator, through his most recent manifestation, gave us teachings and principles specific to our modern time, which are necessary for our spiritual growth and development. I have been discussing these principles with you for some time now. I also shared with you that no former prophet or manifestation of God emphasized these specific principles before, although they may have encouraged them. Do you recall this?"

Smiling, I looked at her and nodded.

"So, to support the elevation and acquisition of knowledge and wisdom in today's world, Bahá'u'lláh enjoined compulsory education for all children. This means children must be taught the basics necessary for them to be of benefit to society, to their family, and to their true selves. This education might initially include the fundamentals most of us learn in grammar school, such as reading, writing, math, science, arts, music, history, and so on, but hopefully in more spiritual and comprehensive ways than with current methods. I'm talking about an education that teaches children **how** to learn, not just a memorization of facts—an education that teaches the relationship of knowledge to real life, and not those things that are impractical or rarely applicable. I'm talking about an education that evokes wonder at the interrelationship of science and the natural world—one that **inspires** children to want to learn and not dread it. I'm talking about an education that teaches true history instead of those versions stemming from or supporting political, religious, racial, or national agendas."

"Wow!" I interrupted. "That's a far cry from what school was like when I was a kid."

Rose nodded in agreement. "Not only should children be taught these subjects in elementary school," she added, "but they should also be educated in spirituality and true religion. You already know I'm not talking about the kind of religious instruction you are familiar with. I'm not talking about rigid, fear and guilt-based education. I'm not talking about religious instruction steeped in superstition, mythology, and thoughtless imitation of past behaviors."

Rose was quite worked up. She sat up straight, talking loudly and emphatically. Without pause, continued. "What I'm talking about is a whole new approach to spiritual education and learning. I'm talking about learning spiritual qualities, traits, and virtues that are beneficial to themselves and others, essential to both this life and the life beyond. I'm talking about learning spiritual qualities based on reality, taught in the most kind, loving, and meaningful ways. I'm talking about spiritual education that is supportive of our true purpose to acquire knowledge for the purpose of being able to express love in the form of service to others. I'm talking about an education that creates loving, kind, peaceful, and joyous relationships among the human beings. I'm talking about a spiritual education that harmonizes with and is supportive of the basics acquired in elementary schools. I'm talking about spiritual education that is exciting, fun, and meaningful, that helps children want to seek out truth, explore, and learn for the rest of their lives. I'm talking about a gentle, loving, nurturing education that trains children in spiritual qualities and builds character. Good education gives understanding and joy to life, whereas ignorance only leads to frustration. What greater gift of inheritance could one leave their children than this? Surely, there is no material legacy to compare."

Exhaling loudly, Rose finally stopped. She sat back in her seat as though she had completed a major task. She was silent for some time. Although I didn't have anything to say in response, her words inspired me. They made perfect sense.

"To me," Rose maintained, "the need for compulsory education is obvious. Children left uneducated can easily become socially handicapped—ignorant and vulnerable to wrongful persuasion, superstition, and deception. You can see how children turn out when left ignorant of their true self or their true purpose, how easily they can become self-centered when they have no spiritual education or training. You can see how rebellious they can become if their education is too stringent or authoritarian. You can also see how they frequently develop a sense of entitlement when their training is too lenient."

Rose was still, staring at the dash, focusing on her next thought. "Part of our purpose as human beings," she continued on the subject, "is to acquire knowledge and wisdom. Learning is what we are created for. It's what makes us feel alive. It gives meaning to our lives and contributes to our purpose of being loving people. It causes us to engage in service to society and forever be involved with change, growth, and development. When one quits learning, well, it's a type of death. When people quit learning, they become depressed, remote, and unfulfilled. Acquiring wisdom through learning helps a person feel good. It helps us in our efforts to be better at expressing love to others, which strengthens all our relationships. It makes us better mothers, fathers, friends, workers, and contributors to society. It helps us attain better understanding of others and ourselves so we can act in ways that support peace, love, and unity among the human beings. Learning, exploring, wondering, and discovery! It's what gives us joy!" she cried.

After a long pause, Rose reiterated, "I want you to know, Grayson, I'm not talking about learning just for the sake of remembering facts and figures or trivial information. I'm talking about learning for the sake of developing spiritual qualities that are harmonious with our purpose as human beings. The possibilities of meaningful learning are endless, but a learning that promotes kindness, generosity, forgiveness, tolerance, and appreciation of beauty—now that's an education! But it must be based on what is real and true. Those who have been around for a while, like me," she snickered, "know that wisdom takes a lifetime to develop. It comes from living with the courage to engage in trial and error. It requires an open mind and a willingness to change our perspectives often, so we don't get locked into a stagnant conservatism. It takes effort and sacrifice. Most elderly people would agree that the best treasures you have at the end of a lifetime are the knowledge and wisdom you have acquired from your life experience. Treasure learning! Engage in it fearlessly! Every moment is a learning experience. And integrate everything you learn with your true purpose to know and love God. That's the nature of a true spiritual life."

Rose grew thoughtful and quiet as if there were something more on her mind. "I don't have the time or energy to give you more detailed examples for each of these principles I am sharing with you. There is so much more I could say. What is important to me, Grayson, is that you take the principles into your heart and meditate on them. Observe within your own self and in the behavior of others whether or not what I say is true. I am proposing that these principles and truths are the spiritual remedies for what ails modern human beings, both individually and collectively as a society of world citizens. Ponder them—think them over carefully, and observe." She was silent again and staring at me. I nodded my head in agreement.

Rose was silent again for some time. Suddenly she said, "Just one more thing on this subject. If people assess their daily experiences in light of the reality portrayed to us in the teachings of God through his manifestations, then all of life's experiences will make sense, have purpose, and integrate harmoniously. Otherwise, life's experiences can appear meaningless and without purpose when attempts are made to integrate them into materialistic or superstitious belief systems."

I looked at her, puzzled. "What do you mean?" I asked.

"If people believe there is no life after death, no God, no consequences to our actions, no eternal purpose to life and no spiritual reality, then their life experiences can cause confusion and chaos. They often quit exploring or learning anything different, causing rigidity and unhappiness. Integrating life's experiences with the truth of our reality helps us feel free and happy. It allows us to fulfill our lives with joy, radiance, purpose, and meaning. The difference is obvious to anyone who observes with an open mind. Exploration, discovery, skill building, the acquisition of virtues and character development, understanding, love—these are what make us human! It's what fulfills our reality as spiritual beings. We are human beings! We are spiritual beings! We are, in our reality, human spiritual beings." Her infectious laugh started up again. She was laughing. I was laughing. Wow, was she wound up! She had spouted out those words like they were going to evaporate if she didn't hurry up and get them out. It was funny, and she knew it, and I knew it! We were laughing with great joy.

It was near the end of the day, and we were cruising through the town of Hope, British Columbia. We had planned on staying the night somewhere nearby. A four-lane street went through town with a notable increase in traffic, so I was attentive at the wheel. Suddenly, I heard a short blast of a siren right beside me! I looked quickly to my left, and there was a Canadian Mountie, vigorously waving me over.

Fortunately, I was in the right lane, and there was a large parking lot immediately to my right with plenty of room for me to pull over and park.

I rolled down my window in anticipation of talking to the officer. The Mountie parked at an angle in front of my truck, exited his vehicle, and approached me.

"Good evening, sir," he began. "Can you tell me why you didn't pull over at the weigh station?"

We had passed a weigh station about a block or two back. I didn't stop because I didn't think I had to. "We're coming down from Alaska," I explained. "Before we left Alaska, I called the Alaska State Police to ask if I had to have any kind of special driver's license or permits or if I was required to stop at the weigh stations in Canada with the truck I was driving. The State Police told me it wouldn't be necessary. I asked the person I talked to for his name. I wrote it down, along with his phone number, just in case. I have it here somewhere. I can find it for you."

The Mountie was unimpressed. He instructed me assertively, "You turn that truck around and go back to the weigh station and get in line with the others. You are required by law to stop at each weigh station that's open. I'll be right behind you."

I looked at Rose and shrugged. "I guess I'll have to go back," I said in dismay. Rose shrugged her shoulders and nodded. I radioed my fellow travelers about the situation. Sonia had already pulled in right behind me. Franklin and T.J. had seen me pull off and were stopped somewhere up ahead. I proceeded to turn around and maneuver my big truck and camp-trailer northbound onto the Alcan Highway.

I only had to wait for about ten minutes before it was my turn to pull forward and weigh in. I followed their instructions. When finished they asked me to pull forward and park, then come into the office to talk to the officials there. I didn't like the sound of that! However, I did as they asked. When they asked me why I hadn't stopped on my first time through, I told them the same story I had told the Mountie. They informed me that the Alaska State policeman was wrong. After about twenty minutes or so an official came to the counter and called out my name. He was carrying a handful of papers which I didn't like the looks of. "Well," he said with a sigh, "You have several violations here, and I am going to go through each one of them with you." When he finished, I was astonished. I had racked up $2,300 worth of fines! I felt a wave of heat move up across my face and especially my ears. I was angry. I proceeded to tell the official again that I had, in good faith, checked with the officers in Alaska before making this trip and I thought I was in compliance with the law. I told him I had the name and number of the officer who assured me I would be okay. He took the name and number down and asked me to have a seat as he went back to his cubicle.

I silently fumed for another ten minutes before the official came back to the counter and called my name again. "This is what I can do for you," he said. "I have been able to reduce your fine to $210. You need to pay this before you can proceed with your truck. And, if I were you, I'd make it to the border as soon as possible."

I felt relief. Two hundred and ten dollars was a lot better than twenty-three hundred! I paid the fine and went out to tell the others the outcome of my situation. We all moaned and groaned a bit, but we didn't want to tarry any longer. Road weary and agitated, we headed south again.

Soon we found a nice place to stay at the Wild Rose RV Park. It was a beautiful park surrounded by huge evergreen fir trees. We were hungry and tired—too tired to seek out a restaurant. So we ordered pizza delivered, to our trailer, in the park! Now that was a first.

After dinner T.J., Alene, and Rose left to find a motel. Sonia and I took a relaxing walk around the park. When we got back to the campsite, I did some reading. We had just gone to bed when we heard the rumbling of a train coming. It kept getting closer and louder until the trailer began to shake. We hadn't realized there was a train track right beside our spot at the campground. A width of fir trees and underbrush had obscured any view of the tracks. But it was too late to do anything about it. All night long we were visited by noisy trains.

DAY EIGHT

OH, MODERATION

I t was so hard to get up. I was tired. The rush in preparing to move, the stress of disconnecting all our ties in Alaska, the pressure of the trip, and worrying about everything that could go wrong so far away from home had taken a lot out of me. And now, on top of all of that, those noisy trains all night long! It was all taking a toll, and it took every bit of determination I could muster to get moving. Sonia and I, and Franklin and Annie, were to meet T.J., Alene, and Rose at a little café nearby for breakfast. Rose was sitting on a bench in front of the café when we arrived. She looked at me with a beaming smile when we pulled in.

"Good morning, Rose," I greeted her.

"Good morning, Grayson," she beamed with a smile. "How was your night?"

"I'm exhausted!" I exclaimed, recounting to her the night of horrendous trains!

She laughed as we unhappy campers shared our stories of being intermittently awakened all night long. Her eyes sparkled with amusement. Before I knew it, I, too, was laughing, but not about our overnight situation. Rose's child-like, innocent laughter always seemed to lighten my spirits. When she laughed, it was hard for me not to.

We ate breakfast, and soon we were on the road again. Everyone knew the preflight routine—what to check, what to fasten, what to have in place for whatever was to come next—which seemed to reduce the stress level that had existed earlier in the trip. We were all tired of traveling, but knew if we kept up our steady pace we would soon be home.

We rode along for ten minutes or so before Rose asked, "Do you have any questions about what we have recorded so far?" I glanced at her, wondering if she was probing for something specific.

"No," I said, looking out the window and checking my mirror for the others in our caravan. "I mean, yes, I have lots of questions, but it's hard for me to think about them right now," I explained.

"What do you mean?" Rose asked.

"I mean right now my mind wants to focus on this trip. I have all our belongings in this truck. I'd like them to arrive in Oregon intact. That's why I can't focus long enough on what you've been saying to engage in a long discussion about any of the topics you have shared, even though they are all extremely important to me. And I really want to. I have longed so much for this kind of conversation, yet at the same time I have all these responsibilities tugging at my mind. At least at this moment, today, I don't have any specific questions."

We were both silent for some time. Finally, Rose resumed. "I suppose I might as well share with you another spiritual principle from Bahá'u'lláh." She waited for me to respond, but I didn't. "Do you recall me explaining to you that the creating and sustaining Force behind all things in the universe, what we call God, gives us guidance periodically through his manifestations to help us fulfill our purpose as human beings?" I nodded to indicate I remembered. "Do you recall that these spiritual teachings and principles I am sharing with you from Bahá'u'lláh are specific to modern conditions and times?" She stopped and looked at me for acknowledgment.

"Yes, I understand that." And I did. I understood it, and I liked it. In fact, I was so mesmerized by the possibility of it being true that my attention to worrying about everything was suddenly redirected. "Yes, I remember," I continued, "and I am very excited about such a hopeful possibility, and I do want to understand it better." She looked at me with a blank face. Looking back, I think she probably was puzzled by my definition of her discourse as being a 'possibility.'

She arranged herself more comfortably in the seat, and then proceeded with her point. "Another spiritual principle for modern times given to us by Bahá'u'lláh is to individually and collectively practice moderation in all things. Specifically, on this matter, he wrote,

'In all matters, moderation is desirable.'[42]

"The implementation of this principle means to always seek the middle way that does the least harm, the golden mean, if you will, which avoids the harmful effects of extreme or excess. Moderation suggests we observe reasonable limits in our decisions and behaviors and restrain ourselves from that which is severe or overly intense."

"Oh yeah, I know this one," I interrupted, "moderation in all things. I have heard you say it many times . . . in fact, my parents often used that phrase. Like the Buddha," I continued, "the middle way." I stretched out my hand to make a horizontal sweeping motion in front of me to demonstrate the middle way. I glanced at Rose with a smile.

"Yes, it's not new," she said, pausing momentarily before adding, "but the broad scope of its intentional implementation is new and specifically emphasized as critical in dealing with the problems that currently face mankind. Because of the extreme possibilities available to individuals, it is equally critical and important to the development of our very soul."

I frowned at her, questioning such a strong remark. She gazed steadily back at me; her face completely serious as she restated, "Yes, critical."

She further explained, "Moderation means that middle way that does the least harm. It means we are obligated to think ahead—to project the consequences of our behavior or decisions before we act on them hastily. Obviously there are consequences to all choices. Some are more beneficial while others may be more destructive. Let's take child rearing, for example. Isn't it obvious that exercising extreme discipline upon children is really a form of cruelty? Surely you know that children disciplined with verbal, emotional, or physical abuse become rebellious, which negates any goodness you try to instill in them. Furthermore, they often are emotionally affected for life in the most undesirable ways. That is the natural, predictable consequence of hostile or violent parenting. On the other hand, children brought up without firm guidance and self-discipline are more prone to become selfish, crass, immature adults." She stopped and sat with her shoulders up and her arms crossing her chest, a little like she was trying to look tough. She was getting quite emotional again. I looked at her, then back to the road, then back again. She just sat there.

"You look a little upset," I remarked. "That was a pretty emotional moment for you, wasn't it?" She stared at me, red-faced, without remark. "You look like a puffed-up old grizzly bear," I said, teasing her.

She exploded into laughter. "I feel like one!" she exclaimed. We both laughed freely.

"Sorry, Grayson," she apologized. "I have some deep-seated emotions about this issue." Rose closed her eyes and took in a few breaths, exhaling slowly after each one. After a bit, she opened her eyes and went on with her thoughts. "There is a moderate way, you know—where children are taught **self**-discipline, where they become aware of normal and natural consequences of certain behaviors because they have been gently, kindly, and wisely nurtured to understand. There is a moderate way that results in emotional, mental, and spiritual strength and maturity—one that avoids the more extreme methods of either a controlling aggression or a passive leniency. Surely you have witnessed this in your life and in the lives of those around you?" She paused.

"Yes, I sure have," I agreed.

"Let me give you an example," Rose said. "I know a couple who have two little boys they both adore. They love those little boys so much they give rigorous attention to everything they do as parents. They have decided that children should learn discipline. So they make sure to inflict punishment upon those children so they will learn that there are natural consequences to their behavior. Once when the oldest child was about five, he was distraught with his mother, and he bit her. The mother bit him back. Later she told me that she wanted her son to learn not to bite. But do you know what that kind of violent behavior taught that child?"

I looked at her, expecting her to answer her own question.

"That little boy learned if someone bites you or hurts you, you have the right to hurt them back, only worse! Children learn to do what their parents **do**! If a parent punishes a child with a stick, the child learns to use a stick to hurt others. The point is that if we want our children to be self-disciplined, then we **model** it ourselves! They will then learn to do likewise. This is the wisdom behind moderation."

After a short pause, she continued with another example. "Now on a larger scale, look at what excessive liberty to pursue free enterprise has caused around the world. This extreme leniency alone has resulted in a dangerous interference with the planet's natural balance, as well as the unabated abuse of many of its defenseless people. Excessive freedoms in the pursuit of free enterprise have allowed large companies to do as they please with little oversight or consequences. It has resulted in deadly, out-of-control pollution, destruction of rain forests vital to the planet's ecological balance, and other serious imbalances in the earth's natural equilibrium. Furthermore, it has resulted in a culture so focused on having the unbridled right and freedom to have and to do more that terrible consequences await our society—the advent of which we are currently experiencing. People know this, and they are becoming worried, anxious, and scared.

"Most people now see that something has gone terribly wrong in our society, Grayson, but they don't know exactly what it is or what to do about it. That's why I am telling you about these spiritual teachings—so you can help me share them with the people and give them hope! That's why we are writing this book! I feel confident that the salvation of the people and our wonderful planet depend upon the implementation of these sacred principles from Bahá'u'lláh. So I urge you to think carefully and observe how well these spiritual principles fit the needs of our modern times.

"Moderation is one of these vital principles. Moderation in our conduct—so we avoid the extremes of either a passionless life or one based on excessive excitement, thrills or pleasure-seeking. It is in our best interest to find the middle way. Moderation in dress, appearance, speech, and expressions in art are all part of this. The outcomes of vulgarity and nudity are becoming unmistakably evident, as is the other extreme of wearing clothing that veils the entire body, for example. Either extreme, as you have surely witnessed, can result in undesirable personal and social conditions. The middle way is far more conducive to a unified, peaceful, fear-free, conflict-free society. When the principle of moderation is elevated in the minds and hearts of the human beings, the destructive consequences of extreme behavior become more avoidable.

"We would do well to consider what happens historically to societies when extremes are not kept in check. Extremes between those with excessive wealth and those living in dire poverty have repeatedly resulted in social breakdown. Aren't we close to that now? Aren't extremes in entitlements equally as destructive to social disorder as the accumulation of most of the wealth by the very few? Aren't the ideologies of the extreme right and the extreme left, the extremely conservative and extremely liberal, demonstrating their futility? Isn't a life balanced between extreme austerity and extreme pleasure seeking the more desirable path? Yes . . . moderation! Isn't the path somewhere between zealous, frenetic behavior and passive, dispassionate apathy a more desirable, intelligent, and practical way? Isn't the middle road between excessive rights and freedoms and overbearing restrictions and oppression more assuring to all being well served? Isn't a middle way of governance preferable to bickering by extremists who can so stifle government that it can become nearly impotent in its ability to be of service to the people?

"Do you see how extremism is causing such damage in today's world? We are living in a time when it has never had so much opportunity to express itself. I offer this for your consideration: Is it possible that what allows extremism to thrive is the development of material civilization in the absence of sensible moral and spiritual discipline? And aren't the resulting consequences evident?" She turned to look at me and sat motionless for a moment. "I suggest to you that moderation in all things is one of the spiritual principles whose time has come, and is, in fact, long overdue."

Rose then turned and fumbled around in her travel bag to look for something. Apparently she couldn't find whatever she was looking for. She then sat up and proceeded with the subject at hand.

"Now, even though we are in the midst of dire circumstances in our world, many believe it will require radical measures to correct the direction we are going. I disagree. I think we still must remain true to principle, and make choices affecting change in a moderate fashion. Change, even that which corrects an undesirable trend, should be approached with proportionate moderation that will cause the least harm. We have to be careful not to upset the balance of things to such a degree that destructive consequences would be forthcoming.

"Perhaps you have noticed that I have been avoiding giving specific suggestions or examples when addressing some important issues. I am doing this for a reason. I am personally unable to propose specific solutions to the numerous problems that face our society. Each problem requires a thorough investigation of relevant facts, a collective agreement upon those facts, comprehensive consultation on proposed solutions, collective agreement upon the decisions, and harmonious cooperation in carrying out the agreed upon plans. What I am proposing to you, though, is that the spiritual principles of thinking and behaving given to us by Bahá'u'lláh are the most prudent approach to solving the problems that face humanity. So, if we want to improve the conditions of our lives, we would do well to practice moderation in our personal lives, our families, our organizations, our businesses, and governing bodies. That's my point. Moderation in all things is a **real** tool for living, behaving, decision-making, and problem solving. Observe around you, and in your own life, the consequences of extreme behaviors, decision-making, and policy-making as compared to those that employ this spiritual principle. I suggest to you that mature observation and contemplation will conclude that moderation is not only desirable, but also critical to our survival and eventual prosperity and happiness. I want to share with you this caution from the writings of Bahá'u'lláh pertaining to moderation:

'*If carried to excess, civilization will prove as prolific a source of evil as it had been of goodness when kept within the restraints of moderation.*'[43]

Rose was silent for a while. I was pondering what she had just quoted when she started in again.

"You know, Grayson, I think I would like you to put an appendix at the end of this book, listing these spiritual principles given to us by Bahá'u'lláh for this new age. Yes," she said with certainty, "and I'll help you do that. People then would have immediate access to a list of these spiritual principles, making it easier to apply them in their lives. What do you think?"

"Sure, I can do that," I said. "I think that's a great idea. In fact, I think I have already forgotten most of those you spoke about." I looked at her childishly. She started laughing as though something really funny had occurred. I was swept up in her levity and we belly-laughed to the point of tears again. *Thank you, God, for this sweet woman!* I thought. *What a treat she is in my life.*

Suddenly, I noticed numerous brake lights up ahead. We were at the Canadian-American border. I hadn't been paying attention to where we were, so I was surprised. When we approached, I noticed there were optional booths to accommodate several automobiles at once. We each took a lane and waited our turn to be checked out by the officials. It took some time, but eventually all of us went through and pulled off into a large parking lot, except for Sonia.

One of the officials had checked out the Bronco and noticed the houseplants in the back. One of them was a two-foot spruce that our daughter had planted in the first grade—eight years ago. The officer insisted a representative from the Department of Agriculture check out the tree. It took a while before someone came to investigate the plants.

The representative officer asked Sonia, "What kind of tree do you

STEVEN E. ELLIS

have there, ma'am?" Sonia told him she didn't know. He looked it over and then informed her that it was only a pine tree and that she was free to proceed. I had to chuckle. Here was a department of agriculture representative that didn't know the difference between a pine tree and a spruce. *Oh well, so much for bureaucracy*, I thought. Sonia was waved through, and we all were back in the lower forty-eight.

We took a little break in the parking lot before proceeding to our evening destination of Lakewood, Washington, which was just south of Tacoma. Franklin's step-parents lived there, and he had made arrangements for us to spend the night at their house. We walked and stretched a while before reloading into our vehicles and hitting the road again.

Except for the normal engine sounds and routine hum of the tires over the pavement, it was quiet in the truck. *Moderation—hmm. I like this*, I thought, remembering what Rose had been talking about before we approached the border. I had oftentimes been an extremist in my life, and now that I looked back on it, I could recall the painful outcomes. I thought of how I could have chosen a more moderate way that would have been easier on me and all those affected by my behavior and choices. I could have done better, much better. *I will*, I vowed. *I will be more moderate in my decisions and behavior. I can see now that the results will be less destructive or troubling, and more useful and meaningful to my purpose.*

Yeah, my purpose! I wondered aloud, "What was our purpose in life again?" Rose had already spoken about it several times, but I wanted to hear her state it again.

Rose saw that I was unsure. She looked straight ahead, motionless for a moment, and then said, "Our purpose in life is to acquire knowledge and wisdom, to love, and more specifically, to know, love, and glorify the one true God, and to contribute to the advancement of our society and civilization."

"Okay," I murmured. "I guess I remember most of that. My mind just went blank there for a minute."

"Let me quote for you what Bahá'u'lláh has written regarding our purpose," Rose offered. He wrote,

'Having created the world and all that liveth and moveth therein, He, through the direct operation of His unconstrained and sovereign Will, chose to confer upon man the unique distinction and capacity to know Him and to love Him—a capacity that must needs be regarded as the generating impulse and the primary purpose underlying the whole of creation.'[44]

"Wow!" I marveled.

"Yes, wow!" Rose mimicked before continuing. "Moderation, as well as all the principles I have told you about, help us do just that. You will find that the moderate way will improve your ability to express love in all its aspects. It will help you apply knowledge and wisdom, while it equally and simultaneously teaches you knowledge and wisdom. And let me tell you this about your purpose: all things you know and love will pass **except** your relationship with the one true God. That is the only thing that is without end. It is eternal! So really, everything you learn, all knowledge and wisdom, is a knowledge and wisdom about God and your relationship with him. And all your expressions of love are ultimately an expression of love for God because he created all things. Eventually, we come to glorify him because we understand that everything comes from and has its origin in him." She raised her hands, palms upwards, and just sat there looking at me. I didn't know what she just said, but I got it, or it got me; I don't know. Whatever it was, she had answered my question. I couldn't repeat it if I wanted to, but it hit a place in me that I knew was right and true. I felt good. I felt a kind of peace come over me—at least for the moment. *This is good*, I thought, *this is really, really good.*

She had done it again. Every time I had doubts, Rose would allay them. Every time I became cynical, she would bring me around to hopefulness. Whenever I was too serious, she would cleanse me with laughter. *This is love!* I thought. This was pure love coming from her and lifting me from my darkness into the light of goodness. *How does she do that?* I wondered. I hope when I'm eighty-something I'll be able to do that—make people feel loved all the time. What kind of magic is that? What kind of spirituality is this? What kind of saintliness? *That's it*, I thought, *Rose is saintly. She is holy! She's a holy person! She's a holy man!* The sudden realization smacked me right between the eyes. All my life I wanted to find a holy man. And here he was—a woman! Rose! Right here before me! I started to tremble and tear up at the thought. In a short time I found myself sobbing. Rose didn't say a word. She just put her warm hand on my shoulder again and kept rubbing it. I don't know—it was cathartic, I guess— whatever. *No self-analysis needed here, just gratitude*, I thought. I felt loved, and free somehow, and it felt good.

DAY EIGHT

LEADERSHIP AND MORE

We stopped in a small town for lunch. I fueled the truck while the others selected a table for us in the restaurant. It was a small restaurant, with tables along two walls, a large round table in the center, and a small room in the back that wasn't in use at the moment. Our party had pulled two tables together so we could share one another's company. Rose and I sat next to each other, but it just happened we were closest to the large table in the center of the room. There were two elderly people, I assumed husband and wife, sitting at the large table with another gentleman who spoke rather loudly. Apparently he was a local host of some kind. He was telling them all about the town, the weather, and the people—not unlike a tour-guide. He kept saying, "They should be here soon," and looking out the window. Finally, I heard him say, "Here they are." Six people came in and joined the trio at the table— four men and two women. They all appeared to be locals by the way they talked to one another and to the waitress. The loud gentleman introduced his two guests to the group, and they all proceeded to chatter while the waitress took their orders. She had taken ours already, so we were now waiting and talking.

After a short time, the loud gentleman began to complain to one of the others about the worthless teachers in his area of the country and asked the other couple if the teachers were any good where they came from. They were all complaining about teachers and how they just weren't like they used to be in their abilities to control and educate children. And from that, their conversation just took off. It was like they were all trying to out-do each other in complaining about people in positions of authority. First, it was teachers, then local school board members, local police and city officials, coaches at the high school—then it really escalated! They started in on politicians! And how our system was broken and how we don't have any leaders anymore that people can get behind and support. The sentiments seemed mutual for everyone at the table.

"Everything is just falling apart!" one concluded.

"I just don't know where it's all going to end," said another.

My table was pretty quiet. This other group was so loud and emphatic about their concerns that everyone else was relegated to listening, like it or not! They went on for quite some time until the food came. Then they quieted down some and began talking about less explosive topics. I was relieved.

We ate and exchanged small talk before proceeding to the parking lot. After a little stretching and tire kicking, we re-embarked on our journey. Rose was happy and jolly. I was generally relaxed and tired after eating, but a little stirred up from listening to the people in the diner carrying on the way they did.

"What did you think of that?" I asked, as I put on my seatbelt and started the truck. I really wasn't interested in Rose's answer as much as I wanted to vent. "That was quite a bitch session, wasn't it?" I noticed Rose reach over and turn on the recorder. "But you know, it's true, Rose—what those people were saying in there. We just don't have any leaders anymore that we can look up to. It's all pretty depressing! It just doesn't seem very hopeful for our future if we can't get decent leadership—in anything! What are we going to do about that? I mean really!" My cynicism was showing.

I wasn't feeling very well. I hadn't rested well the night before; I was tired, and now I was feeling negative and upset. I really didn't want to talk or to have a conversation, and I didn't want to listen to Rose anymore either even though I had just asked her a question. I decided to shut myself up. Thankfully, Rose also remained silent.

After we had traveled for a half hour or so, I could feel myself calming down. I let out a big sigh.

Rose looked at me with a gentle smile. "That felt good, huh?" Then she threw back her head and laughed, and that made me laugh, too. Yes, I was feeling better.

"I am always amazed at how the spirit works," she began. "I have been avoiding this topic for quite some time because I didn't know how to introduce it. And yet today, at lunch, in that restaurant, everything came clear to me." She looked up as though talking to the heavens. "I am so grateful!" She paused briefly. "Today, I have the pleasure of sharing with you one of the most hopeful aspects of the latest revelation from God to the human beings, and that is the promise of just, kind, and effective leadership."

I turned and looked at her in disbelief. "Oh, yeah?" I replied.

She ignored my remark and pressed on. "I am going to introduce you to a whole new leadership style. I am going to share with you some principles given to us by Bahá'u'lláh, that pertain to leadership, decision-making, and governance.

"Before I can give you a vision of hope for our future as it pertains to leadership, first I want to identify the proper attitude individuals should have toward leaders and government if they are going to stay true to the spiritual path. Several times now I have talked about how unity is the overall theme of the Bahá'í revelation. Everything I am sharing with you stems from and reverts back to this theme. I described unity as a heartfelt condition of peace, love, and harmony in human relations, free of conflict and struggle for dominance. Do you remember that?" She waited for an answer.

"Of course," I affirmed.

"So, I did tell you these things, right?" She looked at me inquisitively.

"Why, yes, several times, as I recall."

She started laughing. I wasn't sure if she was laughing at me or not. "I'm getting to a point where I can't remember what I have shared with you and what I haven't," she blushed. This time I felt relief because I knew she was laughing at herself.

"When we consider the question of what our relationship as individuals should be with government and those in authority," Rose explained, "it is closest to righteousness if it is harmonious with unity. This is the spiritual way." She paused for a moment to admire the blooming fireweed along the side of the road, giving me time to contemplate what she had said. Curiously, I felt a sense of calm about the whole issue even though I didn't know why.

"When we were in that restaurant at lunch," Rose continued, "did you feel the anger and tension created by the discussion the people were having at the center table? Did you feel the disgust, the frustration, and the discontent?"

"Yes, I did. In fact, I was getting rather upset listening to them. I wanted to chime in with my two cents worth."

"Yes, that's nearly always the outcome when people engage in discussions or activities related to politics or government. The spiritual principle for our age and time, given to us by Bahá'u'lláh, pertaining to our individual relationship with those in authority and government, is that we take a firm position of unity. This means as citizens we would be doing best to make every effort to be law-abiding, loyal, trustworthy, and honest in all our dealings with government and those in authority." She looked at me and paused.

"What?" I asked, unsure I had been paying attention.

"Yes," she repeated, "exemplifying unity means we are law-abiding, loyal, trustworthy, and honest in our relationship to presiding governments."

"Really?" I remarked, surprised.

"This spirit of unity means we make every effort to avoid anything that creates mischief or could be considered as meddling in the affairs of government," Rose insisted. "It means we do not concern ourselves with its affairs by engaging in dis-unifying arguments, nor do we participate in unruly activities that attempt to interfere or create conflict with the direction government is going. Consequently, it is contrary to the spirit of unity to join political parties or to become engaged in their partisan activities or projects. Politics are, by their very nature, a considerably divisive aspect of human affairs.

Why do I say this? Because partisan politics **takes sides**!" she exclaimed emphatically. She looked at me and said again, "Politics takes sides! When you have people who create groups like political parties, who then support certain beliefs, values, and ways of thinking and invite others to join them, they become opposed to those who think differently! And there's the problem.

"Unity cannot exist when people are committed to opposing other groups. We are instead called to a higher and more unifying condition in human relations in this new day and age. The highest priority, therefore, above all other things pertaining to human relations, should be harmony, agreement, peace, and accord—not conflict, disagreement, and competitive struggle. This is how we express true unity in our relationships with government and those in authority.

"So, to be faithful to the principle of unity, it is best that religion and its believers refrain from engaging in partisan politics. The activities of religion and role of spirituality pertain to the world of the spirit, not to worldly management and control. The role of religion and spirituality is to train and nurture hearts and souls toward goodness, love, and kindness; toward understanding and wisdom, and toward the acquisition of spiritual traits, virtues, and behaviors. Politics, on the other hand, tries to manage worldly affairs—an arena fraught with conflict, contention, dissension, strife, deception, intrigue, manipulation, corruption, and often violence. The true spiritual path naturally avoids such activities."

She quieted again. I was mulling over what she had said. I asked, "So, are you saying we shouldn't get involved with politics or government?" She didn't respond. "What about voting, or, let's say, protests and stuff like that? Are you saying we shouldn't even be engaged in discussing important issues of the day? What are you saying here, exactly?"

Rose took a deep breath and let it out with a sigh. "This is harder to explain than I expected," she said humbly. "I'm not doing a very good job of it." She looked down and sank into her seat. I felt for her. I felt like I had said something that made her feel bad. I didn't know what to do. I remained quiet and gave my attention to the driving.

Finally, Rose said, "Let me see if I can be more specific. Joining political parties or supporting them creates serious divisions among the human beings. So, to be harmonious with the spirit of unity, it's best we remain nonpartisan. For example, in the United States people have the option to register and affiliate themselves with several different parties, all of which have their own agendas and philosophies which are in conflict with the others. However, in most states there is the option of registering as nonpartisan, or unaffiliated, or some other similar option."

"I'm going to register in Oregon as an Independent," I announced proudly.

She looked at me in disbelief and said, "Grayson, in Oregon, Independent **is** an organized political party! Checking 'not a member of a party' or something similar on one's voter registration card is about the only way to remain unaffiliated with a political party, a set agenda, or a set of beliefs or philosophies about how human affairs should be conducted."

"You mean Independent **is** a political party, just like the rest?"

"Yes, in Oregon it is!" she assured me.

"Well, I guess I didn't know that," I said, feeling foolish. We looked at each other and laughed simultaneously.

"Another spiritual way to maintain a unified relationship with those in authority is to avoid protests or behaviors that are illegal, aggressive, or hostile toward government. On the other hand, peaceful, legal activities for the purpose of educating and enlightening people to options on a particular issue can be expressed in a unifying way. And that's the key. The spirit of the age is love and harmony! Anything that attempts to divide or cause conflict among individuals or groups of people is contrary to the spiritual path and thus our purpose as human beings. The end results do not justify the means, as the elders and leaders of former times often told us. The spirit of the age is that the end outcome, and the means to achieve it, must be harmonious with unity. So the spiritual principle is that religion should remain separated from partisan politics and political disputes. Our personal role is to be law-abiding, loyal, truthful, and honest in all our dealings with duly constituted governments. This is the way of the spiritual heart. This is the way to a unified people and a peaceful world!"

She sat still and focused before continuing abruptly, "This doesn't mean we should avoid discussions about important social or governmental issues. No, not at all! It means we can have meaningful discussions about the important issues of our time, but not if the discussion becomes divisive or those involved are approaching it from partisan points of view. It's an inherent feature of our spiritual reality to explore truths, investigate options, and discuss important issues and topics. To avoid this would be untrue to our spiritual purpose to acquire knowledge and wisdom. When such discussions turn argumentative or divisive, though, or descend into blaming and shaming, or when anger becomes evident, or when partisan views are blindly injected into the discussion, it's time to withdraw from the conversation. It's time to find the path of least resistance and either change the subject to one of agreement or disengage from the discussion all together. To discuss important issues for the purpose of exploring options, trying to understand the varying views, and seeking out wise and meaningful solutions to ongoing problems is part of being human. No real harm can come from it. In fact, it's valuable beyond measure! Unless, of course, those engaged in the discussion are presenting their points of view from some kind of a fixed belief system, like a political party.

"In many ways, political parties are like a secular religion, with founding fathers and a fixed system of beliefs and ideologies. When people attempt to have a discussion on an important topic and their opinion is dictated by the agenda or platform of a political party, they are no longer engaged in a discussion for the purpose of exploring truth. Instead, they are engaged in a debate." She paused for some time. I could tell she was thinking seriously about what to say next.

"I want you to know there are better, more mature ways of problem solving than debate. By its very definition, debating starts out by taking a side and holding on to perspectives commonly dictated by political affiliation, a system of beliefs, or some other agenda. Debate, by its very nature, is competitive, conflicting, and divisive. The object of a debate is winning, not arriving at truth or understanding. It is not unifying and there are rarely any meaningful outcomes. There is an alternative approach to exploring truth called **consultation**, which is another teaching given to us by Bahá'u'lláh. When used properly, it is a far more mature form of problem solving than debate."

I looked at her with puzzlement. "Consultation?" I asked.

"Consultation, guided by the spirit of unity, is a form of discussion wherein participants offer their varied opinions, not with narrow minded attachment, but with humility." She paused for a moment, thinking. "More about this later," she declared. "For now, I want you to be clear about the spiritual approach to politics I have shared and the attitudes necessary for a unified relationship between individuals and government."

She looked at me as though I was supposed to know something or answer her. I looked at her then looked away in silence. Finally, I said, "You know, I think I'm getting something here, and I really like it! It seems no matter what the topic is, or what the issue is, you have an answer, or suggest a spiritual approach to it. Whatever the case, it seems it always has to do with unity, which for me means peace and love. Those are the words that I use to describe the feeling of unity. It's like you always go to that place in your heart where peace, love, and unity prevail, and whatever it takes to approach that, or maintain that spiritual feeling, is how you answer a question or approach a subject. Now, I don't know if that's right, or if that's what God wants, or if it's what Bahá'u'lláh said, or what you're really doing, but it feels like it." I looked at her, hoping for understanding.

"Well, Grayson, I don't know any better way to express it than what you just said," Rose murmured. She smiled a gentle smile, but there were tears welling in her eyes. I couldn't look at her. She seemed to be looking right through me with light. She seemed radiant. She finally turned and reached into her bag for a tissue. We rode silently for some time. I was so excited about this understanding I felt like I was trembling. I even held out my hand to see if I was shaking, but it was steady. I was trembling inside, though, with exhilaration! If this was what Rose had been saying to me all along, if everything she had been telling me was real, then this **was** it! This was what I had been searching for my whole life, and I knew it. This spirit of unity—this was the key to being a human being and living the spiritual path. I knew it because I had felt it before, but I was never able to encapsulate the concept before the way Rose did. If this Bahá'í Faith was really as she was describing it, and not just something in her mind or in the cab of this truck, then I was in with both feet. And my heart! And my soul! My mind was racing. My being was trembling, and my breathing was accelerated. I felt like I was going to wind up too tight if I didn't come down off this spiritual high I was experiencing. I took a deep breath and tried to think of something else, but I couldn't. I just kept smiling and wondering: *Is what I think is happening to me really happening?* I felt hope again that hadn't been there for a long time. Not this depth of hope. I was full of hope, and joy—yes, joy—that was it! "Thank you, God!" I cried out loud.

"Yes, thank you, God," Rose whispered prayerfully. Rose turned to gaze out the window. We rode again in silence.

A while later, Rose cleared her throat, signaling to me she was about to say something. "Leadership is always a hot topic because it has to do with human beings having say over other human beings," she began. "Generally people don't like others telling them what they can or can't, or should or shouldn't do. But leadership is a necessity of life if we are going to achieve any sort of collective undertaking with quality. All tasks require some order, and all order requires some kind of management to organize and guide it to its proposed end. I'm going to define leadership in a very general and simple way. Leadership, essentially, is the responsibility to see that a task is accomplished by a particular group of people. Teachers and school administrators, for example, have the responsibility of educating children. Police officers have the responsibility of protecting people and enforcing the laws of the land. Business leaders have the responsibility to see that their organization produces products or services with efficiency, and as with most businesses, at a profit. All these responsibilities include multiple tasks that must be accomplished if successful outcomes are to be achieved. So the subject I want to talk to you about at this point has to do with the style or methods used to carry out the leadership roles. It has to do with **how** we effectively infuse the role of leadership with spiritual qualities and traits that will create unity between the seemingly polar positions of leaders and their subordinates.

"I have already shared with you the role individuals have in relationship to governing bodies. It is one of honesty, truthfulness, and loyalty, which essentially means if we are to play our part in expressing and seeking out a condition of unity we must be sincerely willing to abide by laws and rules and obey those in authority. But the other side of this relationship, the leadership side, also must have unity as both the means of achieving their task and as a co-equal objective to the task itself."

"What do you mean by that?" I interrupted. "What do you mean by co-equal?"

"Well," she arched her back to stretch her shoulders, and then said, "Most of the time leadership has a specific task to perform. The general rule is for leaders to accomplish their given tasks by nearly any means possible, providing it is legal, and within certain other agreed upon parameters, which means, for the most part, they practice the principle of 'the ends justify the means.' In this new age, we are being called to a greater maturity. The major spiritual principle of leadership specific to the age we are now living in is that the tasks assigned to leaders must be accomplished with the equal objectives of **performing** the tasks in unity, and assuring that their eventual **outcomes** are harmonious with unity as well. This is of major importance." Rose turned to look directly at me while raising her hand to point her finger in a gesture that emphasized the point. "The Creator of all that is, through his manifestation Bahá'u'lláh, has given us this new principle to employ in everything we do. Unity is the central spiritual theme for the current age of man, even in leadership, which historically has been expressed with force or dominance. Now, however, in order to be effective, leadership must adopt unity as both its means and its ends!"

I looked at her doubtfully. *How?* I wondered.

"Yes, I know! That sounds highly idealistic, implausible, and even improbable. But I am suggesting to you that we have been given the means to accomplish it by observing and employing the spiritual principles given to us by Bahá'u'lláh. That is what I am going to share with you now. There are spiritual principles that can help us apply and achieve unity, even in the most volatile of relationships: between those in positions of decision-making authority, and those who are under their governance.

"The style of leadership historically employed by most of the human beings is modeled on those inherent in the various animal groups. Animals use various types of force to ensure compliance with the desires of those in authority. Walruses, for example, bite and stab with their tusks and exile others from the herd in order to force them to comply with the desires of the herd leader. Chickens, I have heard, have a so-called 'pecking order,' which means the head chicken can dole out consequences to every other chicken in the flock unchallenged. The number two chicken in authority can exert violence on all the chickens except the number one chicken. This pecking order goes down the line to the chicken at the bottom. That poor chicken has no power and can be picked on and controlled by all the others. Wolf and dog packs are similar. There is usually an alpha-wolf or dog that has achieved top position and compliance by the pack through physical strength, cunning, and the application of force and violence. The leadership styles of human beings have been similar to these and other animal groups. History is full of examples of physical force and violence used to ensure compliance with those in authority. It still goes on today even though people are weary of it. It continues because no better alternative has been demonstrated.

"Admittedly, leadership styles have improved over time because of the implementation of rules and laws, making violence, for the most part, unacceptable. Thank God for that! Yet leadership still functions on the principle of the ends justify the means, where the violence that was formerly used to achieve compliance is merely watered down to deception, coercion, manipulation, intimidation, misinformation, deceit, secrecy, bribery, and endless other aggressive psychological tactics. I am sure, Grayson, I don't have to convince you that the people are tired of ineffective, inefficient leadership. They are additionally disgusted with those forms of leadership that are physically, emotionally, or mentally aggressive." Rose stopped and turned to look out the window. She was motionless, but tense. I remained quiet, waiting for her to compose herself.

"Over the ages there have been strides in the development of progressive leadership styles that have helped us move away from the more violent forms evident in some animal groups, to the more common types used today. However, they too are limited in their ability to exemplify unity," Rose continued. "One is the authoritarian leadership style. It functions with a hierarchy of unquestioned authority strictly enforced from the top to the bottom of the power structure. Dictatorships and totalitarian states are obvious examples. Also, most military organizations employ this style. Authoritarian leadership style has exposed its abusive potential and dis-unifying means and outcomes that are too numerous to recount. I can tell you it does not create peace, love, and harmony among the people. In fact, the authoritarian leadership style **predictably** creates just the opposite. It will always, sooner or later, provoke opposition and rebellion against those in authority.

"Another leadership style is termed paternalistic. These leaders act like loving fathers or mothers who take care of everything on behalf of everyone else. It has some value in specific circumstances, especially in parenting very young children. But paternalistic leadership among adults creates dependencies and eventually fails because the leaders take the responsibility for doing nearly everything important while the rest of the people are left untrained, never learning how to function without their leaders. When a paternalistic leader leaves, moves on, or dies, the group is no longer able to function because it has been taught by its leaders to be dependent. It is said: 'If you give a man a fish you feed him for a day, but if you teach him how to fish you feed him for life.' Paternalistic leadership just gives people the fish, while doing all the fishing for them. It creates dependencies that are doomed to fail because it cannot sustain their collective accomplishments.

Rose took a short pause and then continued with an explanation of another style of leadership. "Nowadays people often endeavor to employ a democratic leadership style. The democratic leadership style appears to be effective, except it, too, degenerates to a watered-down authoritarianism which still employs manipulative leadership tactics. We see sincere attempts to practice democracy in both business and government, but they still practice the principle of 'the ends justify the means.' Since most leaders don't know of reasonable alternatives to ensure compliance with their desires, they continue to employ the same manipulative styles used for centuries—bribery, coercion, threats, guilt, shame, intrigue, intimidation, manipulation, deception, propaganda, and numerous other mental and emotional control tactics. So I think it is evident, if one observes without prejudice or attachment, even the democratic style seriously lacks the ability to be a unifying form of leadership or governance. So, if the leadership styles currently developed and employed are ineffective and dis-unifying, then what will work? What could work?

"Let's consider some additional principles given to us by Bahá'u'lláh," Rose suggested, "to see how they help us move out of this terrible condition of disunity, to one of harmony, agreement, peace, and accord.

"I would first of all like to give you a list of some Bahá'í leadership principles, and then I'll talk a little about each one. For leadership to be unifying in this new age, it will have to take on a sea-change in perspective. That is, we have to collectively employ a whole new set of principles as a world community if we are to become a peaceful, unified humanity.

"First and foremost, as I mentioned, is the principle of unity as both the means and the ends in all we do.

"Second: we have to think of leadership not as a position to seek, but as a service to which we may be called.

"Third: we employ skills that transmute leadership from a position of dominance and control to one of a facilitator of what is right, good, and true for the sake of all people.

"Fourth: we employ consultation as a means for achieving good decisions instead of debate and compromise.

"Fifth: we apply the high standards of moral integrity emphasized by Bahá'u'lláh in everything we do.

"Sixth: we transform pride and self-superiority into humble fellowship.

"Seventh: we employ all the other spiritual principles I have shared with you in the application of leadership. And those were..." With her right index finger, Rose ticked off the spiritual principles she was referring to on the fingers of her left hand, "Number one, a humble recognition of the one true God. Number two, a recognition and employment of the principle of the oneness of humanity. Number three, the equality of women and men. Number four, the elimination of prejudice as well as the elimination of blind imitation and superstition. And number five, the focused application of justice, wisdom, knowledge, and science."

"In other words, everything I have been talking to you about up to this point is all part of the new leadership style being infused into the consciousness of humankind. In fact, I don't like to think of it as 'leadership' anymore because the word 'leadership' has such negative power-mongering connotations. But because we have no other terms for it, we appear stuck with the word," she complained.

"We can think of the new leadership style envisioned in the Bahá'í writings as one that **facilitates** the tasks at hand while creating and employing peace, love, and unity, Rose explained. "A facilitator style of leadership is one that strives to be comprised of fair administrators, of loving and kind trainers, and of associates, activators, explainers, and strengtheners who exemplify certain outstanding qualities. Specific among these qualities are,

' . . . *unquestioned loyalty, of selfless devotion, of a well-trained mind, of recognized ability and mature experience.'*[45]

"They additionally include humble fellowship, frank expression, open-mindedness, candor, modesty, and devotion to the welfare and interest of the common good. This is the kind of leadership we are talking about as a servant to the new world. These are spiritual leaders who facilitate unity and exemplify mutual cooperation." Rose paused for a moment to catch a breath but quickly resumed.

"Do you remember me talking about truth being relative and not absolute?" She looked at me for a response. She must have seen from my face that I was not sure what she was hinting at because she turned away quickly and proceeded to explain. "Let me say that it should be evident in modern times that truth is relative. That is, the truth about any given issue depends upon one's perspective. Everyone has an inner map of the world, so to speak. It's the inner map of your perspectives of reality that you have developed over time from your life's experiences, your education, your beliefs, your emotions, your relationships with others, your genetic makeup, and numerous other influences. It is your own personal perspective of things. It's the way you understand and make sense of everything in the world. This personal inner map is relative—relative to you and everything that has contributed to making you who and what you are today. Everyone has his or her own personal inner map of the world, and every single map is different from everyone else's. You know this by the fact that when anyone asks a question and posts it on the internet, for example, there are endless different answers proposing solutions, all of which are relative to the perspective of the person giving the answer.

"There are even studies showing a marked difference in the way eyewitnesses perceive an event or incident. If you have a circle of witnesses to an event, staged central to the circle, everyone will have a different perspective. Some will witness one thing and others will witness something else. The truth of the matter is that no one person has a truly complete perspective to the event. However, if everyone were to add their view to a collection of perspectives, then the truth about the given event could be more closely determined.

"This is the way it is with most everything. Everyone has a piece of the pie of truth, so to speak, but no one has the whole pie of truth. This is called relative truth. That is, something is true to you, given your perspective, and someone else may have a different perspective that can be equally true. So, in complex social and spiritual issues, how do we know what is true when there are so many perspectives, each containing a portion of the truth? Can any one person have a complete understanding of an issue? Perhaps, but how will any of us know who has the correct perspective when ours is different enough from theirs that we can't even recognize that they might have a completely clear and true understanding? We can't! So how can we expect to find leaders who can or will make enlightened decisions on our behalf when there is no one out there with a completely clear and true understanding of things? Do you see the dilemma?" Rose asked.

"Well, yes, I see the dilemma, and I have seen it my whole life. I just want to know what to **do** about it," I answered anxiously.

"Do you know anyone who is right, accurate, and fully trustworthy to make good and accurate decisions all the time, or even most of the time?" Rose asked.

"Mmmm, not hardly!" I retorted.

"No, I am sure you don't because no mature adult does," Rose avowed. "So is there any wonder that we struggle to appreciate our leaders when they are nearly as incompetent as anyone else might be?"

I almost laughed at the unintended humor in her question, but when I looked at her I saw real sadness in her eyes. She silently waited for my reply.

"Well, then, what are we supposed to do?" I asked. "No one is perfect. We have to do the best we can, I guess." I looked at her for agreement.

"Yesssss," Rose breathed through a smile. "So you see the limitations individuals have as leaders and the problems that arise when one individual is given absolute decision-making power. They have a limited perspective and therefore have limited potential for making meaningful or accurate decisions. However, if you were able to combine the perspectives of a number of wise, understanding people, then you could have better potential for meaningful decision-making. Here is one of the most profound leadership principles of the new age, given to us by Bahá'u'lláh. He said,

'*From two ranks amongst men power hath been seized: kings and ecclesiastics.*'[46]

"What this means is that single individuals in positions of power and authority, at least in religion and government, are no longer able to be effective in making meaningful legislative, executive, or judicial decisions. The power to do this has been lost, or maybe it simply has run its course in the evolutionary history of mankind. Whatever the case, the principle of the new age is that power, authority, and leadership decisions are best wielded by wise, mature, consultative **groups** of people, not individuals."

Rose waited to see if I had anything to say before continuing. I was silent.

"Everyone has heard the saying 'absolute power corrupts absolutely.' This is because individuals given great decision-making power can easily slip into cruelty, corruption, bribery, and other undesirable behaviors because there is no one to counterbalance their power. Essentially, it is rare that any individual given endless power will not abuse it. If you have a number of individuals responsible for collective decisions, however, individual abuse is thwarted, and the chances of collective abuse become minimal. This was the very issue that concerned the founders of the American government when they set about to form a new system of government here in America."

"I just don't see how you are going to do this," I spouted hotly. "I mean, how do you expect people to be able to employ these principles, as you call them, any differently than they have before or differently than they do now? I mean, just because you say 'use these principles' doesn't mean people can or will! Do you really think it can be different? Do you really think a leadership can be created that will behave or perform the way you are suggesting? I mean, **really?**"

Rose didn't even look at me. She just sat motionless and stared out the front window. I was feeling bad, like I had burst her bubble of hope and joy again. I wished I hadn't said anything. We rode in silence.

After several minutes, Rose gently asked, "Remember me suggested to you that people can change the way they do things by practicing these principles consciously, constantly, and confidently?"

"Yes," I said, still wishing I hadn't flown off the handle.

"I know people who are practicing these spiritual principles regularly. They believe in Bahá'u'lláh as the manifestation of God and believe the teachings he brought us are guidance from the Great Spirit that created and sustains all things. It is the power of this belief that makes it possible for them to apply the principles I am sharing with you. Faith is the most powerful faculty a human being has. It gives one the power to change undesirable behaviors into more spiritually mature characteristics.

"This change for the better is inspired by the words of the manifestations of God," Rose emphasized. "God's teachings have a transforming effect on the human soul. Whenever a soul takes the Word of God into their heart, that soul is then energized and inspired. That inspiration effects a behavioral transformation that can then manifest a loving, kind, and unifying form of leadership. This has always been the way of bettering the behavior of the human beings, and it will remain so. I ask you to remember when I quoted Bahá'u'lláh before:

" . . . *the still greater task of converting satanic strength into heavenly power is one that We have been empowered to accomplish . . . The Word of God, alone, can claim the distinction of being endowed with the capacity required for so great and far-reaching a change.'*[47]

"Do you understand what's being said here?" She looked at me intently.

"Yes, I think so," I responded.

"Do you recall me suggesting, too, that all the good in the world was because of the effects of the teachings of the manifestations of God throughout the ages? And how without their influence the humans would have degenerated into the most savage of beasts?"

I acknowledged her statement with at nod.

"Let me assure you that I have seen this new style of leadership, or facilitatorship, as I like to call it, in action. It is not only possible, but the Bahá'í community of some five million souls is employing it right now throughout the world. Your question was: 'Do I think it's possible to employ leadership in a whole new way, one that is unifying, effective and efficient?' My answer is yes, without a doubt! I know this because we have been given the means and the power to achieve it! I have confidence about it because I see it being practiced regularly and exemplified in the structure of the Bahá'í community worldwide.

"I'll explain a little more so you can have a better vision of how it works and be more confident in its possibilities. Grayson, when I say good decision-making is best made by groups of people, I'm not talking about people getting together with their own personal agendas, platforms, or policies and debating or arguing over an issue. I'm talking about something totally different. I'm talking about a method of communication and decision making called **consultation**, which I mentioned before. Consultation is a type of spiritual conference. It happens when people subjugate their undesirable passions and come together humbly, offering their personal perspectives to the discussion with the intention of making decisions that are unifying and best for the common good of all those affected by the decision. Consultation is frank and loving. It's one person offering his or her perspective at a time. Consultation requires careful listening—true listening with the intent of clearly understanding the opinions and perspectives of others. Consultation is not debate. It is not the presentation of different sides of an issue and then compromising. Insistence or bickering or maneuvering to influence others to side with one's opinion has no part in consultation. Instead, it is spiritual discussion where one presents their personal perspective with humility. It takes time. It can take a lot of time! It takes delving into the depths of one another's souls for understanding, so that unity and consensus may be forthcoming. Yes! It takes willingness, patience, and faith to explore the dark tunnel of different opinions, knowing you can come out into the light of unity, agreement, and consensus by employing the principles of true consultation."

Rose stopped suddenly and turned in her seat to face out the side-window. She sat motionless. I didn't say anything. After a short time, she turned in her seat to face me again. "As I said," she continued, "consultation is not arguing, and it's not debating. It is not yelling or manipulating others with powerful emotions. It is not swearing to emphasize a point. It's not persuasion or attempts to convince others of one's perspective. It is not deceptive and it's never demeaning. It does not attempt to denigrate the opinions of others. It is not about who's right and who's wrong. It's not about winning. It's not about assigning blame or shame. It is not loud, hostile voices.

"Consultation is speaking forth one's perspective with kindness, sharing one's inner map of the world and humbly offering it to the collective pool of opinions. It is a searching of one's soul to offer something of value to the collective perspective. It is an offering of one's opinion frankly and lovingly. It is a search for the truth of the matter at hand. It is listening to others with a sincere desire to understand fully. It is asking questions of one another to clarify what another is expressing. It is an honest, truthful, respectful, humble, and caring spiritual conference. It is patient and persevering, with confident knowledge that true and thorough consultation can and will, conclude in agreement and consensus. And that consensus of opinion will arrive at a decision that is the best of all possible choices relative to the circumstances that currently exist on an issue. It will be the closest to righteousness you can get.

"Consultation is the principle given to us by the manifestation of God for our age as the best means for making decisions among individuals, families, businesses, organizations, and all levels of governance. It's a way of communicating that is spiritual in nature—harmonizing the human beings while allowing them to retain individual expression. This is the way to peace in the world. This is the way to healthy, loving relationships. This is the way of governance for our future. In fact, it's already happening. The old ways are slowly giving way to these more mature ways. Each generation understands this a little better than the one before it. Each generation senses the need for a kinder, more loving, gentler way of interacting with one another, and a kinder, more loving, gentler form of leadership. We are moving in that direction, slowly but surely."

Rose looked at me with a great big smile. I just looked at her and grinned. What else could I do? I loved everything she said. I hoped for it so much. I hated aggression and conflict. Here she was, telling me we can nearly eliminate it, even in governance and leadership! She was **so sure** that I, too, felt sure. I felt hopeful for our future. Perhaps it wasn't so gloomy after all. *There is hope. I can see it now. I can see a way forward for myself and for the world.* I felt giddy. A few of my demons of doubt were struggling to make themselves heard in my head, but my heart felt this truth and it was winning! I looked at Rose. She didn't look the same to me as usual. She was glowing. She was some kind of a special being opening up a renewed vision of hope in me that I knew was there, but it had been dormant for so long. Without Rose, I never could have put it together enough to make sense of things. This little Native woman was redrawing my 'inner map of the world,' as she called it. I felt confident. I felt free— free from the apathetic 'what's the point of trying' perspectives I had in the past. I felt detached some way. I felt like I was above the pettiness of my life and the life of the world. I felt high in a real way—high above the mundane hopelessness that surrounded me. I had vision today. I could see the future, and it was good! It was gloriously good!

I can do this, I thought. *We can do this. We, the 'human beings,' as Rose calls us.* I was trembling again. I held out my hand, but it was steady. I was trembling inside with hope and wonder. *Please God, don't let me lose this!* I prayed silently. I got it. I got the vision, and I was not going to let it go. Not this time. I had it, and I had it good.

"Big Koala, let's take a break up here." I snapped back into my truck seat with a thud. I grabbed the CB and responded, "Find us a place, Tail-gunner." T.J. and Alene went around me on a mission. I smiled as they went by. I loved them. Right now, I think I loved everybody. I was high on life and truth. I looked over at Rose. She looked back and smiled as though she was listening to my thoughts and knew exactly what I was thinking. We drove on, waiting for T.J. and Alene to find a place where we could stretch and have a break.

Rose said, "I have more to share about the hope and the means for better leadership. Here is another spiritual attitude or perspective necessary for good leadership. The Bahá'í writings uphold representative government as a good development. I suppose we could say that the United States government, for example, uses representative leadership, in that we elect representatives from our specific areas to work on our behalf in government. Bahá'u'lláh clarifies the proper attitude representatives should have if they are to serve the people in a way that will facilitate unity. Pertaining to this, Bahá'u'lláh said,

'*It behooveth them, however, to be trustworthy among His servants, and to regard themselves as the representatives of all that dwell on earth. This is what counselleth them, in this Tablet, He who is the Ruler, the All-Wise.*'[48]

"Did you get that?" Rose asked. "They should regard themselves as representatives **of all** that dwell on earth! This means that people in representative governing positions would be more efficient in their service if they considered what would best benefit all people, not just what was good for one's own state, or one's own party, or one's own nation. This suggests that the human beings would do well to reconsider how they want their representatives to function. It suggests that it would be more mature for those in leadership positions if they were to make decisions based on what is best for the **common good** and move away from the divisive type of representation that places them in the position of having to please their constituents, or their party, or their organization, or their people, or whoever it is they represent.

"The forms of leadership where the representatives make decisions based on what they perceive is best for their constituents or their parties is similar to how special interest groups and lobbyists function. They are, by nature of their job, selfishly oriented, serving only the needs of a few. This is nearly always divisive. In contrast, the spiritual principle conveyed by Bahá'u'lláh contains greater potential for making decisions that better serve **all** the people while simultaneously enhancing unity.

"So again you see that all the principles given to us for this age, even those that pertain to leadership and governance, facilitate unity, peace, and harmony among the human beings. Not only does Bahá'u'lláh give us the ideals, principles, and truths to attain unity, he also provides us the power to achieve it." She looked at me, grinning.

I grinned back. I hadn't heard a thing she had just said. My heart was too full of hope and excitement to let any more in. I just knew that I liked what she said, and I loved this woman. Red brake lights glowed up ahead, which meant we were stopping for a break. I was ready.

After stretching and walking about for twenty minutes, and after everyone had the chance to use a restroom and get drinks or a snack, we were back on the road. Rose was ready to continue talking.

"Grayson, there is still more I would like to share with you this afternoon related to the subject of leadership. I know I have mentioned this many times, but I want you to remember that the spiritual principles I am sharing with you from the manifestation of God, Bahá'u'lláh, were given to him by God to help us cope with the issues of modern times and to assist us in our progress as human beings. Most of these teachings were not vigorously promoted by former manifestations of God because humanity was not mature enough for them, nor were the conditions right yet for them to be implemented. But now, in this day, in the time we are now living, they are critical to our survival.

"One of those principles that relate directly to both our spiritual and physical survival is the need to abolish war by laying the foundation and building the charter for an enduring international peace agreement."

I looked at Rose with raised eyebrows. She must have seen the doubt in my face because she went on insistently. "Yes, a binding international peace agreement, signed and supported by leading representatives from all nations, agreeing to abolish war and all that pertains to it." She paused for a moment, eyes toward the sky as if remembering something. "Chief Joseph, Chief of the Nez Pierce Indian People," Rose explained, "once made a famous statement that captures the essence of this commitment." Rose sat up erect, and while gazing out the windshield and holding her arm straight out in front of her, she quoted the great Chief: '*From where the sun now stands, I will fight no more, forever!*'"[49]

"Oh! I like that!" I exclaimed.

"Yes, they are good words," Rose agreed. "Bahá'u'lláh calls for a convocation of the leaders of all nations to come together and make a solemn oath and to write a binding agreement that they will collectively abolish war. This agreement must be so sincere as to further agree to collectively and simultaneously disarm themselves, over time and with oversight, of all armaments produced for the purpose of waging war on one another. The only exception is such weaponry as may be necessary to protect and manage the **internal** affairs of each independent nation. He says that if any one nation should break this agreement and wage war on another, all the nations of the earth would be obliged by the agreement to immediately and collectively stop that nation from its aggressive action. Furthermore, such an agreement would oblige each nation to gradually and significantly reduce taxation upon the people for what was formerly considered a defense budget. This means the peace agreement must include the commitment to eliminate war and eventually any supporting organizational structures, which in our country would include a major portion of the army, navy, air force, and marines.

"Furthermore, it would include the eventual destruction of most weapons produced for the purpose of war, including nuclear, biological, and other weapons. Bahá'u'lláh makes it clear that this agreement must be upheld by an international governing body, comprised of elected or appointed representatives from each nation of the earth. The representatives are to be chosen or appointed on their integrity that they can and will uphold the international agreement and make decisions pertaining to the good of **all the people** of the earth, and not just for the select interests of the nation they represent.

Pray God!" Rose nearly shouted. "We won't have to have an all-out war again before we can make this binding agreement! Pray God! We don't have to engage in another world conflict before we are intelligent enough to fully implement this guidance. Pray God! We don't have to have another serious crisis before our leaders preemptively take these vital steps to prevent it."

Rose stopped speaking and turned to look out the window. She was breathing heavily. She had been so emphatic and serious that I was afraid to say anything. I was thinking to myself, *Is she really expecting this to happen?*

She suddenly continued, "This might sound like an awfully big order to accomplish, especially given the current condition of international posturing. This directive for the abolition of war was given to us in the 1800s. At that time, it seemed completely impossible, but there have been great strides forward since then. The development of the League of Nations, and its evolution into the United Nations is an example. I would hope that we have learned the futility of war. I hope we will continue to make every effort to attain international peace."

She paused long enough for me to ask, "Rose, how can we do anything about it? We, the common people, don't have much to say about how our leaders carry out international affairs."

She looked at me and smiled. "Oh, yes, we do!" she exclaimed. "First of all, we have the power of the vote, which is becoming more and more powerful around the world as democratic-style governments are being formed wherein people are given the opportunity to vote for their leaders. More and more of us can appraise the qualifications of those running for office and vote for those who are more supportive of peaceful problem solving rather than those who support the use of force and war as a means for resolving differences. The international peace agreement and its supporting governmental organization advocated by Bahá'u'lláh will be created by the governmental leaders of the world's nations. They are the only ones that can make a binding and enforceable agreement to end war. However, the common people can have influence on this process by selecting those who are most supportive.

"Further to this I have to say that women will have a significant role in advancing this effort. Once women have attained an equal position to influence the affairs of the world, they will collectively and emphatically refuse to send their husbands, sons, and daughters to war! May they take this stand soon—now, if possible—throughout the world! And may they maintain the pressure until such time as this great agreement and its supporting structures are fully established."

Rose paused for a short time, and as if she were reading my mind, she acknowledged, "I know this sounds idealistic and nearly impossible to achieve. The people are ready, but the governmental leaders need help. I have assured you before that great things come about through the power of faith in the manifestation of God and with confidence in carrying out his message! This is the way all good things materialize. The process of peace has already been set in motion, and the people can either support it and assist its forward movement or resist it. To resist only increases the chances of further calamitous wars, the horrors of which are too awful to even consider. Pray God this peace agreement will come about soon."

During the lunch break T.J. had insisted that when we approached Seattle we should take the 405 to avoid downtown Seattle rush hour traffic. We all thought it was a good idea at the time, so we agreed. It was three in the afternoon. We had just turned off I-5 onto the 405 maybe twenty minutes earlier, and now the traffic was getting heavy and slow. We had automobiles all around us. Driving suddenly became intense. Sonia was staying right behind me, but even that was becoming challenging. Rose could see that I was distracted by all the traffic, so she remained quiet. Finally, she commented, "I thought T.J. said we would avoid the rush hour traffic if we took this route." She snickered. Curious, I looked over at her. She sat stiff with tension against the door. Her eyes were fixed on the traffic ahead. Her legs were braced as though we were about to crash and her right hand was gripping the hand rest. I burst into hearty laughter. It was my turn to laugh at her for a change.

"K-kind of s-sscary, huh?" I managed to sputter as I laughed.

"It's just been a long time since I have been in traffic like this," she remarked.

"Me, too, but thankfully it's going slow." I no sooner said it when we slowed to a crawl. I hadn't experienced stop-and-go traffic for many years—the kind where you drive a little ways at twenty miles an hour, and then stop completely.

Annie came on the CB, reporting, "Dad said they call this gridlock."

Welcome to the city, I thought.

It took us three hours to travel from the north side of Seattle to the city of Lakewood, Washington. It was a long and tense drive, but we got out of the city, off the highway, and began slinking down back streets toward Franklin's stepparents' house. When we arrived there, I put the truck into park and shut it down. I looked over at Rose and let out a big sigh. "Whew! I'm glad that's over!" I exclaimed.

"Me, too," agreed Rose, as she shuffled around to gather her things.

Rose called her family and made arrangements for them to come pick her up. The rest of us sat around in the yard talking. At the request of Franklin's stepparents everyone decided that we would stay an extra day in Lakewood. Rose came over to me and asked if she could speak to me privately before her family came to pick her up.

We walked out to where the truck was parked before Rose stopped and turned to look straight at me. "I'm not finished yet!" she said in desperation. "I had planned on staying here with my family, but I am not finished with the recording yet. I heard the rest talking about going shopping tomorrow. Do you think you and I could spend some time together and maybe finish up this book?"

I was glad she said that. I was not in favor of staying an extra day in Lakewood anyway, and if Rose needed more time to finish, then I was committed. We had come too far not to complete this project in a way that was satisfying to her. "You can come back here tomorrow if you want. We can sit out in their beautifully landscaped garden and continue our project. I don't want to go sightseeing or shopping anyway," I assured her. She gave me a big grin and sighed with relief.

DAY NINE

THE ENVIRONMENT

Franklin's family lived down a long, narrow lane, near a stream, on the outskirts of Lakewood. It felt isolated from the city, in a way, because it was surrounded by tall trees and dense, coastal foliage. They had a large backyard that long ago had been beautifully landscaped with stone walkways, retaining walls, water features, flowers, exotic plants, and trees. Because Franklin's stepparents were now elderly and unable to keep it up, it was mostly overgrown, with just a few trails leading through it. There was a uniquely pleasant, beautiful little clearing near the center with an old couch-like swing that had a tarp recently thrown over it. Rose liked the swing, so we decided to sit there and continue our project. The swing was low, so it was easy for Rose to use. She pulled the recorder out of her travel bag and motioned for me to sit down. I was tired of sitting. "If it's all right with you, Rose, I would like to mosey around this little clearing while you talk. I can hear you just fine. Would that be all right?"

"Sure, Grayson," she said with a smile.

"Ah—today is a beautiful day, indeeeed," Rose crooned, giggling at her attempt to sound Canadian. "The sunshine, the beautiful blue sky, and the smells of the earth this early in the morning are exhilarating!"

"Yes, it is beautiful," I agreed, looking around me at the wonder of the little garden. We were both silent as we admired our surroundings. But my immersion in the natural world wouldn't last, as it sparked a thought in my mind. "I can't help but feel a bit of grief at the thought of our rampant assault on the earth's beauty, you know, the environment. It seems we are rapidly losing our natural world, and there isn't much hope of us saving it from its eventual destruction. I mean, this whole global climate change is scary!" I looked at Rose to see if this line of discussion was okay with her. She just sat still, swinging gently, looking straight ahead. I continued, "It appears to be proceeding just as the scientists said it would, only faster. Even in my lifetime, I have seen obvious consequences of the unrestricted destruction of our natural world. Do you know," I continued with disgust, "there is a trash pile in the Pacific Ocean—a floating island of garbage and plastics twice the size of the state of Texas? It's so large that it can be seen from the space station! There are so many things." I trailed off, pausing long enough to catch a breath. "The ice melting in the polar regions, the consequential rise in seas level, the extremes in bad weather, the acidification of the oceans and its loss of sea life, species going extinct with more disappearing every day, unregulated deforestation, the pollution of water and air—**where will it all end**? How can it end if we keep living the way we are? Our populations are growing worldwide, each demanding its right to exploit the earth's resources—until what? Until they're all used up? It seems to me that we human beings, as you call us, are consuming the earth's great gifts at such a pace there is little hope of reversing it in time to prevent a serious worldwide calamity. I mean, it took millions of years, billions in fact, for the earth to form its natural beauty." I waved my arms outwards as if to welcome an embrace from the garden before us. "And once it's destroyed, it will take centuries for it to stabilize. How can we do this? I am so upset about it. Driving through Seattle yesterday in all that traffic after traveling through Canada reminded me of what's going on. I don't like it! What do you think, Rose? You speak about our spiritual life and how we should be treating each other, and that's good and all, but in the meantime we're indiscriminately destroying our own home." I looked at Rose to see if she was concerned. She sat stationary in the swing, just looking straight ahead without showing any emotion.

I bent over to inhale the fragrance of a small yellow rose that was blooming near the trail. Finally, I continued. "Oh, there are good things happening, I suppose. People are recycling. We have started using solar and wind power. We're concerned about our personal carbon footprint, and people are talking about it. Still, there doesn't seem to be enough meaningful action—fast enough, you know—no urgency! I know you suggested moderation in all things, but this seems urgent to me!" I looked at her again, waiting for a response. Nothing.

"And the corporate world just keeps right on with their destructive ways—like fracking, for example, as though there will be no serious consequences. I think the corporate world, and maybe even the government, promote personal involvement in saving the environment mainly to divert public attention away from them—the biggest violators of all. They encourage everyone to focus on their personal contribution to save the environment so they can keep right on with their destruction, unabated! That's what I think!" I growled. I was worked up now, feeling my heart rate and blood pressure rising. I was upset. I felt powerless to do anything about a looming disaster from our indiscriminate destruction of the planet. I walked over to an old stump where I had carefully placed my coffee mug. Taking a big gulp, I walked over to the swing, turned around, and backed up to sit down. I felt powerless and on edge. Here I was, taking in the beauty of this wonderful garden in Washington State while feeling upset that too little was being done to save the earth from being destroyed!

"What do you think, Rose? Do you think we're doing enough? Do you think we can slow down the destruction enough to avoid disaster? I heard one scientist explain if the water continued to warm up in the polar regions and melted enough ice, it could cause the ocean currents to nearly stop! He said it was the melting of the polar ice sheets and their consequential fresh water rivers plunging into the oceans that cause the ocean currents to move about the earth. He was saying that the slowing of the ocean currents had already caused some weather changes, and there were now areas in the oceans where the current has slowed sufficiently to decrease the oxygen level—enough so, that sea life can no longer live in some areas! They call these regions 'dead zones.' And this scientist said if the ocean currents slow enough, they would be unable to deliver enough warm water back to the polar regions, eventually producing a mini-ice age! Yeah! He said it could be cold enough in North America to produce a solid ice pack throughout Canada and into the northern areas of the United States within a ten-year period. This would also mean solid ice pack over a large portion of Europe and Asia! Now that's scary! So, did Bahá'u'lláh say anything about this? I mean, doesn't this matter?" I looked at Rose pleadingly, wishing for some kind of hopeful response. She remained still. I thought, *Maybe I shouldn't have started ranting on this subject. Rose probably had something else she wanted to discuss.* I was already wound-up and into it before I knew it, though. As I crossed my arms and looked out at the garden, Rose broke her silence.

"Yes, he did!" she declared emphatically, slapping the seat between us. She shut her eyes and took a long pause. "He said, and I quote directly,

'*If carried to excess, civilization will prove as prolific a source of evil as it had been of goodness when kept within the restraints of moderation. Meditate on this, O people, and be not of them that wander distraught in the wilderness of error.*'[50]

"He also wrote,

'*Strange and astonishing things exist in the earth but they are hidden from the minds and the understanding of men. These things are capable of changing the whole atmosphere of the earth and their contamination would prove lethal.*'[51]

"It should be clear from these quotations that he duly warned us of potentially disastrous consequences associated with excessive use, or misuse, of the earth's resources. It is also clear in the Bahá'í writings that the impending calamity can be lessened if mankind collectively turns toward its Creator for guidance and assistance and follows that guidance. The human beings would do well to listen to their loving hearts, opening them up to the message of the one who speaks as the spirit of God for our time! I believe this is our greatest hope in lessening the evident calamity looming from overutilization of the earth's great bounty." She looked at me with the most serious expression I had yet seen on her face.

"It means the human beings would do best to remember that we have repeatedly shown, generation after generation, civilization after civilization, that we are too selfish, too ignorant, and too immature to solve our problems on our own or with foresight. The Creator has made us this way that we may humbly discover and understand this, and turn to him for guidance and protection. We do this by deferring to the teachings of the manifestations of God. And, as I have repeatedly stated, the teachings of the manifestations of God are given to address the needs of the age and time in which they are delivered. So, yes, Bahá'u'lláh did give us the knowledge and the power to avert or lessen the destructive process we are now so foolishly engaged in. The guidance he gave requires conscious application of the truths and principles he revealed. Even so, the mindful application of these outstanding principles is not enough by itself. The power to accomplish a meaningful outcome takes a real and heartfelt faith in God that he knows what he is doing! It takes faith in the fact that God sends true guidance through his manifestations, a faith that Bahá'u'lláh is the manifestation for our time, and a faith that the truths and principles he gave us are right for what is good. I don't mean a blind faith, mind you, but a conscious knowledge and understanding of who we are as human beings and what our purpose is in life."

She stopped and returned her gaze to the garden. It was then I realized I was sitting on the left side of the swing and she on the right, just like when we were in the truck! She was silent for a time, but I couldn't stand the silence.

"I don't get it," I said, jumping up from my seat. Pacing about the clearing, I fired off the questions on my mind. "Did Bahá'u'lláh say anything specifically about the environment then? Did he give us a direction or a plan of action to prevent us from eventually destroying ourselves? What? What did he say about it, Rose?"

Rose stopped swinging and stared at me. She stared with such intensity it was as if she were seeing through to my core. I had to look away. "Oh, Grayson," she intoned quietly. "**Everything** I've been sharing with you these past several days **is** his plan of action—don't you see? If we human beings turn whole-heartedly to him and his teachings, we will discover that they give us the best possible outcomes for all the issues we are concerned about, including the environment. That's what I have been trying to tell you! When the humans turn to God and humbly approach him for guidance, they find that his manifestations have always given the answers." She paused for a moment, sitting still, looking at the ground. "I am reminded of this quotation from Bahá'u'lláh," she said, before reciting,

'*The All-Knowing Physician hath His finger on the pulse of mankind. He perceiveth the disease, and prescribeth, in His unerring wisdom, the remedy.*'[52]

"Let me show you what I mean. Let's take our concern over the loss of the natural environment, and its predictable outcome, and apply the teachings and principles of Bahá'u'lláh to the issue to see how they help resolve it. Are you up to that?" she asked with a smile.

"I sure am!" I replied.

"First, let's consider the principle of the oneness of God. 'What does this have to do with the environment and nature?' you might ask. I think most people sincerely do want to preserve the natural environment; it's just they disagree how it should be done or what's causing its destruction. Some are afraid of losing what they have, so they don't want to consider too much change. Most everyone revels in the beauty and wonder of nature and knows we would be deprived of one of the greatest gifts of life if we had to live without it. So what is it about nature that is so valuable, other than the obvious fact that it supplies us with everything necessary for life?"

Rose paused for some time and looked about the garden. "You know what it's like to gaze on a beautiful piece of artwork, say, at an upscale gallery?" She looked at me, asking further, "Have you ever done that?"

"Well . . . yes," I replied.

"You know that feeling of admiration you have when you view a piece of artwork that's beautiful, or adorable, or fascinating? Do you realize that when you find a piece of artwork you are attracted to, you are, in reality, admiring the artist?"

I frowned at her in confusion.

"When you admire a fine piece of art," Rose explained, "you are really admiring the artist—because—everything about that piece of art came from the artist. Everything!" She was silent for a moment, letting that soak into my conscience. "Or, let's say you have a high quality piece of fine furniture, or a hand-woven rug, or a tall, beautiful building, or a song, or a poem, or a story—whatever— something you think is beautiful that is man-made. Whenever you admire something outstanding made or created by human beings, you are really admiring the maker of those fine things, because they created it, or invented it, or built it. They conceived it within themselves and then brought it into creation. And so it is with nature. Everything you admire or find awesome or beautiful in the creation—like the natural forests we drove through for the last eight days—everything in the natural world reflects, comes from, and has its origin in the Creator, that is, the one true God! When you go into nature to find your peace and serenity, you actually are having an experience with God, the Creator of all things, whether you know it or not. That's why people love nature so much. It puts them in touch with the Great Spirit. Everyone loves it, and everyone needs it, even if they don't admit it, or if they choose to think of it in some other way. The principle of the oneness of God, then, inspires a love for the natural world, which is vital to motivating a determined effort to preserve it.

"The Creator and Sustainer of all things in the universe and beyond has made the human beings the most advanced, the most intelligent, and the highest life form on this planet. Therefore, we, and we alone, have the capacity and responsibility to conserve the natural world. The dinosaurs couldn't do it! The insects can't do it! No! Just us. We are the stewards of the planet—its caretaker, its manager, its governor, and its preserver. We have the capacity and responsibility to use its bountiful resources wisely and to preserve them sufficiently for infinite generations to come. The Creator of all that is has infused us with the capacity to meet this responsibility. When we consider the principle of belief in the one true God, and believe in his guidance through his manifestation, we then acquire the **means** to be good stewards of the earth and the **power** to achieve it through a collective, unified effort. Belief in the one true God, and faith in him, is imperative to addressing the concerns of the environment successfully. The environment, or nature, does not exist separate from its Creator. It is integral.

"Now, let's consider the principle of the unity and oneness of religion," Rose continued. "If the human beings perceived themselves as all being part of one common faith, their ability to mobilize collective action with wisdom and intelligence on most any issue would be without question. I suggest to you that the empowerment necessary to solve complex or threatening issues is best created by unity in faith. There is no power like it. It is clearly demonstrated in our history, and every generation knows it to be true. The oneness of religion is not just a 'warm-fuzzy.'" Rose crooked her fingers to show quotation marks. "It's becoming more evident how necessary it is for our survival and our ability to flourish on this planet. But so long as religions perceive themselves as separate from one another, or superior to others, or more special than others, they will not be able to contribute adequately to agreeable solutions nor rally their believers to collective action. It should be obvious to any mature observer that it will take a unified, collective, worldwide, agreed upon plan of action to combat the unrelenting attack that has been launched on the natural world.

"While we're on the subject, I want to include the principle of the importance and need for religion. Remember, I'm referring to true, pure religion, based on reality, and not religion steeped in superstition or meaningless tradition. If you listen to the people, you will hear they are seriously concerned about the order of society, as we have known it, coming unraveled. People are worried about the decline in morality, or human virtues as some call it, or Godly qualities, or spiritual characteristics, or ethics, or whatever you want to name them. They see them disappearing, and many are alarmed. These qualities are essential to everything that makes us human, and they know it. Some of these vital qualities include truthfulness, trustworthiness, kindness, respect, tolerance, good work ethics, compassion for others, responsibility, and so forth. People are worried about their children and their grandchildren and what kind of world they are going to inherit. They see the good things around them collapsing and know it is ominous. At the same time, there is a steady decline in the respect and value of religion in the lives of the people, which is adding to the perpetual decline of these virtues and a consequential decline in the integrity of our society. I tell you this: the common perception that there is no need for religion in modern times will continue to spread. Each generation, for some time now, has dissociated itself from organized religion while perceiving themselves as being spiritual without it. After a time, the people of the earth will realize they cannot live without the true spirituality of religion. There will be a collective understanding that we cannot live or survive without knowing our true purpose in life and engaging in that purpose. They will realize that only religion can fulfill that spiritual need. Not religion as we might have known it, mind you, but religion as we know it should be. Then, there will be a spiritual revival, a collective search and awakening, a rebirth of religious faith and true spirituality. As a result, people will acquire a truer understanding of the religions of the past and see them in a new light. They will see them in their proper relationship as being necessary chapters of one ongoing, progressive unfoldment of the Creator's guidance to the human beings. They will see themselves as one people, of one planet, created by one God, and cohorts of one common faith. This renewed perspective of faith, religion, and spirituality will empower the people to rightfully and effectively engage in their destiny and make the necessary decisions to act, care for, and preserve the natural environment and its resources for generation to come."

Rose sat motionless, erect in her seat, and staring straight ahead. I knew there was more to come. I waited.

"And the sooner, the better," she continued. "The deterioration of true religion and spirituality is taking a toll on society. How far do we have to decline before there is a collective awakening? I don't know. But the longer it's postponed, the more society will degenerate, as will the natural environment and its dearly-loved resources. Furthermore," she looked at me sternly, "we cannot wait for this mass awakening. Each one of us that hears the call to action in our hearts must engage!" She put her hand over her heart. "The sooner we put these spiritual principles into action, the sooner the ongoing decline of our societies and the loss of the environment will begin to diminish."

Rose sat back in her seat; she lifted her feet off the ground and began to swing ever so gently. Letting out a big sigh, she turned to look to her right as though she was still in the truck looking out the side-window. She was quiet for some time, and then she said, "I'm sorry I became so emotional and direct there. My passions sometimes overtake me, and I express the urgency I am feeling. I hope you understand." She looked over at me with apologetic eyes.

"I love everything about you, Rose," I said without thinking, "and I love everything you say, and the way you say it. You have nothing to apologize for. Your love is great, and the vision of hope and love you are sharing with me needs no apology."

I walked over and sat down on the swing again. She looked at me through tearful eyes, put her hand on my shoulder, and then turned to sit restfully in her seat. "Okay, thank you, Grayson," she said. "I will try to stay focused and just share this as it comes. I hope it is okay."

"I'm sure it is," I assured her.

"Let's continue," she said softly. "Let's consider the spiritual principle of the oneness of mankind and how its application would affect the preservation of the environment. When people really and truly believe and act on the belief that all human beings are one people, then everything we do will change. When we realize that harm to another is really harm to ourselves, that another's joy is our joy, another's pain and suffering prompts our pain and suffering, then we will act in ways that assist and benefit others, and not in ways that take advantage of another's weakness, ignorance, or vulnerability. The oneness of humankind means we modify our behavior so that we cause no harm to others, no matter who they are or where they are from.

"Generally, this is not the case in the world today. Some of the human beings are seizing and consuming the various resources of the planet at terrible costs to others. It is blatantly inhumane for one to think that their company, or their nation, or their people, or their skill set, or their particular knowledge and power gives them a right to take advantage of others at their expense. Right now in the world, little consideration is given to the long-term collective effects of the exploitation of the earth's resources. Rich and powerful countries take or buy-off poorer nations and sometimes completely strip them of their abundant resources, leaving serious destruction in their wake. The same thing happens with wealthy, powerful companies. At the present rate, unchecked utilization of many of the planet's natural resources could become depleted in just a few decades, leaving future generations with nothing but devastation. However, when the common people and those in business or government consciously, constantly, and faithfully apply the principle of the oneness of mankind to all their decisions related to natural resources, thereby treating all people, cultures, and nations with loving kindness and respect, then this inconsiderate destruction of our planet can be averted."

We were both silent for a spell before Rose resumed.

"Next we'll consider the principle of equality for all people, more specifically, for the moment, the equality of men and women. Women, more so than most of their brothers, are naturally more compassionate and more attuned to the oneness of humankind. They naturally are more aware of the intimate and complex relationships between people as well as between people and the environment. When the equality of men and women becomes universally applied, it will naturally result in a more compassionate humankind, allowing us to respond more effectively to the needs of the natural world. Shameful indeed is man for not lovingly embracing the equality of women."

She paused for some time again, thinking. "Not only does this principle propose equality for women, but it means equality for all people. Let each person, each group, each people, and each nation of people carefully consider how they perceive those who appear different from themselves. May they all sincerely search their hearts to find that place where true understanding abounds. May they find within their hearts the love it takes to subjugate their prideful feelings of superiority over others. May they come to see themselves as true and equal fellow human beings. May it be so!" she pleaded as she gazed up at the blue sky overhead. I saw her wipe her eyes with the back of her hand. Even though she tried not to show her heart-felt grief over this serious issue, that had clearly caused much pain in her life.

Finally, Rose sat upright quickly, shook her head as though dispelling any unwanted thoughts or emotions, and then picked up where she had left off.

"I would hope that the principle requiring harmony between science and religion speaks for itself on this issue. Religion can no longer cling to superstitious interpretations of the spiritual truths given to us by the former manifestations of God. Science proves certain truths, and religion should conform to these truths. For example, global climate change and the unmistakably overwhelming impact the humans are having on it are indisputable. It is scientific fact. Scientists have proven that the global climate changes now taking place are caused by an unprecedented increase in the release of carbon dioxide gas. They also have reported that the amount of carbon dioxide in the atmosphere necessary to propel the current rate of global warming and climate change is exactly equal to the amount of carbon dioxide being expelled into the atmosphere by the activities of the human beings. This tells us there is a direct causal relationship between human-produced carbon gasses and global warming. This global climate change is not a natural phenomenon. It is not part of a natural cycle. It's the earth's response to flagrant abuse of the environment. It is human caused. There is no intelligent debate on this issue anymore. There is, however, plenty of false information being propagated by politicians, religious leaders, special interest groups, and media conglomerates who fear they have something to lose unless they deny these facts.

"Conversely, science has the responsibility to remain true to the scientific method, to interpret its findings free from preconceived theories, and to adopt ethics and morals that harmonize with our reality as spiritual beings. Obviously this would create more favorable conditions for religious believers to adopt scientific facts. With that in our favor, we could have a more unified effort at addressing environmental concerns successfully. In addition, the application of good science will help us devise more effective ways and means to deal efficiently with all concerns pertaining to the environment. Essentially, it will require the truths of science and the faith of religion to combat the ongoing destruction of our natural world.

"I invite you to consider carefully these spiritual principles and truths given to us by Bahá'u'lláh. Surely you will find hope and assurance in our ability to devise plans and find means to a better future. All these truths I have shared with you, when collectively applied, give us the best possible chance for abating the destruction of the environment and the consequential impending doom."

I was up again, pacing about the little twenty by twenty-foot clearing in the garden. I had been listening intently and was feeling energized.

"Another spiritual principle," Rose continued, "is compulsory education for children. Consider how if children were properly educated, which includes true spiritual education, their loving concern for others would give them the capacity and the will to behave in caring ways toward other children and people on the planet, as well as the great mother earth herself. Well-educated, kind, and loving children make for intelligent, caring adults.

"Proper learning and education also protects us from being

influenced by those who are self-serving, deceptive, and misleading, which leads us to appreciate the value of emphasizing and employing the principle of giving high merit to knowledge and wisdom. Without the careful application of knowledge and wisdom to the environmental issue, we can only expect continued immature, ineffective responses to the crisis.

"The application of justice to this issue—another spiritual principle we talked about—demands that we do what is right, good, true, and fair. Can this be argued? What if we were to weigh all proposals against the principle of justice? What if, before we did anything, we asked ourselves, 'Is this behavior, this decision, or this action just? Is it right? Is it true? Is it truly good? Is it fair as it pertains to the people of the earth and the preservation the earth's natural resources?' If the answer is no, then we should work on it until we can answer with a resounding 'Yes!' This is how we apply the spiritual principle of justice to everyday problems.

"And what about the principle of universal peace upheld by global governance? Have you considered the environmental impact of nuclear war?" I stopped pacing and turned to look at Rose. Our eyes locked as we both imagined the outcome.

"Nearly total destruction of the planet—for centuries!" I shuddered.

We were both quiet for some time.

Rose continued, "Peace! I can only hope we will all do everything we can to foster and promote an international agreement by our governments to end all war. May the people rise up and demand it of their governmental leaders worldwide. May God help us!"

"Next let's consider the spiritual principle of fair distribution of wealth and services and its impact on preserving the environment," Rose proposed. The key word here is 'fair.' When we consider the effects of eliminating extremes of wealth and poverty, we can predict more moderate lifestyles and a lessening of the exploitation of the world's natural resources for the sake of having more. This is also true of the principle of moderation. When people consciously, constantly, and confidently apply the principle of moderation in their lives, the destructive consequences of excess become naturally averted.

"As you can probably tell by now, these spiritual principles given to us by Bahá'u'lláh can be applied to everything. I suggest they are the means to cure the spiritual ills that currently afflict the human beings. Our social sickness is a spiritual sickness, in that we have given up on religion and spirituality, when in fact, it is our surest remedy and greatest hope! Not religion as we may have known it, but religion as we know it can be.

"I have not been able to cover all the spiritual principles that apply here, but you get the idea of how it's done. When we apply these God-given spiritual principles to our lives and to the issues that confront us, we can be assured of the best of all possible outcomes, no matter what the problem or concern. This is the promise. This is the essence of what I am sharing with you."

Rose was done, or at least I thought she was. She sat slumped and relaxed, gently swinging back and forth in her seat, gazing at the garden vista. I, too, sat quietly on the old stump where I had kept my coffee mug. I started thinking about being here in Washington, how we were getting closer to our destiny, and of all the things I would need to do once we arrived in Oregon. Suddenly, Rose perked up and started talking about the environment again.

"Other vitally important spiritual principles to consider when assessing the truth about the environment, and more specifically global climate change and its effects on the earth, are independent investigation of truth and the elimination of thoughtless imitation and superstition. Do you remember us talking about these principles?"

I nodded.

"Independent investigation and freedom from both mindless imitation and the foolishness of superstition mean we are obligated as human beings to be true to ourselves and the greater good. It means we believe and act in ways that are free from the control, influence, and opinions of others. It means we make efforts not to be unduly influenced by our friends, families, associates, or co-workers, and certainly not by the extremists in religion, politics, media, and government. It means we resist the temptation to let others rouse our emotions and enlist our support of their personal, financial, or nationalistic agendas. It means we dispassionately, in the best way we know how, investigate and find the truth of matters for ourselves, and then take a firm stand to support that truth. It means we re-evaluate what we believe to make sure it is true and not based on false traditions, beliefs, or behaviors. It means we take a conscious look around us at the world, gathering the best information from the most reliable and trustworthy people—the truly wise and loving souls who have no personal or group agenda. Then we take action by personally doing our part to reduce the greenhouse gases contributing to global warming. It means we support those who do the same and support all the other plans of action collectively devised as we apply these principles. It means we get behind businesses, organizations, and nations that work to reverse the deadly trend we have inherited. It means we are true to the spirit of the age and supportive of all that is good. Above all, it means whatever we do—or don't do—we do without anger, hostility, or violence. Instead, we set love and unity as our highest priorities and proceed with the utmost kindness. This is the true way of spirituality."

I was strolling about the clearing, listening and enjoying the fact that I didn't have to drive while Rose spoke. I didn't know if there was more, but soon Rose proved there was.

"It will take consultation," she said, "another Bahá'í principle I shared with you. It will require frank, loving, and dispassionate consultation among the peoples of the earth, the experts, and the policy maker to assess the situation. Together they can plan actions that will be effective in turning the current climate toward a more stable condition. Those plans of action will require sacrifice on everyone's part to set limits to our individual and collective use of the earth's resources. Excesses will need to be trimmed to necessity. Necessity itself will have to be redefined. It will require us to employ the spiritual principle of moderation, both in the future use of resources and in the methods of planning for action. Maturity is needed here, which I think is best expressed in a collective mirroring forth of the spiritual principles submitted by Bahá'u'lláh. It is the most effective plan for the human beings to collectively abandon their adolescent-like behaviors and arise to the challenge of spiritual maturity and adulthood. This issue over the stewardship of the environment and the earth's natural resources is like all other issues facing the human beings. No single approach can adequately address them. It will take a collective change in the world society.

"Just as I have outlined the spiritual principles necessary to deal with the issue of global climate change, I furthermore suggest the employment of these same spiritual principles to address all other human concerns—from our daily personal activities to more complex global matters. The issues are complicated. People feel anxious and confused. If you carefully consider with mature contemplation how the collective application of these spiritual teachings and principles given to us by Bahá'u'lláh would affect society, you will surely conclude that this is the surest way forward for dealing with global climate change and all other problems facing us on this great and wondrous planet.

"Reflect deeply upon any of the multiple social concerns and carefully consider how these truths and principles enunciated by Bahá'u'lláh would affect them. Whether it be the decline in health or the inefficiency of the healthcare delivery systems, the difficulty in educating our children, the moral and ethical decay, the trends in aggressive and violent behavior, or the excessive substance abuse." Rose gasped for air, took a couple breaths, and then continued. "Consider their influence on the trends toward anarchy or the concerns of over-controlling governments, the devastating effects of excessive freedoms, the excessive accumulation of power and wealth by the few, the disunity among the varying political, ethical, national, or religious groups, the confusion over the basis of the family or the conflicting opinions over the rights and wrongs of human behavior!"

Rose stopped talking. She had given me a long list of issues that would take a long time to ponder.

As I arose from my stump, I interjected, "I remember in the early seventies feeling that we were, as a society, doomed. I felt that greed, corruption, and immorality were on the rise and that they would eventually cause our demise. People use to call me Chicken Little, because I was always warning them things were going to fall apart. For the most part, most people didn't believe me. Now nearly everyone sees the declining trends that you just noted! Oh, there are those who try to be positive—if you want to call it that—who try to paint a rose-tinted picture of everything. It's an admirable quality, I suppose. Unless, of course, they are simply in denial and use their rose-colored glasses to obscure what's really going on. People are concerned and confused. They have had no reasonable solutions proposed to them. Until now, I had never heard of such a comprehensive proposal with such a reasonable approach to dealing with just about everything."

"It's more like a **means** of dealing with everything," Rose corrected. "More like **the spirit** with which we deal with things."

"Yes, I get that," I assured her.

"It's a means of living in harmony with our purpose as human beings, which is to acknowledge the one true God and find favor in his way," Rose went on. "It's 'the way' spoken of by the manifestation of God, Jesus. This is *'the way and the truth and the life,'*[53] more fully revealed for the needs of modern human beings. Remember that Jesus said,

'Though I have been speaking figuratively, a time is coming when I will no longer use this kind of language but will tell you plainly about my Father.'[54]

"Well, that time has finally come."

It was over. I got it, and I knew it. Something happened within me that infused my soul with a deeply felt contentment. I just smiled at Rose as I looked over at her from my stump. I had arrived at my true destiny, and it wasn't Oregon! It was everything Rose had been telling me for these last several days. This was for me, and I was for it. *I'm a Baháʼí*, I thought. *That does it! I want to be Baháʼí, just like Rose!*

I was up again, pacing around the garden while Rose sat in the swing, rummaging around in her travel bag, looking for something. I was reveling in my certainty when Rose started in again.

"Grayson, there is more. The problem with the rampant over-utilization of the earth's resources is profound and complex. It's been going on for a long time. The essence of the problem is that the human beings collectively abandoned a spiritual view of reality and adopted a materialistic concept of the purpose and reality of life on this planet. It is understandable how and why there has been a gradual abandonment of religion. Its authoritarian style of leadership, its misinterpretation of the words of the manifestations of God, its subsequent superstitions and fantasies, and its insistent attachment to purposeless and meaningless ways, are collective evidences of its internal degradation. For these reasons organized religion feels irrelevant to the human beings of modern times. As a consequence to the abandonment of what we knew from religion, a more sinister, destructive, and insidious model of reality moved in to take its place—a model for perceiving reality I call 'secular materialism.'"

I looked at her, a little confused. She caught my glance. Raising her palm toward me, she reassured me she was about to explain.

"The materialism model of reality focuses primarily on this short lifespan. Human values become based on self-gratification and the so-called successes of this life, which primarily revolve around the desires to have and to acquire. People want to have a job that pays substantially, irrespective of its effects on the environment. They want to have remarkable possessions, despite the cost to the environment to acquire them. They want to have unlimited use of fuel and energy in spite of the damage it takes to obtain it and aside from the consequential devastating pollution that results from its production and use. They want to have unlimited rights to entertainment, whatever the costs. They want to have, have, have! All this 'having' comes from somewhere, and that somewhere is ultimately the earth! This great mother earth has limitations to its giving. Sooner or later human 'taking' and 'having' is sufficient enough to create significant responses from the living earth, many of which are unfavorable to the human beings."

Rose stopped. She was sitting upright and rigid, staring right over my head to the trees beyond. Her stare was so fixed I turned to see what she was looking at, but she wasn't looking at anything in particular. She was looking into her own being to see if there was more to say on this subject.

"Now I want to contrast this materialistic, man-made model of perceived reality with the true spiritual model given to us by the manifestations of God. The spiritual model of reality teaches that we are eternal beings with a spiritual reality and purpose. Life on this planet is temporary and short compared to our eternal life. To over-emphasize the material aspects of this life leads to the selfish development of wants that divert and distract us from our true spiritual purpose. The spiritual model teaches love of others, not love of self. It embraces moderation, not excess. It values truthfulness and trustworthiness, not deceit is okay, as long as you can get away with it. The spiritual model teaches respect for the source of our having, the great mother earth, and not unfettered and indiscriminate taking. The spiritual model helps us take personal responsibility for our own actions. It does not support irresponsibility the way the materialistic model of reality does."

She paused in thought. "Unlike the materialistic model of reality that focuses attention on getting and having, the spiritual model of reality draws our attention to our relationships."

I looked at her, surprised.

"Yes, relationships!" she asserted. "Our relationship with God, our relationships with people, and our relationships with the earth and its creatures. The spiritual model of reality gives relationships the highest value in our hearts and minds. That was one of the things Jesus was talking about when he said:

'No one can serve two masters. Either he will hate the one and love the other, or he will be devoted to the one and despise the other. You cannot serve both God and money.'[55]

After a short pause, she added, "The excesses of materialism are about to wreak havoc upon the human beings." She looked over at me to see if I was listening.

"About to?" I questioned. "It looks to me like it's already happening!"

"Yes, it is," Rose replied. "But it will continue to worsen even if we make immediate changes because we have been too slow to respond appropriately. The human beings are awakening to the consequences of their collective actions, and change is on the move. Many still want to blame certain groups of people or specific behaviors, but this, too, will change. Slowly the human beings will come to understand that it takes a complete transformation in the model by which we live our lives—a change from the materialistic model of reality to a spiritual one. The spiritual model is what the manifestations of the past were trying to convey to us all along, and it's what Bahá'u'lláh elaborated on extensively in the entirety of his teachings.

"I just hope the people will take to heart the seriousness of the environmental issues. They are hurting themselves and passing hurt to their descendants. I hope they will look at the bigger picture, the whole planet and the life of the human beings here. I hope they will lay down their fears and prejudices and explore with open hearts and minds the spiritual reality put forth by Bahá'u'lláh. Not only do I hope for this, but I can promise you they will. I can say this because Bahá'u'lláh has assured us the human beings will live through the current crises that are troubling mankind, to witness the birth and development of a divine world civilization, providing and sustaining all that is known to be good. The sooner and more energetically we act on these principles, the sooner we will experience that spiritual civilization."

Rose was quiet for a time, then she suggested we take a walk. We strolled about the short trails in the garden, admiring the plants, flowers, and trees that someone had so laboriously nurtured and cared for. It was an inspiring place to spend some time. After a short walkabout, we returned to the clearing. Rose sat down in the swing and began to rummage in her bag. "Would you like a peanut-butter and jelly sandwich?" she asked with a smile.

"I'd love one," I said eagerly.

We sat in the garden and ate our sandwiches, sometimes quietly, and sometimes making small talk. Sometimes I sat with Rose on the swing, sometimes I sat on the stump, and sometimes I paced about as was my habitual behavior. It was a very pleasant time.

Day Nine

I Declare

"Grayson, I have some things I have prepared to share with you today. I hadn't planned on talking about the environment, but I am glad we did. I wanted to address it earlier, but I never found the time. So if I may, I would like to begin with a short recap of the last eight days." She looked at me as she shuffled into a comfortable position on the swing.

"I shared with you our purpose as human beings—to know and love the one true God, and I assured you we are spiritual beings, having a material experience with a spiritual purpose. I spoke to you about the evidence of the one true God and gave you a different perspective of the limitless reality of God in all his attributes. I shared with you that the Creator—God—has never left mankind alone or unaided, but has always guided us, nurtured us, and infused our souls with his spirit of goodness, through the steady flow of spiritual truth from the successive manifestations of God. I illustrated how true religion is the source of spiritual knowledge and goodness in the world. I carefully explained that all major religions are like individual chapters of one ongoing book of God's guidance to the human beings, and that these religions are part of one continuous, relative, progressive truth. I informed you that each major religion started out like the refreshing light of dawn—crisp, clean, and pure. Slowly each one warmed the earth of men's hearts until it rose to its midday, erasing before it the shadows and darkness of ignorance and conflict, bringing forth the light of unity among those it influenced. Gradually, the outer forms of each religion faded into the long shadowy sunset of doubt and fear, eventually to enter the dark night of ignorance and superstition. Each one was again renewed by the following dawn of a restored spirit of faith, coming to be known again in what was believed to be a new religion, but which was, in actuality, a continuation of the one ongoing faith of God. I talked to you about the religions all conveying the same basic spiritual truths, but providing different social guidance, depending upon the needs of the people at a particular time and place in history. I explained how each religion had a central theme, which each manifestation of God emphasized. I told you the central theme given to us by Bahá'u'lláh—the manifestation of God for our time—is unity, a heartfelt condition of peace and love, free of competitive conflict."

She paused and sat motionless, gazing into the forested surroundings before continuing with her summary. "I spent the last several days sharing with you the social principles given to us by Bahá'u'lláh to help us through this critical time in history. In addition to those just mentioned, those specific spiritual principles included the oneness of all people; the elimination of prejudice, superstition, and mindless imitation of others; the world-wide adoption of one universal language and script; that religion and science must be harmonized to address truth; that all people should be considered as equals; that all people have the right and obligation to independently and impartially investigate truth for themselves; that the extremes of wealth and poverty should be overcome by a fair distribution of wealth and services; that education for children should be compulsory and include spiritual guidance; that religion should be kept separate from politics; that we should adopt a cooperative form of leadership; that we be truthful, honest, and loyal to duly formed governments; that we should adopt an international agreement to end war and develop a world federation to manage international issues; that we acknowledge and value the development of spiritual characteristics and virtues; that we give merit to the acquisition of knowledge and wisdom and employ moderation and justice in all things, and that we consider work in service to others as a vitally important aspect of life." She paused again, reviewing in her mind to be sure she hadn't forgotten something. "Do you recall me talking to you about all these things?" she asked lovingly.

"Well, now that you brought them up again, yes, I recall most of them. Did we really cover all that?" I asked in astonishment.

"Yes, we did. At least I hope we did!" Rose began to laugh, perhaps wondering if her memory was as good as she thought. "Oh!" she exclaimed as she suddenly sat upright, raising her hand as though to ask a question. "I also just shared with you how these spiritual principles could be effective in addressing the concerns over the environment." Pursing her lips, she sat perfectly still, staring out in front of her. I could tell she was thinking hard about something.

"Even though I have carefully and specifically shared these things with you, there is one most important point I would like to emphasize at this time. I have already shared this with you for the book, but I want **you** to give it special attention. Earlier I told you a little about Bahá'u'lláh. I informed you he was from the land of Persia, now known as Iran, and that he claimed to be the manifestation of God for our time. He taught the human race, through his writings and his words, what the one true God inspired him to reveal. He wrote and spoke about spiritual matters for forty years. Not only did he convey to the human beings the spiritual principles I have just reviewed with you, but considerably more. He wrote extensively about our reality as spiritual beings. He wrote hundreds of prayers, poetic odes of a mystical nature that cause the heart to soar, and numerous books. In his teachings, he elaborated on spiritual codes of behavior and conduct. He revealed necessary religious rules and laws and left instructions in personal spiritual disciplines. He proclaimed a new day, and a new phase and cycle in human social and spiritual evolution. He wrote letters to the heads of the world's major religions and to the leaders of many nations, proclaiming his station, the advent of a new day, a new age, and the renewal of pure spirituality and religious faith. He explained with detailed clarity the symbolic language of the sacred scriptures of former religions. He was tortured, imprisoned, poisoned, and exiled four different times simply because of the spiritual truths he was teaching. He endured his sufferings with complete composure and submission without lifting a finger of protest or complaint for himself. Now, who does this? I ask you. Who **can** do this? He would write or reveal spiritual teachings as inspired by the Holy Spirit without forethought or need for correction for hours at a time. Who can do that? I ask you! I suggest to you that Bahá'u'lláh's claim to be the manifestation of God for our time is thoroughly supported by the evidence of his life, the timeliness of his teachings, and the loving power and influence of his words.

"Now I say to you, any man who claims to be a manifestation of God, who claims to speak for the one true God by the influence of the Holy Spirit, is either delusional or he is telling the truth, and he is that One for our time. So to be true to one's self, doesn't it seem natural that every soul would feel a sacred obligation to investigate this astonishing claim once they hear it? Isn't it our spiritual duty as a human being to determine independently for our self, within our own heart, whether Bahá'u'lláh's claim is true? Isn't this a divine opportunity to decide whether to believe and whether or not to take up our life and embellish it with the spiritual knowledge and goodness made available by immersing our heart in his spiritual teachings?

"The whole point of me wanting to write this book, Grayson, has been to say to you that Bahá'u'lláh is the One. The One promised by all the religions of the past, the One that fulfills the hopes, dreams, and expectations of the great seers, writers, poets, thinkers, prophets, and manifestations of former times. Here it is. Here is the chalice of immortality, pristine and radiant. Here is pure, true religion raised from the tomb of ignorance and superstition. Let him who has faith drink his fill of this wondrous spiritual truth and light."

I didn't intend to say anything right away, and then it just came out. "I believe that," I said with assurance, as I looked straight at Rose. "I believe all of that is true."

Rose smiled. After a long pause she joyfully announced, "I guess that means you are Bahá'í then!"

"Yes, I am!" I resounded immediately. "In fact, I was thinking that earlier today."

Rose paused and looked around the garden. She had a radiance to her face that was nearly too brilliant to gaze upon. She said, "Anyone who believes that Bahá'u'lláh is the manifestation of God for this day and is willing to affirm it either verbally, as you just did, or in writing, or in some cases with a couple clicks of a mouse," she laughed, "is a Bahá'í. So may I say to you, welcome, Grayson, to the Faith of Bahá'u'lláh."

She put her hands on the swing to push herself forward so she could stand up. She then turned directly to me and stood motionless. I don't know why, but I, too, stood up off my stump. She walked toward me, reaching out with both arms and gently embraced me. It felt loving and genuine. She then put both her hands on my shoulders and looked up at me with tear-filled eyes and a warm, gentle smile. "Congratulations, Grayson, you have attained!" she said firmly. Then she turned to sit down again on the swing.

We were both quiet for some time, neither of us saying anything. I could hear people talking across the creek on the other side of the forested draw. I noticed the sound of traffic in the background and the singing of birds. Time stood still there for a few minutes. It was a significant moment for me in that little garden, and I knew it, but I didn't know how significant until later.

"Would you like to affirm yourself as a Bahá'í and become a member of the Bahá'í community at this time?" Rose asked, finally breaking the silence.

"I guess I would. But how do I do that?" I asked.

"I'll show you," she said as she reached down to pick up her bag.

I couldn't think of any reason not to, and I felt certain in my heart that what Rose had talked about this whole trip was what I believed and what I wanted to be part of. Everything she had said to me seemed to reach down inside me and pull out things I already believed, or wanted to believe, but didn't know it, or didn't know how to say or express it. I liked what she had said. It was me, and I was on board.

Rose retrieved the same cloth-covered book I had seen her with before. Opening the book, she removed a small card and then placed the book down on the swing beside her. Holding the card up, she said: "This little card is one way you can register with the Bahá'í community. If you fill it out, I'll send it in for you. That's all there is to it," she said, handing me the card. The card had a place for my name and address and a statement, which read: "I have declared my belief in Bahá'u'lláh as the Manifestation of God for this age. I wish to register as a member of the Bahá'í Faith." Rose remained quiet while I filled out the card and signed it. When I handed it back to her, she looked it over carefully and placed it in her little book.

"I want to give you a website to put in our book so others who believe this way and want to register as a Bahá'ís can do so easily. I have written it down on this piece of paper for you, and I am also going to say it into this recorder, so you have it in two places and get it right. Think of it as a belt-and-suspenders approach for keeping everything where it should be," she laughed. She then leaned over and spoke directly and slowly into the recorder the following website: http://join.bahai.us/Invitation.aspx. She continued to lean over and talk into the recorder: "And for those who want to find a local Bahá'í community or to request further information, they can access the official website of the Bahá'ís of the United States at http://www.bahai.us/ or call 1-800-228-6483."

She seemed pleased and contented that she had shared all she had intended for the day. I could tell because she was carefully packing up her travel bag, including the recorder. Before getting up out of the swing and leaving the garden, I remember her sitting on the edge of that swing looking serious as if waiting for the right moment to say more, or perhaps she was wondering how to say goodbye. I didn't know.

Finally, she offered her thought, "I know you will be leaving for Oregon in the morning." She paused and looked down, wiggling her foot back and forth nervously. "I have more to share with you to finish what I feel is necessary to conclude this book. I spoke with my family here in Washington last evening and asked them if it would be all right if I rode on with you to Portland tomorrow. They reluctantly agreed. I have a granddaughter in Portland. Perhaps we could meet her there, and you could drop me off on your way through. I want to know if you feel all right about that?" She continued to stare at the ground, wiggling her foot and waiting for my reply.

"I would love that!" I almost shouted. I was kind of wondering how we were going to wrap this up. It didn't feel complete yet, like we needed, or I needed some closure of some kind.

"Great!" Rose said joyfully, looking up with a smile. She slowly stood and stretched, took hold of the two handles of her travel bag, and reached for my arm. I stepped toward her so she could hold my arm as we walked back along the garden path to the little house where we were staying.

Day Ten

Home

We were late getting started this morning, but it didn't seem to matter. Everyone was happy after taking a little break, knowing today was the last day of our trip. Just three hours' travel to Portland and then two more to Tygh Valley.

Rose didn't turn the recorder on right away. We just drove, talking and laughing about various things. It was a pleasant, happy morning.

Finally, she reached in her bag and retrieved the recorder, laid it on the seat, and turned it on. Neither of us said anything for some time, and then she began.

"Soon after Phillip Eagle told me about his vision, he passed away," she began. "I didn't know what to think of his vision, but I thought about it often. Then, when I was twenty, a middle-aged white couple moved to our village. They were Bahá'ís, but I didn't know it at the time. After a few months, I heard they were having spiritual meetings in their home. A schoolteacher of mine told me about the meetings and asked if I would go to one with her. I wasn't really interested, but to honor her position and the fact she was an elder, I agreed. The people I met there were very kind, loving, and respectful, so it was easy for me to enjoy the experience. There was something about being around them that kept me coming back. Eventually, I found interest in what they were sharing. I began to find it true in my heart and subsequently became Bahá'í.

"Like that couple did in my village, I have tried to convey to you, to the best of my ability, an introduction to the Faith of Bahá'u'lláh. And that vision old Phillip Eagle had about me? Well, this is it. The words I had to speak to the people in his vision are the words I have been sharing with you these last nine days. The instrument I used in his vision to convey this message must be this little tape recorder." She patted the recorder sitting in the seat between us. She smiled at me. "The truth is, I'm not the only one sharing this message. There are over five million Bahá'ís in the world, and all of them share the teachings of Bahá'u'lláh with others in the best way they can. The Bahá'í Faith has no clergy, no paid teachers, preachers, or speakers. Every single soul has the opportunity, the privilege, and the spiritual obligation to do what they can to share Bahá'u'lláh's message with others, as I have done with you for these last nine days."

"So, there is no clergy?" I asked, looking over at Rose, puzzled.

"No."

"Then, how do you, I mean . . . we . . . organize anything? Are there any leaders of some sort?"

"Instead of having priests, ministers, preachers, mullahs, monks or rabbis, we have elected assemblies in each locality that serve the local Bahá'í community. In the United States, at this time, there are some eleven hundred spiritual assemblies. Furthermore, each nation has a national spiritual assembly that serves the members of the Bahá'í Faith in their nation. Each assembly consists of nine people who are elected annually by secret ballot. The elections are unique. There is no campaigning, no nominating, no electioneering, no platforms, and no discussion about any individuals by name. Each year the believers gather and cast a secret ballot for the nine people they think are most qualified to serve the community. If elected, a person serves as an assembly member for one year. This service is a non-paid position. Individuals on the assembly have no personal power other than as a consulting and voting member of the assembly when it's in session. In addition to these local and national assemblies, there is a nine-member body in Haifa, Israel, called the Universal House of Justice. It serves as the head of the Bahá'í community worldwide. It, too, is elected, but every five years instead of yearly.

"So we are organized. Each of the Bahá'í Institutions I just mentioned conveys the Bahá'í Faith in their respective area of jurisdiction the best they can. But primarily, the sharing of the Faith goes on from heart to heart, individual to individual, as you and I have done on this trip. So when you arrive in Oregon, and after I send in the card you filled out, you will probably receive a letter from the National Spiritual Assembly of the Bahá'ís of the United States welcoming you to the Bahá'í Faith. They also will help make arrangements for you to be introduced to the local Bahá'í community where you live. Furthermore, you can look in the yellow or white pages or do a search online to locate the Bahá'í community in your locality.

"The Bahá'í friends in the local community make every effort to address the specific needs of those who would like to know more about the Faith or would like to participate in some way. You can ask for literature, and they will see that you receive some. There is a smorgasbord of optional activities to consider. You can attend public speaking events or personally hosted firesides, which usually include a short talk with questions, answers, and discussions about the Faith.

"Bahá'í communities have study circles you can attend on a regular basis where people study the basic teachings of the Faith and learn how to put the teachings into action and service. You can attend devotional meetings that are usually offered in people's homes or sometimes in public places for the purpose of inviting all people of all faiths to pray and meditate together. You can also ask to sponsor one in your own home.

"There are deepenings, where people study together with others to acquire a deeper understanding of a specific spiritual topic or subject. If you want, the Bahá'ís will come to your home to pray with you, to introduce the Faith to you, help you deepen in the spiritual teachings, or do whatever you need to assist you in your spiritual journey. For the young people, there are children's classes, pre-youth classes, and youth classes geared to different age levels to facilitate their spiritual discovery and development. There is no shortage of

Bahá'í experiences available that will accommodate most everyone's needs.

"I am telling you these things because I want you to know there are endless opportunities in the Bahá'í communities for you to enhance your spiritual life. All around the globe the Bahá'ís are engaged in a collection of activities for the purpose of developing our spiritual qualities and enhancing our abilities to be of service to mankind.

"Bahá'í communities worldwide currently are involved with teaching children's classes—open to all children—for the purpose of assisting them in developing spiritual characteristics and virtues. We talked about the importance of teaching children spiritual characteristics and virtues as being valuable for their personal development and necessary for them to become useful, contributing citizens. These classes are not characterized by teaching children dogma, ritual, or superstitious beliefs. They instead consist of the same teachings I have shared with you on this trip with an emphasis on developing such spiritual qualities as honesty, truthfulness, trustworthiness, kindness, tolerance, unity, respect, thoughtfulness, forgiveness, peace, thankfulness, equality, fairness, justice, the value of work and service, and much more."

"So, who pays for these activities?" I asked. "I mean, how is this Faith financed? Is there tithing or what?"

"The Bahá'í Faith operates on voluntary contributions made by the believers only. The Faith does not accept donations from people or organizations that are not Bahá'í. If an individual who is not a Bahá'í insists on donating to the Bahá'í Faith, then those monies will be used for charitable purposes only, not for promoting or administering the Bahá'í Faith in any way."

"Well that's certainly unusual," I declared.

We rode quietly for some time. Traffic was heavier here in Washington than any I had experienced in several years, so driving was a little tense for me. Rose must have noticed my tension. Reaching down into her travel bag she pulled out a small book I had seen her with before, titled *Bahá'í Prayers*.

"I mentioned to you about devotional meetings, right?

"Um . . . ," I answered, without really remembering.

"How about we have one right here in this truck?" she said with a smile. "I'll do the reading and you do the driving. How about that?"

"That's a very wise idea," I smirked, looking over at her.

"Here is a prayer from Bahá'u'lláh that I especially like." She then sat very still, with her eyes closed and her head bowed. After a few seconds she slowly, and with what seemed like great reverence, read the following prayer:

'*Create in me a pure heart, O my God, and renew a tranquil conscience within me, O my Hope! Through the spirit of power confirm Thou me in Thy Cause, O my Best-Beloved, and by the light of Thy glory reveal unto me Thy path, O Thou the Goal of my desire! Through the power of Thy transcendent might lift me up unto the heaven of Thy holiness, O Source of my being, and by the breezes of Thine eternity gladden me, O Thou Who art my God! Let Thine everlasting melodies breathe tranquility on me, O my Companion, and let the riches of Thine ancient countenance deliver me from all except Thee, O my Master, and let the tidings of the revelation of Thine incorruptible Essence bring me joy, O Thou Who art the most manifest of the manifest and the most hidden of the hidden!*'"[56]

She remained still and quiet for a short time before closing her little prayer book and placing it back in her travel bag.

"Well, that was beautiful," I said. I thought, *I'm not sure I understand it totally, but it was beautiful, and it makes me feel— detached! Yeah, that's it, detached, and light as a feather.* "Thank you for that, Rose."

"You're welcome."

We drove in silence again for quite some time. I thought about everything Rose had said to me the last several days, trying to think of something that felt unfinished, or something I didn't understand or had questions about. I couldn't think of anything, so I remained silent. Rose must have been doing the same because she rode along, relaxed, looking out the side-window at the scenery. Finally, she took a big breath and let out a sigh.

"The human beings are ready for this, you know, for this Bahá'í Faith," she said. "They are sufficiently dissatisfied with the other options they have before them, and many are just waiting for something to happen to make the world change. Some, unfortunately, see a great collapse coming and are resigned to it—like there is going to be a zombie apocalypse or something." We looked at each other and laughed.

"The time appears right for a great spiritual awakening or movement in the world. I want to point out that this Faith has demonstrated its tremendous potential to inspire a spirit of hope, a rebirth of positive thinking, and a true condition of love and unity so desperately yearned for by the human beings. I ask you in all sincerity—if not this Bahá'í Faith, then what?" She paused and gazed at me lovingly. "If not now, this generation, then when, or what generation will have the collective positive energy to bring society into a forward movement? If not by this Bahá'í Faith, then how will the human beings avert war and deal with the myriad dis-unifying problems that plague it? If not this, then what possible force has the spirit and vision to unite the world and avert its predictable catastrophe? If not the Faith of Bahá'u'lláh, and you, and I, and all those who read our book, and all those who associate with this Faith—then who will do it? Who will propel any true vision of hope forward among the people? If not this Bahá'í way, then what way, I ask you, what way forward with hope? And if not now, then when? Why wait when the path forward to hope is so clear?" She paused.

"I say this, Grayson, for the people who will read our book," she laid her hand on the recorder. "I say it in the hope they will seriously contemplate these things in their heart. I say it in hope that they will independently investigate this Faith, discover its message of hope, love, and truth, adopt its message as their own and get involved in it—for their own sake and for the sake of generations to come." She was just sitting there staring at me. I looked at her and could see in her face that she was finished.

I nodded my head at her and said with assurance, "I'm on it!" She smiled and looked at me with happy, tear-filled eyes. *It was accomplished*, I thought. *Her vision was complete. Her mission— concluded.*

"I have one more thing," she said, reaching into her travel bag and removing what looked like a few pieces of folded up copy paper. "I want you to keep this and use it as a closing to our book. It's a farewell address by the son of Bahá'u'lláh, who visited and toured the United States from 1910 to 1912, sharing his father's message. His title name was 'Abdu'l-Bahá, which means servant of Bahá. Please quote it word for word."

I assured her I would.

We were getting close to Portland. The traffic was getting heavy. Rose was pointing out landmarks and talking about her family and the area. She didn't mention the Faith again that day. There was no need for more, I guess.

I took the 205 highway across the beautiful Columbia River to the east side of Portland and followed Rose's instructions to meet with her granddaughter at a truck stop on I-84. Things began to happen quickly. As we pulled into the truck stop, Rose lifted her travel bag to her lap. The recorder remained on the seat where it had been riding for ten days. She took a small carrying case out of her travel bag and lay in on the seat beside the recorder. It was full of the cassette tapes she had used to record our trip. After we parked, I helped her out of the truck and transferred her suitcase from the Bronco to her granddaughter's car. She gave me a big hug, gently laid the palm of her hand against my cheek, and looked deeply into my eyes. No words were spoken. She then turned and seated herself in her granddaughter's car and began conversing with her. As they drove off, Rose turned to give me a quick wave and she was gone.

It was a quiet ride up the Columbia River Gorge, and a hot one. I hadn't felt the outside air warmer than my body now for nearly eight years! It felt good. The scenery in the Gorge was remarkably beautiful. Finally, I passed through The Dalles and headed up the long, steep auction-yard grade. My big truck was straining. I was watching the temperature gage—hoping it wouldn't overheat. In my mirror, I could see Sonia in the Bronco behind me, and Franklin and

Annie behind her. T.J. and Alene were no longer with us as they had left us at Portland and headed for their home in Tillamook. After thirty minutes or so we were up on top of the high plateau with Mount Hood looming in the foreground out my passenger window. It was all so familiar, as this is where I had spent most of my life as a young person.

Soon we were coasting down the long, steep Tygh grade into the Tygh Valley. "Home," I said to myself. "Home at last!" It felt good, but I knew it wasn't just this place that was making me feel so elated. No. It was the contentment in my heart and the hope for the future that was stirring in my being. I was smiling and happy, for this had truly been a road-trip home—not to my home in Tygh Valley, but to that true home in my heart.

The following is from a talk given by 'Abdu'l-Bahá, the son of Bahá'u'lláh, who had been traveling in Europe and America to share the Bahá'í Faith in the West. This was his last address to a small group of devoted believers who had come aboard to bid him farewell on a December day in 1912 as the steamship *Celtic*, in view of the Statue of Liberty, prepared to sail out of New York Harbor. I share his words with you, as Rose requested.

> "This is my last meeting with you, for now I am on the ship ready to sail away. These are my final words of exhortation. I have repeatedly summoned you to the cause of the unity of the world of humanity, announcing that all mankind are the servants of the same God, that God is the creator of all; He is the Provider and Life-giver; all are equally beloved by Him and are His servants upon whom His mercy and compassion descend. Therefore, you must manifest the greatest kindness and love toward the nations of the world, setting aside fanaticism, abandoning religious, national, and racial prejudice.
>
> "The earth is one native land, one home; and all mankind are the children of one Father. God has created them, and they are the recipients of His

compassion. Therefore, if anyone offends another, he offends God. It is the wish of our heavenly Father that every heart should rejoice and be filled with happiness, that we should live together in felicity and joy. The obstacle to human happiness is racial or religious prejudice, the competitive struggle for existence and inhumanity toward each other.

"Your eyes have been illumined, your ears are attentive, your hearts knowing. You must be free from prejudice and fanaticism, beholding no differences between the races and religions. You must look to God, for He is the real Shepherd, and all humanity are His sheep. He loves them and loves them equally. As this is true, should the sheep quarrel among themselves? They should manifest gratitude and thankfulness to God, and the best way to thank God is to love one another.

"Beware lest ye offend any heart, lest ye speak against anyone in his absence, lest ye estrange yourselves from the servants of God. You must consider all His servants as your own family and relations. Direct your whole effort toward the happiness of those who are despondent, bestow food upon the hungry, clothe the needy, and glorify the humble. Be a helper to every helpless one, and manifest kindness to your fellow creatures in order that ye may attain the good pleasure of God. This is conducive to the illumination of the world of humanity and eternal felicity for yourselves. I seek from God everlasting glory in your behalf; therefore, this is my prayer and exhortation.

" . . . Your efforts must be lofty. Exert yourselves with heart and soul so that, perchance, through your efforts the light of universal peace may shine and this darkness of estrangement and enmity may be dispelled from amongst men, that all men may become as one family and consort together in love and kindness, that the East may assist the West and the West give help to the East, for all are the inhabitants of one planet, the people of one original native land and the flocks of one Shepherd.

"Consider how the Prophets Who have been sent, the great souls who have appeared and the sages who have arisen in the world have exhorted mankind to unity and love. This has been the essence of their mission and teaching. This has been the goal of their guidance and message. The Prophets, saints, seers, and philosophers have sacrificed their lives in order to establish these principles and teachings amongst men. Consider the heedlessness of the world, for notwithstanding the efforts and sufferings of the Prophets of God, the nations and peoples are still engaged in hostility and fighting. Notwithstanding the heavenly commandments to love one another, they are still shedding each other's blood. How heedless and ignorant are the people of the world! How gross the darkness which envelops them! Although they are the children of a compassionate God, they continue to live and act in opposition to His will and good pleasure. God is loving and kind to all men, and yet they show the utmost enmity and hatred toward each other. God is the Giver of life to them, and yet they constantly seek to destroy life. God blesses and protects their homes; they rage, sack, and destroy each other's homes. Consider their ignorance and heedlessness!

"Your duty is of another kind, for you are informed of the mysteries of God. Your eyes are illumined; your ears are quickened with hearing. You must, therefore, look toward each other and then toward mankind with the utmost love and kindness. You have no excuse to bring before God if you fail to live according to His command, for you are informed of that which constitutes the good pleasure of God. You have heard His commandments and precepts. You must, therefore, be kind to all men; you must even treat your enemies as your friends. You must consider your evil-wishers as your well-wishers. Those who are not agreeable toward you must be regarded as those who are congenial and pleasant so that, perchance, this darkness of disagreement and conflict may disappear from amongst men and the light of the divine may shine forth, . . . so that the East and West may embrace each other in love and deal with one another in sympathy and affection. Until man reaches this high station, the world of humanity shall not find rest, and eternal felicity shall not be attained. But if man lives up to these divine commandments, this world of earth shall be transformed into the world of heaven, and this material sphere shall be converted into a paradise of glory. It is my hope that you may become successful in this high calling so that like brilliant lamps you may cast light upon the world of humanity and quicken and stir the body of existence like unto a spirit of life. This is eternal glory. This is everlasting felicity. This is immortal life. This is heavenly attainment. This is being created in the image and likeness of God. And unto this I call you, praying to God to strengthen and bless you."[57]

SPIRITUAL PRINCIPLES
FOR MODERN TIMES

1. **Belief in the One True God of Creation and Revelation.** There is only one true God, the Creator and Sustainer of all things and the Source of inspiration for the founding Prophets and Messengers of the world's great religions.

2. **The Oneness, Continuity, Relativity, and Progression of Religions.** All the world's major religions are inspired by the one true God, are equal phases of one continuous source of spiritual guidance, each revealed in a manner relative to the times and people they addressed, and each more advancing, expanding, reforming, and evolving than its predecessor.

3. **The Oneness of All People.** All people are of the human family and should be treated lovingly with equal concern, irrespective of race, nationality, gender, social status, class, religion, country of origin, or other differences, culminating in a unified world in all aspects including spirituality, trade, finance, language, scientific pursuits, governance, and fellowship.

4. **Unity – Paramount in All Things.** Unity is the ultimate moral value and our highest priority. Unity is a heartfelt condition of peace, love, and harmony in human relations, free of conflict and struggle for dominance.

5. **The Elimination of Prejudice, Blind Imitation, and Superstition.** To eliminate from our lives harmful irrational prejudices, mindless imitation of pointless beliefs and behaviors of the past, and any beliefs and behaviors not based on what is true or real.

6. **The Harmony of Science and Religion.** For the teachings and concepts of religion to be true and free from superstition, they must remain harmonious with science and reality, while science is best protected from materialistic and unethical practices by embracing the spiritual wisdom of true religion.

7. **Adoption of One Universal Auxiliary Language and Script.** Essential to the unity of mankind is the creation or adoption by the world community of a single language and script to be taught to all children as a supplement to their native language.

8. **Equality of Women and Men.** Women are to have equal opportunity, rights, freedoms, privileges, and status as enjoyed by men in all aspects of the human experience.

9. **Independent and Impartial Investigation of Truth.** The search for truth and reality, especially pertaining to spirituality and religion, is best approached independent of the influence of others and impartial to possible outcomes.

10. **Spiritual Solutions to Economic Disparity.** The extremes between wealth and poverty should be eliminated through equitable sharing of profits between capital and labor and by fairness in the distribution and allocation of wealth, goods, services, and work.

11. **Universal Peace Upheld by a World Commonwealth of Nations.** The time has come to formulate a World Federation of Nations that will create and uphold an international agreement to end war and regulate all issues of international concern.

12. **Religion Should Remain Separate from Politics.** Religion should abstain from political affiliation and partisan disputes as its true purpose is unity, harmony, and agreement, making it spiritually incompatible with the inherent divisiveness of partisan politics.

13. **A Facilitative Approach to Leadership.** A facilitator style of leadership is most desirable, consisting of consultative groups characterized by mutual cooperation, moral integrity, and devotion to the welfare and interest of the common good.

14. The Necessity of Religion for Progress and Development. True religion has always been the source of spiritual, ethical, and moral goodness in the world and when universally fostered nurtures humanity to its divine purpose and protects it from degradation.

15. Compulsory Childhood Education. Meaningful education in elementary subjects, and kind and loving training in spiritual qualities and character, is to be provided to all children for their own sakes and for the advancement of society.

16. The Development of Spiritual Characteristics and Virtues. A requirement of our true purpose as human beings is to acquire and develop spiritual qualities, traits, and virtues that reflect the spiritual light of our Creator.

17. The Importance and Value of Justice. The realization of justice requires conscious effort in all matters to conform our behavior to what is right, good, true, and fair so that order, fellowship, and unity may reside in the world.

18. The Distinction of Wisdom. The acquisition and application of wisdom, as it pertains to our true purpose and reality, should be appropriately recognized and highly valued that all may benefit from its illuminating influence.

19. The Wise Application of Moderation in All Things. Moderation should be sensibly practiced that desirable benefits may be forthcoming and the harmful effect of extremes avoided.

20. Truthfulness, Honesty, and Loyalty to Government. Obedience to legitimate government invites social order and peaceful relations that avoid the damaging and harmful outcomes of mischief and conflict.

21. Work in Service to Others is Worship of God. Exerting effort to excel in one's trade, profession, art, science, or work is a demonstration of love, appreciation, and honor to others, and is considered an expression of worship to the one true God.

WEBSITE LINKS

To Join the Bahá'í Community in the US:
www.join.bahai.us/Invitation.aspx

Official Website of the Bahá'ís of the United States:
www.bahai.us

Website of the Worldwide Bahá'í Community:
www.bahai.org

Bahá'í Book Store:
www.bahaibookstore.com

Newsletter of the Bahá'í International Community:
www.onecountry.org

Bahá'í World News Service:
www.news.bahai.org

References

1. Dante Alighieri, *The Divine Comedy*, trans. Allen Mandelbaum (New York, NY: Knopf Doubleday Publishing Group, 1995), canto I, lines 1-3.

2. 'Abdu'l-Bahá, *Paris Talks*: *Addresses given by 'Abdu'l-Bahá in Paris in 1911–1912* (New Delhi: Bahá'í Publishing Trust, 1971), 72.

3. Bahá'u'lláh, *The Kitáb-i-Íqán*: *The Book of Certitude*, trans. Shoghi Effendi (Wilmette, IL: Bahá'í Publishing Trust, 1931), 211.

4. The Báb, *Selections from the Writings of the Báb*, compiled by the Research Department of the Universal House of Justice and translated by Habib Taherzadeh with the assistance of a committee at the Bahá'í World Centre (Haifa: Bahá'í World Centre, 1976), 123.

5. Bahá'u'lláh, *The Hidden Words of Bahá'u'lláh*, trans. Shoghi Effendi (Oxford, England: Oneworld Publications Ltd., 1986), Arabic no. 12, 14.

6. Bahá'u'lláh, *The Kitáb-i-Aqdas*: *The Most Holy Book*, (Haifa, Bahá'í World Centre, 1992), 85.

7. Bahá'u'lláh, *The Kitáb-i-Íqán*, 211.

8. His Divine Grace A.C. Bhaktivedanta Swami Prabhupada, *Bhagavad-gita: As It Is*, complete edition with original Sanskrit text, Roman transliteration, English equivalents, translation and elaborate purports (New York, NY: The Macmillan Company, 1972), chapter 4, text 7, 224.

9. Bahá'u'lláh, *The Kitáb-i-Aqdas*, 85.

10. Bahá'u'lláh, *Gleanings from the Writings of Bahá'u'lláh*, trans. Shoghi Effendi (Wilmette, IL: Bahá'í Publishing Trust, rev. ed. 1971), 52.

11. 'Abdu'l-Bahá, *The Promulgation of Universal Peace*: *Talks Delivered by 'Abdu'l-Bahá during His Visit to the United States and Canada in 1912*, compiled by Howard MacNutt (Wilmette, IL: Bahá'í Publishing Trust, 1982), 341.

12. Bahá'u'lláh, *Gems of Divine Mysteries*: *Javahiru'l-Asrár* (Haifa: Bahá'í World Centre, 2002), 24.

[13] Bahá'u'lláh, *Gleanings from the Writings of Bahá'u'lláh*, 286.

[14] Bahá'u'lláh, *Tablets of Bahá'u'lláh Revealed After the Kitáb-i-Aqdas*, compiled by the Research Department of the Universal House of Justice and translated by Habib Taherzadeh with the assistance of a committee at the Bahá'í World Centre (Haifa: Bahá'í World Centre, 1978), 221.

[15] Bahá'u'lláh, *Epistle to the Son of the Wolf*, trans. Shoghi Effendi (Wilmette, IL: Bahá'í Publishing Trust, 1971), 14.

[16] Ibid.

[17] Shoghi Effendi, *The Advent of Divine Justice*, (Wilmette, IL: Bahá'í Publishing Trust, 1974), 31.

[18] Ibid.

[19] Bahá'u'lláh, *Epistle to the Son of the Wolf*, 14.

[20] Bahá'u'lláh, *Gleanings from the Writings of Bahá'u'lláh*, 250.

[21] Ibid.

[22] *The Bahá'í World: A Biennial International Record,* vol., 11 (Wilmette, IL: Bahá'í Publishing Trust, reprinted 1981), 788.

[23] Bahá'u'lláh, *The Hidden Words of Bahá'u'lláh*, Arabic no. 27, 23.

[24] Bahá'u'lláh, *Gleanings from the Writings of Bahá'u'lláh*, 265.

[25] Bahá'u'lláh, *Tablets of Bahá'u'lláh Revealed After the Kitáb-i-Aqdas*, 12.

[26] Ibid., 125.

[27] Ibid., 171.

[28] Shoghi Effendi, *The Advent of Divine Justice*, 22.

[29] 'Abdu'l-Bahá, *The Promulgation of Universal Peace: Talks Delivered by 'Abdu'l-Bahá during His Visit to the United States and Canada in 1912*, 49.

[30] Ibid.

31 Ibid., 394.

32 'Abdu'l-Bahá, *Paris Talks: Addresses given by 'Abdu'l-Bahá in Paris in 1911–1912*, 145.

33 Bahá'u'lláh, *The Hidden Words of Bahá'u'lláh*, Arabic no. 2, 9.

34 Bahá'u'lláh, *Tablets of Bahá'u'lláh Revealed After the Kitáb-i-Aqdas*, 67.

35 'Abdu'l-Bahá, *Selections from the Writings of 'Abdu'l-Bahá*, compiled by the Research Department of the Universal House of Justice, translated by a committee at the Bahá'í World Centre and by Marzieh Gail (Haifa: Bahá'í World Centre, 1978), 24.

36 Bahá'u'lláh, *Gleanings from the Writings of Bahá'u'lláh*, 200.

37 Bahá'u'lláh, *Tablets of Bahá'u'lláh Revealed After the Kitáb-i-Aqdas*, 173.

38 Ibid., 125.

39 Shoghi Effendi, *The World Order of Bahá'u'lláh: Selected Letters by Shoghi Effendi* (Wilmette: Bahá'í Publishing Trust, second rev. ed. 1974), 186.

40 Bahá'u'lláh, *Gleanings from the Writings of Bahá'u'lláh*, 149.

41 Bahá'u'lláh, *Tablets of Bahá'u'lláh Revealed After the Kitáb-i-Aqdas*, 66.

42 Ibid., 69.

43 Bahá'u'lláh, *Gleanings from the Writings of Bahá'u'lláh*, 342–343.

44 Ibid., 65.

45 Shoghi Effendi, *Bahá'í Administration* (Wilmette: Bahá'í Publishing Trust, rev. ed. 1968), 88.

46 Shoghi Effendi, *The Promised Day is Come* (Wilmette, IL: Bahá'í Publishing Trust, rev. ed. 1980), 20.

47 Bahá'u'lláh, *Gleanings from the Writings of Bahá'u'lláh*, 200.

[48] Bahá'u'lláh, *Epistle to the Son of the Wolf*, 61.

[49] Howard, Helen Addison, *Saga of Chief Joseph* (Lincoln: University of Nebraska Press, 1978), 330.

[50] Bahá'u'lláh, *Gleanings from the Writings of Bahá'u'lláh*, 342–343.

[51] Bahá'u'lláh, *Tablets of Bahá'u'lláh Revealed After the Kitáb-i-Aqdas*, 69.

[52] Bahá'u'lláh, *Gleanings from the Writings of Bahá'u'lláh*, 212.

[53] Ryrie, Charles Caldwell, *The Ryrie Study Bible: New International Version* (Chicago, IL: The Moody Bible Institute of Chicago, 1986), John 14:6

[54] Ibid., John 16:25.

[55] Ibid., Mathew 6:24.

[56] *Bahá'í Prayers: A Selection of Prayers Revealed by Bahá'u'lláh, the Báb, and 'Abdu'l-Bahá* (Wilmette, IL: Bahá'í Publishing Trust, 1991 edition), 142–143.

[57] 'Abdu'l-Bahá, *The Promulgation of Universal Peace: Talks Delivered by 'Abdu'l-Bahá during His Visit to the United States and Canada in 1912*, 468–470.

www.ingramcontent.com/pod-product-compliance
Lightning Source LLC
Chambersburg PA
CBHW031108030726
47496CB00002BA/449